DECEPTION COVE

ALSO BY OWEN LAUKKANEN

Gale Force

STEVENS & WINDERMERE NOVELS

The Professionals

Criminal Enterprise

Kill Fee

The Stolen Ones

The Watcher in the Wall

The Forgotten Girls

DECEPTION COVE

OWEN LAUKKANEN

MULHOLLAND BOOKS

New York Boston London

The characters and events in this book are fictitious. Any similarity to real persons, living or dead, is coincidental and not intended by the author.

Mulholland Books / Little, Brown and Company
Hachette Book Group
1290 Avenue of the Americas, New York, NY 10104
mulhollandbooks.com

First Edition: May 2019

Mulholland Books is an imprint of Little, Brown and Company, a division of Hachette Book Group, Inc. The Mulholland Books name and logo are trademarks of Hachette Book Group, Inc.

The publisher is not responsible for websites (or their content) that are not owned by the publisher.

ISBN 978-0-316-44870-3
LCCN 2018962441

10 9 8 7 6 5 4 3 2 1

LSC-C

Printed in the United States of America

For Lucy, of course. And for Sassy May, too.

Let the thief no longer steal, but rather let him labor, doing honest work with his own hands, so that he may have something to share with anyone in need.

—*Ephesians 4:28*

DECEPTION COVE

PROLOGUE

Certain moments *came back to her, or maybe they never left. Images, sounds. Marshall fumbling around on some shale slope at daybreak, looking for what was left of his leg, trying his best not to scream and give away their position. Hawthorne, dropped by a sniper as he came out of the latrine, dead before he could fasten his belt, the sound of the shot coming across the valley a split second after he'd fallen.*

It was Afia, though, whom Jess saw most of all.

Sometimes it was different. Sometimes it wasn't so bad. Sometimes, when Jess saw her partner again, it was when the sun was still shining. No snipers, no RPGs, no Taliban ambush.

Sometimes it was Jess and Afia bonding over back issues of Betty and Veronica *in Jess's bunkhouse at the OP. Afia had confessed, teasingly, that she'd seen Jess as Veronica at first—the dark hair, sure, but she'd confused Jess's quiet reserve for something more judgmental, condescending.*

"Of course, you're Betty," she told Jess six or seven months after they'd started working together. "Kind, cheerful, hardworking. I see it now, but when we first met . . . " She winced. "I was scared of you, Private Winslow."

"And you?" Jess asked. "If I'm Betty, who does that make you?"

Afia cocked her head, thought about it, frowning everywhere but her eyes. "Jughead Jones," she said finally. "A good meal is more interesting to me than any romance, definitely."

Sometimes Jess remembered Afia in a village down valley, sharing a joke in Pashto with a group of local women, then translating for Jess so she could laugh too—something about the gunnery sergeant in the platoon Jess was attached to, a southern guy named Atkins, his voice like a bleating goat when he got mad or excited.

And sometimes she saw Afia with those same local women, cradling a baby, six weeks old at the latest, smiling down at him, cooing and singing softly—and then passing the bundle to Jess, who'd been surprised at first, apprehensive, afraid the women would take offense at an American sharing such an intimate moment. But she'd looked up at the women, at the baby's mother, and seen nothing but warmth and community there, women who knew next to nothing about one another sharing the one thing they all had in common.

It had been, perhaps, her favorite moment of that first deployment, of any deployment. She'd felt that little bundle in her arms long after she'd given him back, could picture his tiny hands, his scrunched-up face as he slept. She'd tried to write to Ty about it, in an email, but she hadn't found the words, hadn't been sure he'd understand anyway.

She'd shared that moment, instead, with Afia, and Afia alone. Afia, whose husband had died in a mortar attack before they could start a family; Afia, who in her grief had vowed never to marry again, and who had taken advantage of the sudden vastness of time spread in front of her to learn English, to volunteer, to work with the American marines, and with Jess in particular, her conduit to the women in the valley and the secrets they wouldn't share with men.

Those memories of Afia were painful, sure, but it was a different pain: delicate, bittersweet. It was a pain Jess savored, no matter how much it hurt, because that was how she wanted to remember Afia. Those were memories she cherished.

But mostly it was the last memory, that final, bloody day, that stuck in Jess's head and kept coming back. Afia was gone, but every night in her dreams Jess saw her friend's face again, saw the blood in the dirt and heard the screams, the screams she'd later learned were her own.

Something had woken her. Just what it was, Jess Winslow couldn't be sure, but she was awake now, wide awake and lightning fast, too, like she was back in that OP in the Hindu Kush, strapping on her body armor as someone triggered the alarm, listening to the sound of mortars launching, waiting for the boom.

Except she wasn't over there anymore. She was here, America, home, sacked out on the couch under a Pendleton blanket, the TV blaring infomercials, and God only knew what time it was. Dark outside; no light but the moon.

Lucy whined. Lifted her head from the floor, looked around, those big black ears perked. She looked up at Jess and whined a little more.

Whatever it was, it had scared the dog, too.

"Never mind, you big baby. It's probably just a deer." Jess sat up, rubbed sleep from her eyes. Found the remote and turned down the TV. "For a big, scary guard dog, you're kind of a wuss."

Lucy grumbled like she wanted to contest the point, but decided better of it and laid her head back down. Kept her eyes fixed on the front door, though, and her ears at high alert.

Though Lucy might have looked the part, the truth was she wasn't really a guard dog. There wasn't much that Jess owned that needed guarding. "Companion animal," the VA doc had called her. "Something to help you keep your mind over here."

Lucy helped, sort of.

She was a mutt, probably pit bull but not entirely; she had that square, blocky head and that big, dumb pit smile when she panted, but her body was long and more lean than stocky. A boxer, maybe, or some kind of retriever. Her hair was short and fine, jet black save a white snout and a stripe up her forehead, a patch on her neck and one on her belly, white socks on all four paws, and another patch like paint on the tip of her tail. She was a rescue, the lady at the agency had told Jess, a refugee from somewhere back east, from some assholes who'd aimed to fight her.

The agency lady had sworn Lucy had never actually fought, the law having caught up to the assholes in question before they could actually chuck her into a pit. They hadn't even snubbed her tail or clipped her ears, and for that Jess was glad. Lucy's ears were her most distinctive feature: velvet smooth and floppy like a Labrador retriever's, they channeled the dog's mood better than her perpetually sad eyes or even her bullwhip tail.

Right now Lucy's ears were standing rigid. There *was* something outside. Jess could sense it out there, was 98 percent sure she wasn't stuck in her head again, hearing phantom Taliban creeping through her front yard. Lucy whimpered once more, stood up straighter, glanced over at Jess, and took a couple of tentative steps toward the front door, and Jess knew neither she nor the dog was imagining anything. Whatever was out there, it was real.

She pushed the blanket from her lap. Stood, the light from the TV casting a bluish glow around the small living room. She crossed the room to the window and peered out into the night, saw nothing but empty road and dark forest—and then she caught the glint of moonlight against American steel, thirty yards down the road and almost invisible.

Jess stepped back from the window. Felt her heart rate ramp up. Hers wasn't a road that saw much traffic, especially this time of night. It dead-ended about a quarter mile in the other direction, petered off into second-growth fir and cedar. Weren't many other houses, either, not close by. The road wasn't close to the highway, or even the water; unless you lived nearby, you wouldn't think to come this far down—and that truck outside didn't look like the neighbors'.

Damn it, Ty. Her husband had promised her a new house when she came home from her tour, something closer to town, something better than this: one bedroom, one bathroom, and a patch of grass in the backyard, which she'd fenced in so Lucy could do her business without Jess needing to worry she'd run off after a chipmunk and never come back.

Ty had been full of promises. A new house. A better truck. Hell, a family. Instead, Jess had come home a widow, come home to a load of debt and the same shack as ever, come home with not much more than bad memories and no clue what to do with herself next.

She stole another glance out the window. The truck hadn't moved. She squinted, looked hard, but it was too dark to see inside, look for a driver. Too dark to catch the make and the model, even. *Maybe just some hunter got lost,* she thought. *Some kids hooking up or something.*

Beside her, Lucy was still staring at the door. And Jess saw the way the dog's hackles were raised, saw the way she stood stiff, square, like she really *was* a guard dog, and she knew this wasn't just a couple of horny teenagers fooling around. This was something else, something worse, and though Jess wasn't sure exactly what it was, she knew Ty must have had something to do with it.

Boot steps on the wooden porch interrupted that line of thinking. Heavy, slow, deliberate. Then a knock at the door, three knocks, the same measured pace. Like whoever was out there knew she was at home, knew she had nowhere to run.

Beside Jess, Lucy began to growl.

ONE

A man goes into a cage for fifteen years and he's bound to change inside, though in the end it's up to him whether that change is for the better or the worse. Sometimes even he won't know until he's let back out into the world again, and at that point, there isn't much that can be done but to stand back and keep watch, hope he isn't broken beyond fixing.

Mason Burke had been eighteen years old, a boy and a wild one, when he walked into the Chippewa state pen on Michigan's Upper Peninsula, and when he walked out again, his time served and fifteen years passed, he was no longer a boy and no longer wild, but still a mile shy of manhood and not fully tame, either.

He'd served his sentence quietly and without complaint, and he harbored no grudges. He was guilty of doing what the law said he'd done, what the courts had determined deserved fifteen years' penalty, and in consequence he'd spent nearly half of his life a prisoner—though as far as he was concerned, he'd been treated fair.

But he hadn't enjoyed prison. He'd learned how to survive, and how to pass the time, but just surviving fifteen years had forced him to stifle parts of himself he'd once thought were fundamental. He'd walked into prison a human being, albeit a flawed, reckless one, and as he stood outside those gates for the first time in one full decade and another half, buffeted by a chill November wind that swept across the barren parking lot, Mason couldn't even be sure of his own humanity anymore, couldn't be sure his time incarcerated hadn't reduced him to something lesser, something base, something unfit for the world that awaited him.

He didn't want to leave. That was the sickest part, the part that told Mason maybe something was broken inside him that could never be fixed. He wasn't the first prisoner to have panicked at the first breath of free air, and he wouldn't be the last, but as he stood gazing across that parking lot to the flat, dull land beyond, the whole world seemed impossibly large and alien, no walls and no boundaries, no structure, just a suffocating expanse of empty space and a lifetime's worth of codes and social norms he'd missed out on learning.

He wanted to turn around and walk back in through the gates, return his civilian clothes to where they'd stored them all this time, go back to his old cell and stretch out in that bunk and let the prison walls envelop him, protect him from the outside just as much as they protected the outside from people like him. He'd have said he was scared to be out in this world, except fear was a reaction you learned to hide damn fast on the inside. You learned to push it down, ignore it, until it just went away and you didn't feel scared anymore. The guys who got scared were the guys who didn't survive.

But there was no turning back, and Mason wouldn't have anyway, even if his sister hadn't been standing leaned up against a dusty Dodge Grand Caravan, hands in her coat pockets, squinting across the lot at him, studying her younger brother as he took his first steps back out into the world.

She took her hands from her pockets, gave him a little wave, shy and stilted. "Hi, Mase," she said, avoiding his eyes as he came across the pavement toward her. "Looks like you made it."

"We thought you could live with us for a while, me and Glen and the girls," Maggie said as she drove out of the parking lot and set the minivan on a two-hundred-mile course to the south. "There's a spare room in the basement you can stay in, rent-free, just so long as you keep out of trouble."

She was two years his senior, but it might as well have been twenty; she kept sneaking glances across at him like she was wondering who he was, wondering if he was still capable of doing the things he'd done long ago. Mason sat in the passenger seat and felt her eyes on him, and he looked out at the world as it passed his window. His stomach churned with the first stirrings of motion sickness.

"Glen said he could line up a job for you too." Maggie's voice was all forced cheer and fragile hope. "He says they're always looking for good, hardworking men."

Mason cleared his throat. "What does he do again?"

"Glen?" Maggie blinked. "Well, he's a real estate agent, Mase." She looked at him again. "Anyway, it wouldn't be like you were working *for* him, exactly, just they sometimes need people to clean the houses they're selling, do minor repairs, that kind of thing."

"Clean houses," Mason said.

"I mean, it wouldn't have to be forever, just until you got on your feet, right?"

"I thought I might stay at Mom's old place," he said.

Maggie's look was half pity, half wishful thinking, like she and Glen had probably had a hell of a fight about giving Mason that spare room, and familial duty had only barely won out.

"Oh, Mase," she said. "We sold Mom's place after she died, didn't we tell you?"

"I guess I must have just forgot," he replied, more for her sake than his. Maggie hadn't done much to keep him filled in on the family news while he'd been inside, and they both knew it.

"It was all falling apart anyway, needed so much work. Glen got us a good price, and—well, anyway. You didn't want to be fixing a bunch of plumbing and redoing a roof first thing after you got home, right?"

There was only one right answer to that question, and that was to lie, so Mason just didn't say anything. And Maggie waited long enough that his silence became an answer in itself, and then she sighed and reached for the radio, and Mason knew she was thinking the same thing that he was, that they'd driven just ten miles and they still had one hundred ninety more to go.

The first thing Mason did at Maggie's house—after he'd set his bag down in that basement spare room, after he'd enjoyed a cold beer and a scalding hot shower, scrubbed as much of that fifteen-years-in-captivity stink as he could from his skin—was to find a picture in his bag of a big black-and-white dog, set it on top of the nightstand beside his new bed.

Then he borrowed Maggie's phone and placed a call, to a Ms. Linda Petrie at the Rover's Redemption agency.

He'd kept Ms. Petrie's number since the last time he'd seen her, about six months before his release, had spent that whole stretch of time plotting this phone call. But Mason still felt the nerves as he listened to the ringing, drummed his fingers on his thigh and couldn't help pacing, knew this was probably against some kind of regulation, knew he should hang up the phone.

But Linda Petrie picked up before Mason could make that decision, and then there was no sense in anything but moving forward.

"Rover's Redemption." She sounded the same as Mason remembered: tough, take no shit.

"Ms. Petrie." The name came out rough, like he was out of practice. Like it took something extra to speak as a free man. "It's Mason Burke calling you."

Silence. Then, "I'm sorry, Mason . . . Burke? I don't—"

"I figured you might not remember," Mason continued. "You probably work with a lot of guys like me. I was up in the Chippewa pen this last go-around. Lucy was my dog."

"Oh, Lucy," Linda Petrie said. "Yes, I remember now, of course."

Mason waited, but she didn't say anything else, and he could sense by her tone that she wasn't exactly comfortable hearing his voice. He wondered if this was how he was going to feel for the rest of his life, like he was asking a huge favor just hoping people would look at him straight, have a conversation.

"Well, I was calling because I'm out now," he said. "And I got that postcard picture you sent of Lucy, and I wanted to check in and see if you knew how she's doing." He paused. "You know, how she's adjusting to her new home, and such."

Another pause. Then Mason heard Linda Petrie suck in her breath. "I really can't discuss what happens to the dogs after they leave the program, Mr. Burke—"

"Mason please, ma'am."

"Mason," she said, but there was still that *something else* in her voice. "I'm afraid I just can't give you any information," she said. "It wouldn't be appropriate; I'm sorry."

"Did she find a good home?" Mason asked. "I don't need to know where she is or anything, just that I set her up okay for when she went out into the world."

That long silence again. "I can't be talking about this," she said.

"Not with you. They'd pull the program if they found out I'd given this information to a—to a . . ."

She wanted to talk. Mason could tell. Something had happened, something was wrong, and the trainer was itching to talk to him about it.

"Is she alive, at least, Ms. Petrie? Tell me she's still alive."

But she couldn't even do that.

"There was an incident," she said. "Your dog attacked someone. From what I understand, she had to be destroyed."

"Destroyed." The word hit Mason like a roundhouse punch.

Petrie breathed out. "Listen, whatever happened, it wasn't your fault. Sometimes a dog just goes bad."

"Not Lucy," Mason said. "I know that dog. Something must have provoked her."

Petrie didn't say anything, and Mason realized he was pacing, his body tense, muscles clenched tight. He wasn't willing to believe it, not his dog, not Lucy. Not the dog he'd trained.

"Mason?"

"Yes, ma'am?"

"You just have to forget about this," Petrie said. "I'm sorry it didn't work out, but these things, you just have to move on."

She sounded scared. Like she thought she'd made a mistake telling him, like he was going to run off and do something crazy now.

"It's okay," he told her. "You don't have to worry about me."

He ended the call. Replaced the handset and went back down his sister's stairs to his basement bedroom. Found the picture of Lucy he'd propped up on the nightstand, and sat on the edge of the bed and stared at it for a while.

TWO

The dog wasn't *much to look at, the first time Mason saw her. Just a scared little black-and-white thing crammed up against the back wall of her crate with her tail between her legs, shaking, not making eye contact with Mason or anyone else.*

She was a pit bull—at least partially, anyway—but she didn't look like the pits Mason had seen growing up: solid, rough-looking dogs jacked front to back with heavy muscle, collared in chains, and boasting foul dispositions. The pit bulls Mason had known had been mean animals, goaded into aggression by owners who used the dogs to intimidate and impress—and, occasionally, to punish.

This creature, she wasn't impressing anyone. And she sure wasn't intimidating.

"That ain't a dog," Bridges Colson said, laughing, looking in at the little runt. "That there is fucking bait*."*

Bait. They all had a laugh at that, the lot of them—hell, Mason included. Laughed all the way until Ms. Linda Petrie pointed him over to that crate, told him the little runt dog was his dog, no two ways about it.

Mason looked over at the other guys, their own dogs—puppies, yellow Labrador retrievers, German shepherds, a couple of gangly, hairy mutts—all of them strong, all of them happy as a TV commercial, big pink tongues lolling out, chasing balls, shaking paws, the whole doggie dream, and he looked in at his own little wretch and felt damn cheated.

But Linda Petrie was talking again, and there was something about when she talked, you wanted to pay attention. Like she didn't give a shit, like she'd march right into the Chippewa pen and stand up in front of a couple of dozen hardened felons and not even worry if the two guards behind her would have her back if the whole show went sideways. And that's pretty much how she did it.

"This won't be happy hour," she was saying. "And there's nothing that says we have to keep you here, with these dogs. This is a privilege the warden has extended you, and if he or these two gentlemen behind me come to believe you're abusing that privilege, well, hell, they'll find someone else who appreciates the opportunity a little more. Are we clear?"

She looked hard at the men, each of them in turn, and when she looked at Mason, he nodded like the rest. Wanted to ask what happened if your dog washed out before you did, but Ms. Linda Petrie had moved on.

"This isn't the start of some lifelong friendship, either," she said. "You'll work with your dog for six months, train them up, and then we'll place them in homes with people who'll care for them. You won't get to see them again, so don't bother asking. Anyone have a problem with that?"

Nobody had a problem. The trainer went over some other stuff, like from a script, how the Rover's Redemption agency was truly grateful for their time and effort, and how if they let them, the dogs might just teach them something about themselves in the process, but Mason was kind of tuning the whole spiel out; he peered back into the crate at the pitiful creature within and wondered what in the hell this dog was supposed to teach him; it couldn't even come out and say hi.

Wouldn't last an hour on the yard, *he thought*. These hard boys would mess you straight up.

Beside Mason, Bridges Colson's dog—a big, dumb golden retriever—was all over him, a real sight to behold; the meanest guy in the room, and he was giggling like a child as his dog gave him the most slobbery face wash Mason had ever seen.

Meanwhile, the little black-and-white runt at the back of the crate stared out at him, with big brown eyes that looked away fast when she caught him looking back. Must have weighed thirty pounds, tops.

The name on her crate said LUCY.

"Bit of a fixer-upper, that one," a voice said beside him, and Mason looked up to find Linda Petrie standing there, didn't even realize she'd finished her lecture. "Come out of a dogfighting sting down in Muskegon, about thirty dogs on the property, most of them too far gone to be saved."

Mason looked at her. "They killed them?"

"Yup. Either too mean already, or too tore up by the mean ones. By the time we heard about it, they'd destroyed all but six." She looked off into the middle distance a moment. Then she shook her head clear. "So you're going to have to work a little harder with her, is what I'm telling you."

"Why'd they even save her?" Mason asked. "She looks damn scared."

"She's scared, sure, she's been on the bum end of the stick every day of her young life. But we're going to show her she's got better days ahead, right?" The trainer hunched down beside Mason, reached into the crate with both hands. "Lucy," she said, her voice transformed to pure sweetness. "Come on out, girl."

This was the closest to Mason a woman had been in fourteen years. He could smell the soap she used, feel the other prisoners staring, knew the guards were somewhere nearby, tensed up in case he should decide to do anything foolish. Knew the other guys would give it to him if he didn't try a move. But somehow Linda Petrie had coaxed Lucy out of the crate, the poor dog hunched over and folded in on herself like a dang paper clip, long spindly legs shivering, eyes darting everywhere.

"There you go," the trainer was saying. "There's a good girl. No one's going to hurt you out here."

The dog wasn't convinced. She tried to bust back into that crate, but Petrie had the door closed and locked, trapping her outside.

"There we go," she said, standing. "Now you two can get acquainted."

She walked over to Bridges Colson's magazine-cover golden, left Mason sitting there with a dog who wanted nothing more in the world than to not *get acquainted with anyone.*

Mason put out his hand. "Hey, girl," he tried. "Hey, Lucy."

Lucy shivered. Backed away. Ignored the peace offering. She scratched at her crate like she was sure he was trying to kill and eat her. Mason looked at her some more. Rubbed the back of his neck.

"Damn," he said, and he reached over and wrapped his arms underneath Lucy's front legs, dragged her back to him squirming, lifted her off the ground, and held her up to face him.

"I don't mean you any harm," he told her. Tried to get her to meet his eyes with her own. "I'm here to help you, dog. Just a friend."

Lucy looked at him, met his gaze briefly, and for that instant Mason could swear he maybe felt something, a connection, like the dog had heard what he'd said and understood, and for that one moment he felt like he knew why he'd been partnered with this *dog, like this was something with some deeper meaning.*

Then Lucy looked away, and Mason felt something warm on his legs, and he looked down and the damn dog had pissed all over his lap.

THREE

"If you could spare a little money, I'd be grateful," Mason said. "I'll pay you back, soon as I can."

Across the table, his sister swapped a glance with her husband. Set down her fork. "Girls," she said. "Go finish your homework."

Mason waited while his nieces pushed back their chairs and carried their plates into the kitchen. Brianna, ten years old, and Natalie, eight; they were Mason's blood, but neither of them had known him before today. The girls looked at him like they were scared of their uncle, put off by his sudden appearance in their lives.

He couldn't fault them for it. Just his physical presence alone was bound to be off-putting. He'd always been tall, even as a kid, and so many years in a prison gymnasium had built his body into a form that seemed cartoonish and threatening out here in the real world, a menace come to life who couldn't even maintain eye contact.

And here he was, asking for money.

Mason hated to do it. He knew he was only giving life to his sister's worst fears, her no-good brother come to leech as much as he could from the family before he did another bad thing and got himself locked up again.

But Mason had done more than just lift weights up in the Chippewa pen. He'd read a fair bit too, whatever he could find. Trying to prepare for the moment he stepped out from inside the prison walls and found himself a free man again; for the years that lay ahead of him; for what meager atonement he could seek for the damage he'd caused.

He hadn't found answers; what he'd found were first steps. And though he wished he didn't have to start the journey begging for a favor, he couldn't see any other way to set about getting started, not as fast as he needed to go. He could only hope that his sister would see that *this* path of his was a true one, unlike so many of the paths she'd seen him walk before.

When the girls were gone, Maggie's husband cleared his throat. Glen, a decent guy, kind of boring. He'd always been decent, always been boring, from what little Mason could remember, a clipped-beard, pleated-khakis kind of guy. But then, boring seemed to be Maggie's type; she seemed happy, anyway.

"How much money are we talking, Mason?" Glen asked. Even the tone of his voice had a decency to it.

"However much you can spare," Mason said. "There's something I have to take care of, now that I'm out."

"We're giving you room and board," Maggie said quietly. Eyes down at her plate. "A room to sleep in and hot meals. That isn't enough?"

"I know I'm putting you out, Mags, and I'm grateful for all of it. But you don't want me hanging around here forever. Sooner I can get my life together, the better for everyone."

"So how much?" Glen said. "How much are you thinking you'd need to make a start, Mason?"

"A couple grand ought to do it, I figure."

"A couple *grand*?" Maggie was looking at him now, half laughing, incredulous. "Where do you think you are, Mase? Trump Tower?"

"I'll pay you back," Mason told her. "I swear, I'll be good for it."

Maggie and Glen looked at each other again. For a long while nobody said anything.

Deception Cove, Washington. That's where Lucy had gone.

Linda Petrie had given every inmate a photograph of "his" dog, taken by the new owner somewhere out in the real world. Mason had kept his close; the edges were rough worn now, and there was a crease down the middle, but there wasn't any way in the world he would ever part with it.

In the picture, Lucy had filled out since that first day in the pen, put on some muscle. She was sitting in the grass in a sunlit field, sitting proud, head held high and that big, goofy smile on her face, that tongue lolling out of her mouth. She looked happy. She looked good, as good as Mason had ever seen her.

There was a note on the back of the picture. Linda Petrie's handwriting. *Lucy—with thanks, LP.* That was all it said.

Mason had studied that photograph and that handwriting in his basement bedroom after the telephone conversation with Linda Petrie. He'd known Lucy six months, practically night and day, trained her, never known her to tend toward violence. Yet she'd gone and attacked somebody? That didn't make sense.

There was a building behind Lucy in the photograph, across the grassy field. Looked like a school, one story, nothing special. A sign on the cinder-block wall, the words cut off in the middle: N COVE H.S. HOME OF THE RAVENS.

Mason had set the picture aside. Left the basement bedroom and climbed the stairs to the kitchen. His sister and her husband kept a computer in a den off the living room; Mason found the den, found the computer unlocked. Brought up an internet search window, typed: "N Cove High School Ravens."

The results loaded: a high school, a small town in northwest

Washington State, the Olympic Peninsula, way out on the farthest edge of the country. Mason ran another search, just the town name, got a few pretty pictures: the ocean, forest, a few fishing boats. An Indian reservation nearby, the Makah tribe, a big museum, and a few ecotourism outfits. The town of Deception Cove was too small to have its own animal control people, so Mason dialed up the Makah County seat in Neah Bay, figured he'd start with the central office.

"Calling about a dog," he told the woman who answered. "Supposed to have got in an incident, bit someone."

"Got more than a few dogs who'd fit that description," the woman replied. "You want to be more specific."

"Black-and-white dog, medium sized," Mason said. "Name's Lucy, or it was. This would have been over in Deception Cove."

"Oh," the woman said. "Yeah, all right. You're talking about that pit bull who went and bit the sheriff's deputy."

Mason blinked. "She bit a *deputy*?"

"Yes, sir. Bit him pretty good, from what I heard. Left him in a whole mess of stitches."

"A deputy," Mason said. "I mean, dang. What were the circumstances?"

The woman sucked her teeth. "A house call gone bad, I guess. Who knows? The sheriff's deputies down at Deception Cove handled that one themselves. We just heard it through the grapevine."

"Who's the owner?" Mason asked. "I mean, how'd he let this happen?"

"Some ex-marine, and he's a *she*. But like I said, I don't know the specifics. Listen, what's your interest in this dog, anyway? You writing a news story or something?"

"Just a concerned citizen," Mason replied.

"Yeah, well, no cause for concern," the woman told him. "That dog's due to be destroyed any day now. I don't know why they haven't put her down already."

"We aren't exactly flush with cash at the moment, Mase," Maggie said finally. "Glen's business slows up in the winter, and with Christmas on the way—"

"I understand that," Mason said. "I'm not trying to take food from the girls' mouths. But you must have cleared about a hundred grand when you sold Mom's place, right?"

Maggie glanced at Glen. Glen nodded, started to say something. Mason beat him to it. "You paid down the mortgage, I imagine. Probably socked money away for the girls to go to college, and I'm fine with that, Maggie. I'm not asking for half of what you made from that sale, or even a quarter. Just a couple grand to get me where I need to go, and you can count on getting that money back."

Maggie looked down at her plate, seemed to be working out what she wanted to say next. Finally, without looking up, she went for it. "What do you really need that money for, Mase?"

Mason hesitated. "I'm done with all that old stuff," he told Maggie. "I swear it. But I've got a friend from inside who ran into a jam out west on the coast. I need to head out there, try and make things right."

Maggie raised her head to meet her husband's eyes. But she didn't say anything.

"It's important, Maggie. I wouldn't ask if it wasn't."

Another long silence. Mason studied his sister. On Maggie's other side, Glen was doing the same. Finally she closed her eyes. Shook her head, slight, almost imperceptible, as she blew out a breath and muttered, *"Fine."*

"Thank you," Mason said. "I won't ask for another dollar."

They didn't believe him, he could tell. But they were polite enough not to say so to his face.

"The bank's closed already," Glen said after a while. "We'll have to get the money to you tomorrow."

"Tomorrow's fine," Mason told him. "Early would be best."

FOUR

"Do not withhold good to those to whom it is due," Proverbs said, "when it is in your power to do it."

Mason hadn't grown up religious. His mom had dragged both him and Maggie to the local Baptist church when they were youngsters, and as far as Mason knew, his mother had kept going long after she'd given up trying to force her son's attendance. He was already sloughing off the Sunday services by the time he turned a teenager; figured he'd given the Lord twelve years to make his gospel stick, and it hadn't. There were better things to do on a Sunday.

Maggie had kept going, more to placate her mother than out of any religious fervor. Mason wondered how long she'd kept it up, if she still went, if she ever felt she gained anything from it.

The library at the Chippewa pen had been a limited one, but Mason figured he'd read every book in there at least a couple of times before he finally picked up a Bible. The library had had plenty of those.

By that point in his incarceration, Mason was through feeling sorry for himself. He was through wishing he'd done something different, through being angry: at the world for how it had raised him, at himself for all the ways he hadn't resisted. He felt guilt, above all, and an encompassing shame, a desire to be better than the angry, violent boy he'd been when he arrived there.

He built his body in the gym, day after day. He kept his head down, and he stayed out of trouble. And he read, every night, from the Bible and anything else he could find, and little by little, he laid himself guidelines, a blueprint for living better when he was finally free.

"Let the thief no longer steal," read Ephesians, "but rather let him labor, doing honest work with his own hands, so that he may have something to share with anyone in need."

The bus ticket to Deception Cove would cost Mason $161.50. Glen and Maggie drove him to the bus station directly from the bank, where Glen had handed Mason an envelope with twenty crisp hundred-dollar bills inside. Glen had played it cool, even cracked a joke, like, "You don't have to count it, it's all there," but Maggie had shushed him, avoided looking at Mason as he climbed back into Glen's Grand Caravan, and Glen had pulled out of the lot.

They were like a whole other species, Mason thought, watching his sister and her husband from the back seat of the minivan. Or Mason was the other species; his sister was living the normal life, doing exactly what a thirty-five-year-old woman was supposed to be doing: raising a family, paying a mortgage, saving for retirement. Meanwhile, Mason, thirty-three himself, had no skills, no money, no job, had wasted nearly two decades when he could have been learning self-reliance and normalcy and how to open a checking account.

He would start with Lucy, and then he would deal with the rest.

"Fifty-seven hours," Glen said, shaking his head and laughing a little when Mason purchased the bus ticket. "Cripes, Mason. Are you sure you don't want to fly out there?"

Bus would be fine, Mason replied. He figured he would need to save the money, figured he'd spent fifteen years in prison; what was three days on a bus? He didn't mention he had never been on a plane before and didn't expect he'd ever feel the need to change that. The bus would be fine.

When Maggie excused herself to use the restroom, Glen pulled Mason aside. Took him by the arm and leaned in, spoke softer. "Listen, Mason," he said, "you're sure you're not in any trouble? I mean, this whole trip and whatever, it's a little . . ." He gestured back over his shoulder. "Maggie's worried about you. I told her you were fine, but she wanted me to make sure."

Mason glanced toward the restrooms, no sign of Maggie. Wondered if his sister really cared, whether this wasn't just Glen's decent streak shining through all over again.

"If there's anything we can do," Glen said. "You know, if you're in any trouble. You can always talk to us. To *me*."

"It's nothing like that," Mason told him. "I just need to help out this friend."

Glen rubbed his chin. "Yeah?" he said. "Well, look, you play it safe, okay? No sense in your getting mixed up in anything, now that you're finally out."

Mason promised he'd be careful. Held out his hand, and Glen shook it, firm, looked at Mason like he wanted to say something else but didn't quite know how to put it.

Then Maggie was back, and Mason's bus was announced, and the moment was over. Mason hugged his sister quickly, thanked her again and told her goodbye, and boarded the bus. And that was the last Mason saw of his only family in the world for a good long while.

Fifty-seven hours. Transfers in Chicago, Minneapolis, Billings, Missoula, Seattle. Bleary-eyed breakfasts in bus station diners. Long, lonely hours on the road. Mason made himself comfortable. Bought a *Time* magazine at a newsstand in Chicago, a *Car and Driver,*

Rolling Stone. Paged through them as the bus traced the shore of Lake Michigan up to Milwaukee, recognized few of the musicians and none of the politicians, the cars nothing like the cars he remembered.

Fifteen years. He left the magazines on a bench in Minneapolis. Stared out the bus window and thought about the dog.

"Our job is to prepare these dogs for lives of service," Linda Petrie said, walking patrol in front of the men and their dogs, three days into the program. "For some of you, this will mostly be a matter of basic obedience. . . ."

She looked at Bridges Colson, at his golden, and smiled. The dog was named Rascal, and the dog's name was an apt one. Rascal couldn't sit still, couldn't help causing mayhem, tug-of-war with his leash, roughhousing with other dogs and with Bridges, chewing on everything he could get his teeth around. He was a good dog, and funny, the class clown. He was pretty well the dog Mason had had in mind when he'd signed up for the program.

Linda Petrie resumed her patrol. "For others," she said, looking Mason's way, "it's going to require a little more work."

Bridges Colson looked over too. "Bait," *he said, smirking. "Might as well save the kibble and put that runt out of her misery now. Be the only* humane *option, my opinion."*

A few of the other prisoners laughed, and Mason joined in. Figured Bridges was probably right, couldn't see this dog serving anyone, anywhere. He didn't laugh as loud as he had on day one, though; the bait shit was starting to get old.

Mason was still working on coaxing Lucy out of her crate and into the great beyond. She was still shivering plenty when she saw him, still terrified, but Mason liked to think she wasn't so much scared of him *in particular; she just wanted him to know she was scared of just about everything else in the world.*

She hadn't pissed on him again, anyway; he'd learned his lesson. And she took treats from him now, haltingly, nibbled on them from his fingers, then retreated, then came back, cautious, to nibble again. She'd let him scratch behind her ears, even leaned in a little when he found the good spot. But then someone had slammed a door somewhere, and she'd spooked and bolted into her crate again.

"She's got to learn to trust you," Linda Petrie told him. "You're going to have to be patient, and show her that you're kind." She looked at him, appraising. "Can you be kind?"

Mason didn't quite know how to respond. Kindness wasn't exactly a prized quality inside the Chippewa pen. Kindness meant soft, and soft meant you were a pussy, and pussies didn't survive long inside. He'd spent fourteen years trying to erase anything in his person that might be construed as vulnerability. Kindness wasn't really in his vocabulary anymore.

But the trainer was still watching him, studying him. Like she was looking, hard, for some hope for this dog's future, and she wasn't seeing it in the piece-of-shit convict in front of her.

Something about the way she looked at him made Mason angry. Like she'd written him off already, like everyone else in his damn life had, inside and out. Like Bridges Colson had written off the dog without even knowing her. Shit.

"Yeah, I can handle this," Mason said, and he dug into his pocket, found another treat, a piece of the dried beef liver he'd noticed was Lucy's favorite. "You don't have to worry about us."

It was a Wednesday morning when Mason boarded his first bus. On Friday night the sixth bus turned off of state Route 112 and pulled to a stop in an empty ARCO parking lot, and the driver opened the door and stood and called "Deception Cove" back to the half dozen passengers still on board.

Mason was the only one to get off the bus. He thanked the

driver and stood in the cold drizzle, watching the bus pull away, listened to the sound of its engine until the taillights disappeared around a bend in the road and the sound diminished to nothing, until the only thing he could hear was the buzzing of the lights above on the ARCO canopy and, somewhere in the distance, the sound of the surf.

Mason stood there and thought for a while. He wanted to talk to the sheriff, the deputy in question, see if he could tease out the real story. See if there was any way the local law enforcement could be swayed to break toward leniency. At the very least, figure out what had happened and why.

But it was too late at night to start anything now. From the looks of the town, anyone with any sense had already gone to bed. Mason drew his coat tighter, squared his shoulders. Set out into the rain down the highway, the way the bus had come in, remembered seeing a motel a ways back, a bright VACANCY sign. Figured it would do to get out of the rain, get some sleep. First thing tomorrow he'd have to buy some dry clothes.

FIVE

Looking back, Jess *realized the whole op had felt wrong—or maybe that was just hindsight. In her dreams, anyway, she could think of a million reasons why she and Afia should have just walked away.*

They figured out pretty quick that the preliminary intelligence was wrong, or at least wildly optimistic, as they walked down from the forward outpost and south into the narrow, high-walled valley, that place of shale and pine they'd been fighting Haji over for the better part of their deployment, and seemingly every marine deployment before that, back to the dawn of the corps itself. The sun was baking hot, as usual, and it glared down from on high like an insurgent sniper, another malevolent force in that hostile land.

They were headed down the valley to check up on a lead Jess had unearthed with Afia, whispered rumors about the enemy falling back, redeploying men and machine guns to other places, other valleys, other fights with other Americans. It had sounded too good from the outset, but the marines didn't give points for shying away from the tough stuff, and anyway, as far as the guys in the OP were concerned, they'd been brought here for one purpose, and that was to kill insurgents. If Haji thought they were crafty enough to outfox the baddest fighting force on the planet, well, let the motherfuckers try.

It sounded good in theory, but in practice, filing down goat trails with a parched throat and grit in your eyes and every fucking snapped twig the shot that might kill your best buddy? Jess figured most of the guys in the patrol felt like she did: i.e., this was a very bad idea.

They'd given her the dog for nights like this. For the desolate, lonely, desperate nights, the rain hammering down on the roof above her, the wind gusting through the trees like voices from beyond. These were the nights when even Ty's little four-room shack seemed impossibly vast and filled with ghosts—Afia's ghost, Ty's, all the others Jess had collected. These nights, when the dreams came back visceral and cinematic, the memories inescapable. These were the nights when Lucy earned her keep.

The dog knew her; Jess couldn't argue that point. They'd spent a month on a ranch together in eastern Washington, feeling each other out as the trainers watched. It wasn't long before Lucy could pick out by Jess's breathing that an attack was coming. Soon the dog learned to scout around corners in the grocery store for her, watch her six for surprises when they walked into town. And when the nights got long and empty back home, and Jess dreamed of the valley and woke up screaming herself hoarse, Lucy would climb into bed beside her, snuggle up close and lick her face, cuddle, until the nightmares were gone, and the valley gone with them.

But Lucy hadn't been here since the night Kirby Harwood knocked on Jess's door, a month or so back. As far as Jess could surmise, the dog wasn't ever coming home. So now, with a storm raging outside and the dark house cold and empty, there wasn't anyone to turn to when the memories came clawing back, nobody who could save her. Jess lay in bed amid tangled sheets, the rain pouring down outside and a bitter wind howling, and still she couldn't escape the valley.

The feeling of foreboding only got worse as they neared the village, the sun directly overhead now and scorching hot, sweat dripping down Jess's back beneath the body armor she wore. It was the noise, she realized, or the lack thereof; the closer they got to the objective, the quieter the valley seemed to get. No birds, no animals, no human voices. The air was still, waiting for what happened next.

The village was three or four clicks down the valley from the OP, nestled plumb on the frontier between American-controlled territory and the enemy. Go much farther down the road and you'd better have the whole damn corps at your back, unless you were suicidal.

The village was built up along the east side of the valley, the terrain so steep that no house sat level with its neighbor, and each row of houses stood entirely above the last, the whole place tied together by narrow, labyrinthine passages cut into jagged shale, the valley above choked with rock and dense forest.

They didn't have the whole damn corps, but they did have Second Platoon spread out on the western side of the valley for cover, mortars and shooters alike, a couple of 240s, machine guns, and a .50 cal to boot. There were even supposed to be Apaches for air cover, so as far as command was concerned, all bases were covered. The Apaches never showed, diverted to more pressing concerns a couple of valleys over, but as it turned out, none of that would matter anyway.

They were almost at the village when Jess saw the boy. He was hiding behind a low stone wall, peering out at the marines as they passed, his eyes wide and serious. She recognized Selab, one of the villagers' children; he was eight or nine years old, and precocious, if a little shy. He'd watched Jess and Afia drink tea with his mother and the other women in the village, lurking on the margins of the room, clearly curious but always silent.

He'd looked at Jess in awe then, as though he'd never expected to see an American woman in combat attire, as though she were something larger than life and fantastical, a comic-book heroine. Now he just looked worried, and when she waved to him and smiled, he didn't wave back, just ducked down quickly and didn't reappear. And still the air was quiet.

Nobody else had noticed Selab.

Their contact, a woman named Panra, watched from the shade beside one of the village houses as the marines fanned out, forming a perimeter. She wore a chador, a scarf over her head, and a traditional patterned firaq partug, *a flowing, billowy garment over loose, baggy trousers. Her expression was inscrutable.*

Jess caught the eye of her platoon CO, Lieutenant Grieves, who nodded up toward the village and shook his head, frowning. His meaning was clear: no matter how many marines they brought to secure the area, the topography would give any enemy the advantage. From the cliffs overlooking the houses, any number of Taliban soldiers could camp out with rifles and RPGs, raining hell on any marine unlucky enough to be caught out in the open. It was not an ideal place to be spending time, not if you had an American flag on your gear, but Panra had sworn to Afia that her elders had good information, and Panra had always been reliable in the past.

Sweat had drenched Jess's combat gear by the time she and Afia crossed the twenty yards from Grieves to where Panra stood in the shade. Afia and Panra exchanged a few words in Pashto, and Panra gestured up into the passageway behind her, a narrow stair cut into the mountainside, so steep it was impossible to tell exactly where it led. She smiled quickly at Jess, then gestured again, her eyes darting back to the marines spread out behind, ducked down behind low walls with rifles at the ready, waiting on the first shot that would reveal the ambush.

Jess might have woken at this point if she'd had Lucy with her. She might have called out in her sleep to Afia, a warning, or she might have moaned slightly or whimpered, and the dog, attuned to any sign of anxiety, would have saved her from what was to come. She would have woken to Lucy's rough tongue on her cheek, or the dog might even have barked to rouse her. Jess would have opened her eyes, heard the rain outside, and the wind; she would have felt the dog's presence, and she would have known, suddenly and clearly, that she was safe.

But the dog wasn't here. Jess was alone, imprisoned in her nightmare. And there was no way she knew of to escape what happened next.

SIX

Avoid eye contact.

Mason had learned it pretty quick in the yard. Eye contact was a challenge. A challenge meant a fight. And a fight in Chippewa only led to a couple of outcomes: you kicked someone's ass and you pissed people off, guards or the guy's friends; or you got your ass kicked and the yard decided you were easy prey. Fights sucked. Mason had worked hard to avoid them.

Out in the free world, though, you couldn't just go through your days not looking people in the eye, not if you wanted anyone to trust you.

Mason was still learning that. Still retraining his eyes to maintain a connection, training his face out of the slack, expressionless stare he'd cultivated inside. He was still learning to look like a human being again.

He woke at first light, a dull gray through the motel room's thin curtains. The parking lot outside his door was empty, ditto the highway beyond. The rain was still falling, a chill, endless trickle that somehow seemed colder and less inviting than a blizzard back home.

Mason slid the curtain back. Made the bed. At the foot of the bed, he did push-ups and sit-ups, one hundred of each. He'd been lax on the bus ride; no way to exercise. He could feel it now; even a lapse of three days was like a major setback. He wouldn't let it happen again.

He showered, and dressed again in yesterday's jeans and his only spare shirt, then locked up his room and walked across to the lobby. He'd woken the owner last night, an older man who'd come out of the back room rubbing his eyes and yawning, handed Mason a key and told him to come back in the morning, settle up then.

The man was at the front desk when Mason walked into the lobby. He looked up and smiled, and Mason reminded himself to meet the man's gaze.

"Morning," the man said. "Sleep okay?"

"I did," Mason said. "Thank you. I'm going to stick around a couple of days, if that's okay."

"That'd be just fine. Forty dollars a night, or two hundred a week." The man flipped open a black binder. "You have a driver's license?"

"No, sir."

"Credit card?"

"No, sir. But I'd be glad to give you a deposit up front, if you need one."

The man looked him over. He was probably fifty or so, Native American, shorter than Mason, but thick, muscles gone to fat. On the wall behind him was a framed picture, a man in desert fatigues, sun-bleached earth and sand in the background. It was an older shot, and Mason realized it was the same guy.

"Heck," the man said, "you're not going to trash my room, are you?"

"No, sir," Mason said.

"So give me the three nights up front, and if you wind up staying longer, we'll throw it into the weekly. What's your name, son?"

"Burke," Mason said. "Mason Burke."

The man wrote Mason's name in his binder. "Where you from, Mr. Burke?"

"Michigan," Mason said. From his back pocket he removed Glen's envelope. Removed a hundred-dollar bill and a twenty, and slid them across the counter.

"Here on vacation?"

"Come to see a friend," Mason said as the man tucked the money into the cash register. "You wouldn't know where I could find the sheriff in these parts?"

The man chuckled, gestured up the highway, west. "Sheriff Wheeler's up the road at the county seat in Neah Bay, but at this stage of the game, he's largely ineffectual," he said. "You want to talk to the law around here, you want Kirby Harwood, and his office is just down the hill with what's left of the town. Second building up from the government wharf; you can't miss it."

"Harwood," Mason said. "He the deputy got bit by that dog?"

The guy cocked his head. "You heard about that already, did you? Yeah, Kirby's the one. Bit him right on the ass, that dog did. Likely had a good reason, though I can see how Kirby'd disagree. Anyway, sounds like it was the last night of fun that dog's ever going to have."

"Heard that, too. The owner, she's a veteran or something?"

"That's right, Afghanistan. Dog was supposed to be some kind of therapy animal."

"You know how I would find her?" Mason asked.

The man paused and kind of narrowed his eyes. "What's your business there, Mr. Burke?" he replied. "This whole fiasco doesn't sound like the kind of thing that'd make the nightly news back home in Detroit."

"No, sir," Mason said. "It didn't make the news. I'm just wondering why that dog would want to go and bite someone that way."

The man studied him a little longer. "I'm afraid I can't help you," he said, closing his binder. "This is starting to sound like trouble, and more trouble is the last thing that woman needs right now."

"It's not trouble I'm after," Mason said. "But I—"

The man set his hand down on the counter. "Enjoy your stay here in our little town, Mr. Burke," he said. "Whatever your reasons for being here, I'd appreciate if you didn't bring them back to my establishment."

The town of Deception Cove was a rainy-day kind of place, and would have been so even if the sun had been shining. As Mason walked the main road down the hill to the water, he passed more than a handful of abandoned homes in the trees, fallen-down hulks reclaimed by the rain forest, moss-covered and rotten doorways and windows like black, empty eyes.

At the bottom of the main road was the town proper, a handful of ramshackle buildings spread along a thoroughfare far too wide for the meager business it was conducting. Beyond this abbreviated downtown was the water, the ocean, and Mason imagined that on clear days the view from the hill must be spectacular.

It was not a clear day, though, and the view was more gray: thick clouds and low fog obscuring the horizon, slate-black seawater pebbled with rain. The government wharf extended out from the foot of the road on pilings, and from it extended a number of floating docks, empty save for half a dozen decrepit fishing trollers, of which all but a couple looked moments from a watery grave.

There was a building on the water too, to the west of the government wharf, on the left from Mason's standpoint. It extended out on stilts, corrugated metal gone rusted brown-red, a half-sunk floating dock of its own. DECEPTION COVE SEAFOODS, the sign on the roof would have read once, though it was now rendered nearly illegible by a succession of graffiti artists of varying levels of talent.

Nothing much seemed to move as Mason descended the hill. A

pickup truck pulled out from somewhere, came up toward Mason, its engine struggling with the incline, windshield wipers working hard, its headlights dim yellow smears against the gray backdrop.

Mason reached the buildings, found a couple of bars, a grocery store. A marine outfitter and a diner. The sheriff's deputy's office and a boarded-up gas station. He stopped at the diner first, ordered eggs, hash browns, and bacon from a tired-looking waitress, ate his breakfast and drank coffee and looked out at the sheriff's deputy's office. It was a one-story building, a couple of cruisers and a big, jacked-up red pickup truck out front. Mason paid for his meal, left a generous tip, and walked across the street to the marine supply store.

The business appeared to function as part machine shop, part general store. It was a small, crowded space, shelves piled to the roof with fishing gear and tackle, rope of various sizes, engine lubricants, tools, and hunting knives, much of it covered in a thin film of dust. Behind the cash register sat a bored-looking man in his seventies, reading a paperback adventure novel through bifocal lenses. He nodded when Mason walked into the store, went back to his reading. Behind him, in a locked display cabinet, was a selection of rifles and shotguns for sale.

Mason found a package of Jockey shorts and some thick socks. A couple of T-shirts with fishing company logos on them, a Stanfield's wool sweater, and two pairs of Wrangler jeans. He carried them to the front and deposited them on the counter, waited as the man finished his page and dog-eared the novel and stood, wearily, to sort through Mason's purchases.

The man moved at a deliberate pace. Mason stood back and looked out through the doorway, watched the rain fall. Read the notices tacked to the bulletin board by the door, someone selling an outboard motor, someone selling a car, a couple of different men looking for deckhand jobs.

The store owner caught him reading. "Hope you're not looking for work," he said, his voice gravel. "There isn't any."

"I'm not looking for work." Mason glanced out at the rain again. Turned and came back to the counter holding a green oilskin rain jacket. "But I am hoping to stay dry."

The man let Mason change clothes in a little bathroom in the back of the store. Mason pulled on the Wranglers, a fresh T-shirt, the wool sweater, new socks. Let himself enjoy the feeling of being clean, dry, warm. Bagged up his dirties and thanked the man at the counter, pulled the oilskin jacket tight and set out into the rain again.

He didn't have far to go; the sheriff's deputy's office was next door. Both cruisers remained outside, and the big pickup, too. Mason looked it over as he passed. Imagined a life where he drove something like that, something flashy and powerful and gleaming and new, something that screamed *Look at me, I'm important* to everyone who saw it.

The deputy's office was an open-plan kind of deal. A large room, a receptionist by the entrance, a couple of desks, and a private office in back. Somewhere in the building there was bound to be a lockup. Maybe that was where they were keeping Lucy.

The girl at the front desk looked to be about sixteen, Mason figured, unless people grew up different in this part of the world. She snapped her gum as she looked him over. "How can I help you?"

"Looking for Deputy Harwood," Mason told her. "Is he around?"

The girl swiveled on her chair, hollered into the back. *"Kirby!"*

Shortly, the door to the private office swung open, and three men came out, one after another. They were young, all of them in their twenties, ruddy faced and windburned and tall. They were laughing and shoving one another, pistols on their hips and badges over their hearts, a swagger to their step that Mason couldn't miss. These kids were the law in this town, and they knew it.

Kirby Harwood turned out to be the eldest of the bunch, though even he couldn't yet be thirty. He had blond hair, a tight crew cut, a square jaw, and a smirk. He looked at the receptionist and then at Mason, and he nudged the other two men aside and strode to the front of the detachment, a politician's smile on his face.

"Kirby Harwood," he said, his hand outstretched. "What can I do for you, sir?"

Mason shook the deputy's hand. "Mason Burke," he said. "Come to talk to you about the dog that attacked you."

Harwood's smile flickered, just for an instant. Then it was back. "Well, all right, Mr. Burke, was it?" he said. "Why don't you come on back to my office."

Mason could feel the eyes of the other men watching him as he followed the deputy back through the detachment. Wondered why Harwood even bothered with the pretense of privacy; Mason was pretty certain there weren't many secrets in this town. But he let the deputy guide him into the office anyway.

The deputy walked with a slight limp, Mason noticed, though he didn't appear to be in much pain. If he hadn't recovered fully from Lucy's bite, he was close.

The office was small and cluttered, with a cheap plywood desk and a couple of chairs, and a view out over the alley in back, more rain and rust, not exactly a vista. On the desk sat a new-looking iMac computer and a handful of pictures mounted in black frames: a sleek white powerboat, Harwood with some fish. No wife or children, no dog.

Harwood caught him looking. "Grady-White Express Three Seventy," he said, proud. "Thousand horses back there, hell of a boat. You do any fishing?"

"No, sir," Mason said.

"You ought to. Best halibut fishing in the world just offshore here. Catch you a hundred-pounder, easy, if you know what you're doing."

"I don't," Mason said. "But maybe I'll give it a try sometime."

"I suggest you do." Harwood sat back, tented his fingers. "Now, you wanted to talk about that dog, you said?"

"Yes, sir," Mason said. "I thought I could take her off your hands, if you all haven't gone and destroyed her yet."

Harwood studied him. "Now, why would you want to do that?" he asked. "Take a vicious dog off my hands. You know dogfighting's a felony around here?"

"Yes, sir. I don't want to fight her."

"Did Jess put you up to this, then? This some kind of play you all are trying to make?"

"No, sir," Mason said. "I just hate to see a good dog put down."

He produced Glen's envelope from his pocket, counted out five hundred-dollar bills. Laid them on Harwood's desk. "I have five hundred dollars if you'll sell me that dog," he said. "And I give you my word I'll take her out of your hair, out of your jurisdiction, as soon as she's in my possession."

Harwood didn't answer right away. He leaned back in his chair, tapped his finger on the desk, and looked Mason over some more.

"What's your angle here, Mr. Burke?" he said at last. "There's plenty of dogs that need homes in the world. Plenty cheaper than five bills, to boot. What exactly is so special about this particular dog?"

"Nothing," Mason said. "Not a thing. It's just that I trained that dog, and I know she's a good one. And before you all go on and get rid of her, I'd like to try to work with her again, see if I can't iron out whatever mean streak got in her."

Harwood studied Mason a little longer, like he was trying to take the measure of the man across his desk. Then, abruptly, he sat forward.

"Well, I'm sorry, Mr. Burke," he said. "That dog you say you trained is a proven menace, and it's the opinion of the county of Makah that she needs to be destroyed. It would be irresponsible of me to do anything else."

"She hasn't been destroyed yet," Mason said. "Looks like you've healed up pretty good, so I guess it's been a while. What's the holdup?"

Harwood colored. "These things just don't happen overnight," he said. "But I assure you, that dog's good as dead." He stood. "Now, Mr. Burke, if you'll excuse me, I have a few other issues to deal with today. I wish you the best of luck in your search for a dog."

He held out his hand. Mason shook it, let the deputy guide him out of the small office. He crossed the detachment toward the front door, felt every eye in the place watching him, knew there'd be plenty of chatter the moment he stepped outside. Didn't care.

The dog was alive. That was a start.

The motel owner was still behind the front desk when Mason walked back into the lobby.

"Her name is Lucy," Mason said before the man had even looked up. "The dog that bit the deputy. I know her, I trained her, and I'm just not willing to believe that she attacked that man without cause."

The owner stood up slowly, and for about the tenth time already that day, Mason felt himself being studied. Scrutinized. He fought his prisoner's instincts, made himself hold the man's eyes.

"You're a dog trainer?" the man said finally.

"No, sir." Mason hesitated, but there was no way to do it but just come out and say it. "I'm an ex-con. There was a program where I was locked up; they brought in dogs who needed rehabilitation, gave them to guys like me who needed something to do."

The man didn't say anything. "That dog was a scared little runt when they brought her to me," Mason continued. "Pretty much nobody gave her a chance. But we got to each other somehow. And I didn't train a dog who'd go attacking people for no reason."

"Oh, son," the man said. He said it gentle, like maybe Mason would freak out and get violent if he pissed him off, like Mason was some kind of damaged person who needed extra care.

"Son, sometimes a dog just goes crazy," he continued. "We think we know an animal, and then something triggers and it's all of a sudden something wild again, something we've never seen. Happened to me more than once—I've had dogs. There's nothing to it but to move on."

"Not this dog," Mason said. "All due respect, but I know this dog, sir. I just can't accept that she acted out of turn."

"So what are you asking? What is it you're thinking you'll do?"

"I want to talk to the dog's owner at least. Deputy Harwood didn't want to play ball, so I'd like to get her side of the story, hear what happened. If nothing else, I just want to understand why Lucy did what she did."

The man said nothing for a while. Looked Mason in the eye and seemed to be weighing something.

"You were in prison?" he said.

Mason nodded. "Yes, sir," he said. "There's a man dead thanks to me, and I deserved to be in there because of it. And I don't have any designs on going back, but this dog gave me a reason to get up in the morning. I figure I owe her something in return."

The motel owner thought some more. Mason held his gaze. Had

he made the right decision, being honest with this man? He hoped he hadn't erased any glimmer of goodwill he'd cultivated here.

But he realized he felt comfortable, for the first time since his release, telling somebody who he was. He had no choice but to own it, build trust through integrity, and rely on human decency. He'd gambled that this motel owner was as decent a man as any in this town.

Finally the man squared up, seemed to come to a decision. "Winslow," he said. "Owner's Jess Winslow. Lives up on Timberline, little red house a quarter mile from where the road peters out. If she's home, you'll see a Chevy S10 in the front yard. Be careful out there, mind; she saw plenty of action, and she brought most of it back. You're going to want to make your intentions clear."

"Timberline," Mason said. "I'm much obliged to you."

"Don't bring her any trouble, son. She's been through enough as it is."

"I promise," Mason said, and he turned for the door.

"Son?"

He turned back.

"It's a couple, three miles up to where Timberline meets the highway. If you're planning on walking, you might want to wait for the rain to let up."

Mason looked out into the parking lot, the same steady drizzle he'd been seeing all day.

"I might have just goosed Harwood into killing that dog," he replied. "I don't think I have time to spare."

SEVEN

The stranger appeared down the road in the middle of the afternoon, toward the end of the day's long decline into night. If there'd been any sun for shadows, the shadows would have been long, but as it was, there was no way to mark the evening except for the world outside Jess's window seeming to lose definition, slow and imperceptible, minute by minute, a steady diminishing of color and detail until, all at once, it would come dark.

Jess watched as the man walked up the road toward her house. He didn't look like anyone she knew, though it was hard to tell: he wore a green rain slicker like Ty used to keep on the boat, the hood up over a baseball cap, hiding his face. She couldn't see a vehicle, so he must have walked a ways; she wondered if he knew where he was going, if he knew there was nothing worth seeing this far up the road. Then she wondered if he was coming for her.

He walked steadily, with a purpose, and as she watched, he looked up at her house and changed direction toward it. Jess drew back from the window, felt ice down her spine. She wondered if the stranger was even real, if her mind might be playing tricks again, conjuring enemies where none existed.

This was what Lucy had been good for. If Lucy responded to a visitor, Jess knew they were real, and if that visitor had bad intentions, Lucy might very well scare them away. But Lucy had sure responded to the last man who'd come knocking, and that hadn't exactly worked out, had it?

Jess drew back into the living room, thankful she'd kept the lights off. Her truck was parked up alongside the house, but that didn't mean anything. Maybe if she kept quiet and didn't move, this guy would just leave her alone.

She stood in the stillness, listening to the rain on the roof, hardly daring to breathe. Waited, and prayed the stranger would keep walking. Then she heard the sound of his boots on the front porch, and she closed her eyes. She was fucked.

He knocked, three times, like the last guy who'd come. Jess didn't move. The man knocked again. "Ms. Winslow?"

She drifted back, farther away from the door, ducked into the shadows where the living room met the kitchen, stood stock-still. Watched the man's shadowed form as he peered through the window. She didn't move. Her heart raced. She still couldn't make out his face.

Go away, she thought. *Go away go away go away.*

Time seemed to still. The man called her name again, and she didn't reply. She heard his boot steps on the porch again and prayed that was the end of it.

But it wasn't, of course. Nothing ever came easy. The man left the porch and circled around the side of the house, and Jess caught a glimpse of him through a side window, knew he was headed around back to keep looking.

Damn it.

Quiet as she could, she crossed to her bedroom, the shades drawn in there, the lights off. She knelt by the bed and reached underneath, felt around until her fingers found the soft case she'd stashed. Quickly she unzipped the case and removed the shotgun.

She'd purchased the gun from Chase Ogilvy at the marine supply store in town, after Harwood and his tagalongs had come back for Lucy. She'd let them take her dog, okay, but she'd be damned if they were going to take anything else from her. It was a Remington tactical shotgun, twelve gauge, model 870 Express. Seven-round capacity, and Jess kept the gun loaded.

She stood. Hesitated. Strained her ears for any sound of the man through the rain. Heard nothing. Maybe he'd gone, but she doubted it.

The house was getting darker, daylight disappearing. Shadows played on the walls, and Jess squinted to see. Squinted too hard, and she was somewhere else suddenly, back in the valley with an M4 in her hands, another shitty situation, another bad feeling.

Pull it together. Come on back, marine.

She let the sound of the rain bring her back to reality. Cradled the shotgun and moved back to the living room, the kitchen. Looked out over the sink into the backyard, the fenced-in weedy patch and the green-black forest beyond.

The man was out there. He'd come up to the back door, must have looked in through the window. Now he was turned around, headed out across the weeds to the edge of the fence line. Ty had built a shed out there for the lawn mower and whatever else, and Jess watched the man check it out, look around the yard, slow, and then start back across to the gate.

Quickly, Jess hurried to the front door. Opened it and slipped through as stealthy as she could, like she *was* back in the shit, patrolling Haji's turf. She crept across the front porch and around to the edge of the house where the path came up the side. Waited there, stilled her breathing, clutched the shotgun two-handed, and tensed for the man's approach.

He wasn't trying to be sneaky. Or he was really bad at it. Jess heard his boots on the gravel path, practically heard him breathing.

Timed it so just as he reached the end of the house, she stepped out toward him, swinging the butt of that Remington into his belly.

The blow punched the wind out of him. Knocked him flat on his ass, knocked the hood off his face. She flipped the shotgun around, showed him the business end, made sure he could see her finger inch toward the trigger.

He was older than she was; in his thirties, she guessed. Crow's-feet starting to show around his eyes, his face winter pale. Jess didn't recognize him, but that didn't mean anything. It sure didn't make him a friend.

The stranger caught his breath. Stared up at her, past the shotgun, like he wasn't all that worried she'd use it. "I guess you'd be the army vet, then," he said.

"Marine," she replied. "And who does that make you?"

"Well, I'd be the guy trying to piece together why his dog bit a deputy," he said. "Are you going to shoot me, or can I stand up?"

She didn't answer. Replayed his words, couldn't make sense of them. "Harwood send you?"

He laughed. "That deputy? No, ma'am, he did not. In fact, I'm fairly sure he'd take issue with my being here."

"What you said just now, about *your* dog biting him," she said. "What the hell's that supposed to mean?"

"It means I trained that dog, Lucy—you still calling her Lucy?" He gave her space for an answer; she nodded. "Good," he said. "I know that dog pretty well, and she wouldn't just up and attack somebody. I came to figure out what went wrong."

She stared down at him. Held the gun square, center mass. "They said it was prisoners who trained her," she said slowly. "Some jail back east. You a criminal?"

He nodded. "I was."

"And what, you heard the dog was in trouble and you escaped?"

"No, ma'am," he said. "I served my time, and the first thing I did when I got out was call and check on Lucy, make sure she was all right. I wasn't looking to see her again, nothing like that. I just wanted to see that she was happy."

She opened her mouth. Closed it. Figured she'd have some harsh words for the woman at the agency, sending this ex-con out in her direction. But the stranger caught her expression.

"She didn't tell me anything," he said. "Just said Lucy was in trouble and due to be destroyed. I figured out the rest on my own."

"How?" she asked.

"You sent a picture, Lucy in some school yard?" He shrugged. "Deception Cove Ravens, that's how I got it."

Jess stared down at him. How in the hell was this real, any of it? "What are you planning to do?"

"I already talked to that deputy; he didn't say much. I thought I'd look you up, get the real story. And then I was planning to do what I could to get that dog out of trouble."

Jess didn't say anything. After a beat the man laughed.

"Ma'am, I'd be glad to tell you anything you want to know about my plans and whatnot, but do you think we could do this inside? I'm getting pretty well soaked, and you . . ." He gestured to her feet. "You aren't even wearing shoes."

She looked down, saw he was right, felt the wet soak through her thin socks, and realized she was freezing. Shit.

"You try anything, I'll cut you down," she said, backing up a few steps. "I've got no problem with defending my home."

"I can see that," he said, pushing himself to his feet. He brushed himself off, then held out his hand. "Mason Burke," he said.

She looked at his hand. Didn't let go of the shotgun.

"All right, then." Burke pointed toward the front yard. "Shall we?"

Jess kept the shotgun on him, stepped back so he could lead, and followed him up the porch stairs to the front door and into her living room. The house was dark, there was almost no daylight, and Mason Burke was a silhouette in the center of the room as she felt along the wall with her free hand for the light switch.

"You want my boots off?" he asked her after she'd turned on the light.

She shook her head. "You're not staying long."

"Well, what about my jacket? I don't want to drip water all over your floor." He was half smiling again when he said it, like the Remington didn't bother him, like this was some kind of joke.

"Look," he said, nodding over her shoulder. "You have a coat hook right there. You want to swing around so you can keep that gun pointed at me while I'm hanging it up?"

She hesitated a moment, not liking being told what to do, but then she stepped aside anyway because he *was* dripping all over the rug.

"Might as well take your boots off too, then," she said, backing around him and toward the kitchen. "Take a seat on the couch, and don't try anything stupid."

"Yes, ma'am," he said, and as he knelt to unlace his boots, she ducked into the kitchen, pulled out a chair, and installed it opposite the couch, a clear line of sight to the front door.

Burke hadn't sat down. He'd kicked off his boots and ambled over to the mantel above the fireplace, was studying the pictures she kept there in frames. "This you?" he asked, motioning to the first one, a snapshot from the Kunar Province, her with her flak jacket and M4 and helmet, her hair down to her shoulders so the local women would know from a distance she was a girl too.

Jess nodded.

Burke studied it a beat longer. Then he moved down the line, the wedding picture, her and Ty outside the church in Neah Bay, Ty in a rented tux and her in that borrowed white dress from her cousin, her smiling and those stupid freckles showing across the bridge of her nose, and Ty looking at her all proud anyway, like he'd never seen anything so beautiful in the world.

Shit.

"Where's the old man?" Burke asked.

"Dead," she replied. "Drowned. Been almost four months."

"I'm sorry."

"You didn't do it," she said. "He got drunk one night on that old boat of his, misjudged the distance jumping across to the dock. They found his body the next morning, stuck under a float." She shrugged. "It happens every few years; people get careless. And Ty had a tendency to get that way when he'd been drinking."

Burke turned from the picture to look at her, the skin around his eyes crinkling. She wondered what he was seeing, what he was thinking about.

She motioned with her Remington over to the couch. "You going to sit down, or what?"

He gave up on the photos and went over and sat. "Okay." He set the palms of his hands flat on his thighs. "You want to tell me how Lucy came to bite that deputy?"

She sighed. "Not really," she said. "Look, what are you planning to do here? Are you thinking you'll just pile that dog in your truck and take her back home with you?"

"I don't have a truck," he said. "I took a bus here. And I hadn't thought that far ahead yet. But, ma'am, she's your dog. I just want to see to it that she stays alive."

She said nothing. Chewed on her lip and lowered the gun slightly.

"So you want to tell me what happened, or what?"

Jess closed her eyes. "Not really," she said again.

Lucy was growling, her hackles raised, and Jess tried to shush her as she slipped past to the front door, tried to chase the fear from her voice, hoped the dog couldn't hear it.

But the dog knew something was wrong.

Whoever was outside knocked again. Startled Jess so bad she thought her heart had stopped. She nudged Lucy away from the door with her knee. Brought her hand to the lock, hesitated. Then she turned the lock and pulled the door open.

"Good evening, Jess."

Kirby Harwood stood on her porch, Stetson in hand, smiling that plastic smile like he was already running for Sheriff Wheeler's job, that same plastic smile she remembered from high school, when he was a lock for all-state and the homecoming king, and still the asshole who got his kicks locking freshmen in their lockers when he didn't think anyone was looking. Harwood was taller than Jess by a fair sight, outweighed her by about a hundred pounds, most of it muscle. He filled her doorframe, and the sight of him did nothing to calm Lucy down.

Jess nodded to Harwood. "Deputy."

"Was wondering if you'd had the chance to think over what we talked about last time," Harwood said. He looked past her. "You mind if I come in?"

She did mind, very much, and judging by the growling noises by her right knee, Lucy did too. But Jess and Harwood both knew he hadn't really asked a question, and she stepped aside and grabbed hold of Lucy's collar, let the deputy walk into the house and stand in the middle of the living room, looking around the place like a real estate agent, like he was trying to decide how much he could sell it for.

But that wasn't it at all.

Harwood's eyes landed on Lucy. "Hey, girl," he said, smiling even broader, oblivious to Lucy's clear lack of cordiality. "How you doing? That's a good girl. Jess, you can let her go, she just wants to say hi."

"I don't think that's a good idea, Deputy," Jess replied. "She's feeling kind of territorial tonight."

This is her territory, Deputy. You'd better step off.

"How many times do I have to tell you, Jess? Call me Kirby. We certainly go back far enough. Hell, we almost dated, if I'm remembering right."

He wasn't remembering right at all. She wondered if it was an honest mistake, or if the deputy had talked himself into an alternate version of the facts. He'd asked her out, sure, sophomore year, but she'd seen how he picked on the freshmen, targeting the weak, told him she'd rather they just stay friends.

Later she found out he'd told the whole football team she'd gone down on him in his dad's old F-150 late one night out by Shipwreck Point Beach. By that point, though, she'd found Ty, and all the rumors and gossip didn't matter.

Harwood sat down, heavy, on the couch. Glanced at the TV, watched what was playing, another infomercial, then felt around for the remote and hit the mute button like he owned the damn set. The sound died, but the blue light remained, casting flickering shadows on the walls, on the ceiling, on Kirby Harwood's face.

"Now," Harwood said. "What was I saying?"

"I don't have it," Jess told him. "Whatever you and Ty were into, he carried that to his grave. He sure didn't share it with me."

Harwood's smile remained, but his eyes got harder. "You look for it, Jess? I mean, really look?"

"Of course I looked." She gestured around the house. "There really aren't that many hiding places, in case you couldn't tell. Maybe if you'd give me an idea what I was supposed to be looking for, I could help you."

"What about the boat?" Harwood said. "You check the boat?"

"Checked the boat. Checked the truck, checked the shed, checked under the porch. Deputy, whatever you're looking for, I don't have it."

"There's no need for that tone, Jess," Harwood said, and he had a tone too. "I'm an officer of the law now, don't forget."

Sure aren't acting like one, *she thought.*

"Here's the thing," he said, planting his boots and pushing himself to his feet. "Like you said yourself, there aren't too many hiding places in this little house of yours."

Lucy tensed as the deputy turned toward them. Pulled at her collar, whined a little. Hackles still raised.

"You've been back, what, a good couple months now; that's plenty of time to look. Doesn't seem like you're doing much with your free time besides."

"That's right," Jess replied. "I've got nothing to do all day but sit around and clean up Ty's messes. So if I haven't found this particular mess yet, Deputy, maybe it just isn't here."

"Or maybe you're hiding something yourself." Harwood's smile was gone; he took a step toward her. He filled the room, so she had nowhere to go. "You holding out on me, Jess? Because I'm telling you, if you're trying to play hardball, you picked the wrong man."

Jess shook her head. "And I'm telling you I have enough problems without getting into Ty's little calamities. Now maybe you'd better run along, Deputy, before you do something you'll regret."

Harwood smirked. "That a threat?"

She didn't say anything. Lucy tugged again toward Harwood, front legs off the floor, clawing at air. She was growling still, low in her throat. Harwood didn't seem to notice.

"You and Ty were always a pretty good match," he said. "White trash,

through and through. But Ty isn't here to protect you anymore, sweetheart. And I'm not much given to negotiation."

He chuckled, as if impressed with his own cleverness, and Jess could see more than meanness in his eyes, could see hunger, too, like he'd just talked himself into something worse than he'd intended, something he'd been wanting for a long while.

He made a grab for her shoulder. As she twisted away, Lucy wrenched forward, pulled out of Jess's grasp to lunge up at Harwood.

"Shit!"

Harwood scrambled back, lost his balance, and crashed down hard to the floor, Lucy on top of him, faster than Jess had ever seen, jaws clamped on his blue jeans, tearing through denim and the soft flesh underneath.

"God damn it! Get this fucking dog off of me!" Harwood squirmed to get free, but Lucy's grip was too tight. Jess dashed forward, intercepted the dog. Bodied her off of the deputy and over to the corner.

"Sit," *she said. "You sit down, Lucy. Sit down and stay."*

Lucy sat. Didn't look off from Harwood, though; kept growling, licking her lips. But she stayed put.

Slowly, Harwood pulled himself up from the floor. The ass of his jeans torn to shreds, striped boxer shorts underneath. Jess couldn't see any blood; most of it, she figured, was in the deputy's face. He'd gone red with anger, and he turned around to stare at her, fire in his eyes.

"That was a mistake, Jess," he said. "That was a real big mistake."

"They came for her the next morning," Jess told Burke. "Kirby, Dale Whitmer, and Cole Sweeney, the whole detachment. Said Lucy was a menace and she'd have to be destroyed. Took her away from me, and there wasn't a damn thing I could do to stop them."

"Nobody you could call?" Burke replied. "State police, even? You'd have grounds, the way he came after you."

Jess laughed. "What would I tell them? The deputy stole my

dog? She bit him, Mr. Burke, that's indisputable. The rest is my word against his."

Burke took this in. Studied the rug for a while. "And this thing with your old man," he said. "You don't know what he's talking about?"

"The hell if I do," she said. "They're looking for something, but I'll be damned if I know what it is. Ty got into all kinds of schemes; that's just what he did. He was a fisherman—salmon, like his dad—but that's no way to make a living around here anymore. But he swore he was going to get rich, one way or another. Told me when I came back from overseas, he'd have built me a brand-new life."

Which he did, she thought. *Just not the way either of us intended.*

"Sounds like some guys I might used to have known," Burke said. He let another silence stretch between them, kept looking down at that rug, scratching his chin. "What about the dog?" he asked finally. "You know where they're keeping her? Didn't look to me like she was at the detachment."

"She isn't," Jess told him. "They couldn't keep her there. And she isn't at animal control on the reservation in Neah Bay, either."

"So where is she?"

Jess shrugged. "Who knows?" Then she stopped. Felt, suddenly, the hopelessness of the whole situation. She'd already accepted that Harwood was going to put Lucy down. And in accepting it, she'd resigned herself to the notion that her own story was going to meet its end soon enough. She couldn't survive without Lucy, not alone. Not for very much longer, anyway.

But even if the dog wasn't dead yet, so what? What was this criminal proposing to do, attack an entire detachment of deputies to save her? The whole idea was reckless, and stupid, and destined to fail. Lucy was as good as dead, and Jess figured she was well on her way to joining her. "Shit," she said, wiping her eyes, turning away. "I think you'd better go."

Burke was looking at her. "You sure about that?" he said. "I'd be glad to—"

"Just go," she said. "I'll be fine."

Burke waited a beat. Then she heard him stand, shuffle over to the door. "You think on where that dog could be," he said as he laced up his boots. "We put our heads together, maybe we can spring her loose."

EIGHT

The motel owner called out to Mason as he walked through the empty parking lot to his room. Night had fully fallen, and the rain remained, constant, making the gritty black pavement between Mason's feet feel slick and oily and dappled with reflected yellow light.

"Did you make it all the way to Jess's place?" the older man asked when Mason had detoured over to where he waited by the lobby.

"I did," Mason said.

"How's she doing?"

Mason lifted a hand to his stomach where Jess Winslow had hit him with her shotgun. He laughed a little bit. "She's heavily armed," he said. "And she kicked my ass."

The man looked him over. "Good," he said. "You get what you want?"

"Maybe." Mason glanced down the long row of doors, then back toward the warmth of the lobby. "You got time to talk for a little bit?"

The motel owner's name was Henry Moss—Hank, he said, to his friends. He led Mason into the lobby, switched on the coffeemaker in the corner, and set himself up behind the front desk.

"So," he said, "what is it you want to know, Mr. Burke?"

Plenty. "That deputy, Harwood. What's his story?"

"Kirby?" Moss laughed. "That's a subject that's ripe for examination. More or less the town's prodigal son, hell of a quarterback back in his varsity days. Went off to the U. of Washington on some kind of scholarship, supposed to have a shot at the pros."

"Guess that didn't work out," Mason said.

"No, sir. Kirby washed out after a year of not exactly living up to his potential. Came on back to Deception Cove, got himself deputized, and now we all figure he's just marking time until Kirk Wheeler up in Neah Bay retires."

"Wheeler's the sheriff?"

"In name, anyway," Moss told him. "Though he mostly concerns himself with fishing these days. He's pushing seventy, been threatening to call it quits for years. One of these days he's actually going to do it, and then Makah County is all Kirby's."

"Kind of seems like he's already assumed ownership," Mason said. "Based on my limited interaction. You figure he's an honest cop?"

Moss studied him for a beat. Looked out over his shoulder at the parking lot behind. The lot was still empty, the highway, too.

"There's whispers," the older man said. "Maybe you saw that truck he drives—"

"The boat, too."

"The boat, too," Moss agreed. "Hard to say how he'd scrape up that kind of cash on his county salary, but everyone has a theory."

"What's yours?"

Moss hummed something tuneless. "I mean, here's the thing," he said. "We have a bit of an amphetamine problem in Makah County. Now, I'm not saying Kirby's directly involved, but he hasn't exactly focused his efforts on curtailing the local operation."

Mason said, "Was Jess's husband involved in that stuff?"

"Ty?" Moss frowned. "I thought this was about a dog, Mr. Burke. What exactly are you thinking is going on here?"

"I don't know yet," Mason said. "Just a couple things struck me as funny, that's all."

The coffee machine burbled. "Just one second," Moss said, disappearing into the back room. He returned a moment later with a bottle of Irish cream. He winked at Mason, poured them both mugs, spiked each with a splash from the bottle, and slid Mason's mug over.

"To your health," he said, and lifted the mug to his lips. When he put the mug down again, his expression was focused.

"I don't know much about Ty Winslow," he told Mason. "We didn't exactly run in the same circles, you know how I mean?"

Mason tried his coffee. Surprisingly good, and hot enough to chase the damp cold that had followed him since he'd stepped off the bus last night.

"Let me put it this way for you," Moss continued. "There's two bars in this town. We got Spinnaker's, across from the government wharf. Tim Turpin owns that one, and Tim sees himself as a real gourmet-type individual, has the locally sourced veggies and the gluten-free bread, sustainable salmon, that kind of thing."

"And the other place?"

"The other place is the Cobalt, and it isn't the kind of spot you want to take your sweetie for dinner," Moss said. "Kind of the epicenter for all the bad news in this town." He took another drink. "See if you can guess where Ty Winslow did most of his drinking."

Mason nodded. "I think I get the picture."

"You want to know about Ty, you want to check out the Cobalt. Someone there will have answers for you, if you're really interested." Moss squinted at Mason. "Though I'm still not clear on why you'd care."

Mason hesitated. Tried to choose his words. Looked past Henry

Moss to the picture the motel owner had hung on the wall, a younger Moss in combat fatigues, somewhere in the desert.

"Jess Winslow's husband was mixed up in something with the deputy," Mason said. "That's why the deputy came to bother her that one night, and that's why he took the dog from her. He thinks she has something, and he's using that dog as leverage to get it back."

Moss laid his hands flat on the counter. Leaned forward. "And what's your play here, son? Are you thinking you'll just wade right into the middle of this whole thing and rescue that dog?"

"I was thinking about it," Mason said.

"Must be a hell of a dog."

"She's more than a dog, sir. She's a friend in a bad spot, and I can't just sit idle while there's still a shot at helping her." Mason gestured past Moss at the picture on the wall. "That you?"

Moss turned, checked out the picture like he was seeing it for the first time. "That's me," he said. "Forty-First Infantry, Desert Storm. Seems like a long time ago now."

"You see much combat?"

"Did we see combat?" Moss laughed. "Son, we were first across the Saudi border, the tip of the spear. We saw plenty of combat."

"I guess I should have known that."

Moss waved him off. Drained his coffee.

"Sounded like Jess saw her own share of action," Mason said. "I must have been away a long time. I didn't know they let women be marines now."

"I guess you never heard of a female engagement team," Moss said. He caught Mason's blank look and shook his head. "Yes, sir. For a Marine Corps that didn't want to send women to the front lines, they sure as hell gave Jess her share of the loud and scary stuff." He looked off again, into the parking lot. Pursed his lips.

"Yes, sir," he said again. "There's a reason they gave her that dog when she came back, and it's not because they figured the dog needed a friend."

Mason bid the motel owner good night. Retreated to his room, unlocked the door, switched on the light. Half expected to see Kirby Harwood waiting in the dark for him, and when the deputy wasn't there, Mason wondered if Harwood's presence would have unnerved him any more than the emptiness he found instead.

Fifteen years in a cell. Three squares a day. Lights on, lights off. Doors open, doors closed. Fifteen years with no agency, no privacy, no personal space. He'd grown used to the structure, made his peace with his relative powerlessness. He'd matured in that prison cell, accustomed himself to the strange rituals on the inside, the hierarchies, rules written and unwritten. Fifteen years, nearly half of his life so far. He'd never been comfortable inside the prison, but at least he'd known what to expect.

And now, on the outside, Mason felt the vastness of possibility like a heavy stone on his chest. There was no one to tell him what to do, a thousand paths to walk and no clear way to choose. He felt rootless, adrift, drowning in his freedom, surrounded by a population of normal, law-abiding people who all knew the roles, the social mores, who could look a person in the eye without feeling they were revealing their monstrous selves.

Shit.

He'd landed here, in this motel room at the end of the world, utterly on his own. He would wake up on his own, bathe on his own. He would choose what to eat, and where, and when. And he knew this was an incredible luxury, something he'd dreamed about over countless nights inside the Chippewa pen. He'd imagined eating at nice restaurants, going for long drives. Hell, meeting a woman, making actual friends. It had all seemed so simple when he was still inside. Now, on the outside, Mason Burke had no idea what he was doing.

He needed structure. Mason knew, somewhere in his subconscious, that coming to Deception Cove in search of a dog wasn't the sanest idea in the world. He knew it wouldn't make sense to most anyone who knew what he was doing. The dog was just a dog, after all. And from the sound of it, the dog was mixed up in something a lot bigger than Mason had anticipated. He knew the sane answer was to turn around and go home.

And do what? Where was home, exactly? What did he have in this world to look forward to? Where would he start? Cleaning houses?

"Greater love has no one than this," the Bible said, "that someone lay down his life for his friends."

The dog needed help. Mason needed a purpose. He undressed for bed and slipped beneath the sheets. He'd be sticking around for a while.

NINE

Mason had only *ever seen the dog riled up one time.*

As with most fights inside prison walls, it started over something trivial. Something stupid. In this case, it was a chew toy.

Less than a week left to go in the program, before the dogs would graduate out of the Chippewa pen and move on to a month or two with real trainers on the outside, men and women who would work with Linda Petrie to polish the dogs into genuine companion animals. In a few months, all things going well, Lucy would have a new home, a forever home, with someone who needed her, who deserved her a lot more than Mason did.

It wasn't like it didn't hurt, just a little bit, knowing the dog was leaving, knowing he'd never see her again. She'd come a long way in the months they'd worked together; she wasn't scared of her food bowl anymore, for one thing, had put on some healthy weight. She wagged her tail when he looked her way, covered him in dog-slobber kisses when he came to get her from her crate in the morning. She sat, she fetched, she heeled when they walked around the yard together. They were working on rolling over; they'd mastered high fives. The dog had found her confidence; she looked happy. She was going to be a good dog for somebody, Mason knew. But that didn't make it hurt any less, thinking about saying goodbye.

Heck, though, in six months or so he'd be out of this prison himself. He could find his own dog, train her like he'd trained Lucy. He figured he'd picked up a few tricks, and though it wouldn't be the same bond as he'd built with this dog, it would have to do.

Except he very nearly messed up his chances of getting out, and Lucy's, over one stupid rubber tire toy.

The tire, by rights, belonged to no one. It had come in the canvas bag of rope toys and tennis balls and stuffed animals that Linda Petrie brought with her each day, that she dumped in the middle of the yard for the dogs to play with when they weren't learning how to behave themselves. The tire belonged to the group; it was fair game for anyone. But in practical terms, that tire belonged to Marques Alvarado and Meatball.

Alvarado was a banger from somewhere in Detroit. He'd taken ten years on a manslaughter conviction and, like the rest of the men in the program, was due for release sometime within the next year. Alvarado palled around with a guy named Porter Trammel, who was serving five to seven for boosting cars down in Flint. Trammel's dog, Reggie, was a German shepherd from the slums. And Meatball was a big, beefy rottweiler.

That tire belonged to Meatball, and when Meatball didn't want it, Reggie took over. They'd wrestle over the damn thing all day if they could, and they generally did, and the rest of the dogs left them alone, left the tire alone.

Until the one day, three days before graduation, when Lucy and Mason found themselves alone unexpectedly in front of the pile of toys, having finished the morning's training before anyone else. Lucy saw the tire sitting there and, as best as Mason could figure, finally saw her shot and snatched it up and jogged away happily, tail wagging furiously and a gleam in her eyes, looking back at Mason every couple of steps to make sure he knew just what mischief she'd pulled off.

She looked so damn happy, he couldn't take the tire from her. And so he didn't. He let her have her fun, played tug-of-war with her, let her sit down and chew the thing until it was covered in drool and a whole host of new bite marks, until Meatball and Reggie—and Alvarado and Trammel—finished their own training and discovered the tire was missing.

Funny thing was, it wasn't like the dogs gave a shit. Meatball found a piece of frayed rope she seemed to like just as much, and Reggie chased her off to a corner where they could gnaw on the thing together. But Alvarado saw Lucy, saw the tire, and Alvarado took it personal.

"Burke." *Alvarado's voice could turn heads across the yard, and it did. Mason heard him approach, knew what was coming. Turned and saw Alvarado and Trammel steamrolling across the yard toward him, and knew immediately that this wasn't about a tire toy anymore.*

Confrontation at Chippewa, no matter the spark, burned over one fundamental question, and that question was power. Didn't matter if it was the guy butting in on you in the cafeteria line, or a hard foul on the basketball court in the yard. Everything inside came down to which man was tougher, which man would give way. And once you found yourself challenged, there was no easy way out. There certainly were no points given for peace.

Not that Mason didn't try. He took the tire from Lucy, who'd already seemed to sense the new tension on the yard. Tossed it to Porter Trammel, who caught it and grimaced at the amount of drool that coated the thing.

"Come on, Luce," Mason said, standing and starting toward the pile of toys. "We'll find you something else."

Except to get to that pile of toys, Mason had to walk past the two men who'd challenged him. And Alvarado wasn't about to let the issue die. He moved over as Mason passed, bumped him, stood in his way.

"Stay in your lane, hillbilly," Alvarado said. "Keep that dog in line."

Conversations stilled. Heads turned. It wasn't so much the words Alvarado chose; it was the tone in his voice and the fact that he and Mason Burke were having words at all.

"Take it easy, Marques," Mason said. "You got your little toy back. What else are you looking for?"

"What am I looking for?" Alvarado smirked. Cracked his knuckles. "Well, shit, hillbilly, an apology would be nice."

This was where Lucy drew her line, apparently. She tensed beside Mason, let out a long, low growl in Alvarado's direction, and when Mason looked down at her in surprise, he saw that her hackles were raised, and she was staring at the banger with menace in her eyes.

"Hell, even the dog wants some," Alvarado said. "This is going to be fun."

Lucy's back was up like Mason had never seen before, and worse, Alvarado had the gleam in his eye Mason had seen in other prisoners, men who didn't care anymore, who'd given up any dream of a new life outside and had settled for causing mayhem wherever they could, with whomever they could, inside the prison walls. Mason knew Alvarado would enjoy what was coming; he knew, also, there was no way to escape it. Hell, he just hoped Lucy survived.

She has your back, *he thought.* It's too bad it's going to cost you both.

Then Bridges Colson stepped in.

"The fuck are y'all doing?" he asked, looking hard at Mason and at Alvarado and Trammel in turn. "You boys figuring to start a dogfighting ring up in here?"

Mason said nothing. Neither did the other men; they were hard guys, but Bridges Colson was harder, and he had numbers at his back, out in general population. Nobody took up against Colson and enjoyed the experience.

"You all got a week before these dogs are graduated," the big man was saying. "Less than a week. And you want to risk all of that over some petty shit, really? You want to fuck up these dogs' lives over a goddamn little chew toy?"

He looked at Mason again, as if expecting an argument, like Mason was going to tell him it was more than a chew toy; it symbolized something.

But it didn't, of course.

"You two," Colson said, addressing Alvarado and Trammel. "You all got your little tire back, so quit being bitches. Go on off and play with your dogs and don't start shit no more, understand?"

The men said nothing, but their posture spoke for them. They were beaten without even throwing a punch; Bridges was the alpha dog here.

"And you, Burke," Colson said. "You seen how this dog was, the first day she got here. You seen how she changed since she's been here. You going to throw that away?"

Mason shook his head. "I'm not looking for trouble."

"Yeah, well." Colson reached down, scratched Lucy's head, and the dog, damn her, had the gall to wag her tail and look happy about it. "You're almost out of here yourself, man. You gotta be smarter than this."

He had a point. But what stuck with Mason as Alvarado and Trammel slunk away wasn't so much how close he'd come to ruining his life again, or how funny it was that Bridges Colson had been the stabilizing influence, but rather the look in Lucy's eyes when Alvarado had stepped to him, the menace in her growl as soon as Mason was threatened.

She has your back, buddy, *he thought as he fed Lucy a Milk-Bone and threw a tennis ball for fetch.* That dog cares about you, and that isn't some small thing.

TEN

The twelve gauge was a piss-poor companion.

Jess had set the shotgun down on the table in the living room after Mason Burke left, and sat down on the couch next to it and stared at it most of the night.

She didn't sleep. If she slept, she'd dream of Afia, and if she dreamed of Afia one more time, she might well blow her head off with that shotgun the moment she woke from the nightmare. So Jess didn't sleep. She didn't blow her head off either.

She'd bought the shotgun from Chase Ogilvy with that eventuality in mind; she could admit that, now that she wasn't going to do it. Sure, she would use the weapon to defend herself in the interim, but once she'd scared Kirby Harwood and his buddies away, once she'd found herself left alone in Ty's house again?

That shotgun was meant for one purpose, and that purpose was to rid her head of the nightmares, of Afia and the valley, forever. Jess figured she could live with the side effects.

But she didn't blow her head off, alone as she was with her thoughts. And the reason she didn't do it was that every time she looked across the living room at that shotgun on that table, her eyes would skim past the gun and scan the room a split second, and she'd catch a glimpse of Lucy's worn leather lead hanging on a hook by the door.

She hadn't been able to throw the lead out, not yet. Same

for Lucy's water bowl in the kitchen, and the bag of pepperoni treats stashed in the fridge. The dog was as good as dead, but to trash her stuff would make it final, and Jess wasn't ready to take that step yet.

Except now she couldn't look at the shotgun without seeing that lead, and she couldn't look at the lead without hearing what Mason Burke had told her, how Lucy was still alive and he planned to rescue her. And if the dog was still alive, and Burke planned to save her, then damn it, the notion of Jess blowing her head off kind of made it seem like she was abandoning the damn creature, giving up too easy.

Jess didn't give Mason Burke a snowball's prayer of rescuing Lucy from Harwood and his buddies, but the dog was still alive, and that meant she still had a chance, however infinitesimal. Jess wasn't sure she had the energy for a fight, but damn it, the last thing she needed was to pile more guilt on her head, feel like she'd let someone else down.

She stared at the shotgun on the coffee table some more. She didn't know what to do.

She'd always known, more or less, what to do. Her whole life Jess Winslow had had plans, a path spread out before her, and growing up had been as simple as putting one foot in front of the other.

Marrying Ty, that had been simple. He'd asked her out shortly after Kirby Harwood did, sophomore year, and he was ambitious and funny and cute and didn't bully the freshmen, and she'd said yes and they'd gone into Clallam Bay to the movies, and afterward Ty had kissed her, and then they were going together, and that was pretty well how it happened. She felt safe with Ty, liked his dimples and the way he looked at her, and the way he talked about making something of himself, a real man, a highliner like his daddy used to be, resurrecting the family name and Deception Cove at the same time, doing something important. She liked that.

And even after they'd graduated, and Ty's big ideas didn't pan out the way that he'd planned, he always had other ideas, more schemes, and anyway, Jess was enlisting and there was no sense in waiting—kids in Deception Cove married their high school sweethearts, that's just how it went—so they married before she set off to South Carolina, and then overseas, and by the time she came back from that first tour of duty, she'd been gone so long and seen so much that she wasn't even sure she could recognize herself, much less the man she came home to.

He was up to no good then—he must have been, those big schemes gone sour—but Jess was so stuck in her own head that she didn't catch on. And anyway, there was still some of that magic left sometimes, like she'd come out of her fog now and then, and there was Ty, like the old days; they'd watch a funny movie together, or he'd drive her out to the cape and they'd walk in the woods, the stillness of the rain forest a salve on the wounds she carried inside her. Ty still knew her better than anyone else in the world, still loved her, and she supposed she'd still loved him, too, and still did.

But she'd reenlisted anyway, and gone back over, and he'd gone and gotten himself drowned.

The corps, too; she'd always known she'd be a leatherneck. Her dad had fought in Iraq with the First Marines, Operation Desert Storm, and growing up, Jess had wanted nothing more than to emulate her father, impress him. So she'd enlisted after graduation, joined a female engagement team, and found out pretty quickly that she was just as good a marine as she'd ever hoped she would be.

It wasn't just the fighting, though she was plenty good at that part too. Working with Afia was less about shooting M4s and more about talking to people, listening, mediating. Gathering information and assessing its value, helping your team leaders make tactical decisions. And Jess, who'd never been much of a student, realized she was good at the engagement stuff. Working with Afia, she'd been better than good.

But Afia was gone, and Jess was too fucked up in the head to fight anymore, a medical discharge and some combat ribbons and a never-ending barrage of nightmares her only souvenirs of a four-year engagement she'd hoped might become a career.

Her dad was dead, Ty was dead, Lucy was gone; for the first time in years, maybe even a decade, Jess Winslow had no idea where she was going, what she was supposed to do. No path to guide her but her memories of the valley, and the blessed relief offered by the shotgun that lay before her.

And she might have done it too. She might have eaten that barrel, put an end to the guilt and the horrible thoughts, the hopelessness and aimlessness and apathy. She might have welcomed the silence, the sudden end.

But damn it, every time she looked at the gun, Jess saw Lucy's lead on its hook in the background. And every time she saw that lead, she saw Lucy, languishing somewhere, terrified and alone. She saw Mason Burke and the look in his eyes, and she knew there was still a path she could follow, if she could only find the starting point.

She'd given up on Afia. She wouldn't give up on Lucy. Jess supposed that meant she'd have to find Mason Burke.

ELEVEN

The drizzle had dissipated into a fine mist by the time Mason left the motel room the next morning, and as he walked down the hill into town, he could sense the sun, somewhere above, trying to burn through the clouds. He stopped at the diner and ate the same breakfast as yesterday, at the same table as yesterday, and when he'd finished his meal, he crossed the street to the sheriff's detachment and asked to speak to Deputy Harwood again.

Harwood looked less pleased to see him the second go-around, though he made a nice try of keeping his smile fixed. He led Mason back to his office again, closed the door behind them. Went behind his desk and stood and spread his arms and looked at Mason.

"Well, Mr. Burke," he said. "What can I do for you this time?"

Mason took his bankroll from his pocket. Counted out ten hundred-dollar bills. "One grand," he said, laying it on the table. "A thousand dollars, cash money, and I'll take that dog off your hands."

Harwood clucked, tried for a sympathetic smile and didn't quite get there. "That's a generous offer," he said, "but like I told you before, that dog's not for sale. You want an animal, the pound out on the Indian reservation is sure to have a good selection of—"

"Thousand won't cut it," Mason said, interrupting. "I guess that means whatever Ty Winslow took from you is a sight more valuable."

Harwood's smile flickered. He looked Mason over again, and when the smile came back, it was something harder, something meaner.

"Are you looking to go back to jail, Burke?" he asked.

Mason said nothing.

"I did some reading about you." The deputy gestured to his computer. "Mason Burke, thirty-three years of age, the last fifteen years a tenant of the Chippewa County State Penitentiary, Chippewa County, Michigan. First-degree murder, if I read that part right."

Mason held Harwood's gaze. Still didn't say anything.

"Does that pretty young widow know you're a murderer, Burke?" Harwood asked. "Did you tell her that part, when you told her you'd get her dog back?"

"I served my time," Mason said. "What I did fifteen years ago has no bearing on what we're doing here today."

"What we're doing." Harwood clasped his hands together, cracked his knuckles. "What I'm doing, Burke, is attempting to dispose of a menacing dog, while simultaneously aiming to protect my town from the murderer who just showed up out of the blue."

"That's how you're going to play it," Mason said. "That's fine."

"That's how it is, Burke. You want my advice, you'll get back on that bus and ride off to where you came from, forget you ever heard of Deception Cove." Harwood's smile was gone now. "Because if you stick around here and keep stirring up trouble, I'm liable to get angry. And I bet you've pissed off enough cops in your life already."

Mason gathered his cash from the deputy's desk. "I'll take that under advisement," he said, turning to leave. "Anything else?"

"Get out of my town, Mr. Burke," Harwood called after him. "Next time I won't be so polite about it."

Harwood watched Burke walk out of the detachment. When the drifter was gone, the deputy walked to the door of his office, called across the room to his men.

"Sweeney, Whitmer. My office."

The deputies looked up from the coffee machine, fell in line. Came over to the office, where Harwood sat behind his desk, waiting for them.

"Close the door," Harwood told them. "We've got trouble."

The younger deputy, Cole Sweeney, sat across from Harwood. Dale Whitmer closed the office door, remained standing. Harwood tented his fingers.

"I heard from Okafor," he told the men. "He gives us to the end of the month."

Whitmer nodded. Sweeney glanced at the calendar on Harwood's desk.

"Three days," Harwood told him. "Three days, we get Okafor that package, or we get him his money. Or not, and we're all in one hell of a shitstorm."

"Jess isn't panning out," Sweeney said. "Maybe she really doesn't know where her old man hid the package."

"Maybe she's not looking hard enough," Harwood replied. "We didn't give her the proper motivation, and now this asshole's come sniffing around, distracting her from the task at hand. We need to set her mind back on what's important."

"How do we do that?"

"The dog," Harwood said. "We haven't been severe enough. First thing tomorrow we start sending pieces. We run out of pieces, we start in on Jess herself."

Sweeney made a face. "Jeez, Kirby."

Harwood looked at him, stern. Watched the younger man wither.

"I'm just saying, we got into this to make money, boss," Sweeney said. "Nobody said we were going to have to be killers."

"Them or us." This was Whitmer, from the door. "You see eight hundred grand sitting around, Cole? What do you think Okafor is going to do if we don't make him whole?"

Sweeney went paler. "I know, but still."

"We don't have to worry about Okafor," Harwood told them. "Because once we lean on Jess harder, she'll get us that package. We just have to up our game."

Sweeney didn't reply. Whitmer was smirking.

"Yeah, what is it, Dale?" Harwood glared at him. "You got something to say?"

"Just thinking on how you and Jess used to have that thing together, back in the high school days, remember?"

"Yeah," Harwood said. "So?"

Whitmer winked at Sweeney. "Well, I guess you mustn't have impressed her all that much, boss," he said. "Seeing as how she sure hates your guts these days."

Harwood felt his muscles tense up, involuntary. "I used her up till I was good and done with her, Dale, and then I traded her in on the cheerleading captain," he said. "I guess Jess still holds a grudge."

Whitmer nodded, still smirking. "Yeah, I guess so." Then his smile faded. "And the drifter, boss? What do you want we should do about him?"

Harwood relaxed a little bit. Pushed Jess from his mind. "Run him out of my county," he said. "By any means necessary."

TWELVE

At first pass, Mason had assumed the building that housed the Cobalt Pub was abandoned, if not condemned. But today, looking past the graffiti tags, the boarded-up windows, and the wind-worn posters for long-ago musical acts, he found a black, windowless door, and when he pulled the door open and peered inside, he found himself in a bar, just like Hank Moss had promised.

Barely nine thirty in the morning and already doing business, the Cobalt was a long, narrow room, a bar along the right wall and a row of tables on the left. The place stank of sweat and stale beer and urine, the light dim enough to hide most of the filth on the walls, the floor, the countertops, though nobody would ever have made the mistake of calling the place clean.

A couple of old men sat drinking alone at the bar. Toward the back, three more men sat at a table. They looked middle aged, though in the shadows Mason couldn't be sure. Their eyes followed him as he found a seat at the bar.

The bartender was an older guy too, a white beard and thick, muscled arms. He nodded at Mason as he sat down. "What can I get you?"

"Beer," Mason replied, and the man took a greasy glass from a rack and filled it from an unmarked tap.

"Three bucks."

Mason slid him a five. "Looking for someone," he said. The

bartender raised an eyebrow. "Guy named Ty Winslow. You know him?"

The bartender snorted. "You're a little late, bud," he said. "Ty drowned in the chuck about four months back."

"Well, dang," Mason said. "I guess that's that."

"Guess so." The bartender moved on, and Mason nursed his beer. Wondered what he was drinking, where it had come from, whether it was branded or somebody's basement home brew. Figured it didn't matter; nobody who came to this place was going to be a connoisseur.

He drank, and minded his business, and the bar was quiet, save the hushed voices of the three men in the back. There was a mirror along the back of the bar, and Mason used it to survey the room, found nothing worth writing home about. The old-timers beside him looked weathered and beaten, looked like they'd been here since the door opened, and would be until close, and back first thing tomorrow.

The men at the rear of the bar wore flannel shirts and work boots. They had beards, wore ball caps. Every now and then they looked over at Mason, not long looks, just checking. Mason recognized the behavior. He'd done the same thing in the yard, keeping tabs on his surroundings, anyone who didn't like him, anyone he didn't know. A survival instinct, safety mechanism. Mason figured the men weren't looking for trouble, but they'd be ready if trouble found them. He left them alone, avoided eye contact.

He finished his beer, motioned the bartender for another. The bartender obliged, set his glass back in front of him. "You're not from around here."

"Back east," Mason said. "Just finished a bid, thought I'd come out this way and maybe find a boat needed crew."

"And you heard Ty was your man, did you?" The bartender

laughed again, shaking his head. "Mister, Ty Winslow was a lot of things, but he sure wasn't much of a fisherman."

"Wasn't looking for Ty to give me work, no," Mason said. "I heard he was the man to talk to if a guy needed something sharp to get him through the day."

The bartender lowered the glass he was polishing. Squinted at Mason, looked him up and down. Mason held his gaze. Finally the bartender turned around. Caught someone's eye in the mirror, cocked his head, and Mason heard a chair push back behind him, one of the three men from the table in the corner.

He waited. Tensed, watching the mirror, ready for the fight, if that's what was coming. But the man slipped beside him, pulled the stool out, and sat down. Found Mason's eyes in the mirror. "You a cop?"

He was the youngest of the three. Late thirties, probably, though it was hard to tell behind his wiry, rust-colored beard and the sallow skin beneath. His gaze was direct, his tone no-bullshit. Mason shook his head. "Not a cop."

"What are you looking for?"

"Whatever you've got," Mason told him. "Something to pick me up, keep me going. Been on the road a long while already."

"How much?"

"About a week's worth, if you got it."

"Not here. Got cash?"

Mason nodded. "I do."

The guy stood. "Come on."

The man's friends remained inside the bar. Mason followed him out and around the side of the building, to a Ford F-150 the same color as the man's beard.

"How much you're talking, I don't have it on me," the man said. "You want it right away, we gotta take a little ride."

"All right," Mason said. He opened the passenger door and climbed into the truck. The man slid behind the wheel, turned the engine over.

"You got a name?" he asked Mason.

"Burke," Mason replied.

"Yancy," the man said, pulling away from the bar. "You come looking for work, you said?"

"That's right. Thought I might try fishing."

"Sounds like timing just ain't your strong suit," Yancy said. "Ain't been much fishing for years now. This whole town's dried up."

"Used to be, though?"

"Sure," Yancy said. "Used to be you couldn't throw a stone on Main Street without putting a dent in a brand-new Corvette. You had a boat and a salmon permit, you had a license to print money. But the bottom fell out; the granola types and the Indians saw to that, and now . . ." He gestured around. "Shit."

He'd driven east, away from Main Street, past a collection of ramshackle houses and down a narrow road winding through the forest, the ocean somewhere nearby out the driver's-side window.

"You ever fish?" Mason asked him.

"With my dad, yeah," Yancy said. "He was supposed to give me his boat, his license. Then the license got worthless all of a sudden, and the boat was worth more in insurance money. As luck would have it, that boat had a fire."

"As luck would have it."

"Yes, sir."

Yancy drove a few miles, drove in silence, the only sound the Ford's engine and the squeak of the wipers, the tires on uneven pavement underneath.

"Ty didn't fish, though?" Mason asked after a while.

Yancy slowed the truck, pulled over; it looked like the middle of nowhere. At the last minute Mason saw a dirt road coming up out of the rain forest, mostly mud and washed-out gravel, and that's where Yancy pointed the tires.

"He *tried,*" Yancy said. "Ty's dad was about the biggest highliner the town ever saw, back in his younger years. Supposed to run in the family, but Ty never had the knack. He'd go out on that boat of his every now and then, try and catch something to sell to Tim down at Spinnaker's, a nice king salmon or a halibut, whatever, but it wasn't his game. It ain't anyone's game."

The road dropped ahead, following the general declination of the land. Mason let the conversation die, watched out the window as the road narrowed and curved through the rain forest, lush green all around, moss and ferns and tall pines and spruce. In some places the forest was so dark it looked night black, in others it opened up into swampland, big skunk cabbages and reeds growing out of the mud. Yancy had his window cracked, and the air was cold and damp, refreshing after the stale air in the bar.

Yancy let his foot off the gas, let the truck coast down the last of the drop, rounded a corner and the road petered out into a small clearing and the ocean beyond, a narrow, half-sunk dock leading out over the water, the remains of a derelict freighter going to rust at the far end.

Yancy stopped the truck. Killed the engine. "Here we are," he said. "Come on out."

Mason opened his door. Stepped out onto a carpet of pine needles, smelled wet earth and low tide and something else, something chemical.

He walked around the front of the truck, surveyed the clearing, a few rusted cars and some junk alongside, and then the ship out on the water. It couldn't have been more than 150 feet long, rust red and faded, filthy white, no nameplate visible. The wheelhouse at the stern, windows dark, the hull secured to the dock and the shore by a collection of mismatched and fraying lines. The dock looked well used, though, and there was a rope ladder down the hull; Mason surmised this was where Yancy cooked his product.

The sound of a hammer cocking back chased the notion from Mason's mind, and shortly thereafter the barrel of a gun pressed into the nape of his neck.

"You sure ask a lot of questions, Burke," Yancy said from behind him. "Are you *sure* you ain't a cop?"

THIRTEEN

Mason made his body relax as Yancy prodded him again with the gun. "I'm not a cop, Yancy," he said calmly. "You're seeing this situation all wrong."

"Maybe I am, and maybe I'm not." Yancy was scared, Mason could tell, though the dealer was trying not to show it. "And maybe I just drop you right here and walk away with your cash and it doesn't matter if you're a cop or you're not."

He pushed the gun harder into Mason's neck, and Mason laughed, a little bit. "What the fuck is so funny?"

"I'm about the furthest thing from a cop you can think of," Mason said. "And I can't say I'm too big on our having this conversation with that gun of yours at my back."

Now it was Yancy's turn to laugh. "Man, fuck *you.* Maybe you don't fully understand the situation here, but I—"

Mason ducked down and to the left, swung his right arm up and knocked Yancy's pistol hand away from his head. Yancy squeezed the trigger but not nearly in time. The pistol fired, *loud,* above Mason's head, the shot somewhere high and wide, nowhere near its target.

Before Yancy could recover, Mason swung around, tackled him in the midsection, driving him back across the clearing and into the hood of the Ford, Yancy hammering down on his head with the pistol the whole time. Mason ignored the blows, launched Yancy hard against the front of the truck, and swung him around. Crashed down to the ground, landed on top of him and knocked the wind from Yancy's lungs. Pinned the drug dealer's pistol hand to the mud and focused on prying the weapon out of his fingers, while Yancy focused on battering Mason's face in with his free hand.

But Mason had taken worse shots, and Yancy wasn't much of a fighter. In short order, he had the pistol prized free, and he squared it at Yancy and watched him quit fighting, just lie there and breathe heavy and glare at the gun.

Mason stood, kept the pistol trained. "Get up," he told the dealer.

Yancy stood, and Mason kept a couple of yards between them. Caught his breath and let Yancy catch his.

"I'm not a cop," Mason said again. "But I'm not here to buy your crank, either. I just have a couple more questions for you. You think we can have an actual conversation?"

Yancy nodded, his eyes still on the gun. Mason tasted blood, touched his mouth; the drug dealer had busted his lip.

"That ship back there," he said, gesturing to the water. "I guess that's where you cook."

Yancy spat some blood of his own. Nodded again.

"Ty cook there too?"

Yancy studied the gun for a moment. Then he shook his head. "Ty had his own setup inland, up in the hills a ways," he said. "Somewhere off the main-line logging road, tucked behind some old clear-cut. Wasn't nobody but Ty knew the actual location."

"Ty ever come around here?"

"Maybe once or twice. Would have been a social call, though; we didn't never do business together."

"What about Harwood?" Mason asked. "He come up here?"

"What, the deputy?" Yancy laughed. "Shit, every now and then."

"You all do business?"

"Me and Harwood? That depends on your definition of 'business,' I guess," Yancy said. "He come around when he wants some shakedown money, make sure we know we only exist 'cause of his good graces."

"Same with Ty?"

"I assume so," Yancy said. "There's not much goes on in Deception Cove that Kirby Harwood doesn't know about. I don't imagine Ty Winslow would constitute an exception."

"Yeah," Mason said. "All right."

Yancy cocked his head. "What's with all the interest in Ty Winslow, man? You go through all this shit just to ask me about a dead man?"

"Just trying to get a clearer picture," Mason said. "You think Harwood could have killed Winslow?"

"What, over a few points on some fucking crank?" Yancy laughed again. "Listen, Burke, I'm telling you, Harwood and his boys don't give a shit about small-time like us. Even when he comes around, it ain't about the money, it's about proving he's the biggest dick swinging in this town. We're just a game to that man."

Mason considered this. It fit with what he'd seen of the deputy. Unless the whole of Makah County subsisted on crank alone, Harwood hadn't bought that truck or his fancy boat with shakedown money from outfits like this. Mason didn't figure Ty Winslow's setup in the woods would prove otherwise, though he would have to check.

But none of this explained why Harwood was so damned determined to muck up Jess Winslow's life. The deputy may not have taken Yancy's operation seriously, but the marine's husband had put a bee in his bonnet, that was for certain. And Mason still didn't have a clue how he'd done it.

"So what's the story here?" Yancy asked. "You Ty's kin or something? Why are you so interested in what he was up to?"

"It's not Ty I'm concerned with," Mason told him. "It's his wife."

Yancy blinked. Mason watched a slow smirk spread over the dealer's face. "Well, shit," he said. "You could have saved us a whole lot of trouble if you'd opened with the fact that you're trying to get laid."

"It's not like that." Mason gestured around the clearing, the dock, the rusted machinery piled up along the margins. "You got any wheels that still run in this place?"

Yancy surveyed the clearing like he was seeing it all for the first time. Scratched his head. "I might got a dirt bike with a little life left in her," he said. "Assuming we can agree on a price."

The bike was a thirty-year-old Yamaha, mud spattered and banged up almost beyond recognition, but the engine turned over, and Yancy swore he'd taken her for a ride just a couple of months back.

"Ain't going to get you to Denver," he told Mason, "but she'll get you around town, anyway."

They settled on $350, three bills for the bike and fifty for Yancy's time.

"And your rounds," Mason said, dropping the magazine from the pistol and racking the slide to clear the chamber.

"What about the piece?" Yancy asked. "You can't just . . ."

Mason held it out to him. "You aren't going to shoot me, are you?"

Yancy looked at the gun. Looked at Mason. "Now, why would I go and do that?"

"Kicked your ass, didn't I?"

"Bullshit," Yancy said, nodding to Mason's busted lip. "I got you just as bad as you got me. Maybe better."

He took the pistol back. "Shit, Burke, if you were a cop, you'd be the most fucked-up cop I ever met, you know that?"

"I'm not a cop, Yancy," Mason said. "Now give me those keys."

It had been a long time since he'd been on a dirt bike. Hell, he'd been fourteen, maybe fifteen, visiting cousins on the Upper Peninsula. He'd bailed within a half a mile, nearly killed himself. Busted that bike bad enough that his cousin kicked his ass, and that had been that.

He managed to ride out of the clearing without causing a crash. Waited until he was out of Yancy's sight to try changing gears. The engine ran, anyway, just as the man had said, and Mason found if he took the gravel road slow, but not too slow, he could get along fine.

He pulled off every now and then, paused and tried to listen, half expecting Yancy to come flying down in that truck of his, pistol loaded and blazing. Had he made the right choice giving the dealer back his weapon?

But you had to give respect to get respect, and Mason wasn't one to make enemies of men who had no cause to hate him. He figured he'd earned Yancy's trust when he hadn't shot his ass, figured the dealer cared more about keeping his business afloat than measuring whose dick was bigger.

Mason took the magazine from his pocket, chucked it deep into the rain forest. Pulled out again onto the rough road, took it down to the pavement, and followed that pavement east until the road widened out and the rain forest parted, and he was at the blacktop of the highway.

Now what?

He could try to find Ty Winslow's setup, or he could try to find where Harwood was keeping Lucy. He figured he'd turn the bike back toward town, grab something to eat at the gas station, and then see if Hank Moss knew anything. But before he could fire up the dirt bike again, Mason heard tires on wet pavement approaching, saw headlights reflected on the blacktop. In short order a car appeared and blew past Mason, and as it did, he saw it was a Makah County sheriff's Ford Explorer. The SUV's brake lights came on about ten yards past Mason, and as Mason watched, the SUV came to a stop, made a quick U-turn, and idled back to where he waited on the bike.

The driver's door opened, and one of Harwood's deputies climbed out. "Well, hot damn," the deputy said, adjusting his Stetson and grinning at Mason. "I *thought* that was you."

FOURTEEN

"License and registration?"

Mason watched the deputy walk slowly up the gravel shoulder toward him. The rain had started again, that fine, insidious drizzle, and it had seeped under the neck of Mason's slicker, soaked through his jeans and his boots and socks, chilling him with that damp that somehow seemed colder than any Michigan winter.

The deputy was the younger of Harwood's two buddies. SWEENEY, it said on his jacket. As he approached Mason, his right hand crept down toward the holster on his hip. He glanced up and down the highway; the road was deserted. The lights from his truck smeared blue and red reflections against the wet pavement.

Mason said nothing as the deputy approached. Thought about the pistol he'd given back to Yancy, and decided for once in his life he'd been smart about something. No way he'd walk out of here if the deputy found a gun on his person; not a free man, anyway. These Deception Cove lawmen were itching to be rid of him. Heck, the deputy might well have shot him dead, claimed self-defense.

He still might, Mason thought.

"You hear me, Burke? License and proof of registration for this bike." The deputy stopped a few feet away. Kept his right hand at his hip, eyed Mason over.

Mason shook his head. "No registration. I just bought this thing."

"Driver's license?"

"No, sir."

The deputy's lip twitched. "Proof of sale?"

Mason laughed. "Come on."

"Yeah, okay." The deputy took a step back, drew his pistol. "I'm going to need you to come on over to that truck with me."

"Are you arresting me?" Mason asked.

"*Now,* Burke." The deputy drew a bead on Mason's forehead. "It wasn't a suggestion."

Second time in an hour that someone had drawn a pistol on Mason, and he figured this deputy wouldn't be quite so easy to shake as Yancy had been. He climbed off the bike, kept his hands visible and his movements slow, walked up the edge of the highway to where the Explorer sat parked.

"Hands on the hood," the deputy told him. "Spread your legs. I'm gonna search you."

Mason obeyed. Stayed motionless as the deputy frisked him. Waited as the deputy pulled the wallet from his back pocket, the envelope with his cash.

"Guess you got used to this kind of treatment inside," the deputy said. "Fifteen years of strip searches and group showers, huh?"

Mason smirked. "Are you flirting with me, Sweeney?"

"Am I . . . " The deputy might have laughed; Mason couldn't be sure. But then something clocked him, hard, on the side of the head, and suddenly he was down on the grit beside the Explorer, staring up at the deputy and his gun. The deputy wasn't laughing now.

"You're a real piece of work, Burke," he said. "You'd think a guy like you would have learned something the first go-around, but you can't keep your nose out of trouble, huh?"

Mason said nothing. Assumed he'd been pistol-whipped from the way his ears were ringing. He put his hand to the side of his head, felt blood.

"I should just put you down," the deputy continued. "Right here and right now. You think anyone would give a shit if some murderer bought it?"

"Have to be pretty gutless to shoot an unarmed man," Mason said. "Then again, you all are already terrorizing a combat-wounded marine, so maybe this kind of thing is right in your ballpark."

The deputy flinched a little bit, and he couldn't meet Mason's eyes.

"That make you feel big, Sweeney, what you're doing to that woman? That kind of thing get you off?" Mason gave it a beat, but the deputy kept his mouth shut. "Or maybe you're just Harwood's little bag boy. Is that it?"

"Fuck you." Sweeney glared down at him. "You don't know what you're kicking over, coming around here. It don't concern you any more than your bullshit Michigan life concerns me."

"I'm just here for the dog, Deputy. You going to shoot me, or what?"

The deputy looked up and down the road again. Then focused back down on Mason. "I could do it," he said. "I could put you down, easy. Leave your body in the woods for the bears and the cougars to fight over, and wouldn't nobody care one way or the other."

"So do it. Put me out of my misery. Make your boss happy."

"I should." Sweeney's gun trembled in his hand. His finger massaged the trigger. Mason stared up at him, rain soaking his face, figured at least if he died, it was warm where he was headed.

But the deputy didn't shoot him. He relaxed his trigger finger, took a step back. Motioned with the pistol.

"Get up," he told Mason. "We're going to take a ride."

"You want my advice, you need to forget about that dog," Sweeney said.

They were in the deputy's SUV now, headed east along the highway. Sweeney had made sure to knock over Mason's bike as he pulled back out onto the road, ran it over a couple of times for good measure.

"Thing was a piece of shit anyway," he'd said, smirking at Mason in the rearview mirror.

Mason hadn't replied. Sat in the back seat and shifted his weight, his hands cuffed behind him, the steel digging into his wrists. Sweeney drove in silence for a few miles, still smiling to himself. Every now and then his radio squawked static. Otherwise, the ride was quiet.

Then Sweeney brought up the dog. "You need to let it go," he told Mason. "The mutt's not long for this world anyway. Outlived its usefulness, I guess you could call it. Kirby thinks it might help the widow remember if she sees her little doggie in pieces."

Mason closed his eyes. "She doesn't have what you're after," he said. "You haven't figured that out yet?"

"Maybe not, but she was hitched to the guy who did. And that means she knows stuff that the rest of us don't. Kirby says it's just a matter of getting her to play along."

"Kirby's a tool," Mason said. "You ever think for yourself?"

Sweeney didn't reply, sneered at him in the rearview.

"What are you all into, anyway? What exactly did Ty Winslow steal from you?"

"That's a need-to-know," Sweeney said. "And you don't."

"Sure, but you should probably tell the Winslow woman what she's looking for."

"You need to forget about her, too, Burke. Matter of fact, you should just forget about Deception Cove altogether, you know? There's nothing here for you."

They'd reached another town, bigger than Deception Cove but not by a whole lot. The sign on the side of the highway said CLALLAM BAY. Sweeney turned off the highway, drove down the main street, pulled off into a gas station lot, and parked alongside the building.

"Won't take but a minute," he said, killing the engine and reaching for the door. "Don't you go anywhere."

Mason waited, squirming to get comfortable in his cuffs. Watched through the windshield as Sweeney disappeared inside the gas station, came out five minutes later holding a piece of paper in his hands. The deputy slid in behind the wheel, twisted back to show Mason what he had.

"This here's a bus ticket to Seattle," he said. "Compliments of the Makah County Sheriff's Department. You want my advice, you buy another bus ticket soon as you hit the city, go home to Michigan, get a good drunk on, maybe get laid, and when you sober up, you can get yourself a real job to occupy your time."

"That's what you suggest, is it?"

Sweeney looked him over. His lip curled. "Kirby wants you gone," he said. "By rights, I should have shot you back there, Burke. If you're looking for something to say, maybe try for 'thank you.'"

It was early afternoon when the bus showed up. Sweeney waited with Mason in the Explorer, the radio tuned to some new country channel, singers Mason had never heard of and was pretty sure he could live just fine without. When the bus pulled into the lot, Sweeney yawned, stretched, climbed from the SUV and opened Mason's door, gestured *Turn around,* and undid the cuffs.

"Don't you get cute now," he said, steering Mason toward the waiting bus. "This is a one-time gesture of goodwill. I see you again, I won't be so kindhearted."

He walked Mason to the door of the bus. Handed him the ticket, and leaned in and spoke to the driver.

"I want this man on the bus all the way to Seattle," he said. "He tries anything stupid, you call the law and have them call back to Deception Cove. We'll send someone down to get him."

The driver was a middle-aged guy, beefy, sleeves rolled up and tattoos. He gave Mason the once-over, nodded.

Sweeney nudged Mason toward the door. "Been a pleasure, Burke," he said. "Bon voyage."

The bus ride to Seattle took five hours. Mason sat in the back and stared out the window and thought about Jess Winslow, thought about Lucy. Eventually the bus stopped at a ferry terminal and drove onto a ship for the ride across Puget Sound, and Mason waited and looked out at the water, watched the Seattle skyline come into view on the other side.

The ferry docked, and the bus drove into the city and found the intercity Greyhound station, and Mason filed off with the rest of the passengers, winked at the driver, who glared back in response. He walked inside the bus terminal and straight to the ticket counter, waited in line some more until a clerk called him forward.

And let us not grow weary of doing good, for in due season we will reap, if we do not give up.

"I need a ticket to Deception Cove," Mason told the clerk, reaching for his cash. "One way."

FIFTEEN

It was just after midnight when the bus dropped Mason off in front of the gas station in Deception Cove. He was the only passenger to disembark; there was nobody waiting at the gas station, no sheriff's deputies or anyone else. The rain continued, ceaseless. Mason was tired and cold and hungry, his busted lip sore, his hair matted with dried blood.

He walked up the highway to Hank Moss's motel. The light was off in the lobby, the VACANCY sign burning bright red in the dark of the night. There were no cars in the parking lot, no other rooms occupied. As Mason dug into his pocket for his room key, he could have been the only person left alive in the world.

He slid his key into the lock, turned it. Before he could push the door open, though, he sensed movement behind him, and he spun, ready to fight, expecting to see Sweeney or Harwood materialize in the empty lot.

Instead it was Jess Winslow who emerged from the shadows.

She wore a black rain jacket, dark jeans, and hiking boots. A baseball cap, her hair in a ponytail. Her movements were cautious, hesitant, though Mason couldn't be sure if it was Harwood she was afraid of or him.

"Hi," she said.

"You scared me half to death," he replied, and it was true; his heart was still pounding, body in fight-or-flight mode. "How long've you been waiting here?"

"A while," she said. "I was beginning to think you'd skipped town."

Mason looked past her, surveyed the parking lot and the highway beyond. He turned the knob and pushed the door open.

"Come on," he said. "It's better if nobody sees us."

She followed him into the room, waited as he turned on the ceiling light and the lamp by the bed, as he pulled out a chair for her from beside the plywood desk. She demurred when he offered to hang up her jacket, and he shrugged and hung his slicker up all the same. Then he sat down on the end of the bed, looked her over.

"How'd you find me?" he said.

"There's only one motel in town," she replied. "And Hank Moss is a friend of mine. He gave you up pretty easy. Though if you weren't bunking here, I was out of ideas."

She was scanning the room, her eyes never resting in one place for long, and Mason noticed she'd backed her chair against the wall.

"What happened to your face?" she asked.

He laughed a little. Touched his lip. "Turns out my presence isn't appreciated in this town. So much so that Deputy Sweeney was willing to pay out of pocket for a bus ticket home."

"Cole ran you out?"

"Yup. Put a gun to my head and swore he'd be fine with just shooting me, but I guess he had a change of heart."

Jess stared across at him, studied his face, and Mason wondered just how bad he looked. He'd caught glimpses of his reflection in the window on the bus, but he hadn't seen a mirror yet, wasn't sure he wanted to.

She pursed her lips, seemed to be considering something. Mason waited. Listened to a car pass on the highway outside, the *hush* of the tires on the pavement. Finally Jess came to her decision.

"Dale Whitmer's brother keeps dogs on his property," she said. "He has a farm a couple miles west of town."

Mason said nothing.

"You asked if I had any idea where they're keeping Lucy," she continued. "I gave it some thought, and I think that's the likeliest story. I've been watching the deputies' houses, and I don't think they have her, but Bryce Whitmer has the space, and a kennel to keep her."

And other dogs, Mason thought. *And guns.* "You been out there yet?"

She shook her head. "Couldn't risk it in daylight. Harwood and his boys know my truck. They see me lurking around, they'll either move that dog or they'll kill her."

Mason stood. Went to the closet, pulled on his coat. Gathered his duffel bag, his spare clothes and gear.

"What are you doing?" she asked.

"There's no sense waiting," he said, bending to retie his boots. "Those boys are getting desperate over there."

She looked at him.

"Are you coming?" he asked. "Because if not, I'm going to need you to draw me a map."

But she was already on her feet. "Yeah, I'm coming," she said. "Let's get this done."

She'd parked her truck around back of the motel, tucked into the shadows and well out of sight of the road. Her shotgun lay in a soft case behind the passenger seat, a couple of boxes of shells beside. Mason glanced at it as he climbed into the truck, and Jess caught him looking.

"I don't leave home without it," she said, turning the key in the ignition. "Not anymore."

She pulled out onto the highway, and they drove in silence. The highway was empty, the forest looming in beside and above. As the lights of the gas station dwindled in the rearview, the night outside was suddenly very dark.

"How far did Cole take you, when he ran you out?" Jess asked after a while.

"Next town over," Mason said. "Bought me a ticket to Seattle, told the driver to call the law if I tried to get off before. So I rode that bus to Seattle and caught the next one back."

"You think about not coming back?"

"No, ma'am."

"Would've been easier." She kept her eyes on the road, hands at ten and two. Gripped the wheel tight, didn't look at him. "Unless you're looking for an excuse to get back at the world, cause some mayhem, go down swinging."

He didn't say anything, waited until she'd looked his way.

"You aiming to go back to jail, Burke?" she asked. "Or maybe you just have a death wish, revenge fantasy? Want to kill a few cops on your way out of this world?"

"I want to see that dog safe," Mason said. "That's all."

"Yeah, well." She slowed the truck. "Just try and remember that some of us have to live in this town when it's all said and done."

He started to reply. Jess cut him off with a shake of her head. Pulled the truck off the highway, killed the engine, and pointed out through the windshield.

"Farm's just through those trees," she said. "Best if we walk from here."

SIXTEEN

Bryce Whitmer's place wasn't much of a farm anymore. When Jess was growing up, Bryce and Dale's dad had tried keeping horses on the property, a couple of dairy cows and a handful of chickens, but there was less money in farming in Deception Cove than there was in fishing. Soon as the old man died, the horses disappeared, the cows were sold, and the chickens were cooked and eaten, and Bryce, who was the eldest, set about filling the land he'd inherited with every manner of junked vehicle imaginable.

Now Bryce ran something of an impromptu pick-a-part: for a ten-dollar fee, Bryce would call off his dogs for you, let you wander around the piles of rusted hulks, dig under the hoods, and when you found what you were looking for, Bryce would assess a value, and you could pay it or you could leave.

Most people just paid, having come that far, and anyway, Bryce was a big, broad guy, six feet five, and he kept two foul-tempered mutts roaming loose among the cars, rumor being those dogs had tasted human flesh now and again, and that they'd liked it well enough to want to try some more.

People didn't mess with Bryce Whitmer. Even his little brother steered mostly clear, and Dale was supposed to be the law. So Jess didn't exactly feel comfortable sneaking around the side of Bryce's property like she and Burke were doing, but if she were Kirby Harwood, she'd have stashed Lucy here, so she'd decided she didn't really have a choice.

She'd hidden the truck off the highway, down a dirt-track road that led up into the hills beyond the Whitmer property line. She'd unpacked the Remington, shoved a handful of spare shells into her jacket pocket, double-checked the shotgun to make sure it was loaded.

"I don't have a gun for you," she told Burke. "I'm hoping we can do this thing without needing mine, either."

Burke just nodded. "That would be just fine with me," he said. "I never shot a gun in my life anyway."

"Well, this is hardly the best time to be learning." She gave him a flashlight instead, closed the Chevy's door, quiet as she could. Through the trees she could see the lights of the Whitmer place, a run-down old two-story house she'd never seen the inside of, but she'd known girls who had, back in high school, and they hadn't come back with five-star reviews. Jess could only imagine what the place looked like these days.

A fence ran up the roadside, into the forest, chain link and barbed wire, security lights. Jess gestured up the dirt road.

"I'm thinking we try and find a way in around back," she said. "Unless you want to knock on the front door."

Burke was studying the fence. "Rather not. You remember the wire cutters?"

She shook her head. "We're going to have to improvise."

Jess could feel her heart rate increasing, feel her senses start to wake up, pay attention, as if she were back on night patrol again, back over there, as if any step she took wrong could blow her legs off, or worse, get one of her guys killed.

She didn't mind the feeling. Figured this was about the only thing in her life she'd ever been good at, sneaking around doing macho man shit. Figured this adrenaline rush was her body telling her she was doing what she should.

She motioned down the fence line, into the dark. "Let's do this."

Burke nodded. Switched on the flashlight, kept it aimed low. Started walking. Jess shouldered the shotgun and fell in behind him.

Mason and Jess followed the road toward the back of the property. He traced the bottom of the fence with his flashlight, looking for a tear in the chain link, a hole, anything they could use to get into the compound.

That's what it was, a compound; it wasn't a farm. Beyond the house, the old fields were filled with the shadowed hulks of old cars, lined up in uneven rows and stacked atop one another, a labyrinth of worn-out American iron. The cars were stacked three or four high; even with their roofs stove in, they still towered above Mason and Jess. Soon the hulks had blocked the view of the house, blocked the view of anything inside the fence line.

They reached the rear of the property, set off through the trees to cover the back fence. Mason walked slow, stepped soft and careful, knew there were supposed to be dogs roaming around. There was a vague path through the forest along the back fence, a deer trail or something, and that helped. He didn't make much noise tracing the line; behind him, Jess made none, and when he glanced back to make sure she was still with him, there was a dim glint of reflected light on the barrel of the shotgun, the same in her eyes, and that's all she was.

"What?" she whispered. "You see something?"

He said, "Just wanted to make sure."

"What, that I'm here? I'm not going anywhere."

He kept moving. Led them to the far corner of the property,

where there was a gate, double wide, and another rutted road. Beyond the fence, through the phalanx of cars, Mason could see an outbuilding, the road leading to it.

The gate was locked with a padlock. The road underneath was muddy from the rain, but the tire tracks looked fresh. He let Jess see the padlock. Then they pressed forward.

But there were no holes in the fence, not even a burrow dug through the dirt at the bottom, no way in or out but the gate in the back or the house at the front.

"I could hop that fence," Mason said when they'd retreated back to the rear of the property, the locked gate. "Those cars back there would block any view from the house."

Jess looked at him funny. "No offense," she said, "but you were locked up in jail, weren't you?"

He nodded. "So?"

"You ever try to escape?"

"I told you," he said, "I served my time."

"So you aren't exactly a fence-hopping expert, then."

He had to laugh. Kept it quiet, though. "You have any better ideas?"

Jess cocked her head, motioned back toward the front. "Sneak in alongside that house," she said. "There's got to be a way.

"Unless you want to put a pin in this," she said. "Go buy some wire cutters and come back tomorrow."

He thought about it. Looked up and down the fence line, didn't see any better ideas. Was about to tell her, okay, they'd try alongside the house, when a screen door back that way slapped open and slammed shut again, and he and she both could hear boots on wood stairs, somebody whistling as he walked back through the yard.

Mason felt his blood go cold. *"Shit."*

Beside him, Jess didn't say a word.

Jess wasn't enjoying this. She'd felt that surge of adrenaline at the start, but as soon as they'd started up the road, the rest had come flooding back. The bad stuff. Patrols gone haywire, faulty intelligence. Ambushes out of nowhere, gunfire from the shadows.

Afia screaming her name as they dragged her away.

It wasn't even the violence that got to Jess; she could take the violence, while it was happening. She'd been trained for that stuff. It was the other parts, the before and the after, that's what killed her. Driving out beyond the wire into a sea of hostile faces, suspicious eyes, not knowing who was coming after them, or where they were coming from, but knowing they were coming all the same.

It was the tension, constant and unceasing, a boot pressing down on your chest, paralysis. It was the flinching every time a car backfired, every time a hand in the crowd reached for a cell phone. It was the *waiting,* that was the shitty part, waiting and knowing the violence was coming, not being able to do a damn thing about it.

And then the after, the blood and the chaos, urgent voices and the smell of burned flesh and shit and piss and fire. Replaying the violence in your head for hours, wishing you'd just done one little thing different, so your buddy beside you, who'd played *Counter-Strike* and showed you pictures of his daughter, so he'd still be alive and intact and not another body bag in the back of a jet.

Right now it was the before. It was the tension. She'd crept around the outside of the Whitmer property knowing the night was going to get greasy, knowing there wasn't a thing she could do about it, not if she wanted to get Lucy back.

And now here it came, someone out of the house, heavy footsteps across the porch and down to the backyard. Whistling, cheerful, not really a tune, but Jess could feel every note creeping up her spine.

She tensed, held the shotgun tight, ducked away from the gate and tried to stay hidden as Burke did the same beside her.

The whistling stopped, and then a man's voice called out. "Here, boys," and Jess could hear the dogs, both of them, panting and snapping at each other, chain collars jangling as they raced across the compound toward the man.

Jess knew the man was Bryce Whitmer.

Suddenly there was light, bright white and blinding. Whitmer must have flipped a switch somewhere, hit the juice on the junkyard, because every light in the compound stayed on, and all at once it was as bright as day beyond the fence.

Jess closed her eyes, tried to steady her breathing. Realized she was shaking, her hands, couldn't make them stop.

Man up.

Whitmer began to whistle again, and he was getting closer. Jess wasn't looking. She was backed against the fence, shotgun to her chest, looking out into the black forest. But then Burke nudged her, and she had to turn.

He was staring through the fence, motioning through the wall of cars to the left, somebody's old Buick crushed and left for dead, just enough space left in the front windshield to see a clear path through the yard to another building, maybe ten feet by ten feet, and Jess didn't know what she was seeing at first.

But then she saw the fencing out front, more chain link, saw the silver bowl on the ground. And then she saw the mass beside the bowl, black and white and oddly shaped, and she saw the glint off the collar, rhinestones she'd bought to try to make her butch dog look more feminine, and the mass shifted and those ears perked up, and she knew it was Lucy.

Before she could do anything else, though, Bryce Whitmer appeared at the front of the kennel, blocking her view, and she couldn't see Lucy anymore, but she could see the light glint off the meat cleaver that Bryce held in his hand.

Lucy whimpered, and Jess felt it like knives.

SEVENTEEN

This was the part Jess was good at.

She pushed herself off the fence. Spun, and leveled the shotgun at the gate. “Move,” she told Burke, and Burke caught the look in her eye and he moved, all right.

She pulled the trigger and the lock was gone, the gate nearly blown off its hinges. The explosion reverberated through the junkyard, the forest, but Jess wasn’t waiting around to bask in the afterglow. She kicked the gate open and stepped through. Hustled, fast, between the stacks of wrecked cars until she came to the clearing where Bryce Whitmer stood with the cleaver in his hand, a dumbfounded look on his face.

“Drop the weapon, Bryce,” Jess told him, aiming the shotgun at him square and closing the distance. “You drop that blade now.”

Whitmer’s expression changed when he recognized her. A slow, mean smile took the place of stunned stupid.

“Now, what the hell do you think you’re doing, Jess?” he asked. “Are you planning to shoot me tonight?”

She responded by raising the barrel and firing over his head, relishing the way he flinched at the shot.

“Drop the fucking weapon, Bryce,” she said. “I won’t tell you again.”

Behind Bryce she could see fully into the kennel now, and the sight broke her heart. Lucy cowered at the back of the enclosure, tail between her legs, trembling, terrified. She was skinny, too, that rhinestone collar fairly drooping off her neck. It looked like Whitmer had neglected her half the time and beaten her the rest. Jess lowered the barrel of the shotgun until it was pointed at Whitmer's midsection again, wanted to pull the trigger right then and there, and to hell with the consequences.

"This ain't going to end well for you, Jess," Whitmer said, bending down to lay the cleaver on the dirt. "You're better off just walking away right now, forgetting you ever came here."

She motioned with the barrel toward Lucy's kennel. "Open the kennel for me," she said. "I'm taking my dog home."

But Whitmer didn't move. He was smiling again. "Can't say I didn't warn you." He turned his head and whistled, loud, over his shoulder. "C'mon out, boys!"

The dogs came running. Careened out from behind a stack of cars near the house and raced across the empty dirt to where Whitmer and Jess were standing. They were big dogs, probably eighty pounds apiece, and they were fast for their size, muscular, and they looked damn mean.

They weren't stopping, either; slavering, barking, lips curled back and teeth bared, and when they saw Jess, they veered off from Whitmer and came galloping toward her instead.

She turned and fired again, quickly, aiming over their heads. The dogs stopped running at the shot, but they didn't bug off.

Shit.

Whitmer was laughing. "What are you going to do, Jess?" he said. "Kill both my dogs to save yours? Something about that just doesn't sound right."

She didn't *want* to do it. Mean as those dogs looked, her beef was with their owner, not them. But if they came at her again, she'd have no choice.

The bigger dog was creeping toward her now, spittle flecked at his jowls, a growl deep in his throat. He wasn't going to stay scared for long.

Jess took aim, but even as she did, the second dog was moving in to flank her, and she knew as soon as she shot one, the other would be on her. And on the other side, Whitmer was reaching for that cleaver again.

Then someone whistled, up toward the house, and Jess and Whitmer and the dogs all turned and stared, turned to watch Mason Burke step out from around another row of stacked cars.

"*Hey,*" he called out. "Hey, dogs, over here!"

Then he turned and ran, and that's all it took. The dogs forgot Jess, and they forgot about Whitmer. They turned and hurled themselves after Burke, kicking up dirt as they covered the yard in a blink.

Whitmer laughed again. "That your new boyfriend, Jess?"

Jess shook her head.

"Good," Whitmer said, "'cause he's about to be lunch."

She leveled the shotgun on him again. "You open the door to that kennel like I told you the first time, Bryce. Are we clear?"

Whitmer didn't move for a beat. Then, chuckling to himself, he walked over to Lucy's kennel and unlatched the metal grate, pulled it open. Lucy shrank back as he approached, stared out at him, shaking harder.

"Lucy," Jess whispered, as calm as possible, nonthreatening. "Lucy, c'mon out, girl. Come on out here."

Lucy perked up at the sound of her voice, but she didn't move. Elsewhere in the yard, Whitmer's dogs were losing their shit.

"Back up," Jess told Whitmer, motioning with the shotgun. She backed him away from the kennel, replaced him at the grate. Kept the barrel pointed at Whitmer, but she bent down and looked into the kennel, clucked her tongue and reached out with her free hand.

"Come on, Lucy," she said. "Time to go home."

Slow, maddeningly slow, and shaking like she had hypothermia, Lucy edged away from the back end of the kennel, slunk around the wall until she'd nearly reached the open grate.

"Here we go, Lucy. Almost there."

Then Lucy stopped. She'd caught sight of Whitmer again. *Damn it.* Jess reached into the kennel, caught hold of Lucy's collar, and pulled as hard as she could, dragging the dog through the open grate. Slammed the kennel door closed, and looked up again just in time to see Whitmer making his move.

She spun the shotgun around. "Don't you fucking try it," she told him. "I'll blow your head off from here, and your dogs can eat your damn brains for breakfast, if they can find any."

Whitmer stopped. He smiled again but said nothing.

"Now," Jess said. "You back away from me and my dog, and you let us go."

She didn't wait for a response. Nudged Lucy back with her knee, toward the fence and the busted gate. Clucked her teeth and spoke softly, soothing the dog, moving her gently to freedom, without ever taking her eyes off of Whitmer.

Mason ran for his life through the labyrinth junkyard. He heard the mutts snapping at his heels, knew they'd take him down without prejudice, tear him to shreds. He veered right, hauled ass up the side of a stack of cars, scraping his hands and his knees something fierce on the rust and bare metal.

The big dogs were fast as heck, but they weren't much good for climbing. He heard the dogs hit the stack behind him, fairly *collide* with it, the stack lurching beneath him from the impact. The dogs leapt up, their claws scraping down the car sides.

One dog got a grip on his boot and held tight, dragging Mason back as its partner tried for the other boot. Mason kicked the dog in the head, once and again, heard it squeal and drop back to the dirt, hit hard, and launch itself skyward again.

He kept climbing until he made the top of the stack. He couldn't see Jess anywhere but hoped he'd bought her enough time. One of the dogs was still trying to follow him up; the other stood in the dirt barking its dang head off like it'd just treed a bear.

Mason jumped down off the other side of the stack. Hit the ground and rolled and knew the dogs wouldn't stay fooled forever. He beat it across the hard-packed dirt and crossed in front of the old farmhouse toward the other side of the yard, where more junked cars lay in various stages of deterioration. From the barking behind him, he could pinpoint the moment the dogs cottoned on, and he hadn't covered nearly enough ground to feel good about it.

He ran faster. Didn't look back. Didn't even glance sideways to see how Jess was doing. She had a shotgun, after all. Heck, she was a goddamn marine; she'd be fine. If *he* made it out of here without winding up dog food, though, it'd be a damn miracle.

He reached another stack of cars, clawed his way up. Sliced his hand open on a loose piece of trim, ignored it. Made the top of the stack just as the dogs hit the bottom. *Now what?*

The fence sat a couple of rows over, just a little lower than the cars, the razor wire curled at the top, the barbs gleaming sharp and vicious in the glow from the security lights. On the other side of that fence was the truck and, he hoped, Jess and Lucy. Mason had but one shot at escape.

Balancing as best he could on the top of the stack of cars, he blocked out the noise of the dogs barking behind him and below him, closed his eyes, and took a leap of faith. Landed with a crash on the next pile of junk, felt something sharp jam into his stomach and knew he'd be paying for it later. He scrambled to the top of the pile, repeated the process. The dogs hadn't figured him out yet, and he made the last stack and climbed to the top, found himself staring out at dark forest so close he could practically touch it.

Home free.

Then the screen door on that farmhouse slapped open, and someone fired a shot, and it wasn't Jess with the shotgun. Mason quit admiring the trees and just leapt straight toward them. Didn't plan to catch a leg on that razor wire, but he did, heard his pants tear and felt skin tearing too as he fell. Landed awkward and rolled an ankle, pulled himself to his feet and half staggered, half crawled toward Jess's Chevy, the brake lights lit up and the engine raring to go.

Mason supported himself on the bed of the truck, limped around the side to the passenger door, and climbed in. Slammed the door closed, and Jess was already moving, the engine howling now, the tires scrabbling for traction.

Lucy was there too, wedged in between them, and the dog licked Mason's face, and wouldn't stop doing it, as Jess hauled ass away from the farm.

EIGHTEEN

Kirby Harwood's cell phone rang loud and insistent. Beside him in the queen-sized bed, not watching the sport-fishing reality TV show, Terri-Lee put down her book and frowned.

"Who could be calling at this hour?" she said. She had that tone to her voice again: disapproval, accusation. As if they wouldn't be getting disturbed like this if only they were living the life they should have been, if Kirby hadn't gone and fucked up his full ride, dragged them back to this shit-hole town. She had that tone of voice a fair bit these days.

Harwood looked at the display, recognized the number. Was already standing when he accepted the call.

"Harwood."

"They got the dog." Bryce Whitmer's voice, deep and steady. "Came in with a shotgun and blew the lock off the back gate. Had the drop on me before I could go for my gun."

Harwood walked into the hallway, leaned against the wall. "Bullshit."

"I wish," Whitmer said. "I was on my way out to piece out that dog like we planned, figured I wouldn't need more than the cleaver."

"Thought those dogs of yours were supposed to be guard dogs."

"They are. But the guy led them off while that Winslow bitch held the gun on me."

Harwood rubbed his face. Why'd this have to be so damn difficult when it should have been simple? A little extra cash for a couple of jobs a month, a little rainy-day money, fix the roof on the house and redo the kitchen, maybe pay for some more visits to that fertility doctor who charged so damn much, give Terri-Lee the family she wanted, so maybe she'd stop acting so damn aggrieved all the time.

It was supposed to be easy. Wasn't nobody supposed to get hurt, not even a damn dog. But Kirby Harwood had seen plenty firsthand how the best-laid plans often turned to shit. He shouldn't have been surprised that this one was no exception.

"The guy with Jess," Harwood said. "Midthirties, tall? Look like a hard case?"

"That's the guy."

Burke. *Who the hell are you, Mason Burke? And why the fuck have you taken such an interest in messing up my little town?*

"I'm headed your way," Harwood said. "Call Cole and Dale, have them meet us. We got to track that bitch down."

Harwood ended the call. Walked back into the bedroom, where Terri-Lee was reading her book again, some self-help manual, visualize the things you want and they will appear in front of you. Snake-oil bullshit.

"Who was it?" she asked.

"Bryce Whitmer." Harwood was already crossing to the closet and pulling on his pants. "Had some prowlers lurking around back of his place."

"So send Dale. He's Bryce's brother, for God's sake."

Harwood buttoned his shirt, grabbed his Stetson. "Dale's off tonight. You know how it works."

His wife sighed, long and expressive. Opened her book again. "They'd damn well better make you sheriff of this county," she said. "For all the bullshit they throw in our lap."

NINETEEN

Jess drove that Chevy fast, headed west on the state route away from Deception Cove, no idea where she was going. As soon as she'd coaxed Lucy away from the gate, she'd booked it for the truck—the dog hesitating a moment, then loping behind, as if she knew she was being rescued and was damned ready for it.

Before she'd had to debate whether to go back in with the shotgun to get Burke or simply drive off, the man had dropped from the sky and come limping around the side of the truck. Panting for breath and bleeding from somewhere, or a few somewheres.

But Jess hadn't had time for triage. Bryce Whitmer wasn't about to concede defeat—and sure enough, he'd come around the front of the farmhouse as the truck sped past. She hadn't seen him, but she'd sure heard his gun going off.

He hadn't hit the truck, though, and now Jess pushed the gas pedal down as far as she dared, taking the twists and turns like a racer, the forest looming out of the dark at the edge of her headlights, the curves coming almost too fast to register.

She was driving on instinct. She'd been working on instinct since she blew that gate open.

Burke sat wedged against the passenger door, gripping the oh-shit bar above his head with one hand and the dog with the other. Lucy leaned into him, whimpering a little bit, twisting her thick neck around to lick his face whenever Jess hit a straightaway, like Burke could somehow stop this ride.

The truck raced past Shipwreck Point, the ocean on the passenger side, right up against the road now. Every quarter mile there was a pullout with a picnic table, and every half mile a flimsy cross dug in along the shoulder, memorial to a drunk driver or a victim thereof. The ocean was a black nothing outside Burke's window; Jess couldn't even see the shore to tell whether the tide was up or down.

The highway was empty. No headlights oncoming, none in the rearview. Jess kept on the gas regardless, knew that by the time she saw Whitmer or the deputies coming up from behind, it'd be too late.

Burke said something beside her a couple of times, but Jess didn't hardly hear him. She was somewhere else, just driving, and he wasn't there with her. After a while he shut up and just held on for dear life and let her get them where she was getting to.

Adrenaline wouldn't last forever, though, and Jess could already feel the comedown. Could feel instinct start to slip away, letting her conscious mind back into the game, and that wasn't good news for anyone.

She didn't know where she was going. There wasn't much west of here, not on this highway or anywhere else; give it ten miles and they'd reach Neah Bay and the Makah reservation, where the highway ended. Beyond that was the lighthouse at Cape Flattery, and that was the end of America, geographically speaking. There was only one road out of Neah Bay too, unless you wanted to brave the logging roads south along the coast, and that was a fool's errand this time of year.

She'd trapped them.

Jess didn't realize she had slowed the truck until she heard Burke say her name. Then she blinked back to now. She'd parked them on the shoulder, one of those pullouts, the crash of the surf audible over the engine. Burke was looking at her, and Lucy whining and trying to get over to her, and Jess wondered how long she'd kept them stranded here.

This was what happened when the adrenaline was used up. When instinct decided it wasn't needed anymore and checked out.

Her mind came back, and her mind remembered: the shotgun and Whitmer's gun and the dogs squealing and barking and the fear and the thrill of it, that galvanizing tension and the excruciating release in the aftermath.

Shit, she was spent. Jess stared at the steering wheel and heard the rain on the roof, and Burke saying her name again, but she just couldn't wrap her head around an answer.

"Jess?"

Mason repeated her name, but Jess didn't so much as blink. She was gone. She sat there with her hands on the wheel, ten and two, the engine still running, gearshift in *P.* She stared down at the dashboard and didn't say a word, didn't move but for the shivering.

She was shaking hard. Mason didn't know exactly what was happening, but he imagined it had something to do with why she'd been given Lucy in the first place. The dog sure seemed to notice; she hadn't taken her eyes off of Jess since they pulled over, kept squirming to get free of Mason and over to her. Mason unbuckled his seat belt and let Lucy go. The dog leapt across the bench seat, tail whipping around like a weapon, sidled up beside Jess, and leaned her weight onto her owner, licking her face like she was covered in peanut butter. Jess's shaking seemed to subside a little bit. She still wouldn't move otherwise.

They couldn't stay here. This highway ran twisted, but there weren't many ways off of it, not that Mason had seen. The ocean on the one side effectively blocked off all means of escape, and aside from the odd logging road disappearing into the woods on the other, you pretty much had a straight shot from the Whitmer property to wherever *here* was.

They'd be coming, he knew. And he didn't want to be sitting here in this truck in the middle of nowhere when they arrived. Not with Jess in this state.

He opened the passenger door. Ducked out into the rain and heard the sound of the ocean beside him, could glimpse the crashing surf just offshore. He circled around to the driver's side and opened Jess's door and hunched down beside her.

He said, "Why don't you let me drive for a while?"

Jess didn't answer. Lucy looked at him with big, worried eyes, looked at Jess and then at Mason again, like she wasn't sure what to do either. The dog had grown since he'd last seen her, he realized, filled out and built muscle. She didn't look like the runt anymore, but he could see in her eyes how she'd likely always carry scars from the men who'd laid claim to her before Linda Petrie came along.

"Come on, Luce," Mason said. "Let's get you guys moved over."

He leaned over Jess to reach her seat belt, caught the scent of gunpowder and sweat and something flowery, too, her shampoo or something.

"I'm going to move you now," he said. "Just a little bit. Just so I can get in here and drive."

"Fine," she said, almost inaudible.

He put his arm under her legs and the other behind her back, guided her over the transmission tunnel and across the bench to where Lucy sat waiting, watching every move Mason made, almost like she didn't trust him to take care of Jess properly. He got Jess situated, leaned over again, and fastened her seat belt, and Lucy promptly laid herself across Jess's lap as Jess leaned against the passenger door.

It seemed to work.

Mason climbed into the driver's seat. Shifted into gear and pulled back onto the highway, trying not to think about how he hadn't driven a car in a good fifteen years, and hoping the rules of the road hadn't changed in the meantime.

TWENTY

"The hell do you mean you let him go, Cole?"

Outside the Whitmer property, Harwood's truck was pulled to the side of the highway, Sweeney and Dale parked close behind. In the pissing rain again, Bryce Whitmer pacing a track in the mud, fondling that six-inch, nickel-plated Colt Python like it was his actual dick.

Sweeney's hat was pulled low, but even underneath it Harwood could see the kid blush. Sweeney shifted his weight, stammered a little bit.

"I mean, heck, Kirby, the guy was unarmed," he said. "He was flat on his back. I couldn't just put a hole in him."

Harwood glared at the younger man. "You couldn't, huh?"

"I just—it wouldn't be honorable, is all. I just didn't think it'd be right."

Harwood crossed to Sweeney in two long steps. Reared back and caught him with a backhand, sent the kid stumbling down into the mud.

"You think Okafor gives a shit about *honorable,* Cole?" Harwood said. "Those Nigerians will cut off your face and feed it to you if we don't get their money back in time. You hearing me?"

"I'm sorry, Kirby," Sweeney said, on one knee in the mud. "I thought I could scare him off. I didn't think he'd come back."

"The man did hard time for murder. You thought waving your little gun in his face was going to teach him anything?"

Sweeney said nothing. Touched his fingers to his lips, examined them.

"Anyway, it don't matter now," Harwood said, turning away. "Doesn't even matter that they came for that dog, though I have to say, Bryce, I'm a little disappointed in the security measures around here."

Bryce didn't reply, just glowered back at Harwood like he was itching to use that Python. That was a good sign as far as Harwood was concerned; the Whitmer boys were far more effective when they were pissed the hell off.

Harwood was worried, but he wasn't shitting his pants yet. He hadn't counted on Mason Burke's tenacity, hadn't imagined Jess Winslow had any juice left in her batteries after three tours of duty overseas. Taking the dog had been a tactical error; they should have shot the thing immediately and leaned on Jess instead. But hell, even Harwood hadn't much liked the idea of kidnapping a decorated marine, let alone trying to squeeze information out of her. He'd hoped the widow would roll over quick. She hadn't.

According to Bryce Whitmer, Jess and Burke had taken the highway west, and that was about the only positive development of the evening.

"We have them trapped," Harwood told his deputies. "They can't stay up west forever, and they can't get out without coming through here. Dale and I will head up to Neah Bay, see if we can't flush 'em out. Bryce, you watch this road here, and you let me know right quick if you see that green Chevy."

Sweeney was on his feet again. "What about me?"

Harwood looked him over. "You, Cole? Whyn't you head back into town, run the detachment while we're gone. We'll need someone on duty in case Mrs. MacAdam's cat gets stuck in that tree again."

Sweeney went red again. "Yeah, all right. Sure, Kirby."

"All right," Harwood said. He turned back to his pickup. "Mount up, boys. And don't be afraid to use those firearms of yours if the widow needs a little convincing."

TWENTY-ONE

According to the sign on the way into town, Neah Bay and the adjacent Makah reservation had a population of just over two thousand people. Bigger than Deception Cove, it looked slightly more prosperous; there were a couple of motels, two or three gas stations, a longer main drag, and a billboard advertising fishing charters and the tribal museum, with its replica longhouses and dugout canoes. Down at the bay more boats at the docks, a few ragged old trollers and some newer sport boats, a Coast Guard cutter and a big, oceangoing tug.

Mason stopped the pickup outside one of the gas stations. Got the washroom key from the guy inside and circled around back to make use of the facilities. Jess stayed in the car, Lucy still piled on top of her. Jess looked catatonic, and no matter how many times Lucy licked at her face and snuggled against her, she hadn't showed any sign of improvement. It wasn't an encouraging situation.

The little restroom stank of piss and was scrawled over with graffiti. Mason found a clear piece of mirror to examine his face. His lip was fat and red; he had something of a black eye. The side of his head was matted blood where Cole Sweeney had pistol-whipped him. He hadn't shaved in a couple of days, and that was starting to show. Whether it was the harsh light in the restroom or the fatigue, he wasn't going to win any beauty contests until he'd had a long shower and a longer nap.

His hands were cut up from clambering over those junk cars, too. He cleaned the wounds as best he was able, which wasn't very well at all. Splashed some cold water on his face, tried to fix his hair so it covered the blood, tried out a smile for the mirror—quickly saw the error in the notion. He walked out of the restroom, to return the key and head back to the Chevy to see about Jess.

Jess was sitting up straighter when Mason climbed back into the truck. She'd shifted positions and had Lucy beside her now, was scratching behind her ears as the dog leaned in and gave some deep kind of grumble of pleasure. Jess looked up when Mason entered the truck, couldn't quite meet his eyes.

"I'm sorry about that," she said. "I wasn't planning on losing my shit in front of you, but sometimes . . ."

"Don't sweat it," Mason replied. "You saved our asses on that farm. Least I could do is drive for a little bit."

Jess stopped scratching Lucy's neck, and Lucy grumbled a little louder and pressed harder against her.

"So what are you going to do now?" Jess asked him, her voice hollow. "You got your dog back, right, that mean you're just going to screw off and go on back to Michigan or whatever, mission accomplished?"

She still wasn't looking at Mason, was staring straight ahead now, out at the gas pumps and the night and whatever else.

"I mean, your work is done," Jess continued. "You got what you came for, so I guess you can leave now, right? Is that kind of what you're thinking you'll do?"

"No," Mason said.

Jess didn't say anything.

"I didn't come here to take that dog from you," he said. "I came to see that she was kept out of danger. And I can't see how we've accomplished that yet."

She blinked, tilted her head a little bit, but she didn't break. "So?"

Mason sighed. "So I'm thinking we need to stash this truck and hole up somewhere, figure out what we're going to do next."

Jess may have nodded, she may not have.

"Okay?"

Now she did nod. "Okay," she said, but she didn't sound all that convinced.

The sourpuss at the cash register in the Land's End Motel had nothing but dirty looks when Mason and Jess walked in through the front door.

"Only got single bedrooms," she told Mason when he asked for a double room. "Maybe try the Harbormaster's."

Mason and Jess swapped glances. They'd surveyed the town's meager offerings and decided the Land's End—off the highway, few cars in the lot, half the marquee burned out—was their best bet. Mason didn't have the energy to go comparison shopping.

Jess shrugged; he figured that meant she felt about the same.

"One bed is fine," he told the desk clerk. "It's going to be cash up front."

The clerk wasn't having that, either. "Need to have a credit card. I can't give you a room without one."

"Just for the night," Mason said. "We'll pay double your rate."

The clerk looked him over, and Mason could tell she was seeing the black eye, the split lip, the butt end of Cole Sweeney's pistol. He took the envelope of cash out from his back pocket, found a hundred-dollar bill, laid it on the table. The woman looked down at the bill.

"I don't want any trouble here," she said.

"We're not bringing any trouble," Jess cut in. "We just need a room for the night, and then we'll be on our way."

The woman looked down at the bill some more. Muttered something under her breath, reached down and opened a drawer, and came out with a room key. Was about to hand it over to Mason when she looked past them, saw the Chevy in the lot out front, Lucy sitting stock-still on the passenger side.

"No dogs allowed," she said, taking the key back. "Especially not pit bulls. Hotel policy."

"That pit bull is a companion animal for a wounded United States Marine," Mason replied. "Far as I know, the law says you have to accommodate her."

The woman closed her eyes. Shook her head. "Which one of you is the marine?"

Mason pointed at Jess. Jess waved.

"Going to need a pet deposit," the woman said. "A hundred dollars up front."

Mason brought out the envelope again. "Thank you kindly," he said, reaching for the room key. "We'll be out of your hair by the morning."

TWENTY-TWO

Jess and Burke found the room, and Jess brought in the shotgun from the Chevy and some extra shells, and an old blanket from the back seat for Lucy to sleep on. Burke brought in his duffel bag full of gear and laid it on a chair, and then he slipped out again with the keys to the truck, said he'd hide it somewhere far from the motel, somewhere Harwood and his boys wouldn't find it right away.

"You keep that door locked and chained," he told her, standing at the threshold. "Don't open up unless you're sure it's me. The secret password is 'pineapple.' "

"Pineapple?" she said, frowning.

He smiled a little bit. "Because when in the world is Kirby Harwood ever going to have reason to say the word 'pineapple'?"

Then he was gone. Jess waited until the door was closed, and then she crossed the room and locked both locks. Turned on all the lights, and drew the curtains tight, and spread the blanket over the bed for Lucy.

It was your standard motel room: a bed and some worn-out furniture, a bathroom in the back with a little window, frosted glass, looking out to the rear of the property. Nothing special. What struck Jess was the lack of a suitable exit besides the front door or maybe the picture window looking out onto the parking lot. If Harwood and his deputies found their way in, she would die in this room unless she could squeeze out through the bathroom.

Jess took the shotgun out of its case, sat on the bed with her back up against the headboard, the gun in her lap and Lucy by her side. The dog had sniffed around the room when they first came in, checked it thoroughly for new smells and fresh threats, and now, satisfied, she'd turned her attention back to Jess, regarding her with those big, concerned eyes, like she remembered the episode in the truck and was afraid it might happen again.

"I'm okay, you big suck," Jess said, pulling Lucy closer to her, into a pile on her lap. "It's *you* I'm concerned about."

Lucy looked thinner, though she wasn't cut or injured anywhere that Jess could tell. She knew Bryce Whitmer had probably been mean to her, kicked her around some, but safe in this motel room, Lucy didn't seem to care. She seemed entirely concerned about Jess's well-being and not at all about her own.

And maybe that was the worst part about owning a dog, wasn't it, the most wrenching thing.

"I'm okay, baby," Jess said again, and she reached down to scratch between Lucy's ears, watched the dog's eyes close in contentment, and she wished that peace and security came that easy for humans, too.

Burke came back a short while later. He knocked on the door, soft, and she brought the shotgun with her to the door and waited until she heard him say "pineapple" before she let him in. He was carrying a plastic bag, looked like from the gas station.

The rain outside had stopped, but the parking lot was wet, and Burke's hair was damp where it wasn't matted with blood. He'd had his ass kicked a couple of times, by the look of his face, and his hands were scratched up and cut. There was a decent slice through his jeans and the calf of his left leg, too—from Bryce Whitmer's razor wire, she surmised.

"You probably need a tetanus shot, at the absolute least," she said, watching as he tried and failed to slip out of his oilskin slicker without wincing.

"No time for that," Burke replied. He dumped out the plastic bag: energy bars and some bottles of water, chocolate bars and a sad-looking banana. A Slim Jim, some rubbing alcohol, and a box of Band-Aids. "We can't hang around here for long."

"At least let me see to those cuts on your hands. There's no telling what kind of nastiness lives on that Whitmer farm."

"You mean besides Whitmer himself?" Burke picked up the Slim Jim, tossed it to her. "For Lucy. She isn't looking like she's been eating too good as of late."

Jess smiled despite herself. "Oh, she's going to love you forever." She opened the package, peeled back the plastic. Lucy was already on her feet on the bed, tail going ballistic and nose insinuating itself toward the source of the sound, the smell of the pepperoni.

"Yeah, you big goof, this is for you," Jess said, petting her head. "Try and at least have the decency to chew."

But Lucy fairly inhaled the pepperoni stick, no thought to savoring the meal. She polished it off and licked her lips and looked from Jess to Burke and back again, like she was ready for round two.

Jess and Burke met eyes, and Burke laughed and Jess did too. "She always was kind of a pig," he said.

He pulled off his woolen Stanfield's sweater and draped it over a chair, stood by the table in his ripped jeans and a T-shirt. He must have taken care of his body in prison, fifteen years with nothing to do but lift weights; his arms were thick and powerful looking, his shoulders broad. Jess found herself trying not to look too long.

"I don't suppose you've ever given any thought to relocation," he said. Cleared his throat. "I mean, moving out of that little town, starting somewhere new."

"What, and let those boys run me out of my home?" It came out angrier than she'd wanted, but to hell with it.

"They aren't going to stop until they get what they're after. The way I see it, we can either leave them to their game, or try and play it better than them."

"I'm not running away," she said. "Those deputies stole my dog, and they probably killed my husband, too. I'm not just going to forget that. Not after all this."

He didn't say anything for a minute. Just stood there and looked at her and the dog and looked around the room like he was thinking things over.

"We're going to need a new vehicle," he said finally. "If we're ever going to get out of here and get past those deputies, I mean. If we're going to see this thing through."

She nodded. Felt that familiar tension start to take hold of her body, like she was wrapped up in a blanket and it was steadily getting tighter and tighter. *See this thing through.* She knew what that meant.

"I have about five hundred dollars left," he continued. "First thing tomorrow we start looking for something. Doesn't have to be pretty, so long as it runs."

She said, "That's fine," and Burke stood there a little longer, like he was waiting for something else, and then he nodded once more with some kind of finality and disappeared into the bathroom, and she heard the shower start up.

She called Hank Moss while Burke was in the bathroom. The motel owner picked up on the fourth ring.

"It's Jess Winslow," she said. "You have a minute to talk?"

"Of course I do." Moss sounded wide awake immediately. "Everything all right?"

"We got the dog back," she said. "Me and Burke. But Kirby won't be happy about it."

Moss processed this a beat. "Yeah, I guess not."

"You see him around? Like, has he come by your place or anything?"

"Not yet. But I expect he will, if he knows Burke was involved."

"He does."

"Best if Burke doesn't come back, then. You, either, for a little while. You have any idea what you're going to do now?"

She paused. "We're going to fight them," she said. "Find out what Ty was into, and why it got him killed. Figure out what those deputies are trying to get after."

"You sure that's a good idea, Jess? Those boys—"

"Aren't scaring me off, Hank," she said. "I have nothing left but what I have in Deception Cove, and I won't let Kirby Harwood take it away." She gave it a beat, but Hank didn't say anything.

"We're holed up in Neah Bay for the night," she continued. "I think we're good to the morning, but we'll need new wheels if we want to get down that highway again. You still have that cousin has the body shop out this way, all those junkers parked in front?"

"Davis? Sure," Moss said. "I don't know what he—"

"Give him a call, would you please, Hank?" Jess said. "Tell him we'll come by first thing in the morning. Tell him we're bringing cash."

A pause. "Yeah, okay," Moss said at last. "Okay, Jess."

"Thanks, Hank."

"You be careful, all right? You have Burke with you?"

She glanced toward the bathroom, the door closed but for a crack, steam pouring out. "Yeah, he's here."

"All right," Moss said.

"Do you think I can trust him, Hank? I mean, am I going to be safe?"

Moss sucked his teeth. "That boy looked me in the eye and told me his story straight," he replied. "And I can't see as he gave me any reason not to trust him."

"He told you his story? Like, why he went to jail?"

"I didn't ask for specifics," Moss said. "But I believe if you wanted to know, he'd tell you the truth."

Jess didn't answer. She wasn't sure what to say to that. But the shower shut off before she could pursue it any further anyhow. "Shit, Hank, I gotta go."

"I'll call my cousin," Moss promised. "You be careful."

"I will."

"The both of you, Jess."

"Yes, sir," Jess said. "We will."

TWENTY-THREE

Jess had a funny look on her face when Mason came out of the bathroom, fresh scrubbed and changed into clean clothes, applying a Band-Aid to the cut on his palm. Lucy lay curled up on the bed beside her; the dog didn't look up when Mason entered the room, but her tail thump-thump-thumped on the blanket Jess had laid down for her, giving the game away.

Mason chuckled. "What a little shit," he said. "Pretends she don't care to see you, but as soon as you look her way, that tail just fires up, doesn't it?"

He scratched the top of the dog's head and she closed her eyes and sighed, long and low. Jess smiled a little bit, but not much.

"I got a lead on a car," she said.

"Yeah?"

"Yeah. Hank Moss at the motel? His cousin runs a body shop over on the reservation. Hank's going to set something up for us for first thing tomorrow."

She still had that look on her face, studying him like she didn't quite know what to make of what she saw, like when you come across an animal in the wild and you're not sure it isn't dangerous. Mason figured he knew the reason why.

"You talked to Hank just now," he said.

She nodded.

"He tell you about me? What I did?"

"He told me I could trust you," she said. "And he told me if I asked you, you'd probably tell me yourself."

"You want to know?"

She met his eyes. "I think I have a right to, being as we're sharing this crummy motel room and all."

Whoever conceals his transgressions will not prosper, but he who confesses and forsakes them will obtain mercy.

"Yeah," Mason said. "I suppose you do."

Jess watched Burke pull a chair across to the end of the bed, to where Lucy lay with her snout just hanging over the edge of the blanket. He scratched Lucy's head again, and the dog wagged her tail, and Jess felt a pang of jealousy at how familiar Burke was with the animal.

She's mine, she thought. *She's mine, and you're not going to take her from me.*

Burke sat forward. Rested his elbows on his legs and clasped his hands together. Looked at her, earnest, right in the eye.

"It was first-degree murder," he told her. "That's what I went in for."

Jess burst out laughing. "God help me," she said. "Of course it was."

Burke studied her. He didn't say anything. She kept laughing, wasn't sure if she'd ever stop. Just her luck, the one man in her life who seemed a little bit decent and he was a convicted murderer; why the hell not?

Then she thought of something. "You said you never fired a gun."

"I haven't," he said.

So, what, did you stab a guy to death? Beat him? Shit, first-degree murder's the worst of the worst. What the hell did you do, Burke?

He caught her expression. "It was nothing like that," he said. "What it was, there was this guy I used to hang out with—Dev, everyone called him—a couple years older than me. He was like my big brother, my best friend, and my dad all rolled into one. My dad was never around much, so I guess Dev kind of filled that void."

He sat back in his chair a little bit. Rubbed his chin. "We got into whatever trouble you could think of, me and Dev, drinking and drugs and whatever else. I was a pretty angry kid back then, and so was Dev, too, and we kind of fed off each other. I always wanted to impress him, show him I was cool enough to spend time with, you know?"

Burke wasn't looking at her anymore. Wasn't really looking anywhere, down at the floor, lost in his memories.

Then he shook his head, as if to clear his thoughts. "Anyway," he said, looking up. "Sorry. You asked what I did."

"It's okay," Jess said.

"Yeah, well. There was this liquor store Dev wanted to rob. I don't even think it was for any good reason, just for the hell of it. I was going to wait in the car for him to come out, you know, the getaway driver."

Jess nodded.

He laughed, but there wasn't any joy in it. "I remember pulling up outside the store, and you know, feeling kind of excited and nervous and whatever, and then Dev pulls out this pistol. And I don't know where it came from, or how he got it, but I'd never seen it before. But anyway, he told me he was going to use it to scare the shit out of the guy inside."

Burke met her eyes. "The guy's name was Faraz Karim. He was an immigrant from Pakistan, father to a little boy. Dev told me Karim made a move on him, pulled his own gun from under the counter, told me it was self-defense. But they showed me the security tapes later, and it didn't look like the guy did much that required defending."

"So you didn't actually kill anyone," Jess said. "You weren't actually guilty."

"No, I'm guilty. The law doesn't distinguish between who pulls the trigger, not in robbery/homicide. I was there. I took part. I knew Dev had a gun, and I didn't stop him. And because I didn't do anything, Faraz Karim's little boy lost his father. I'm guilty as it gets. I've never argued I wasn't."

"But you were outside. You weren't even in the store when it happened."

"It doesn't matter." He sat forward. "Listen to me: it doesn't matter a bit. I was there; I played my role. The law says what I did was murder, and as far as I'm concerned, the law's right."

She didn't have any answer. After a beat he continued.

"They caught up to us pretty quick," he said. "Dev knew a girl with a place out in the county, and we went over and got hammered on Boone's Farm and raised hell. The neighbors called the law, on account of Dev shooting his gun off, and when the sheriff's deputies arrived, they matched the plates on the car in the driveway to the car at the robbery." He paused. "It was my mom's car, an Olds 88. She never really forgave me for that.

"I knew I was finished as soon as they arrested us," he said. "There was no point in fighting it. They had security tape and my mom's car at the scene, and a witness across the street who swore he could identify the both of us. I copped to what I did and kept my mouth shut about Dev, and they gave me my time, and I served it."

"And what?" Jess asked, suddenly angry at the calm in his voice. "You think that absolves you for what happened that night?"

"No, ma'am," he replied. "I could do good my whole life and not be absolved for what I did to that man and his family. But I don't know that trying to pretend it never happened will ever change anything."

Jess stood. She walked to the window, went to pull open the shade, the room suddenly feeling claustrophobic. Then she thought better of it, kept the shade drawn.

He was still watching her; she could feel his eyes on her. Didn't turn around, didn't look at him. Didn't know what she'd say if she did.

"Let me ask you something," Burke said. "Why is it you think I came here?"

She didn't turn around. Fiddled with the edge of the shade, just for something to do.

"You have to be pretty crazy to come two thousand miles just to see after a dog, right?" he continued. "I mean, it ain't exactly normal behavior; I can admit that."

"I'm glad you said it," she said. "Because it isn't."

"But see, training one little runt dog to help out a wounded marine is about the only good thing I ever did with my life, and that's hardly an exaggeration. I've got a lot of bad things I've done that I can't change, but I'll be damned if I'm going to let the one good thing get wiped away."

She turned around finally. He was sitting as she'd left him, leaned forward, his hands clasped together, staring down at the floor again. He didn't look like the big, rough ex-convict who'd showed up at her house unexpected, the tough guy who'd smirked at her from in front of her shotgun. He looked like someone else now, someone less—and at the same time, someone more. He looked vulnerable for the first time she could remember.

He lifted his head, caught her looking at him. Seemed to read her mind; he went red, a little bit, and turned his eyes away.

She watched him a little longer, tried to think of something to say, and then Lucy rolled over on the bed, snorted loud, and started snoring, and it broke the moment and they both laughed.

"Like trucks downshifting on the highway," Burke said, rubbing his forehead. "She ain't exactly a lady, is she?"

The dog was sprawled out, took up half the bed, the night's trauma clearly forgotten, and Jess couldn't help but smile.

"We should get some rest," Burke said. "If you can spare a pillow, I'm just fine bunking down on the floor."

Jess started to protest. "That's not—"

"No, I insist," he said. "Someone comes in here, they'll trip over my big ass, and you pick 'em off with the shotgun."

She realized she'd feel more comfortable with Burke on the floor, realized she was grateful he'd made the suggestion. Crossed to the bed and nudged the dog aside a little bit.

"There's your pillow," she said, chucking him one. "I think we can probably spare you a blanket as well."

Mason woke up, sat up, his heart beating sixteenth notes. Something had roused him, but he couldn't say what.

On the bed above him, Lucy shifted. Whimpered a little bit. Jess had the shotgun up there, lying in its soft case beside her pillow. Mason wondered if she was awake too.

He pushed himself to his feet, pushed the blanket off. Stood and walked to the window and pulled the shade to the side and looked out into the parking lot.

It was late. Or early. It was four thirty in the morning. By rights, Mason should have been awake, wide awake, given the time difference with back home, and how prison had made him an early riser. He was beat, though, exhausted. He wanted to sleep. He needed some time before the deputies found them, before the next round began. He looked out into the parking lot, searched the shadows for Kirby Harwood's fancy truck, for either of the Whitmer boys, for Cole Sweeney.

But the lot was empty. Nothing moved. Mason gave it a minute, waited it out. Still nothing.

Then Jess cried out behind him, and Mason spun, half expecting to see Bryce Whitmer on the bed with her, choking her out. But Jess was alone, tangled in her blanket, arms flailing and legs twisted, Lucy tucked in close to her, licking at Jess's face and whimpering too.

A bad dream.

Mason crossed to the bed. Sat down beside Jess and touched her arm. "Hey."

It took a couple of tries, but he woke her, and she quit moving and opened her eyes, stared up at the ceiling, breathing heavy.

"Guess you were having a nightmare," Mason said.

Jess didn't react. Just looked up, straight up, like she hadn't really come back from wherever she'd gone. Gradually her breathing settled. She rubbed her eyes.

"I'm okay, Burke," she said. "Nothing to worry about. Go back to sleep."

He stood. "Yeah, okay."

"Burke?"

He looked back.

"Thanks," she said.

"Yeah." He lay down again, settled into his blanket. Laid his head on his pillow, and then he felt movement beside him. Stiffened, just in time to feel Lucy's big, slobbery tongue curl over his face. She gave him a solid face wash, and he endured it, finally pushing her away when he couldn't hold his breath any longer.

"Yeah, I missed you, too, girl," he said. "I missed you a lot."

She turned around in a circle, made to settle down beside him. He stopped her. "You don't have to worry about me," he said. "You sleep with your mom tonight, okay?"

Lucy licked his face again. He nudged her toward the bed, and she turned around, looked back at him once, seemed to get it. She jumped onto the bed and lay down close to Jess.

Good.

Mason laid his head back on the pillow. Stared over at the door and tried to get some rest before morning came.

TWENTY-FOUR

Burke was already awake by the time Jess woke up. There was light coming through the shades, so it must have been morning, but damned if she felt at all rested. Lucy was sacked out beside her, drooling on the pillow and hogging the blanket. Burke was doing push-ups on the floor.

"Morning," Jess said, and Burke banged off a couple more push-ups before he stood, reaching for a bottle of water.

"Morning," he said. "I was just about to head out, pick up the new wheels. You said it's a body shop I should look for?"

"I didn't say you should look for anything," Jess said, swinging her legs out from under the blanket. "Give me a minute. I'll go."

"It's no problem," Burke said. "You hang back here with Lucy, get things ready to go. Soon as I get back, we'll hit the road."

She stood. "That's sweet of you, but no," she said, walking around him to the bathroom. "I know you've been in jail awhile, but they let women do things for themselves now."

She stopped and looked back at him. He was staring at her, openmouthed, like he didn't quite know how to answer.

She softened her tone. "Burke, you've never been in this town in your life. You don't know where you're going or who you're supposed to talk to. Tell me how it doesn't make sense that I handle this one."

He scratched his head. Looked down at the floor and chuckled a little bit, and it was kind of endearing.

"Yeah, all right," he said. "You'll take the shotgun with you?"

"What, some woman walking around at the crack of dawn with her twelve gauge isn't going to raise any eyebrows? You hold on to the shotgun. Keep Lucy company. I'll get us the wheels and we'll go."

She turned and walked into the bathroom before he could argue. Closed the door firm and locked it.

The rain hadn't come back when she slipped out to the parking lot, the remainder of Burke's cash tucked into her jeans pocket. There was even a hint of sky overhead, somewhere above all those clouds. Maybe they'd get some sun today, dry out a little bit. It had been raining so long, Jess had almost forgotten what sunshine looked like.

The motel's parking lot was empty. That was a plus. No cars on the roadway beyond. Hank's cousin's body shop was a couple hundred yards down the main road, but the road was wide open, with no place for cover in case Kirby Harwood decided to sneak up on her. So she headed in the opposite direction, down toward the bay and the docks, the Coast Guard station. Skirted through a couple of vacant lots, cut across a stand of scraggly-looking pine. She'd almost reached the body shop when she saw Kirby's truck.

Up the block, on the main road, pulling into the ARCO across the street. Big and red, jacked up and unmissable, probably the dumbest *sneaking-around* vehicle you could buy. But there he was, stopping at the fuel pumps, climbing out with Dale Whitmer beside him, Dale saying something as he walked past Kirby and into the little store, Kirby popping his gas cap.

Jess tucked away behind a big, gnarly arbutus, knelt down in the shadows and damp, and watched Kirby as he worked the pump. The deputy kept his head moving, eyes scanning the gas station lot and the highway and the body shop, like he was thinking Jess and Burke were dumb enough to see that truck and come running out to meet him.

He looked tired, Jess thought, and though he tried to hide it, she thought he looked worried.

Dale Whitmer, on the other hand, still looked prickly as hell. He came out of the little store with some energy drinks and a pack of Marlboro Reds, his free hand lurking by his holster like he was itching to draw down on some unlucky bastard. Jess had no doubt he would shoot Burke on sight, probably get a little more creative with her, mean son of a bitch that he was, but Dale didn't scare her.

Neither did Kirby, for that matter.

Kirby finished gassing up as Dale climbed back into the truck. Jess didn't move, her knees aching, the damp soaking through. A hundred feet more and she'd be at the body shop, have her crack at some fresh wheels and a ride out of town, but she was stuck waiting for Tweedledum and Tweedledickhead to get their butts in gear.

They moved slow but they got there, and eventually Kirby was back in the truck and the truck was fired up and chug-chug-chugging its way out of the gas station lot. This time Kirby aimed the truck toward her, and Jess thought for an instant he'd made her, but he just turned down the road she'd walked up on, cruised it slow. He was past her and had disappeared before she caught her breath back.

She pulled herself up from the dirt. Brushed off her jeans. Came out from behind the arbutus and walked up the road toward the body shop.

Hank's cousin was a man named Davis. He wasn't surprised to see Jess.

"Yeah, Hank woke me up about five in the morning," he said, coming out from behind the service desk and leading her into the shop's only work bay. "Said you needed a vehicle, and it was imperative that I supply you."

"I'd appreciate it if you could," Jess replied. "Something clean and reliable, whatever you've got. I just need to get out of this county."

Davis reached the back of the work bay, a door. He pushed it open, gestured for her to pass through, and she found herself in a little annexed patch of gravel, a half a dozen cars and trucks arrayed before her in various states of repair.

"Got a Plymouth with a couple hundred thousand miles on her, but she still runs pretty good," Davis said. "How much are you looking to spend?"

"I have five hundred in cash and a Chevy truck that isn't ready to die yet." Jess gave the Plymouth a once-over. It wore those two hundred thousand miles plain to see, dented and dappled with mismatched paint and primer spots. It was probably about the ugliest car Jess had ever seen, and she'd served three tours in the fucking Kunar Province.

"If that's what we're talking, I can do you a sight better." Davis motioned her across the gravel patch to a jet-black Chevy Blazer. "Just redid the brakes, and the engine runs fine," he said. "Hardly any rust underneath. I was going to try and sell it on eBay, but what the hell."

Jess looked the Blazer over. It was a small SUV, two doors, plenty of room in the back for Lucy. It looked good, looked capable. But it wasn't going to happen.

"I think I'm better off with the Plymouth," she said, and she walked back over to the car, hoping it had somehow turned pretty in the time she'd looked away.

It hadn't.

"That Blazer will get you anywhere you need to go," Davis said, following her over. "I guarantee it."

"I know it will." Jess took Burke's money from her back pocket. Counted out five hundred-dollar bills and laid them on the hood of the Plymouth, laid the keys to her truck right beside them. "But that truck of mine is kind of a wanted vehicle right now, and if the law finds it before you do, they aren't giving it back."

Davis looked down at the money, the keys. "Where's the truck now?"

"Hidden behind a dumpster," she said. "One of those old fish plants on Cannery Road."

Davis stroked his chin. He seemed to be thinking. Finally he came to a conclusion. Reached down, picked up the keys. Slid the money back across to Jess. "You'll take the Blazer," he said.

"What?" Jess frowned. "Why? What are you talking about?"

"I don't know you, Ms. Winslow, but I know what you did in the marines, and I know why you came home." Davis looked her in the eyes. "And I don't know what kind of mess you're into right now, but I do know my cousin, and Hank doesn't take sides in a fight unless he's sure it's the right one. You'll take the Blazer, and you can keep your money."

She stared at him. "You don't have to do this."

"Consider it a heartfelt 'Thanks for your service,' " Davis replied. "Now, are you going to let me close this deal so I can find that truck of yours, or what?"

TWENTY-FIVE

Jess took the highway back to the motel. The drive took about thirty seconds, and it was long enough for Jess to catch sight of Kirby Harwood's big red truck again and squeeze her foot down a little harder on the gas pedal.

Harwood's truck was parked outside the next motel down the road, the Harbormaster's, about a two-minute walk from the Land's End. Jess pulled the Blazer into the lot and up to the door to their room. Climbed out, left the engine running, circled around, and rapped on the door a couple of times.

"Pineapple," she said. "You in there, Burke?"

The lock unlatched and the door swung open. Burke was dressed, and he'd piled his overnight bag and the blanket and his junk food provisions by the door with the shotgun. Had Lucy sitting there too; she wagged her tail and stood and came over for a butt scratch, but now wasn't the time.

"Kirby's just up the road," Jess told Burke. "Throw the stuff in the truck and come on if you're coming."

Burke was already slipping past her with the bags. He opened the passenger door and tipped the seat forward, chucked his stuff back there and laid the shotgun down, gentle.

"Come on, girl," he told Lucy.

Lucy gave Jess a look, gave the Blazer a cursory sniff. Then she leapt into the back and settled on the seat.

"Get in the back," Burke said, closing the door to the room. "I'll drive."

She looked at him. "Excuse me?"

"Better if I drive this stretch," he said. "You—"

"I'm not going to have another episode, if that's what you're worried about," she told him, her face flushing. "That doesn't just happen whenever. I can drive."

He met her eyes. "Those deputies know your face too well," he said. "And they're looking for two. I'm not suggesting you *can't* drive, just that maybe I should. You stay back there and keep Lucy out of sight until we get out of here a ways. They aren't going to recognize me at speed."

He had a point, as much as it pissed her off to admit it. So she climbed into the back seat after Lucy, shoved the dog's big butt to the side to clear a space to sit, and pulled the front seat back into position again. Waited as Burke circled around to the driver's side, adjusted his seat, and put the Blazer in gear.

"Nice ride," he told her, pulling out of the lot. "Heck, you did better than I would have done."

"That's for sure." She pulled out the money he'd given her, reached in between the front seats, and laid it on the center console.

Burke glanced down at it, and she watched his eyes go wide in the rearview mirror. "Now, how did you—"

"I told you," she said, sitting back in her seat. "It's better if I do the talking."

Jess gave Mason directions, and pretty soon they were on the highway again, headed back east toward Deception Cove.

The rain had let up, and there were patches of blue sky; Mason figured it was as close as the region got to a beautiful day. The highway wound along the shoreline, and Mason could see the views he'd missed last night: a long, rocky coast, whitecaps on the water, the trees growing almost to the water's edge in many places. There wasn't a soul for miles, and apart from the highway and the ships out in the channel, Mason imagined this was probably exactly how this land had looked for centuries.

He studied the ships as he navigated the Blazer along the highway's sinuous curves. There were three headed inbound toward Seattle, another two pointed west to the open ocean. He wondered what it would be like on those ships, the solitude, hard work, nobody giving a damn about your history. See the world, get a tan, make an honest living. It didn't sound so bad.

In the back seat, Lucy whined a little, and Jess leaned forward between the two seats. "You take her out this morning?"

"No, ma'am," Mason said.

"You have to take her out. Unless you want her to pee in this truck."

"I expected they'd be looking for a dog matching her description in town." He glanced past her in the rearview, saw nobody behind. No one ahead, either; they were alone on this road. "Next pullout, we'll let her go."

"So what are we going to do?"

He'd pulled them off the highway at a picnic spot overlooking the water. Got out, stretched his legs, enjoyed the cool breeze off the ocean and the fresh air. Lucy peed near the picnic table and disappeared into the brush. Mason went to follow, but Jess stopped him with her question.

He turned back, and she was leaned against the hood of the Blazer, looking out at the beach and the channel beyond.

Somewhere in the distance was Canada, but the Great White North wasn't showing itself today, and those ships he'd seen earlier had disappeared too.

"The dog will be fine," Jess told him, catching the way his eyes wandered after Lucy. "She'll come back when she's done. But what about us, Burke? You have any kind of plan whatsoever?"

He'd been thinking about this. As far as he could tell, there was really only one loose thread to start pulling.

He leaned on the Blazer beside her. "Your husband cooked meth," he said, and glanced over to see how she took it. She didn't react one way or the other, just looked out over the water with her mouth set in a hard line.

"I did some poking around yesterday, in between getting my ass kicked," he continued. "Met the lawless contingent of that town, of which your husband was apparently a member."

"You going to get to it or what, Burke? I asked you what are we going to do." Jess's voice was soft, and she still wasn't looking at him, and the way she said it made him feel like a shit-heel.

"Yeah, all right." He shoved his hands in his pockets, studied the ground. "A guy named Yancy said Ty had a spot where he used to do his cooking, up the forestry main line a ways. We go on up there and see if we can't find what those deputies are after. Assuming they haven't been up there already."

Jess didn't say anything. Didn't move. He wondered if she'd even heard him, was about to ask when she straightened and pushed herself off the hood of the Blazer. Wiped her eyes with the sleeve of her shirt and gave a low whistle for Lucy.

"Well, come on, then," she said, circling around to the passenger door of the truck. "Are we going to do this, or what?"

TWENTY-SIX

The old woman at the Land's End knew exactly whom Kirby was asking after. And she sold them out with a smile.

"Unit four," she told the deputy. "Came in late last night, looked like absolute hell. He did, anyway; she was a little better. Still smelled like trouble—*stank* of it, the two of them."

The motel's lot was empty. Dale Whitmer stood outside by the truck, staring down the row of doors with his hand on his holster. Harwood decided it was a good thing there weren't any other guests here; Whitmer was liable to put a hole in anything that came out of a door at this point. It had been a long and fruitless search.

"They have a dog with them?" Harwood asked the woman.

She scowled. "They did. Some mean old pit bull, and it wasn't a small little thing, I'll tell you that."

"What time'd the truck leave?"

"Oh, right away. They got set up in their room, and then they drove that truck off again. It was gone in the morning, when I woke up."

"And around what time was that?"

The woman shrugged. "Dawn or thereabouts, maybe a little after. You want to have a look at the room?"

The woman let them into unit four. Gave Harwood a key, and he had her step back, drew his pistol as Dale did the same. He slid the key into the lock, turned it, and pushed the door open and stepped aside, ready for a gunshot.

But nothing happened. Dale crept closer to the threshold, peered inside. "It's empty," he told Harwood.

He was telling the truth. The bed was made perfect, didn't even look slept in. The room might have been vacant last night, unused by anyone, if it hadn't been for the garbage in the trash bins. Chocolate bars, energy drinks, a banana peel in the bin in the main room. Bloody tissues and bandage wrappers in the bathroom. The towels had been used, and piled in the bathtub. Some of them were bloody too.

"Shit," Whitmer said, studying the mess. "Maybe Bryce actually *got* the son of a bitch."

"He didn't get him good enough," Harwood replied. "Not if they were able to walk into that lobby and rent this room."

"Yeah, but check out all this blood, though."

"I'd rather be looking at a body, Dale, and I don't see one." Harwood turned and stalked past Whitmer and out through the empty room to the parking lot. Pulled out his phone and made a call. "Bryce."

"No sign of them," Whitmer's brother reported. "I kept my eyes open, but I ain't seen hide or hair of that Winslow bitch since last night."

"Well, she isn't here, either," Harwood told him. "They got a motel room, but they didn't stay long. They're on the move again, and I need you stopping everyone who passes by your place."

Whitmer snorted. "On whose authority? You never did bother to formally deputize me."

"You have a gun, don't you? Flag 'em down and search 'em, damn it."

"Okay, boss. Whatever you say."

"Find them, Bryce," Harwood said. "Shit."

He ended the call. Slid the phone into his pocket and turned back to the motel room. He'd have to head back inside and drag Dale out, get back on the road, search the rest of the town on the off chance Jess and Burke were still here. But then his cell buzzed in his pocket, played its electronic tune. Incoming call.

"You forget something, Bryce?" Harwood said, answering.

A beat. "Good morning, deputy." This was Okafor, his voice soft and smooth and lethal. "Have you recovered my merchandise?"

Harwood turned, slow. Took a couple of steps out into the lot. Wet his lips. "Ah, we're working on it, Mr. Okafor. Getting close. I got a real solid lead."

Okafor chuckled. "Ah," he said. "A solid lead."

"That's right. We'll track it down soon, sir. I can promise you that."

"I certainly believe you," Okafor replied. "But just in case you do not, I will need to meet with you and your men this evening. Say, five o'clock?"

Harwood felt suddenly sick. "It isn't the end of the month yet. We still have two days to keep working on this."

"I understand, Deputy, but I'm losing confidence in your ability to handle my business. Perhaps the search will go smoother if I provide some assistance."

Harwood said nothing. His mouth was dry again.

"Five o'clock," Okafor repeated. "I'll come to you, Deputy."

Okafor ended the call before Harwood could reply. He stood there in the center of the lot for a while, his phone to his ear. Stood there until Dale came out of the room behind him, walked up, circled him, looked at him funny. "You all right?"

Harwood lowered the phone. "No, I'm not all right, Dale," he said. "And neither are you. We're all of us in some really deep shit."

Bryce Whitmer set down his phone and stared across the front porch at the highway beyond. He'd been up all night, Kirby's orders, keeping himself upright on Red Bulls and strong coffee, a gram of crank for when his eyelids got *really* heavy. He'd sat on his front porch with his guns close at hand, a Colt Python .357 revolver on the little table with the crank and the coffee beside him, a Bushmaster XM-15 across his lap. Wasn't much going past on that highway out there, hadn't been much the whole night. A few cars, an SUV or two, a couple of newer pickups, and a Shell tanker truck. Nothing that rang any alarms in Bryce's head, nothing that even remotely resembled the Winslow bitch and her boyfriend.

Bryce had been looking. Now he just wanted to crash for a while.

But Harwood and Dale hadn't flushed them out of Neah Bay yet, and that meant the bitch was still at large. Whitmer downed the last of his coffee. Stood up and gathered the Python and the crank, holstered the revolver and hoovered the last of the good stuff. Shouldered his rifle and walked down to the driveway, where his own Ram Heavy Duty sat parked.

Flag 'em down and search 'em.

Shit.

Whitmer climbed in behind the wheel, fired the truck up. Put her in reverse and backed down the driveway toward the highway. He'd almost made blacktop when something crossed his rearview, a vehicle headed east, away from Neah Bay.

"Damn it." Whitmer stopped the truck, climbed out with his rifle, ran for the road. It was another SUV, he saw, a black Chevy Blazer. He couldn't see inside, but when he walked out to the center line, he caught a glimpse through the rear window, saw one head sticking up and it belonged to the driver. No one else in the vehicle. Couldn't be them.

His heart revving to redline in his chest, Whitmer returned to the Ram. Shifted back into reverse, eased it onto the highway, and left it parked perpendicular to the flow of traffic, blocking the eastbound lane. Then he climbed out of the truck again, taking his rifle with him. Circled around to the passenger side and leaned against the door, looking westbound up the highway, rifle at the ready.

Flag 'em and search 'em.

So be it.

TWENTY-SEVEN

Jess peered up from the floor of the Blazer. "Did we make it?"

Burke's mouth was a thin line as he drove. He glanced in the rearview. "Not sure yet," he said. "That old boy was out there when we passed, and he had a pretty big rifle in his hands when he came to take a look at us."

"I guess I'll stay down a little longer, then," Jess said, pulling Lucy closer.

Burke said, "I think that'd be wise."

Jess stayed on the floor, her arms around the dog, as Burke navigated the road into Deception Cove and out the other side. Lucy wasn't much for car rides; she panted nonstop, drooled a small lake, and licked Jess's face obsessively whenever she made the tactical error of coming within range.

"It's okay, girl," Jess told her. "We're almost through, I promise."

Lucy licked at her face again, regarded her with worried eyes, clearly unconvinced.

Finally Jess felt the Blazer slow, though she could see only treetops from her vantage point. The road got rough; she could hear gravel pinging the underside of the truck, and she surmised that Burke had found the forestry main line. He stopped the truck.

"Should be all clear now," he said.

She sat up, the muscles in her legs protesting. Leaned forward and pushed the passenger seat up, released the door, and managed to slip out to fresh air without tripping on the seat belt and falling on her face. She stretched, breathed in deep, the damp, loamy smell of the rain forest, the sun, actual *sun,* on her face.

Then she came around the front of the Blazer to Burke's side. "Okay, out," she told him. "It's my turn to drive."

He frowned but said nothing.

"This road's bound to be muddy," she said. "When's the last time you drove a four-by-four, Burke?"

A pause. "Been a while."

"Exactly. Anyway, I'm sick of being chauffeured. Your turn." She hooked her thumb. "Out."

Burke smiled a little bit and did what she said. He went around to the passenger side and made himself comfortable while she adjusted the seat and the steering wheel.

"Right," she said, shifting back into gear. "So how far up this road are we headed?"

"Past the big clear-cut" was Burke's only input, then up a side road. Jess set the trip monitor anyway, watched the miles count up. The road was in decent shape, actually; it had been graded recently and didn't show signs of too many washouts. She made good time, encountered no other drivers. Found the front of the clear-cut within five miles and the back end another mile past, a spur road heading up into the bush just beyond it.

"Must be up this way," she said, and Burke grunted in agreement like the world's most stoic GPS. She turned the wheel and pressed the gas.

The road got shitty real fast from there. It could hardly be called a road, more a pair of twin trails through the brush. The woods got denser, encroaching on all sides, and winter runoff gutted the tracks, sending the Blazer yawing this way and that, forcing Jess to take things extra slow.

Five minutes of this and Lucy crawled over the center console and into the front seat, dropping herself unceremoniously into Burke's lap. She exhaled a long, put-upon sigh and stuck her nose in the gap between the seat and the passenger door.

Burke groaned. "Dang, you're a heavy dog," he said, but when Jess glanced over, she could see he was smiling. He had his arms around her, stroking her flank.

"She's a big, fat baby, all right," Jess said. "If you weren't in the truck, she'd be crawling on *my* lap."

It took twenty minutes of climbing on that muddy trail before the land leveled out and the grade eased off. Jess guessed if the overgrowth weren't so dense, you could probably look out and see Deception Cove and the water, but as it was, you could barely see sky, much less make out where you stood in the grand scheme of things.

Whatever this road had been used for, the rain forest had reclaimed all but the bare basics. Tall pines and Douglas firs, western red cedar, spruce, deadfall draped with lush carpets of moss, ferns of all variations. This was a primeval place; it was quiet here, it was wet, and it was alive. This was what she'd missed when she was overseas. Even after she'd quit missing Ty and quit missing her town, the rain forest had kept her homesick, and Jess imagined it always would.

You can't leave this place, she thought. *You can't let those boys drive you out of here. You'll never survive somewhere else.*

The time for that decision had come and gone already anyway. She was into it now, and she'd brought Burke along with her. One way or the other, they'd be seeing this through.

She was contemplating this notion when the road widened out

and the forest grew lighter by a degree or two. Up ahead, lodged in between the tall trees, she saw signs of humanity: a collection of trailers, a vehicle. A mountain of junk she couldn't begin to identify. The whole spread looked deserted, abandoned. It looked like a mess, and Jess knew better than to be surprised.

"Yep, this was Ty's space," she said, stopping the truck. "Let's go poke around, and maybe we get lucky."

Mason and Jess split up. Not on purpose, just kind of wandered off in different directions. Jess took Lucy along the left side of the little clearing, toward a couple of moldy, mossed-out trailers on the fringes of the forest. Mason bore right, toward the rusted-to-shit carcass of a Jeep Wagoneer and a couple of burst-open bags of trash, mostly fast-food wrappers and pizza boxes. There was a trailer back there too, looked in slightly better condition than the two by Jess. A couple more cars scattered around.

The whole place stank of cat piss and something chemical. It overpowered the smell of the rain forest such that Mason could *taste* it whenever he breathed. The ground was mud and pine needles, and there were tracks in the mud, boots and tires.

Mason didn't see anything that looked worth killing over. He figured if Ty Winslow had brought the spoils up here, whatever they were, he would have had to hide them somewhere dry, protect them from the elements. Hell, it was already raining again, that irritating drizzle that wormed under your jacket if you let the hood down but wasn't cold enough to not make things claustrophobic with the hood up. Mason left the hood down—he couldn't hear with it up—but he didn't like the idea. He was running out of dry things to wear.

He was halfway to the third trailer, the one in the far back, when the kid stepped out from behind the junked Lincoln Continental, holding the pistol. "That's about far enough," he said. "Don't you come any closer."

He was young, early twenties maybe. A shock of blond hair underneath a dirty ball cap. Rail thin, acne scarred, his eyes wide, his movements electric. High on something, Mason surmised, and that didn't bode well.

"Now hold on," he said, keeping his hands where the kid could see them. "I don't mean any trouble."

"This is private property," the kid replied. His voice was as shaky as his gun hand. "I'm within my rights to shoot you. Best you leave before it comes to that."

He kept the pistol aimed in Mason's direction, though his hand swayed enough that he had Mason in his sights only about half the time. But that didn't make Mason feel much better.

"I just have a couple of questions," he said, slow. "You answer them for me, and I'll be on my way."

The kid's lip curled. "Does this sound like a negotiation?" He took a couple of steps forward. Turned the pistol sideways, Hollywood style. "I'm telling you, get off my property or I'm gonna shoot you."

"Are you going to shoot me, too?" That was Jess, come out from in between the two dingy trailers. She carried the shotgun with her and had Lucy by her side. "And the dog?"

The kid spun, waved the gun around in her direction. "You ain't got but one gun between the both of you," he said. "I'm supposed to be scared?"

Jess gestured at Mason with the shotgun. "Burke over there just finished doing fifteen years for first-degree murder, and he's never pulled a trigger in his life. He doesn't need to be armed to mess your shit up, kid."

The kid looked at Mason. Swallowed a little, wet his lips.

"And this dog beside me is mighty protective," Jess continued. "She'll tear your throat out soon as you make a move."

Now the kid looked at Lucy, who stood at attention beside Jess, watching him, her ears cocked. The dog wasn't pissed off yet, Mason could tell, probably thought this was some kind of game—but the kid didn't need to know that.

"You'll get one of us, sure," Jess said, and her voice was dead calm. "You won't get us all. And if it's me you decide you want to take down, you'll want to make sure your aim's good." She leveled the shotgun at his chest. "Because if I have any life left in me after you pull the trigger, I'll perforate your shit on my way to the ground, you hear?"

The kid stared at her. Swung the pistol around, wild, toward an approximation of where Mason was standing, then back to Lucy and Jess. "Who the fuck are you guys?" he asked. "What do you want?"

"That over there is Burke, like I said," Jess told him. "The dog's name is Lucy, and mine is Jess Winslow, and if we're in the right place, I believe this whole sorry compound belonged to my husband."

The kid's eyes got wider. "Ty?"

"The very same."

"Shit," the kid said. "Ty—he told me all this was mine if anything happened. You can't just come up here and take—"

"I don't want it," Jess said. "What I want is to clear up a few things about my dead husband, and it sounds like you might be the guy who can help. Now, are you going to put the gun away and we can talk, or do we have to keep measuring our dicks in this rain?"

The kid made to talk. Stopped. Started again. "You first."

Jess lowered the shotgun. "Don't get any ideas," she said. "What's your name, anyway?"

The kid gave another beat. Closed his eyes, like he was so messed up he was trying to remember. Messed up, or scared shitless.

"Rengo," he said.

"Rengo, all right." Jess gestured at the trailer behind him. "Invite us inside, Rengo, and let's talk for a while."

TWENTY-EIGHT

They found the truck around two in the afternoon. Dale spotted it—that ugly puke-green paint job—poking out from behind a little one-stall mechanic's shop on the highway into the Makah reservation.

There was someone working underneath an old Buick in the service bay. Harwood walked in, stood by the bumper, Dale right beside him.

"Where are they?" he said.

There was a pause, and the sound of the man setting down his tools. Then he rolled out on a little trolley, looked up at them from the floor.

"Beg your pardon?" he said.

He was an older guy, Native. Salt-and-pepper goatee, ditto for the hair. Going soft around the middle, but his eyes were still hard. The name on his coveralls said DAVIS.

"Jess Winslow and that convict she's running with," Harwood said. "The two who gave you that truck in the back. Don't play dumb with me."

"That old Chev in the back?" Davis wiped his brow. "I think someone's misled you, Deputy. That truck's mine."

"Bullshit it is. That truck's been used in the commission of a crime. Hand me the keys, and I'll take it off your hands."

Davis held his gaze. "You got a warrant?"

Harwood stared at him, speechless.

"You got to have a warrant, don't you, being as you came all the way from Deception for that truck," Davis said. "So you all show me the paperwork and you can do what you please, but until then—"

"How about a big fucking gun?" Dale Whitmer, beside Harwood, his hand on his holster. "How's that for your warrant?"

Davis said nothing. Something moved in the back of the shop, and two more men appeared. Younger than Davis—bigger, too—but definitely his kin. One of the men held a torque wrench. The other held a goddamn camera phone, and it was aimed straight at Harwood.

"You sure you want to go that route, Deputies?" Davis asked from the floor, his voice still infuriatingly easy. "Going to have a hell of a time explaining why two Deception Cove lawmen shot up an unarmed civilian on Indian land, aren't you?"

Harwood looked at the camera phone. The man aiming it at him smiled a little.

"This is obstruction of justice," Harwood said. "This is a mistake, what you're doing here. You're making one hell of a mistake."

"That may well be," Davis replied. "And I suppose I'll find out, one way or the other. But until you all have a warrant, Deputies, I'll ask you kindly to step back off my property. I've got work that needs doing."

He didn't wait for an answer, slid back under the Buick again, and Harwood heard him pick up his tools. The man with the camera phone hadn't moved, though, and neither had the other, with the wrench.

"Son of a *bitch*." Harwood spun on his heel, stalked out of the shop. Crossed to his truck and fired up the engine. Whitmer climbed in beside.

"So what does this mean?" Whitmer asked as Harwood shifted into gear.

"What does it mean?" Harwood repeated, gunning the engine and launching out of the mechanic's lot. "It means Winslow and that asshole swapped out their ride. Means they probably slipped past the farm without your brother seeing, which means if they have any sense, they got the hell gone from Deception Cove and probably from this whole fucking county." He slammed on the steering wheel. *"Shit."*

"Damn, boss," Whitmer said. "So what do we do?"

Harwood drove in silence for a moment or two. He was headed the wrong way, headed into Neah Bay. There was no goddamn reason to be here.

"We got a few hours until Okafor shows," he told Whitmer. "We're going on back to town, and we're going to search that bitch's little house, high and low."

"What, Jess's?" Whitmer frowned. "You don't think she'd have taken the stuff with her if she was going to skip town?"

Harwood gritted his teeth. "Probably, Dale," he said. "You probably have this broken down exactly right." He hit the brakes, yanked on the wheel, spun the truck 180 degrees, and stood on the gas pedal. "But trashing Jess Winslow's house will make me feel better about this whole fucking mess, and right now, bud, that's good enough for me."

TWENTY-NINE

"Cops already been up here," Rengo told Jess and Burke. "Harwood and his boys. Tossed the whole goddamn camp upside down. Believe it or not, I had the place pretty well organized before they came a-calling."

Jess looked around. Made a face. "If you say so."

It smelled marginally less bad inside Rengo's trailer than outside in the compound, but that was only because of the twenty-five or so car air fresheners the kid had hanging from the ceiling like Christmas ornaments. The air wasn't so much fresh as it was some chemical approximation of Royal Pine, and the effect wasn't so much soothing as it was suffocating. Jess had been in some smelly situations in her brief time on Earth, and she wasn't sure she wouldn't take a sewage cesspool in Afghanistan over Rengo's dank little home.

The trailer was set up like the usual: bedroom on one end, and a kitchen and living area on the other.

"Shitter don't work," Rengo said, leading them to a filthy couch and an armchair bandaged clumsily with duct tape to keep the stuffing in. "Still working on those creature comforts."

Burke remained standing. Lucy nosed about, wandered into the kitchen, took a cursory glance down the hall to the bedroom, then came back to where Burke stood by the front door, and lay down at his feet.

"We won't be staying long," Jess replied, brushing off the couch before sitting down, the shotgun in her lap. "Don't want to take up too much of your day."

"*My* day?" Rengo grinned for the first time. It was a wide, boyish smile, and she realized he was younger than she'd pegged him for. "Shit, lady, I wasn't exactly full up with appointments before you all came along."

He sat in the armchair. Leaned forward. "Now, what is it you think I can tell you about?"

"My husband," Jess said. "I want to know exactly what he was into, and why it's got Kirby Harwood and his two useless deputies making my life hell."

Rengo's smile disappeared. "You think I had something to do with that?"

"You worked with Ty, didn't you?"

"Yeah, we cooked together," the kid said. "But shit, that wasn't nothing that Kirby cared about. Not unless he was coming around for a taste."

"He killed the lady's husband." Burke, from the door. "And he tore up your spot, looking for something. We aim to figure out what it is."

Rengo raised his hands. Glanced at Lucy again, tried a smile at her, and the dog—*damn her*—scrambled to her feet and went over to him, wagging her tail and licking at his hands and turning around to put her big butt in his face for scratches. Rengo laughed, a childish giggle, and pet her like a boy would a puppy, delighted.

"Big, tough pit bull, huh?" he said as Lucy twisted back with her long pink tongue, trying like hell to lick his face. "You're a vicious dog, aren't you?"

Jess and Burke swapped looks, and Jess rolled her eyes. *Traitor.*

Burke cleared his throat. "We were talking about Ty," he said. "Maybe you want to focus."

"Now listen." Rengo scratched Lucy's butt once more. Then he looked at Burke square. "Ty drowned under that dock because he drank too much and got stupid. Didn't have nothing to do with Kirby Harwood, the way I heard it."

"Yeah?" Jess said. "And who told you that?"

"People." Rengo fidgeted again. The dog twisted and nuzzled her snout between his hands, and he pet her, absently, as he talked. "I mean, it's just common knowledge. Anyway, like I told Kirby, I don't know anything about whatever it is you all are looking for. Ty never told me nothing, and if he'd have hid something here, I'd have found it by now." Rengo looked at Lucy again, then at Jess. "But listen, if you're looking for what turns Kirby's motor, it ain't what me and Ty was up to out here. This is small-time, comparatively speaking."

"And why's that?"

Rengo sat back in that beat-up old armchair and regarded them, smiling like he had the upper hand now, like he knew a secret. Lucy settled down at his feet, sighing contentedly. It seemed she'd decided the kid wasn't a threat.

"You go down to the docks downtown Deception Cove, look out across the water, what do you see?" Rengo said.

"Canada?" Jess said after a beat.

"Fuck Canada," Rengo said. "Try again."

She thought about it. Burke did the same. Lucy laid her head down on the floor of the trailer, her collar tinkling, metallic, as she shifted. Then Burke let out his breath.

"The ships," he said. "Those cargo ships out there."

Rengo slapped his hand on his knee. "Give the man a prize. It's ships, man, thousands of them, from everywhere in the world you can think of, carrying any*thing* you can think of—legal or not."

"Harwood has that boat," Burke said, nodding. "Seemed awfully proud of it."

"As well he should be," Rengo replied. "Boat's probably paid for itself and that big old truck many times over by now. You don't buy that shit on a deputy's salary. Not cooking meth, either."

"So what?" Jess said. "Spell this out for me, Rengo."

"Coast Guard can't search every ship that comes by here," Rengo said. "Ship comes through, dead of night, pissing rain, nobody's going to notice if someone throws a package off the back. Give it a life jacket, GPS beacon, and you're set." He sat forward again. "Rumor is, Kirby's got a deal going with some heavy hitters from back inland—Nigerians, I believe. I heard it's heroin, but I also heard other stuff. But whatever he's doing, he takes a nice cut for his troubles."

Jess frowned. Rubbed her eyes. This had been a long day already, and it was still only midafternoon. What else was she going to find out about her goddamn husband before her head hit a pillow tonight?

"You think Ty got hold of one of Kirby's deliveries," she said. "That's what we're dealing with here. He took it, stashed it somewhere, and they killed him before he could give it back."

Rengo looked uneasily at Burke. "Well, yeah. But knowing Ty, he was probably out for his end."

"Of course he was," Jess said, disgusted. "And look what good it did him."

Burke shifted his weight, Lucy watching him, her ears perked. "This is good," he told Rengo. "But Ty never told you any of this directly?"

"No, sir," Rengo replied. "He was pretty buttoned up about it."

"He must have told someone. Did Ty have any other friends, anyone else he ran with besides you?"

Rengo gave him a pained look. Glanced at Jess and sucked in his breath. "I don't—I don't know if she wants to hear about it."

Here it comes, Jess thought. *Ty, you worthless sack of shit.*

"I want to hear it," she said. "Spit it out."

Rengo didn't know the full story.

"He was pretty tight lipped about this, too," he said. "Even while we were cooking, I'd try to get him to open up, you know, guy stuff. He never said much about her."

Her. Despite herself, Jess felt it like a knife in her chest. Figured that pretty well marked the end of any residual sadness she'd felt over Ty's passing. She felt pissed off, instead, that she'd let him play her like he'd done. That she'd fallen in love, and all she'd gotten in return was a goddamn drug dealer who couldn't keep his dick in his pants or even stay alive.

The men were watching her like they were scared she was going to break down, and she hated them for it.

"Go on," she said, avoiding their eyes. "Tell me what you know and quit being a pussy about it."

"Wellll, she was younger—"

"Damn it."

Rengo wilted. "I mean, she was *young.* Like, too young for Ty, he kept saying. She worked in the cove, lived in town there. I could never get much out of him."

"Name," Jess said. "Give. Me. A. Name."

Rengo looked at Burke, a helpless expression on his face. Looked to the dog, like *she* could somehow save him. But Lucy couldn't, and Burke wouldn't, and eventually Rengo sighed. "I guess her name's Shelby."

"Shelby *Walker*? The little tramp who works at the sheriff's detachment?"

Burke started. "The teenager?"

"I mean, I think she's about twenty," Rengo said. "And I sure as hell didn't know she worked at the detachment. But that would make sense, wouldn't it? Give Ty a pair of eyes on the inside?"

Jess stood. "I know where she lives," she told Burke. "We need to get her story."

Burke was already reaching for the door, Lucy standing and stretching. Burke pulled the door open, stepped back for Jess to go through. Then he dug into his pockets, came out with cash, a pair of hundred-dollar bills.

As Jess watched, he held them out toward Rengo. The kid was leaned over, scratching behind Lucy's ears, the damn dog loving every second of it, Rengo's smile coming back, Christmas morning and Santa'd brought him a puppy. "What, just for talking to you?"

"No," Burke replied. "For your gun."

"You know they'll send you back if they catch you with this thing," Jess said from the passenger seat, studying the pistol as Mason drove them back toward town. "No record of sale, and you're already a felon? Hell, they'll put you away for a long while."

Mason navigated the narrow road, the wipers working now, sheets of water cascading across the windshield. He'd talked Rengo into throwing in what spare ammunition he had, three magazines' worth of nine-millimeter shells. A couple hundred bucks was probably a bargain, but the kid hadn't had much leverage, what with Jess and her shotgun standing right there in the doorway. Mason figured he should feel bad, but money was getting tight, and anyway, the kid was going to hurt somebody, waving that piece around.

"They'll throw me in jail if they catch me regardless," Mason said, eyes on the road.

"This isn't your fight, Burke," she said. "I appreciate what you've done, but this is serious now. You spent half your life in a jail cell; you haven't even barely lived yet. Why on earth would you risk going back?"

Mason said nothing. They'd come to a steep spot in the road; he focused on braking the Blazer down the slippery terrain.

We do not admire the man of timid peace. That wasn't scripture; it was Teddy Roosevelt. *We admire . . . the man who never wrongs his neighbor, who is prompt to help a friend, but who has those virile qualities necessary to win in the stern strife of actual life.*

"You want me gone, I'll get going," he said when the road leveled out again. "I've still got enough money for a bus ticket home. But it seems to me you could use a friend right now."

She said nothing and Mason kept driving, listening to the wipers across the windshield, and the mud and gravel beneath the tires. They reached the forestry main line, and he turned the Blazer north, toward the highway and the town.

They drove in silence. Even Lucy was quiet in the back seat.

Finally Jess spoke. "You must think I'm really stupid." Her voice was soft, and she was staring out the passenger window at the trees passing by, her face hidden. "Marrying a guy like Ty."

"No," Mason said. "I don't know anything about it."

"He wasn't always like that." She continued like he hadn't said anything. "High school, he was different. He was handsome, and he was smart, he was a smooth talker, always had some kind of plan or a scheme." She laughed, humorless. "I guess he never lost that side of him, anyway.

"His daddy was a highliner, back when that meant something. You know what a highliner is, Burke?"

"I guess it means he was good at fishing," Mason said.

"The best. He built a good life for Ty, and Ty's mom, before the bottom fell out. Wound up drinking himself to death just about the same time the town died. But Ty and me, we were bound for something better, somewhere else. Even from day one, we had a plan."

Mason didn't say anything. He figured he would let Jess speak her mind, tell her story. Truth be told, he'd been curious.

"I joined the marines out of high school," she said. "All *I* ever wanted." She smiled a little bit, and there was real joy in it this time, mixed with a wistfulness Mason could feel in her words. "My dad was in the corps, fought in Iraq. He loved the marines, and I loved my dad, and so that was that, I enlisted, Ty and me got married, and off I went."

"To Afghanistan."

"That's right," she said. "Dad died midway through my first tour. They found cancer inside him, and it caught up to him quick. And then it was just me and Ty."

Headlights on the road ahead. Mason pulled to the side of the logging road, crept the Blazer along slow. Beside him, Jess thumbed the safety off on the pistol.

It was a white pickup truck, a Ford Super Duty. The driver gave Mason a wave as he passed, didn't look twice at the Blazer. Mason waited until the truck disappeared in his rearview. Then he continued down the road.

"What'd Ty do while you were overseas?" Mason asked.

"What didn't he do? He tried to make a go of it fishing, made a little bit of money, but not nearly enough for what he wanted out of life. Then he was going to open a restaurant in town, cater to tourists, and then he was thinking about getting into the septic tank business, but I guess the smell drove him off that."

She sighed. "Long story short, he must have run out of ideas. And I guess somewhere along the way, he ran out of patience with my being gone all the time."

They'd reached the highway. Mason hit the blinker, left turn. "This girl, Shelby, she live in town?"

Jess nodded. "Behind the old cannery, a little white house."

Mason turned left, toward Deception Cove, drove a ways. The wipers, back and forth, the tires in the rain.

"You know it's not your fault," he said after a bit. "None of this, Harwood taking the dog, what happened to Ty. Your man running around while you were off fighting. That's on him, not you."

She laughed. There was a harder edge this time, and when he looked her way, she was kind of smirking at him, like he'd said something wrong and crossed some kind of line.

"You don't have to counsel me, Burke," she said. "I married a real piece of shit, and that's a plain fact. I don't need you holding my hand."

"I'm not . . ." He felt lost. Immature, unprepared. This wasn't a conversation he'd ever had before. "Yeah," he said. "All right."

He kept driving. Felt her eyes on him, didn't look. Jess sighed. "Listen, I'm sorry," she said. "You're only trying to . . ."

She stopped when she saw the look on his face. He was scanning the road in front of them, just coming to the outskirts of town now, a haze hanging in the air, thicker than the rain.

The smell, too. Smoke. Something burning.

"You smell that?" he asked her. "Something's on fire."

THIRTY

Even with the rain falling, the place burned pretty good.

It was a wood house, after all, and once Harwood and Bryce Whitmer had spread a few gallons' worth of regular grade all over the widow Winslow's floors and her meager collection of furniture, the fire was a foregone conclusion.

Harwood and Bryce retreated to the edge of Jess Winslow's weedy, muddy lawn, watched the place burn from there until the flames got too high and the heat overpowering, and then they retreated farther up the road and sat in Harwood's truck and stared at the inferno.

Nobody bothered them. Jess lived at the far end of a going-nowhere road, and Harwood had dispatched Dale Whitmer to stand guard at the head of it, his county cruiser angled across and his blue-and-reds flashing. Harwood knew the odds were nobody would bother old Dale at all, but it was better to be safe. He'd left Cole Sweeney in the detachment, let the kid feel like he was doing some good in the world, playing cop instead of helping Harwood work out his frustrations with a jerry can and a match.

Harwood felt a little bit of remorse as he watched the fire, but not much. The arrangement with Okafor was supposed to be easy cash, a little boost to the community economy. And if Harwood hadn't taken the deal, the boys in Clallam County surely would have.

Shit, the whole goddamn town was dying. Harwood had thought

he might have to let one of the boys go, Sweeney or Dale, wasn't really enough county resources to justify keeping them both on. So if some slick motherfucker wanted to come through waving hundred-dollar bills in Harwood's face, well, damn. It was practically his civic duty to jump aboard, when you thought of it that way.

It was supposed to stay easy. Stay civil. Pick up a package, hand it off to Okafor's guys, pocket ten percent for the trouble. Money rolled in. Terri-Lee got her kitchen redone. Cole and Dale kept their jobs. Hell, the whole town reaped rewards.

And then Ty Winslow got greedy.

In truth, Harwood couldn't fault the guy for making his play. He'd have done the same thing, if the tables had been turned. He might even have been willing to deal, if Ty's number had made sense. But Ty's number was high, too high. It was high enough that it made more sense to beat the story out of Ty than to pay him.

He wasn't supposed to die; that had been a mistake. Shit, though, you play the game, you might could lose. If Ty hadn't foreseen that possibility, he'd been dumber than Harwood imagined.

Jess, though.

So maybe he'd played it wrong at first. Maybe it didn't exactly make sense to go in strong-arming a marine. In Harwood's defense, he'd been freaked the fuck out. No sign of the shipment, Okafor on his ass, and Jess Winslow should have been an easy fix, screwed up in the head as she was. He should have known better, and that was his bad.

But now? This bullshit, and with Mason Burke? Harwood was done feeling guilty. He was done being sorry. There was no reason for Jess to take up with Burke. There was no reason for Burke to be here at all. If Jess'd had any sense, she would have dealt out with Harwood, realized she was better off talking things over, working together. Hell, she might even have made money off the deal.

But Jess had to get cute. And so this, what was happening now, this house fire and whatever came after, this was on her. And Harwood figured he would make sure she understood that, when the time finally came to put an end to this.

Beside him, Bryce Whitmer nodded at the fire. "Best we get a move on, don't you think?" he said. "We don't want to be sitting here with our thumbs up our asses when the volunteers get the memo."

Harwood turned the key in the ignition, felt his truck rumble to life. Shifted into reverse, executed a three-point turn, and drove, smelling the fire in his clothes, the road behind him hazy with low, drifting smoke.

In Harwood's rearview mirror, Jess's ceiling caved in in an explosion of sparks and new flame.

This isn't high school anymore, Harwood thought. *We're playing for keeps now.*

THIRTY-ONE

"We can't go down there."

In the passenger seat, Jess looked sharp at Burke. "What the hell do you mean? That's my goddamn house that's on fire, and you know it."

Burke nodded. "Yep," he said. "And that won't be a coincidence, either. Harwood set that fire, and a hundred bucks says he's waiting down there, hoping we'll do something foolish."

"That's my house, Burke," Jess said again, feeling sick. "That's all my belongings, it's where I live. That's everything I own in that house."

Burke didn't look at her. "It's already gone," he said. "All of it."

In the back seat, Lucy whimpered. Jess felt like doing the same—but on second thought, forget crying. Jess felt like kicking some ass.

"That son of a bitch," she said. "I'll make him pay for this, Burke. You understand?"

"Yes, ma'am," Burke said. "I believe you. But there's gotta be a time and place."

Jess leaned back in her seat, closed her eyes. She could block out the sight of the smoke over the highway, but she couldn't chase the smell from her nostrils.

"Fine," she said, opening her eyes again. "So what are we still doing here?"

Burke glanced at her. She avoided his eyes. He shifted into gear and pulled back onto the highway.

They parked a few blocks from where Shelby Walker lived, stuck the Blazer in a copse of trees on an abandoned lot, hoped the shadows would hide it as the daylight gave out. Nobody should have been looking for a Blazer, but there was no harm in being careful.

"We leave Lucy here, we could lose her again," Jess told Burke, pushing the back seat forward so Lucy could get out. "I'm bringing her."

Burke didn't say anything, just nodded, waited for her to help Lucy out of the truck and close the passenger door. They crept out to the edge of the lot and looked up and down the road, the old fish plant a block down on their right, primer gray and rust red and deserted, a handful of hardscrabble houses to their left, some with lights on inside and vehicles at the curb, some swaybacked and empty, tagged with clumsy graffiti. Weeds and tall grass everywhere, litter, busted crab pots and torn fishing nets and worn rope.

Jess pointed across the road to a row of houses on the next street over. "Probably best if we go in through the back."

Nobody seemed to notice as they crossed the road and slunk between two houses into Shelby Walker's backyard. Lucy followed, obedient, pausing to sniff at a clump of weeds, a corner wall, peeing once in the grass and then jogging to strain on her lead toward Burke. The ex-convict walked ahead of Jess and Lucy, his hand lingering near the pistol he'd stashed in his waistband, even though he had never shot a gun in his life and had no idea where he was supposed to be going.

Men, Jess thought.

She let Burke have his little moment, gave him directions, and soon enough they were crossing the Walker backyard, ducking under a sagging clothesline that seemed almost comical in this ceaseless rain, and climbing up the wooden steps to Shelby's back door.

"Best if I take the lead from here, Burke," Jess said, handing him Lucy's leash. "That's if you don't mind."

Burke stepped back, and Jess rapped on Shelby Walker's screen door, a harsh, angry sound. She tried to push her hurt feelings down, tell herself this was about something bigger than Ty now, that whatever Ty and Shelby Walker had had going on, it didn't matter anymore. And then the Walker door swung open, and Jess found herself face-to-face with the tramp who'd taken up with her husband, and all those nice thoughts went for nothing.

"Oh." The girl's eyes went wide as soon as she saw Jess, and she backed away from the door. She *was* a girl, Jess could see, with an uncertainty to her movements and a childish innocence of expression. Jess hated Ty more and more.

But then the girl's eyes hardened, and she seemed to gather herself and chase that childishness away. She glared at Jess. "I guess you're here about your husband."

Jess guessed that Shelby Walker had been preparing for this moment ever since she'd met Ty, guessed the girl had a pretty good idea how she wanted things to go down.

"I'm not here because you were fucking him, if that's what you mean," she said, raising her hand as the Walker girl began to argue. "But I do expect you have some information as to why he wound up dead."

The Walker girl only stared at her, and Jess figured that meant she'd knocked her off-balance. She tried a smile next.

"You want to invite us inside?" she asked. "It's cold out here in this rain."

The Walker girl looked at her. Looked at Burke, and the dog. Looked at Jess again, and Jess doubled down on that smile.

Finally the girl sighed.

"All right," she said, stepping away from the door.

It was a well-kept little house, neat and cozy and warm. Not much to it—a little living room and an open kitchen and dining area, a hallway leading off toward the bedrooms—but it was tidy, and it was clean; there were dishes drying on the rack by the sink, a couple of magnets stuck to the fridge with old pictures beneath them. The kitchen was lit bright, fluorescents overhead, but the living room was darker, a pair of lamps casting a soft glow, comfy-looking furniture, a room for curling up with a good book and waiting for the rainy season to end. It was a house that looked lived in, looked like somebody's home, somebody who still cared about keeping up appearances, and Jess thought about her own little four-room disaster and wanted to hate Shelby Walker even more.

Then Jess remembered she didn't even have a house to go back to, not after this afternoon, and she felt sad and angry and stupid for even bothering to be jealous. There was nothing she had in her life that someone like Shelby Walker could covet.

Shelby ducked into the kitchen, came back with a bottle of Wild Turkey and three tumblers, an ice tray. She cracked the ice from the tray and dropped a couple of cubes into each glass.

"I don't know about you all," she said, "but if we're going to do this, I need a drink."

She poured for the three of them, generous pours, gestured to the seats at the little table, and took a healthy draw from her glass as Jess sat, and Lucy wandered, sniffing around the kitchen, to the end of her leash. She nosed up to Shelby and sniffed at her, too, nuzzling under her hands until the girl relented and pet her, her tail whapping hard against the legs of the table, Shelby smiling despite herself. The dog was a regular goddamn Benedict Arnold.

Burke remained standing. If he was amused by Lucy's antics, he wasn't showing it.

Shelby set her tumbler down, looked him over. Then she looked at Jess again. "He doesn't sit?"

Jess shrugged. "I guess not."

"Does he talk at least?"

Burke shifted. "I talk."

Shelby looked at him again. Longer, appraising. "Looks like an upgrade from the old man, anyway," she told Jess finally. "No offense."

Jess sighed. "Are we doing this, or what?"

"We're doing this." Shelby sat down opposite Jess at the table. "What do you want to know?"

Jess surveyed the little house again. Wondered if the Walker girl had played house with Ty here, if she'd cooked hot meals for him, if they'd cuddled on the couch, watched movies together.

She wondered if Ty had fucked Shelby Walker here, in this house, while Jess was getting her ass shot at in the Hindu Kush. While Jess was watching Afia die.

"Seem awfully young to be living here by yourself," she said.

"Old enough for your husband," Shelby retorted, and it was so obvious that Jess rolled her eyes, and even Shelby seemed to feel embarrassed. "This is my mama's house," she continued, and gestured toward the dark hall off the living room. "She doesn't move around so much these days, since she had the stroke."

"And your dad?"

"Who knows?" Shelby drained her glass. Reached for the bottle. "Is this really what you came here to talk about?"

"Just trying to get a sense of things," Jess said.

"Yeah, well, don't."

Burke made to say something. Jess raised a hand, stopped him. Shelby watched the exchange, a little smirk on her face. But she didn't say anything.

"We know Kirby Harwood's taking deliveries off the ships," Jess told her. "We know Ty knew about it, and he got hold of one of Kirby's shipments. Probably stashed it somewhere and tried to work Kirby for some money to return it, and Kirby killed him instead. And I figure Ty wasn't smart enough to put all this together on his own; he had to have help on the inside." She met Shelby's eyes. "And that's where you come in."

Shelby sat back, crossed her arms. "Sounds like you got it all figured out."

Jess hesitated. She hadn't expected to have her hypothesis confirmed so damn fast. "You know where Ty hid that package?" she asked.

"No, I surely do not." Shelby laughed, cold. "Lady, if I knew where that package was, I sure wouldn't be sitting here talking to you. That whole score was supposed to be our ticket out of here."

"You and Ty."

"Me and my *mama,*" Shelby said. "Look, I think you're overestimating what me and your husband had going on together. No offense, but he wasn't exactly the missing piece to my puzzle."

"Why don't you tell us how you got mixed up in all this in the first place?" Burke. "What the plan was, you and Ty. Maybe we put our heads together and get a lock on that shipment."

Jess watched how Shelby flinched when Burke spoke. Just a little bit, and recovered fast, but there it was, a break in the girl's armor.

She's just a child, Jess thought. *And she's scared shitless, like the rest of us.*

"We find that package, you can have it, for all I care," Jess told Shelby. "I don't give a damn about the money, and neither does Burke. I'm just concerned with getting Kirby Harwood off my back. After that, I couldn't care less what happens."

Shelby studied her across the table. Spent a long time doing it, chewing on her bottom lip like she was thinking hard. Then Lucy flopped down onto the linoleum beneath her chair, clearly bored, rolled onto her back, and pawed at Shelby to scratch her, her tongue lolling.

Shelby stifled a smile. Leaned down and rubbed Lucy's belly, as powerless as Rengo to resist the dog's charms. With her free hand, she reached for her glass, took another long draw. Tossed it back with a grimace she couldn't quite hide, set the glass down.

"Damn it," she said. "All right."

THIRTY-TWO

It was dumb *luck that did it. Dumb luck and desperation. Shelby was hitching home from Port Angeles one Friday night, her night off from the detachment, her usual routine. Anyway, it was late, more like Saturday morning, and cars headed west were few and far between, the highway so dead that Shelby half thought she'd have to walk the whole way to Deception before she found someone to give her a lift.*

And then there were headlights behind her, and she heard the engine slowing before she'd even turned around with her thumb out, squinted in the bright and saw the pickup ease past her, that ugly puke green; she recognized it as Ty Winslow's ride. Ty leaned over and unlatched the passenger door as she walked up the shoulder, pushed it open, and she climbed inside, just like that, no words exchanged.

They drove for a while, and they didn't speak much besides Ty saying "Hey" and Shelby saying "Thanks." Ty had the radio on, some old outlaw country, and he played it at low volume as the headlights cut a swath through the mist on the highway, and for a while Shelby figured that this was how it was going to be.

And then when they were a couple of miles out of Clallam Bay, Ty broke the silence, looked over at her and sparked the conversation that would end up killing him. "Awfully late to be hitching alone," he said. "Aren't you scared?"

She looked at him, hard. "Scared of what, Ty? You*?"*

Ty glanced across the truck at her, frowning like he wasn't sure how to take that one. Then he chuckled. "Yeah, but what about your parents? What do they think about you running around after dark like this?"

"My parents?" she scoffed. "I guess you didn't hear, but my mama can't hardly get out of bed anymore, much less worry after me."

He didn't bother to ask about her dad. Shelby figured he probably already knew, even if he didn't. Most of the dads in Deception Cove had a tendency toward fucking off, and hers wasn't any exception.

Ty drove a little farther. Fumbled in his breast pocket for a packet of smokes, shook one out, and offered Shelby the pack. She waved him off. Put her feet up on the dash as he lit the smoke.

"You're working at the cop shop, that right?" he said as the lights of Clallam Bay appeared around a bend in the highway. "With Kirby and his boys."

She nodded. "That's right."

"That Kirby, he's sure doing well for himself. New truck, new boat. They must pay those deputies a damn fortune."

Shelby didn't say anything. Wondered if Ty Winslow was gaming her, or if he was really that stupid that he hadn't caught on.

"They pay you *that good?" Ty continued. "Answering phones and what-not? Seems like that whole detachment's straight swimming in cash."*

No, *Shelby thought.* No, they certainly do not pay me that good. *In fact, Shelby was pretty sure Kirby Harwood believed she was mentally deficient; otherwise, how could he believe she didn't know what he was doing? Sure, he carried on all secret and suspicious, dragging the boys into his office when he wanted to talk business, but Shelby wasn't dumb. She'd figured it out, quick. And as she sat in Ty Winslow's passenger seat, listening to him gush about Kirby Harwood's new truck, Shelby realized she'd been waiting for the right time to do something with what she knew.*

She'd been waiting for some way to get hers.

"It isn't a county paycheck," she said, cutting Ty off in the middle of

some spiel about a 6.2-liter V-8 engine. "Surely you got to know that, don't you?"

Ty glanced over at her again. Didn't say anything. Kept driving, through Clallam Bay and out the other side, working his jaw like he was thinking about how to answer.

"Yeah," he said finally. "I reckon I did."

Shelby Walker leaned down and scratched Lucy's belly some more.

"From there, it was pretty straightforward," she told Jess. "Your man had his boat, and I knew how to tell when Kirby had a shipment coming through. We put it together, and presto, voilà. . . ." She drained her glass again. Set it down hard. "It was supposed to be easy, the way we had it planned."

"But it wasn't," Jess said.

"Oh, it was easy. Kirby got the call, and I texted Ty it was on. We messed with Kirby's boat so he couldn't go out, and Ty went in his place. From what Ty said, everything happened perfectly. He got the package, hid it away. All that was left was to convince Kirby to deal, and that's the part that got fucked up, and I still don't know why. Ty was dead before he could give me an answer."

Jess said nothing. She studied Shelby Walker across the table. *What about the part where you fucked him?* she was thinking. *How'd it come about that you were sleeping with my husband; where does that fit into this picture?*

"Did your husband ever call you while you were overseas?" Burke asked, filling the silence. "Ever write you any emails, anything he might have let on where he'd stashed the package?"

Jess shook her head. "He just talked about trucks and the new home he was going to build me, all the usual stuff. And..." She stopped. Felt stupid, so stupid, all of a sudden.

"Yeah?"

"Fishing," she said, and reached for the whiskey. "He sent me a letter that arrived after he died. Fishing was all it was." She looked at Burke. "He said he'd had a real damn good day of fishing."

THIRTY-THREE

The Nigerian man appeared at Bryce Whitmer's front door precisely on time. He was short and lean, well groomed, his hands freshly manicured, his black hair cropped close to the skull. He wore a suit, freshly pressed and onyx black, the white shirt beneath a stark contrast to his dark brown skin.

His face was clean shaved and unblemished, save a scar he wore across his right cheek, a souvenir from another conflict, long ago, another precious commodity, another part of the world. He left a black Chevy Suburban parked in Whitmer's driveway.

Bryce Whitmer answered the door. He looked the man up and down. Took in the suit, the Suburban, and—of course—the color of his skin, almost a photonegative of Whitmer's own wan complexion.

"Guess you must be Okafor," Whitmer said.

The man smiled thin, a humorless expression. "My name is Joy," he said. "I am here on Mr. Okafor's behalf. May I come in?"

"Okafor didn't say anything about any Joy," Whitmer replied. He hadn't budged.

Joy's smile, small though it was, didn't waver. He produced a cell phone from his pocket. "You are welcome to call Mr. Okafor to discuss my presence here, if you feel the need."

Whitmer looked at the phone like it was an alien artifact. Then, wordless, he stepped aside and let Joy through the door—taking care as he did so, Joy noticed, to reveal the Colt Python he held at his hip.

Kirby Harwood, Cole Sweeney, and Dale Whitmer sat in the kitchen. They stood when Joy walked in.

"You're not Okafor," Harwood said.

Joy smiled his thin smile again. "No, I am not," he agreed, "and that is a good thing for you and your friends. I am the man Mr. Okafor sends to clean up situations like that in which you find yourselves." He met each of the men's eyes in turn. "If you and I are talking, it means you still have hope. By the time you see Ateke Okafor, it's already too late."

The men swapped looks with one another. Sweeney, the youngest, shifted uneasily. Harwood was first to speak. "Well, all right, Mr. . . ."

"Joy."

"Mr. Joy." Harwood nodded. "Welcome. We're glad you came; this whole situation has us in a bit of a bind."

"Luckily for you, I am experienced in situations just like this one," Joy replied. "First, of course, there is the matter of the fee."

The men swapped worried looks. Harwood cleared his throat. "We're actually a little short on funds at the moment, Mr. Joy," he said. "I'm sure you understand, we'd be happy to pay as soon as—"

"Let me set your mind at ease, Deputy," Joy interrupted. "It isn't money Mr. Okafor requires, to purchase my service."

Bryce Whitmer snorted. "So what the fuck are we supposed to pay you with?"

"*Life,* Mr. Whitmer."

The room went silent. Harwood cocked his head. Sweeney shrank back and looked miserable, like he knew whatever the punch line, it wasn't going to be good.

"Mr. Okafor requires that one of you dies," Joy explained. "Who, it doesn't matter, but it must be one of you, and it must be now. That is the price of my assistance."

"And if we refuse?" Dale Whitmer said.

"If you refuse, I'll explain to Mr. Okafor that you've refused his offer of assistance. And unless you have the money you owe, or the product, that will be bad news for all of you."

"What if we don't let you walk out of here?" Bryce Whitmer said. "You think we're just going to let you come into my fucking house and—"

The pistol was out before anyone could react, and then there was a hole in Bryce Whitmer's head, and blood and brain matter spattered on the wall behind him. The elder Whitmer fell to the ground as the gunshot resonated. The deputies stared for a beat, shocked stupid. Then Dale Whitmer reached for his gun.

"I wouldn't," Joy told him.

"You fuck—you fucking killed my brother. Why did you—*what the fuck?*"

"I made my position clear," Joy said, calm as death. "There was nothing to be gained from prolonging the negotiation. Now you've purchased my assistance. Shall we discuss how we're going to solve your problem?"

For a moment nobody spoke, and the only sound was that of Dale Whitmer's breathing, hard and furious.

Then Harwood reached out, put his hand on Whitmer's pistol. "Stand down, Dale."

Whitmer didn't respond.

"It's done," Harwood said. "We can't do anything for him now, you hear? *Stand down.*"

Whitmer hadn't taken his eyes off of Joy. "I'll remember this," he said through gritted teeth. "You'd better believe, I'll remember."

Joy gave him that smile again. “Whatever gives you comfort, Mr. Whitmer,” he said. “Now, shall we talk?”

Harwood set Sweeney on disposing of Bryce’s body, had the younger deputy take Bryce outside. He figured they’d have to burn him or something, chop him up and drop him off the end of the Grady-White somewhere far out in the strait. For now, it would suffice to get him out of the kitchen, away from Dale’s eyes. Harwood couldn’t predict how the younger Whitmer would react if he spent much more time around what remained of his brother, but he knew it wouldn’t much help their case with Ateke Okafor.

They adjourned to the dining room. Harwood sat opposite Joy at the table, and Dale stood by the door to the kitchen. And Harwood talked.

“It started like it was supposed to,” he explained. “Like every other time. We heard the clicks on the distress frequency as the ship came past Cape Flattery, three of them, one second in between. We’d been tracking the ship on the GPS, so we knew it was good to go, like always.”

Joy drummed his fingers on the table and studied Harwood. “Except . . . not,” he said.

“Well, no. It was a foggy night, kind of lumpy out on the water. Wasn’t the best night for a drop, but I wasn’t too worried, not with my boat. Except when I got her down to the launch and put her in the water, the damn engines wouldn’t start. Either of them.”

Joy leaned back. Tented his fingers. “Aha.”

“Turned out someone’d fucked around with the starter while the boat was on its trailer,” Harwood said. “They would have had to sneak into my backyard to do it, but there you go. Of course, I didn’t know that at first. All I knew was, I was crippled.”

“Protocol would dictate you immediately call Mr. Okafor.”

"And I did. Okafor said he'd call me back on a better line, and it took a while for that to happen. But when he did, he told me the guy on the freighter claimed he'd made the drop, there was a boat out there, knew the signs and everything."

"The signs."

"Yeah, the drop. We had a procedure. I show up off the stern of the ship, flash my lights three times. The guy chucks it back off the stern, fully sealed and, you know, taped up with flotation devices and a GPS so we can find it. Typically, it didn't take much looking."

"But that night someone else intercepted the package."

"That's right. And it took us a while to figure out who'd done it, but once we realized Ty Winslow's boat was out of the harbor at the same time, we put it together. Ty didn't deny it either, told us the package was safe somewhere, we could buy it back from him."

Joy nodded. "And where is this man now?"

"Dead."

"You killed him?"

Harwood spat. "It's not like we were trying to do it," he said. "We went and saw him down at the wharf one night, me and Dale, figured we'd press the issue. Then he made a try at escaping, but we'd beat him so bad he couldn't hardly stand up. Fell over the side of the dock and drowned somewhere underneath, and they pulled his body out the next morning." He shook his head. "Just bad luck, I guess."

"Perhaps," Joy said. "Who else knew about your delivery arrangement?"

Harwood and Sweeney looked at each other. Dale Whitmer glowered at Joy from the doorway.

"Well, nobody," Harwood said. "Just us and Ty Winslow, I guess."

"False." Joy set his pistol down on the dining table, hard. The

sound reverberated through the house. Joy pushed back his chair and stood, paced the room in front of the men.

"How did the thief know the specifics of your arrangement?" he asked. Raised his hand to quell any response. "Was this Winslow character often privy to your private discussions?"

"No," Harwood said. "Never. We never much dealt with Ty at all."

"Then how did he know that night was the night of the drop?" Joy said. "How did he know the signal to alert the man on the freighter? How did he even know you were accepting deliveries? *Who else knew about your delivery arrangement, gentlemen?*"

Joy's pistol sat on the table, within arm's reach of the owner. Harwood couldn't take his eyes from it. Couldn't think straight, think fast enough, with that gun staring at him. Couldn't stop thinking about what it had just done to Bryce Whitmer.

"Shelby." This was Dale. "Girl who answers the phones at the detachment. She's always around."

"No way," Harwood said. "She's still a kid, damn it, and she don't even know Ty Winslow. She wouldn't do something like that."

"Was she in your detachment on the night of the failed drop?" Joy asked.

Harwood searched his brain. Tried to remember. Then he did, and he felt it like a punch to the gut. "Yeah, she was," he said. "She said she had to stay late, do a little tidying up."

Joy picked up the pistol, tucked it away. "There," he said. "You see? It's amazing what we can accomplish when we simply talk a problem over."

He walked to the front door, looked back at the men.

"I think we need to talk to Shelby," he said. "Would you agree?"

THIRTY-FOUR

Jess could picture where she'd kept that letter from Ty, the one that showed up in Bagram out of the blue a couple of days after word came through the OP that Pfc. Winslow was suddenly a widow. She'd thought it was a joke at first, thought Ty was playing a prank—*how can he be dead if he's writing me letters?*—before her common sense caught up and she realized the obvious: he would have posted the letter long before he fell off the side of his boat.

She'd read the letter and reread it as she sat there at Bagram, waiting on the supply flight that would get her to Germany and on her way stateside. She'd searched Ty's messy, uneven handwriting for any spark in his words, any reason he'd written this last letter by hand instead of sending an email. Any reason to hang on to this, her husband's last communication to her.

She could count on two hands the number of letters, actual letters, Ty had sent her. He'd emailed plenty, of course, talked on the phone when Jess could get access. He'd sent the odd care package, candy bars and a fresh toothbrush, socks. But letters? Ty wasn't the type. So this letter was weird for that reason alone, and all the more so because it seemed so *mundane.*

She'd carried it with her all the way home. Propped it up on the mantel beside the wedding picture, read it again when she came home from Ty's funeral, thinking maybe his words would make more sense now—now that she'd returned to her old life, to Deception Cove. Hoping they'd make her feel less alone.

They didn't.

She'd kept the letter with the rest of her keepsakes—a picture of her parents, a wedding invitation, the certificate she'd received with her Combat Action Ribbon from the corps. A few other odds and ends, the detritus you accumulate and assign enough importance to to keep in a shoe box at the bottom of your closet, if not to actually display or even look at anymore.

The letter sat on the top of that pile, in that shoe box, under her dress blues and the few civilian dresses, sweaters, and blouses she owned. Jess could picture it lying there in its powder-blue envelope. For a second she'd been ready to tell Burke they could just run and get it.

But they couldn't, of course. They couldn't because Kirby Harwood and his buddies had burned her little house to the ground.

Burke was watching her. So was Shelby Walker, Lucy forgotten now. Jess knew they were waiting for her to tell them about the letter, about what Ty had written to her. She knew they knew the letter had all the answers.

But Jess could only shrug. "I never really paid attention when Ty was talking about fishing," she said. "He only took me out on the water with him a couple of times, and that was . . ."

She stopped. She'd caught vestiges of a memory, her and Ty, not long after they'd started going together. The sun sparkling like diamonds on the surface of calm water, Ty's little boat chugging along, Ty at the wheel, Jess on the back deck, sitting on the fish hatch, sunning herself in a halter top. Ty playing the radio loud enough to hear over the sound of the diesel.

"Jess?" Burke asked, breaking the spell. "Where did he take you?"

Even Shelby looked interested.

"This place is my secret," he'd told her, throttling down, aiming the boat toward rocky cliffs and verdant green forest. "I take you in here, you got to promise you'll never tell anyone it exists."

And she'd been in love with Ty Winslow back then, and he was tanned and grinning and sexy at the wheel of that boat, and she'd promised right away, of course she had, and he'd pulled her close and kissed her hard, and kept aiming that boat for those rocks.

He'd stayed on that course and kept kissing her, one mischievous hand creeping down to her ass, copping a feel without being shy about it, and she'd giggled and let him, until she heard the surf crashing and pulled back and pointed out the wheelhouse. "You're going to wreck us."

This only made Ty smile bigger, and he gestured out over the bow at those rocks on the shore and the forest behind, that crashing surf. "Look again."

She did. She looked harder, and then she saw what he saw: there was a gap in the cliff, barely twice the width of Ty's boat. It curled out of sight quickly, but it was there, and it was where Ty was aiming.

"It's called Dixie," he said, both hands on the wheel now, focused. "You can only get through on slack tide. And even then, that's only if you're as good as I am."

Jess could see the letter now. She could see what Ty had written. "He told me the fishing was great," she told Burke and Shelby. "Better than ever before. He told me by the time I got home, we'd be whistlin' Dixie."

Burke and Shelby exchanged a look. They didn't get it.

"It was a place he took me once," she explained. "A secret little cove on a little island out there in the strait. He said hardly anyone knew it existed."

"Whistlin' Dixie?" Burke said. "And you think that's where he hid the package."

"Dixie," she said. "Dixie Lagoon. That's the only place I can think of. It was his secret spot; he only took me the once, years ago. I'd completely forgotten."

"So there you go," Shelby said. "And you didn't even need me to help you."

Jess pushed back from the table. "We should go," she told Burke.

"You know how to find this place?" he said.

"No," she replied, "but I guess I'm going to have to remember."

She pushed her chair in, heard Lucy scramble to her feet under Shelby's table. Burke was already turning to reach for the door handle. Then a car's headlights raked through the living room window. An engine cut out, doors slammed shut. Men's voices.

Lucy whined.

"Damn it," Mason said, peering out from the window's edge at Shelby Walker's front yard. Beyond, on the street, a Makah County cruiser and a black SUV sat parked at the curb. Four men stood talking, gesturing up at the house, and Mason could see they were armed.

"They're here," he said, turning back to where Jess and Shelby stood in the kitchen.

"Who, Kirby and his boyfriends?" Shelby scoffed. "Let them come. What are they going to do, arrest me?"

"They burned down my house," Jess told her. "Killed my husband and tried to kill me and Burke. I think we're a little past the right to remain silent."

Mason crossed the living room quickly. "We have to go," he said. "All of us."

Jess already had the back door open. Lucy slipped through, ears perked. She disappeared into darkness, Jess's hand on her lead the only thing keeping her from finding another chunk of Kirby Harwood's ass to lay her teeth into.

Shelby Walker was still standing by the kitchen table, though. She hadn't moved. "What, and leave my mama behind?" she said. "I'm not going anywhere."

Jess appeared in the doorway. "Why aren't we doing this?"

"Her mama," Mason explained.

"She's bedridden; I told you," Shelby said. She gestured to the open door. "You all go. I won't tell Kirby what she told us, I promise."

Jess stared at her. "Those men will kill you if you don't, Shelby. They'll do whatever it takes. This isn't some game to them."

Shelby turned fast, surprising them all. "I know damn well this isn't a game," she said, and she went into the living room and came back holding a rifle. "My dad's old thirty-aught," she said. "About the only thing of value he ever gave to me."

"And what are you going to do with that? Kill them all?"

Shelby fixed her with that look of hers, defiance and pride. Made sure Mason saw too. "I'm defending what's mine," she said. "You all run if you want to, but it'll take more than a pack of limp-dick deputies to clear me out of this place."

Boots on the porch. A knock at the front door. Harwood's voice. "Shelby? You in there?"

Shelby reached into a cupboard, came out with a box of ammunition. Set the box down and began to methodically load her rifle. Another knock at the front door. "Shelby? Open up, now."

"Better go if you plan on going," Shelby said. "Seems to me that option's about to expire."

THIRTY-FIVE

Jess and Burke had nearly made the Blazer when she heard the first shot. Lucy stopped cold, held the pose for about a second and a half. Then the second shot boomed, and the dog took off, yanking the lead out of Jess's hand and disappearing into the dark of the woods.

Burke went stiff too. Stared back between the houses toward Shelby's back door. Then he turned toward the Blazer and hurried over to it. Jess had her focus on getting Lucy back, didn't really see Burke until he reached into the back of the Blazer and came out with her shotgun. It was then that she decided the dog could wait.

"What the hell are you doing?"

Burke slipped the shotgun out of its case. "Can't just leave her in there," he said. "You coming?"

No, damn it, Jess thought. She'd done this before, over there, doubled back into a firefight with the odds square against her, gambled her own ass to try to save someone else's. Difference was, she'd had marines with her then. And none of them had slept with her husband.

Burke stopped and looked at her, and in the dark all she could see of him was the streetlight glint in his eyes.

"I'm not leaving that girl to those deputies," he said. "This isn't something I can walk away from."

Then he was gone before she could answer, and she glanced back at the Blazer, searched the shadows for Lucy, heard more shots from the Walker house. She swore and hurried to catch up to Burke.

Harwood didn't know what he'd been expecting when he showed up at Shelby Walker's house with Cole and Dale and Okafor's scar-faced psychopath, but he hadn't figured on the little bitch opening fire, that was for sure.

He'd gone up to Shelby Walker's front door, nice and easy. Knocked and called her name like there was nothing the matter, like he'd just swung by because she'd left her purse at the detachment or something. He could see the lights on in the living room window, saw movement, knew she was home.

But Shelby hadn't played along. No matter how hard Harwood knocked, or how loud he called her name, the girl wouldn't co-operate. And Harwood had looked back to the street and Dale's cruiser, and to Joy's big Suburban, and he could feel Dale's eyes on him, and Cole's and Joy's, too, and he'd known his men were waiting on him to do something. He'd known Joy wouldn't tolerate failure.

Damn it.

"Last chance, Shelby," he'd hollered through the door. "We're coming in, girl, whether you like it or not."

Still no response. Shadows shifting in the house, light flickering beyond the curtains, onto the front lawn. Harwood felt movement behind him, Dale coming up to join him. "Are we doing this, Kirby?"

"I guess we are," Harwood replied, and Dale stepped back, drew his weapon, and Harwood reared up and put his boot to the door.

The door gave in easy. It was cheap, the lock cheaper, the wood splintering inward without resistance. Harwood kicked again, sent the door swinging clear of the threshold, saw Shelby's living room, and the kitchen beyond, but no sign of the girl.

And then he heard the shot.

Damn, but it must have whizzed right over his head. Harwood swore, threw himself off the front stoop, landed in Mama Walker's old garden, something thorny and brittle. Dale was somewhere on the other side of the stoop, a similar predicament, and behind Harwood lights were coming on in the few neighboring houses still occupied, faces appearing in windows.

Harwood drew his sidearm. "God damn it, Shelby, what the hell are you thinking?"

A little bit of a pause. And then Shelby's voice, from somewhere within, tougher than Harwood could ever recall hearing before: "I'm defending myself, Kirby. What are *you* doing?"

"You can't just open fire on a sheriff's deputy," Harwood hollered back. "I mean, shit, you could have killed someone."

Shelby laughed. "*That?* Just a warning shot. When I want to shoot you, you'll know about it. Now, you want to tell me what you're doing busting down my front door?"

"You know why we're here, Shelby, you bitch." Dale, beating Harwood to the punch, master of diplomacy. "You and that piece of shit Winslow stole something from us."

"Stole what, exactly?" Shelby called back. "Say it nice and loud, Dale, so my mama and my neighbors can hear you."

Dale didn't answer. Harwood could see him on the other side of the stoop, his face drawn tight and contorted, smoke practically billowing from his ears. Harwood figured Shelby put a little too much faith in her neighbors; nobody in this part of Deception gave a damn about anything besides stretching the welfare check to the end of the month, and maybe finding a way to keep the rain from soaking through the ceiling. They sure weren't about to stick their noses into official police business.

But Harwood was still hoping he could talk this through. "Listen, Shelby," he called. "No hard feelings, okay? Let's all take a step back and cool down for a minute."

He waited. No answer.

"We just want back what we came for," he continued. "You point us to it, and we'll be on our way. Heck, I'll even pay for your door."

Another laugh. It wasn't the kind of laugh that instilled confidence. "Well hey, that's generous of you, Kirby. I wish I could help. But that package you want, that was Ty's department. And he never even showed it to me."

"You're lying." Dale again. Harwood looked over, motioned with his hand, *Calm the fuck down.*

"Am I lying, Dale?" Shelby said. "You think if I had any inkling where that package wound up I'd still be answering the goddamn phones for you all at the detachment? You think I'd still keep my mama here in this shit-hole town?" A beat. "You think, Dale, that if I had that package, I might not have tried to shake you down for money at some point? You think maybe that's how it would have gone down?"

"You must know something," Harwood said. "Shelby, we just want to talk. How about you let us in, and we talk this over. Patch this all up, instead of shooting each other?"

There was no answer, and Harwood took that as a positive sign. He pushed himself to his feet, brushed the mud and the brambles from his clothes, made to climb back onto the stoop and ease his way through the front door.

The second crack from Shelby's rifle chased that thought from his mind.

"Damn it!" He was down in the muck again, thorns scratching bare skin, piercing through his shirt, his sidearm falling away and landing somewhere in the mud. "Look here, Shelby—"

Dale cut him off, came crashing in beside him. Harwood hadn't even noticed he'd moved, but his deputy had been busy. He held a jerry can and a handful of matches, left over from their extracurricular mission to the Winslow residence.

"We gotta smoke her out, Kirby," Dale said, and in his eyes there was already fire. "Get our hands on her, get her somewhere quiet. She'll talk, boss, I can promise you that."

Harwood closed his eyes. Felt, for an instant, as if he stood on the top of a high bridge, poised to take the step that would put him over the side, send him careening out of control to the bottom.

But he'd taken that step a long time ago, he knew. He was already falling, and about the only thing he could control was how hard he was going to land.

Dale was waiting, breathing heavy, his eyes on Harwood. "You wait for my word," Harwood told him.

He stood as high as he dared. Looked back toward the street and the cruiser, to Cole. Looked beyond to the neighboring houses, the faces watching through the windows.

"*Cole,*" he yelled back. "You make sure those neighbors keep their heads down, you hear? Make sure they know this is official police business."

Sweeney hesitated. "Yeah, Kirby," he said finally. "All right, but..."

He trailed off.

"But what, damn it?"

Sweeney didn't answer. Just shrugged and pointed over to Joy's black Suburban, still parked where Joy had left it.

Joy was nowhere to be seen.

Joy had circled around to the rear of Shelby Walker's house.

He'd seen enough of the Keystone Kops show to know the deputies were miles out of their league. This wasn't uncommon in Joy's line of work, young men who wanted to play gangster, men with a strong command of hip-hop lyrics and action movie tropes, an inflated sense of ability.

Joy had worked with real men, before he'd come to America. He'd fought with killers over oil in his homeland, killers who would slaughter entire families before breakfast simply to prove a point. He bore his scars from this work proudly, badges of honor. He'd brought what he'd learned to America, where men like Kirby Harwood liked to pretend they were hard, and sometimes even believed it, right up until the moment when Joy showed them just how wrong they were.

These men were not hard.

They'd made mistakes, as people like Kirby Harwood always made mistakes, and they wouldn't last long, not once Joy had solved this problem. These men had become a gross liability.

But for now they were useful.

Joy circled around to the rear of the house. Found the back door and paused in the shadows, drew his pistol. Then he crept up the back steps and tried the door handle, slow. The handle turned easily. Joy pushed it open and walked into the house.

Shelby gripped her dad's rifle. Behind her, in the bed, her mama lay semiconscious, her eyes half-lidded and drowsy, her breathing heavy. Shelby could never figure out how much the woman gleaned about what went on around her these days. She wasn't sure if she even knew she was still alive at all.

She breathed, anyway. She sipped juice from a sippy cup, and she swallowed the warm soup that Shelby spooned into her mouth. She didn't say anything, and she didn't exactly move, but her eyes followed Shelby around the room sometimes, and when Shelby squeezed on her hand, her mama sometimes squeezed back.

A door swung open, somewhere out in the main part of the house. Shelby sensed movement.

"I'll be right back," she told her mama. Then she stole out of the bedroom and crept down the dark hall toward the living room. She could see darkness out the wreckage of the front door, the Makah County cruiser parked on the street beyond. This was not good.

There were two ways out of the house. Harwood and his boyfriends had the front door covered. That left the kitchen door, and that wasn't going to work either. Because as Shelby got to the end of the hall, she looked through the living room into the kitchen and saw the man there, the black man with the white scar on his face, the man she'd never seen before in her life. The man had a gun, and Shelby knew when she saw him she was in deeper shit than she'd realized.

This guy wasn't Kirby Harwood, or Dale Dumb-Ass Whitmer. This guy was on another level. And Shelby knew just from looking at him that she couldn't outwit him so easy as she could the Deception Cove deputies. He wasn't going to be scared off by a couple of potshots and a few angry words.

She leveled her rifle. Took aim at the man. He hadn't seen her yet. A couple of steps farther and he'd be clear in her line of sight. She tensed her finger on the trigger, waited, prepared to fire.

Never got the chance.

Before she could shoot the man, someone else shot first.

Someone from the front door, Kirby or Dale, the shot catching her in the stomach and sending her staggering back. Now the man saw her, and he was firing too, backing her down the hall and out of firing position, backing her toward her mama's bedroom again, Shelby swearing and stumbling and bleeding all over.

And when she got to the bedroom, Shelby knew she was done.

One of the dimwits—whoever wasn't shooting at her—had come around the side of the house. Put a hole in her mama's bedroom window, poured gas through. There was a fire starting to burn beneath the windowsill; as Shelby backed into the room, it had already caught on the curtains and was climbing its way up the wall. There was no killing this fire. No getting out through the window. Even if she could, there was nowhere to go.

That was it, then. She hadn't run from the bastards. She hadn't run from her mama, turned tail on her home. She'd stood her ground, and shit, that was something to be proud of. One fucking woman against four or five men.

The fire was getting hotter, smoke starting to billow. Shelby stuck her rifle out the bedroom door, fired a couple of shots down the hall to keep the men honest. Then she closed the door, firm. Turned back to the bed.

"We put a hurt on them, Mama," she said. "They won't say we didn't go fighting."

THIRTY-SIX

The shots rang out, two of them. Across the backyard, Shelby Walker's small house went still. There were no other gunshots.

Then the kitchen door opened, and the scar-faced man stepped outside, the stranger whom neither Mason nor Jess had ever seen before. He walked down the steps and stood on the grass, slipping a sidearm into a holster on his belt and turning back to study the house with a preternatural calm.

Crouched in the trees that lined the boundary of Shelby Walker's property, Mason spoke to Jess without looking at her.

"So that's it, then," he said, eyeing the unfamiliar man, little more than a silhouette against the house's white siding.

Jess didn't answer right away. She didn't move, either, and for a moment Mason imagined she'd slipped away somewhere. But then she sighed.

"We weren't going to save her, Burke," she said. "That girl wasn't leaving without her mother."

"We could have—"

"We didn't," she said. "It doesn't matter anymore."

Mason started to reply. Started to argue. Stopped when he saw the look in her eyes. It was anger, and it was hurt, and it mirrored how he felt exactly. She might not have liked Shelby Walker, he realized, but that didn't mean she didn't hate that the girl had to die.

Mason raised the shotgun. Took aim at the man across the backyard, fifty feet away. At this range, he hoped, he could blow the man's head off. At the very least he could be sure he'd do damage.

But Jess reached out, put her hand on the barrel, and pushed it down toward the dirt. "Not yet," she told him. "But trust me, Burke: soon."

The fire department was on scene by the time Joy emerged from behind the Walker house. Harwood stood at the street by Dale Whitmer's county cruiser, watching the volunteers roll up in their pumper truck, a line of pickups with Deception Cove Fire plates behind. The pumper came to a stop beside Whitmer's cruiser, and four firemen jumped out. Three of them circled to the back of the truck, began unrolling hoses. The fourth was Brad Anderson, the Deception Cove FD's lead volunteer. He came directly to Harwood.

"Second fire today, Kirby," Anderson said. "Is this town going to hell, or what am I missing?"

"This one's no accident," Harwood told him. "We come out on a call, routine business, and that girl opened up on us. In the middle of the firefight, we started to smell the smoke."

Anderson looked up sharply at the house. "We got people alive in that house?"

"No," Joy said. Harwood hadn't even seen him walk up, but here he was, acting like he belonged. "The girl and her mother, they did not survive."

Anderson stared at him. "And who the hell are you?"

"Drug enforcement." Joy had a smile on his face that might

have seemed charming if you didn't know what the bastard was capable of. "We had reason to believe Ms. Walker was involved in a trafficking operation. Unfortunately, she shot herself and her mother before we could bring her in for questioning."

Anderson opened his mouth. No words came out. He looked from Joy to Harwood to the house, dumbstruck. The fire had appeared in the windows, smoke beginning to snake out from the busted front door.

"I don't have time for this shit right now," Anderson told Harwood. "I've got to save that house, if I can."

Then he was off, walking back toward the pumper truck, calling out orders.

Harwood watched him walk away. Then he turned back to Joy. "You sure that was wise? That DEA stuff?"

Joy's smile was gone. "No less wise than setting the fire, Deputy. We could have used that information. If you'd allowed me, I could have retrieved her alive. Now—"

"*You* said she's dead," Harwood said, confused. "I heard the shots. You—"

"She was dead when I found her, Mr. Harwood, one bullet to the head." Joy looked at Harwood. "Self-inflicted."

Harwood swore. "*Jesus.*" He swayed on his feet, felt back to the truck behind him, leaned against it for support.

What in the fuck are we doing here?

Cole and Dale appeared, mud on their faces, guilt in their eyes. Joy ignored them. Harwood did too.

"So, we lost Shelby," he said weakly. "What happens now?"

"The widow and her companion were here before we were," Joy informed him. "Whatever information the woman had to share, we can assume that Ms. Winslow obtained it."

"How?" Cole. "I mean, how do you know?"

Joy barely glanced at him.

"Three glasses of whiskey on the kitchen table, two untouched, with ice cubes," he said. "A dog's muddy paw prints on the kitchen floor. They were here, gentlemen, not long ago. If you'd acted with more tact, we could have captured all three."

Cole and Dale looked at each other. Harwood stared up at the night sky. "Shit."

"I assume your professional duties will require you to remain here until this fire burns down," Joy continued. "In the meantime, I'll do what I can to see that this trail doesn't get any colder. Pray, don't keep me waiting too long."

With that, he was gone, walking to his big black truck. Harwood watched him climb inside, watched the headlights come on, watched Joy slowly navigate the mess of volunteer firemen and neighborhood looky-loos, and disappear down the block.

Beside him, Sweeney and Whitmer did the same.

"So what on earth happened?" Whitmer said when Joy's truck was gone. "I was betting for sure we could smoke the girl out."

Harwood stared into the house, at the spray from the fire hoses. "Guess you didn't know Shelby," he said at last. "I guess none of us did."

THIRTY-SEVEN

Lucy was gone.

The Blazer sat where they'd left it, tucked into the shadows in that stand of thin trees. But Lucy wasn't there; she'd spooked out at the first sound of gunshots, and wherever she'd run to, it wasn't here.

Burke lay flat on the gravel and peered under the truck, and Jess watched him, feeling some kind of empty start to grow in her stomach, the sick sense that she and Burke had fucked up, and now the night was slipping away from them.

One street over, Shelby Walker's place was a zoo, and the night sky and low clouds were lit up with the reflection of spotlights and flashers from Harwood's cruiser and the volunteer fire department. The chaos had Harwood distracted for the moment, but Jess knew the deputy wouldn't stop chasing them for long.

We have to get out of here.

Burke pushed himself up from the gravel. Stood and brushed his palms clean on the front of his jeans and squinted off into the dark. "You see her anywhere?"

"I'm still standing here, aren't I, Burke?" she said, feeling her anger flare up, frustration. "You don't think if I'd seen her, I'd have taken action?"

Burke didn't reply. He glanced over at her, and his mouth twitched, and then he walked to the front of the Blazer and surveyed the trees some more. She heard him give a low whistle and call out Lucy's name about as loud as he dared, which wasn't very loud at all, not with Harwood and his men so close at hand.

"Black dog on a dark night," he said, walking back over to where Jess stood. "What do you think we should do?"

Jess didn't have an answer for him, just that gnawing void inside her, getting ever larger with every minute that passed. *Black dog on a dark night. Best-case scenario, she digs a hole somewhere and stays hidden until dawn.*

And the worst case?

Worst case was Kirby Harwood took another thing from her. Same as he'd taken Ty, same as he'd taken her house. Worst case was she'd lose the only damn thing she had left; same as she'd lost Afia in that terrible valley. Worst case was Jess would let another friend die.

She met Burke's eyes. "I need to haul ass for Dixie, find that package Ty stole," she told him. "You stick to the shadows, keep your eyes open, you might just find that dog before Kirby does. Hole her up somewhere safe until I'm home free."

"And if you don't make it?" Burke said.

"If I don't make it?" Jess laughed a little bit, hollow. "Well, shit, I guess that'll clear up the question of who gets to keep Lucy when it's all said and done, right?"

Burke looked around again, as if he was expecting Lucy would just come running out of the trees, save them the tough conversation. But Jess knew better. Lucy wasn't coming back here, she knew. Not on her own.

"You don't make it," Burke said finally, turning to face her again. "I take Lucy back to Michigan. And then, what, we all just forget about Harwood? No. . . ." He shook his head. "I'm not leaving you to finish this thing by yourself."

Jess stared at him. Hating him. Wishing he'd just shut up and play by her rules. Knowing he was right, that she'd need him for this next part, and hating him all the more for it.

She let out a breath.

"I need to track down some supplies before we get out of here," she said. "There's no sense the both of us running errands while the dog's on the loose. Can you find your own way to the government wharf?"

Burke nodded.

"Thirty minutes, Burke," she said. "If you can't find her by then, we've just got to hope she found a good place to hide."

"I'll find her," he replied, already turning to go. "See you in thirty."

"That damn dog is probably going to get us all killed."

He stopped. Looked back at her, and he was smiling a little bit, wry. "Oh, probably," he agreed. "But you know that dog would surely die for us, too." Then he shouldered the shotgun and set off down the road.

THIRTY-EIGHT

Jess drove the Blazer through Deception Cove toward Main Street, her eyes half on the road ahead for any sign of Lucy, half on the rearview in case Kirby or his friends had taken notice. She thought about the dog as she drove, and she felt the dog's absence like concrete crushing down on her chest, as heavy as the exhaustion that dragged at her eyelids and slowed her thoughts to sludge.

She hadn't slept much lately, and neither had Burke, as best as she could tell, and she wondered how much longer they could go on like this, full out, before one of them fucked everything up.

Jess wondered if they'd already fucked up. And she wondered how much it would cost them.

She made it to Main Street and turned south up the hill toward the highway, climbed the hill and slowed at the top and turned into the lot out front of Hank Moss's motel. She guided the Blazer in around the long, low building and parked in back, in front of Hank's apartment back door, cut the lights, killed the engine, and stepped out onto damp gravel. There was smoke in the air, mixing with the salt air off the ocean and the smell of diesel off the highway. That smoke was from Shelby Walker's place, Jess knew, and her own house too. It was a reminder that she'd already lost plenty.

Jess squared her shoulders and walked to Hank's apartment and knocked on the door.

The motel owner swore she hadn't woken him up, though he answered the door bleary eyed and in jockey shorts, his T-shirt inside out. Jess explained the situation, everything she could. Capped off with the shootout at Shelby Walker's house, Lucy gone missing.

Hank's reply was a long string of army-issue curse words. "What do you need?" he asked when he was done with the cursing.

"Firepower," she told him. "And a chart and tide tables for Dixie."

The guns were the easy part. Hank had a duffel bag full of a couple of pistols—SIG Sauer P320 and a Beretta M9, ammunition for both—and one long gun, a Colt semiautomatic that looked a lot like the M4 carbines that had saved Jess's ass more than a couple of times in Afghanistan.

"All registered in my name," Hank told her. "So don't get caught holding, or it's my ass too. I'll give you to the day after tomorrow, and then I'm reporting everything stolen. Can Burke shoot?"

"Not yet. But he'll learn."

"Guess he'll have a decent teacher." Hank handed her a little pamphlet and a folded, well-worn marine chart. "That there is Dixie," he told Jess. "I've only done the pass a couple of times, but I tried to mark it out how I remembered, best I could."

Jess took the chart. "I appreciate it. Are those the tide tables?"

"They are indeed." Hank made to hand them over, hesitated. "Listen, even Ty got nervous running that pass, Jess. There's a lot of good sailors been wrecked at that entrance."

"It's the only good anchorage on that island, right?" she said. "Ty said the rest is all cliffs and exposed beach. We've got no other choice."

"You go in a slack tide, or you don't go at all." Hank handed her the tide tables. "Eight thirty tomorrow morning, that's your next shot. Miss it, and you're waiting all day."

"We can't afford to wait." Jess zipped closed the duffel bag. Lifted it and started for the door. "I'd better get moving. Thanks for your help."

Hank lingered. "You're sure you don't want me to come with you?" he asked Jess. "It's been a long while since I fired a weapon in anger, but I can't see how it's something you forget."

"You've done more than enough, Hank," she told him. "You've got brothers. Family. Just keep an eye out for my dog, would you?"

She didn't have to say the rest. *This might be a suicide mission, what we're talking about here. There's a good chance we don't come back.* She figured Hank already knew that part.

He didn't argue, anyway. Just nodded again and watched her drive off.

THIRTY-NINE

Somewhere in Deception Cove, Lucy was scared.

She'd bolted when she heard the gunshots, the noise of the fight triggering some flight instinct inside her such that everything but her fear disappeared from her mind. She'd run from Mason and Jess, wouldn't have returned even if they'd called to her, run to the Blazer and didn't recognize it in her panic, and kept running into the trees as the firefight continued behind her.

Now she was lost. The guns had stopped firing, but the night was still filled with unfamiliar sounds, threatening sounds. Car doors slammed. Men shouted. Diesel trucks rumbled past. Lucy stayed to the shadows, slunk alongside dark houses, her ears flattened back and her tail tucked between her legs, the leash dragging on the ground behind her. She wasn't panicked anymore, but she was scared nonetheless. She wanted to find Jess and Mason and safety.

And she wanted to see to it that Jess was all right.

Lucy might well have hidden. Curled up in the crawl space beneath somebody's trailer and shivered and been scared and waited for dawn or death or whatever was coming for her. But she was a well-trained animal. And though she felt fear, she also felt a duty to Jess and a kinship to Mason, and it was those instincts that won out over her fear.

She stayed as hidden as possible, but she didn't stop moving.

She skulked through weedy backyards and over crumbling asphalt streets, searching for Mason and Jess.

The man named Joy also searched the streets. He drove slow in his black Suburban, eyes scanning left and right for any movement, any life, anything out of the ordinary. He kept his thoughts calm, and he drove with a patience. The night had been singularly unsuccessful thus far, but Joy held out hope that the widow and her companion would make a mistake. People always did.

Joy would hunt them. He would hunt as he'd hunted years ago, across the ocean, when rivals in the swamps of the Niger delta were stealing oil—*his* oil—from the pipelines, stealing food from his family's table. Joy had been a good hunter then. He'd been patient and resourceful. He'd allowed the rival militiamen to wander so far into his traps, there was no possible escape but the slaughter. His family had eaten well. The oil had remained in his employer's control.

This was not the Niger delta. The widow and her friend were not militiamen. But Joy would hunt them all the same, and he would slaughter them, too.

Something moved in the shadows ahead, at the fringe of the Suburban's headlights. An animal, low to the ground and blacker than the night, trotting alongside the pavement in the same direction as Joy was driving. A dog, he saw, black with white markings. A leash but no owner to hold it. Possibly it was the widow's dog. But where was the widow?

Joy slowed the Suburban as he gained ground on the dog. The dog continued on its way, oblivious to Joy's Suburban or ignoring it. It moved with a purpose, trotting at a steady pace, nose to the ground and hackles slightly raised, as though it knew the night was hostile, but meant to reach its destination regardless.

The dog moved with such purpose that Joy couldn't help but believe it really *was* the widow's animal. Perhaps they'd been separated in the earlier confusion. The dog had been lost. The dog seemed to know where it was going, anyhow. Joy resolved to follow. If he was lucky, the dog would lead him to the widow.

The dog trotted onward. Joy idled behind. He searched the night for any sign of the widow, and he let the dog lead him where it would.

Is this a mistake?

Mason walked the empty streets, searching for the dog. Passed a church and a cemetery, a boatyard full up with decrepit, rotting hulks. Every block he walked had more shadows, more places for Lucy to hide. Mason figured the dog must be too scared to run, must have squirreled down a hole somewhere, must be all but invisible.

Come on, he thought, peering out into the dark. *Come on, dog, show yourself. Come out of your hiding hole and let's haul ass for Dixie.*

He checked the time on his watch and saw that twenty minutes had passed, and he knew it was about time he found his way to the harbor. Knew Jess would leave without him if he didn't show in time.

Lord, lead me in your righteousness because of my foes, he thought. *Make your way straight before me.*

But Lucy still wasn't there when he looked up from his watch, and nothing on the street had moved or changed. And he didn't see any sign anywhere from any higher power that he ought to stay here or go to Jess, and he knew the decision was his to make, and his alone.

And he hoped he was making the right decision, if there was such a thing. He supposed he would find out soon enough.

Find a deep hole, girl, he thought. *Find a deep hole, and stay there until we come back for you.*

He squared his shoulders and turned to walk down to the harbor. And then he saw her.

FORTY

Lucy was a block away from Mason, moving east. South of where he stood, toward the hill and the highway, not the water. He watched her trot into the intersection and pause and sniff the ground, and he knew it was her, recognized the way she was running with her back in a hunch like she was scared, her nose low to the pavement and her tail tucked. Saw the leash dragging behind her and knew she was his dog, all right.

He started after Lucy, but she was already moving again. Continuing east toward Main Street, on a side road parallel to Mason's own, and before Mason could run to her or call out, she'd crossed the intersection and disappeared from view behind somebody's house.

Mason figured to cut her off. He cradled the shotgun and jogged east, past more quiet houses and trailers in various states of abandonment. He knew he should stay careful, stealthy, keep aware of his surroundings, but he didn't want to lose the dog again. There was a vacant lot at the end of the next block, and he imagined he could angle across it and get in front of Lucy.

He ran, the shotgun heavy in his arms and his heart pounding in his ears. Made the empty lot and ran through tall weeds and bare dirt, dodging refuse and varmint holes. Slipped in the mud and almost ate shit, but he managed to stay upright and didn't hardly lose speed. He cleared the lot and came out on the street where Lucy should have been, and she was right there where he expected, still trotting along on the other side of the street, heading for a destination Mason couldn't conceive of.

He called out to her and she stiffened, and he thought he'd spooked her again, but then she turned and saw it was him and her tail wagged and her ears relaxed, and she looked east again toward Main Street and then back at Mason, and then, cautiously, took a step in his direction.

Mason met her in the middle of the street. Took the lead from the ground behind her and wrapped it around his knuckles, scratched Lucy behind the ears and leaned down and let her lick his face, and he could feel her relief in the way she nuzzled against him, and he wondered if she could feel how he was relieved too.

And it was about that moment that Mason's focus expanded, and he became aware of the glare of the headlights and the roar of a Detroit motor as someone in a big black SUV bore down fast on them from the direction of Shelby Walker's place, to the west.

Joy pressed hard on the accelerator, closing the distance between his Suburban and the widow's friend and her dog. He'd let the dog lead him, and now Joy would reap the reward. He would use the ex-convict to lead him to the widow, and the widow would lead him to Okafor's missing product. Joy was certain he could convince both parties to cooperate.

But first he had to relieve the ex-convict of his shotgun. And perhaps the use of his legs.

Joy sped his vehicle toward man and dog, washing the criminal in the bright white of his high beams. The criminal had been fumbling with the dog's leash, but now he reached for the shotgun, swinging it toward the Suburban as the Suburban ate road. Joy didn't waver.

The Suburban would hit before the man could take aim. It would run the man over, maim him, kill the dog. Joy would interview the man as he lay bleeding in the street. Then he would kill him.

The man didn't have time to mount a credible defense. Joy kept his foot planted. Smiled as man and dog disappeared beneath the nose of the vehicle, and waited to hear their bodies break beneath his wheels.

There was no time for the shotgun. Mason grabbed Lucy, shoved her away from the truck, and then leapt clear himself, dodging the wheels but clipping his knee on the bumper, bouncing off hard and skidding across gritty asphalt.

Lucy was running again. This time her leash hobbled her; she stepped on it and stumbled in her haste to get clear. Mason pushed himself to his feet, grabbed the shotgun, ignored yesterday's aches and the fresh pain in his knee, and hurried after the dog as, behind him, the Suburban came to a hard stop. Mason reached the dog and took her lead in his hand without losing a step, without losing his grip on the shotgun. Dragged her off the street and up between two ratty trailers, heard a car door slam behind him and then footsteps as the driver gave chase.

Mason and Lucy cut between the trailers, reached a tangled and unkempt patch of grass in the back. He kept running, and Lucy figured out the game; she loped along beside him, then ahead, until she was dragging Mason forward and he was struggling to keep up.

They cleared the grassy patch and reached a tired shed at the edge of the property line and, beyond it, thin trees and a narrow, deep creek bed. Mason slowed Lucy before she could drop into the ditch, ducked behind the shed and raised the shotgun. Waited, listening for the sound of their pursuer.

He could kill this man now. Somehow Mason knew this was the man who'd murdered Shelby Walker. He'd wanted to shoot the man in the Walker backyard; now he would have his chance. Mason could hear the man approaching, hear him breathing. In seconds he would come around the side of the shed. Mason could put him down, easy.

You're a killer already, he thought, *in the eyes of the law.* But he knew there was a difference, and he wished he wouldn't ever have to find out what it was.

The man murdered Shelby Walker. He aims to kill you. But a shotgun would attract attention, wake people up and bring Kirby and his boys running. The shotgun would hamper Jess's ability to get to Dixie.

Mason tugged Lucy deeper behind the shed until they'd reached the far wall. Turned the corner and strained to hear if the driver had followed, if he'd kept running into the trees and down into the ditch.

Beside Mason, Lucy squirmed, and Mason said a silent prayer that the dog would keep from whining. She did.

Around the far side of the shed, branches rustled, and then Mason heard rocks give out and slide and splash as the driver found the ditch and the creek at the bottom. And he knew this was their chance.

He nudged Lucy back toward the twin trailers and the road beyond, and together they ran fast across the grass and between the trailers to where the Suburban sat waiting in the middle of the street. The engine was running, lights on. Mason dragged Lucy to the driver's side and hustled her into the cabin. Climbed in after her and shifted into drive and peeled away with the dog toward the harbor.

FORTY-ONE

Mason followed the sound of a little marine diesel as he navigated the government pier and the spindly wharves on the water beneath. He'd left the Suburban parked at the foot of the pier, but there was no way to avoid it; Jess would be itching to leave, with or without him and Lucy, and he could only hope he'd bought enough time for a clean getaway, the driver still mucking about five or six blocks behind.

The wharf was three fingers, lit with lemon-yellow sodium lights. A handful of boats, and none of them looking seaworthy but one, tied up halfway down the last finger. Barely forty feet long, a rounded-off stern with paint peeling from the hull, a little cockpit where you'd stand to work the trolling lines. Ahead of the cockpit was a large box with a hatch on top that Mason surmised must access the fishhold, and beyond that was the wheelhouse, a squat, salt-stained structure that didn't look much bigger than Mason's living quarters in the state penitentiary. The wheelhouse windows were salt streaked; there was a tag taped to one, an outdated halibut license, and on the bow faded block letters read BETTER DAYS, and if that wasn't a misnomer, Mason figured he didn't know the meaning of the word.

But the engine was chugging, the stack belching black smoke. This was Ty's boat, and Jess was waiting. She stepped out from the wheelhouse as Mason and Lucy hurried down the dock. Took in

Mason, and then Lucy, and he thought he could see she was glad they'd both made it.

But there wasn't any time for happy reunions. Jess took the shotgun from Mason and laid it on the fishhold. Then she reached over and helped him lift Lucy aboard, the dog grunting and struggling as though the whole operation were a personal affront to her dignity.

Then Jess climbed over the boat's gunwale and onto the dock. She bent down to free the tie-up line amidships and gestured toward the bow.

"Cut her loose and then push the bow out," she told him. "Don't get left behind. I'm not coming back for you."

Mason did as instructed. Loosened the bow line as Jess freed the stern. He chucked the rope over the troller's raised bulwarks, then leaned on the boat and pushed, swinging the bow out from its berth as Jess climbed aboard and went into the wheelhouse.

He kept pushing until he heard her knock on the window, and then he hurried aft to where the stern still nudged against the dock. Stepped aboard and flashed Jess a thumbs-up through the wheelhouse doorway, heard the engine throttle up in response, the propeller churning wash as the boat slipped away.

"Made it," he said when he entered the wheelhouse. It was warm inside, smelled of engine oil and kerosene and old clothes. On one side of the little room was a sink and a stove, a couple of cupboards, and on the other side was a table and a little three-sided settee. Up ahead was the captain's chair, a panel of ancient electronics, the wheel and the throttle and the gear selector. There was a hole in the floor in a forward corner of the wheelhouse, same side as the stove, stairs leading downward.

Jess stood at the wheel, navigating the boat out from between the wharf fingers, aiming it across the harbor to the end of the rocky breakwater, where red and green buoys marked a channel to open water.

"I was beginning to think you all weren't coming," she said.

Mason found Lucy curled up in a corner of the settee, snoring already, her brush with danger tonight apparently forgotten. He scratched her behind the ears and sat down beside her.

"Wouldn't have missed it," he told Jess. "Just figured the dog needed a walk before we cooped her up on this boat."

On the government wharf, Joy stood in the shadows and watched as the lights of the little fishing boat rounded the breakwater. The night was nearly pitch dark, but he could tell nevertheless when the boat had cleared the harbor; the lights on the mast began to rock with the swell as the boat motored out of sheltered waters and into the open strait. It plowed the waves and turned westward, carrying Jess Winslow and her companion with it.

The man and the dog had abandoned the Suburban by the time Joy reached the pier. But that was no matter. He'd hurried to the truck and heard the sound of a diesel engine in the boat basin below, and he'd known what the widow and the man planned to do.

He might have tried to intercept them, but he didn't. He'd waited, hidden on the margins, away from the dim yellow sodium lights, and stared down at the little harbor's three fingers, the derelict hulks moored therein.

For a few minutes he didn't see anything. And then one of the hulks had moved, its propeller churning water, and Joy had watched as the little boat slipped away from the dock and out toward the breakwater.

The widow and her friend were gone now, and Joy wondered

if he would regret not acting more assertively. He doubted it. Jess Winslow and her companion were on board a boat, a boat Joy could still see, those lights rocking in the black distance as the vessel bucked the waves.

The boat was headed west. That was all Joy needed to know.

FORTY-TWO

Jess would never have told Burke, but she was glad that he'd come. And it wasn't just that he'd somehow brought Lucy back, or that she suspected she was going to need someone else to shoot back at Kirby Harwood when the time came. It was something else, too, something deeper than all of that.

And that scared her.

Something had changed between them, though Jess wasn't ready to acknowledge what it was. There was a familiarity now, an unspoken intimacy, and whether it was the events of the day or simply the relief from watching Burke bring Lucy down the dock just then, Jess felt like they'd established something. No longer did she feel like she was fighting alone, like Burke was some guy who happened to share her enemies. If Burke had come this far, stuck around when he could have run, boarded this boat with her, he was all in, just as she was, and even if he'd been that way for a while, now was the first time she could actually *feel* it. She trusted him.

You trusted Afia. Afia trusted you.

She could feel real life disappearing again. The memories coming back, taking her into the valley again, hunkered in the OP under RPG fire, or out on some routine patrol—tired, hungry, unwashed, on edge—and this time she knew how it ended, all of it.

She was exhausted; that was part of it. She'd gone longer with less sleep in more trying circumstances, sure, plenty of times overseas. But apparently she'd gone soft since she'd come stateside; a couple of days of being hunted and she was pretty well spent. Now she was crashing. The adrenaline was gone, and there was nothing to do. The boat motored forward, into the swell, and she could do nothing but stand at the wheel and drink coffee and wait for the morning to come.

But it wasn't just fatigue. It was déjà vu. It was that feeling of kinship, partnership, of liking somebody and putting your life in his power, and him putting his life in yours. It was the fear that she would mess this up again, like she'd messed up with Afia and with Ty, and almost with Lucy. That because of her, Burke would get hurt.

He's a grown man. He chose to be here. If he gets hurt, it's his own fault.

Maybe. But wasn't he also just a few days out of prison? Wasn't he, in many ways, still learning how the world worked after fifteen years inside? She couldn't shake the sense that she'd dragged him into this mess, that she was responsible for him now, and that, inevitably, she would fail in that responsibility.

She felt guilty that she was glad he was here.

So Jess tried not to be happy that Burke stayed awake with her, standing by the controls with his coffee in his hand, staring out at the night ahead, his legs braced against the swell rolling up the strait from the open ocean. She tried not to fixate on Burke's proximity to her in the small cabin, the scent of soap and his sweat, the bulge of his muscles through his shirt. She tried to think about what happened next, what needed to be done—gaining access to Dixie, then finding Ty's stash, then what? Returning it to Kirby? Calling the Feds?

She would think about that. She would think it through, instead of thinking about Afghanistan, watching Afia die. About how it could all happen again.

Beside her, Burke shifted. "You want to talk about it?" he asked her.

He must have caught the expression on her face, because he was frowning, his eyes soft, like he was trying to look gentle. And for a moment she considered being honest with him, unloading everything on him, just to see how he took it.

I'm going to hurt you, Burke. Worse than you've ever been hurt in your life.

But then she thought better of it.

She shook her head. Sipped her coffee. "No," she told him. "I don't."

The sun rose behind them as they continued west, just a dim glow at first behind the clouds on the far eastern horizon, and then, suddenly, a burst of dazzling light, casting warmth over the water and turning the troller's foamy wash golden. In her peripheral vision Jess watched as Burke walked to the Dutch door at the rear of the wheelhouse, opened the top half, and peered out across the stern, watching the sun climb over the clouds and the faint hint of land that lay many miles behind them.

"Might actually be a pretty good day," he told Jess as he came back to the controls, rubbing his hands together for warmth. "Still cold as heck, though."

"It's always cold on the open water," she replied. "Even in the middle of summer, it's cold. But we'll be turning back inland soon enough."

She felt deadened by lack of sleep, clumsy and numb. Far from rejuvenating her, the sun's return only served to make her more tired, as if inviting her to join Lucy on the settee, curl up and cuddle, take a nap for a while and let her worries slip away.

The dog certainly didn't seem bothered. She'd been asleep

since they rounded the breakwater, curled up in a pretzel in the far corner of the wheelhouse. Jess didn't think Lucy had ever been on a boat before, but the dog didn't seem to care; it was warm in the wheelhouse, and there was somewhere cozy to sleep, and sleeping was pretty well how Lucy solved all of her problems.

Close your eyes and pretend it's all okay. Pretend you're somewhere else, somewhere far away. Pretend there's no one chasing you, and no one wants you dead.

Pretend you have no reason to be scared.

They'd passed the lights of Neah Bay in the night, off to port, and as the day found them, Jess could see Tatoosh Island up ahead, the northwestern end of contiguous America. There was a Coast Guard light there, to guide the big cargo ships out of the open seas and into the Strait of Juan de Fuca, point them down toward Seattle and Tacoma, and Vancouver, Canada.

Ty's freighter had come in through here. Whoever'd made the drop had hailed Kirby as the ship passed that light on Tatoosh, and Shelby Walker had intercepted the message and passed it along to Ty, who'd disabled Kirby's boat and set out in his stead, sealing his fate and Shelby Walker's, too.

Jess wasn't headed as far as Tatoosh. There was a bay on the northeastern tip of the cape, just before the mainland petered off into water. A place called Mushroom Rock. And just off that bay, about a mile from the rock, the island called Dixie sat lonely and uninhabited, the smallest of specks on anyone's map.

It was a mile in circumference, maybe. Rock and a few trees, a little beach on the western side facing open water. Ty had brought her to the beach once they'd anchored in the cove, rowed them to shore in the troller's rubber dinghy. He'd brought a bottle of wine and a basket of sandwiches; she could tell he was trying to be romantic, and it *was* romantic, even with the wind blowing and the sand getting everywhere, gritty and painful, as they lay on the picnic blanket and tried to make out.

She'd thought it was paradise, even with the sand and the wind. She hadn't been able to believe her good luck.

The island was shaped like a letter *C,* the rocky shore curling around Dixie Lagoon like a protective embrace.

"You could hide out here through the worst weather imaginable," Ty had bragged once they'd set the anchor in the calm waters inside. "Hide out from everything, for as long as you wanted."

She hadn't been able to imagine ever wanting to hide out, needing to hide out, not back then. She was in love; she was happy; she was going to be a marine—a combat marine, not some pretender behind the lines. She'd imagined she and Ty would come back to Dixie, not to hide out from the world but to celebrate. She had imagined they would grow older and it would always be their spot.

She had never come back, not after that first day. And as she'd grown older, the island and those memories had disappeared from her mind.

They were approaching the bay, and Jess could see Dixie Island now, distinguished from the deep-green, featureless shore behind. It was a quarter to eight in the morning, the sun getting higher in the sky, and by the time she maneuvered the boat to the head of the pass, she wouldn't have much grace before slack water.

"You awake?" she asked Burke, who was leaning on the edge of the captain's chair where it met the front of the settee. Burke looked alert; he looked ready. Clearly, the sun was having a different impact on him.

"I'm awake," he said, straightening. "What's the plan?"

She pointed forward through the windows. Dixie lay dead ahead, though she couldn't see the pass yet, just a wall of rock and trees.

"We're going in there," she said, "and we don't have time to mess around. I need you up on the bow watching where we're going. If you see any rocks, you holler, and loud, understand?"

He nodded. "Yes, ma'am."

"We only get one shot at this. There's no road over there on the mainland, not close, and the current's too strong to swim or paddle. We wreck, we're stuck out here until someone comes out and finds us, and with our luck, it'll probably be Kirby."

"So we won't wreck," he said, and squared his shoulders, started back toward the door. "C'mon, Lucy," he said, and as he whistled, the dog sat up, stretched and yawned, and followed him out to the deck.

Jess watched them circle up the side of the wheelhouse to the bow, where they stood among the anchor winch and the tie-up lines, the stay wires leading up to the mast. Lucy peered over the bow, peered down to the water, her ears perked and curious. Burke gripped a stay wire like an old-time pirate, one foot on the anchor winch, his eyes searching the shore.

It would have been a charming picture under any other circumstance.

As it was, Jess didn't have time to be charmed. They motored toward Dixie, the pass slowly coming into view, just a break in the rocks, impossibly narrow, invisible unless you knew what you were looking for.

It was twenty after eight now. No time to get scared. Jess dug out Hank Moss's chart and the tide table, spread them out before her. Knocked on the front window and signaled to Burke as she idled the troller closer to the wall of rocks and white water.

Time to go.

FORTY-THREE

Mason looked out over the water at the tiny gap in the rocks and wondered how on earth Jess thought she was going to fit the troller through. The cliffs closed in around them, waves breaking white over jagged black, the pass barely twice as wide as the little boat and studded with more rock—cruel, unflinching obstacles—on both sides. Some peeked out over the high-tide waterline. The rest were visible only by the way the flood tide dappled and whirled as it passed overtop of them, invisible undersea mines just waiting to cripple the boat.

Jess kept the troller inching forward, the diesel engine at a low grumble, until the boat rested barely two lengths from the rocky threshold. She poked her head out the starboard window, called up to Mason.

"How's the tide running?" she asked.

He peered over the bow. Beside him, Lucy did too. There was water flowing into the pass, but not much of it. The tide licked at the rocks and at the lowest of the trees that clung to the shore.

"Looks slow," he reported back, though he really had no frame of reference. "Looks manageable."

Jess looked dubious, like she'd just remembered he was a Michigan guy, likely hadn't seen a high tide in his life. But she had no choice but to take his word for it; the dog wasn't hazarding an opinion.

"I'm going to take it slow," she said. "You keep your eyes up ahead, let me know if I'm going to run us up onto the rocks."

He nodded. "Roger."

"You see me heading into trouble, you holler at me, Burke."

"Yes, ma'am," he said. "Whenever you're ready."

She peered out at the pass another moment or two, at the waves on the rocks to both sides of the little gap. Then he watched her retreat back into the wheelhouse, watched her through the front window as she gripped the wheel with her left hand, pushed up on the throttle with the other.

The boat motored forward. Mason hunched over at the very forepeak, gripping the anchor chain and hoping he didn't fall in. The waves carried the boat as it neared the rocks; he could see vast patches of kelp on either side too, and he imagined the thick growth would wreak hell on the propeller if Jess wandered into the middle of it.

He guided her with his hands, like she was backing a truck or maybe parking an airplane. Lined her up at the entrance and gave her the thumbs-up, all good, and then he joined Lucy in staring down at the ocean. The water was shallower now, clearer, the rocks looming like ghosts from the murky depths.

Jess kept the boat on a steady path. They crossed the threshold, the twin rocky shoals on either side, and the low cliffs closed in around them, the trees high above. But Mason hardly noticed the trees. He saw how this passage would work only at high tide; anything lower, and the narrow gap would be littered with rocks, like rapids. He wondered how low the boat sat in the water, how high a rock would have to be before it put a hole in the hull.

He guided her around a big one, stout and mean, off to port—Jess edging the boat clear until the starboard rail nearly touched the cliff over there. Got her back into the middle of the pass quickly;

there were more obstacles up ahead. And after they'd gone about fifty feet, the pass doglegged to the right, and there was more plotting to be done.

The tide had slackened, which was a good thing. Soon it would kick up again, on the ebb this time, pushing against the troller and draining the water from under her keel.

Mason could see the lagoon up ahead now, another hundred feet or so—tantalizingly close—but he knew they had a minefield to run before they got there, and they really had only one chance to run it. He had to plan his moves in advance, look beyond the first rock to a path through the next. Reversing in this tight passage would be near impossible. Mason didn't want to have to tell Jess she was going to have to try it.

Slowly Jess moved the boat forward. She followed Mason's instructions quickly and without question; he could feel the engine rumble when he motioned her forward, and he could sense the rudder turn almost before he'd made the gesture. She was good with the boat, and he didn't want to let her down.

The tide had fully turned when they were thirty feet from safe water. The water was flowing past the bow of the boat, slow at first but picking up speed, inexorable. Driftwood and detritus slipped past, the water whirlpooling around more submerged rocks. Mason watched and felt powerless. Wished he could do something to urge the boat faster, but he knew Jess was working as fast as she could, and better than he ever would.

Three minutes later it was over. Mason stood straight and gestured forward, felt the engine throttle up, and the *Better Days* motored into the lagoon Jess called Dixie.

It was a beautiful little spot, peaceful and idyllic, a couple hundred feet in diameter and ringed by dense forest. To the west, through a thin patch of trees, Mason could see blue sky and water;

he could hear the waves crashing. Inside the lagoon the water was calm. There was no wind, no sound but the surf and the purr of the diesel engine. Somewhere in the trees, a raven called.

Jess stuck her head out the starboard window again. "You want to drop the hook for me?"

"Yes, ma'am," he replied. "What does that mean?"

She rolled her eyes. "The anchor, Burke. Drop the anchor, so I can shut her down for a while."

He let the anchor go, watched it splash, the chain unspooling from the winch behind him. Lucy jumped back at the noise, suspicious, then crept forward to sniff at the winch, eyeing the moving chain warily.

"That should be good," Jess called, and Mason tightened the brake, slowed the chain and locked the winch, waited as Jess tested the anchor's hold with the throttle. Finally she nodded, and he slapped Lucy on her big butt and pushed her down the passageway to the stern.

"Come on, girl. Looks like we're here."

Jess was down in the engine room when Mason and Lucy came back into the wheelhouse. The sun was shining outside still, and the wheelhouse seemed almost too warm now, though Mason would have laughed at that notion yesterday. He dug out some jerky from the lockers for Lucy, had her sit for it, tried High Five and settled for Shake a Paw, gave the dog some jerky and a bowl full of kibble as Jess shut the engine down and the whole boat shuddered into silence.

When Jess came back up to the wheelhouse, she'd stripped off her jacket. She stopped on the third step and looked at him. "Listen, I'm pretty beat," she said. "I'm going to need to sack out for a few before we go find this package."

Mason was glad she'd suggested it. He was tired too, but you try admitting that to a decorated marine. "You sure we have time?"

"That package will wait," she said. "I have a pretty good idea where Ty would have hid it, and the island isn't that big if I'm wrong. We sleep a couple hours, we'll still have plenty of time to get our search in before high slack tomorrow. Can't move this boat until then anyhow."

"Yeah, all right," Mason said. "I could stand a rest too. You want to switch off?"

She shrugged. "I sleep pretty light, Burke. You want to catch some z's, go ahead." She gestured down the stairs. "I'm going to sleep down here, in my bunk. If you fiddle with that galley table, take the legs off, you can fit it down against the settee, make a bed."

"I don't need much," he said.

"I'm glad to hear it," she replied. "Because we don't have much. Get a couple hours in you, and then we'll rig up the dinghy and go looking for trouble."

She disappeared belowdecks again, and Mason watched her go, listened to her move around the fo'c'sle of the boat. Then he turned his attention to the galley table, managed to get the legs off, turn it into a bed. He spread the cushions over the hard surface, saved a cushion for his head, climbed aboard and lay there and stared up at the ceiling. It was a funny feeling, lying there, the boat rocking gently on the water, the sun outside and nothing but nature all around him. He couldn't hear Jess anymore, figured she'd fallen asleep.

He stared out the window, at the thin patch of trees to the west, the blue sky and open sea beyond, the treetops swaying with a wind that didn't make it down into the lagoon. He thought about Kirby Harwood and the other men with him, thought about Shelby Walker and the gunshots he'd heard from inside that house. He and

Jess had probably bought themselves some time, heading out in the boat, but now that it was daylight, Kirby and his buddies were going to find the Suburban at the pier and notice the boat missing, and they weren't so stupid as to miss what that meant.

Mason thought about this, and he thought about the strange man with Harwood. He thought about what came next, and what remained to be done before this whole miserable saga was over.

He lay there and stared up at the ceiling and thought about it, and after a while he stood and went out to the afterdeck and came back inside with Jess's shotgun. He laid the shotgun down on the bed beside him and closed his eyes, and slept for a while.

FORTY-FOUR

Jess couldn't sleep.

Not down here, in the tiny fo'c'sle of the boat, two bunks angled along the curve of the hull to the point of the bow. Not with the waves lapping in her ears, the anchor chain groaning. Not here, where everything smelled like Ty.

It was dark and the air was still; there was nothing to do but lie alone and think, nobody to chase and nobody to run from, no one to shoot and no car to drive. No plan to refine, even; they would take the dinghy ashore, and they would search for the package. And if Kirby and his buddies showed up, she and Burke would deal with that. There was no sense worrying about it now. They would handle Kirby when Kirby needed handling.

Right now nothing needed handling, nothing but self-care and sleep. And Jess was a lot better at planning and shooting than she was at taking care of her messed-up mental health.

She could close her eyes, sure, snuggle into Ty's old sleeping bag, and feel the boat gently rock on its anchor. She could try to pace her breathing, try to think about nothing. She could practice mindfulness the way her old shrink had recommended. It didn't matter, not really. All it took was one little hint, one reminder, and then her mind was gone again, chasing its own tail into a whirlpool of dark thoughts and violent memories. No matter how hard she tried to fight it, that whirlpool dragged her down, pulled her under, choked off her air.

And when it spat her out again, she was back in the valley. Back there with Afia on that final, bloody day.

It was three days after the ambush before Afia reappeared outside the barbed wire, staggering up the road to the OP, blind in one eye and nearly blind in the other, covered in so much blood it was impossible to tell where it all was coming from. Her face was bruised almost black; she cradled her left arm. She was crying, or trying to; no sound came from her lips. Jess had heard shouts from the guys at the gate, yelling at Afia, telling her to stop, stop, or they'd have to shoot. Jess had come forward to see what the commotion was about, ready to back up her guys, then saw Afia and blacked out and started running, fought her way past the guards at the gate and out through the barbed wire, everyone yelling behind her, ducking for cover, thinking those Haji bastards had strapped a bomb on Afia, sent her back to the OP for one big fuck-you.

At that point Jess didn't care; Haji could blow them both up, for all it mattered. This was her friend, and yet it wasn't. They'd robbed her of something before giving her back.

As Jess ran closer, she could see the stump where Afia's left hand used to be, cradled in the crook of her right arm like that baby. She could see Afia's knees give out, watched her fall to the road, and then she heard the shot ring out from across the valley, and Afia pitched forward.

There was no bomb. The fuck-you was personal; they'd sent her back to the OP to show off what they'd done to her, cut her down before she could get to the wire, some Haji sniper lodged somewhere in the forest on the east side of the valley. He'd probably been watching the whole time, just waiting for Afia to get close to the OP to make the kill really hurt. She'd never stood a chance.

Afia was dead by the time Jess got to her, facedown in the dirt and the rocks, and Jess barely had a chance to roll her over, faceup, see the damage they'd done close and firsthand, and then her guys were on top of her, dragging her back to the wire, four of them risking their lives to save hers, and Jess fighting like hell every step of the way.

That was Afia, how Jess's cruel mind remembered her. Facedown in the dirt, bleeding into the dust, abandoned by the Americans she'd worked for and befriended. The Americans for whom she'd given her life.

Fuck this. Jess kicked the sleeping bag away, swung her legs out of the bunk and dropped to the floor of the fo'c'sle. She felt her way to the stairs, not sure yet what she was doing but imagining it was probably a bad idea, and knowing all the same that she couldn't stay down here in the dark by herself any longer.

FORTY-FIVE

Lucy stood and stretched as Jess climbed the stairs to the wheelhouse, and then shook herself off, the tags on her collar jangling. Burke sat up and looked at the dog and saw the dog looking at Jess.

"I can't sleep," she told him. "I'm going to try and sleep up here, if that's okay with you."

She could see how Burke was trying not to stare at her bare legs—she was wearing a long T-shirt over her underwear—and she wondered if he was nervous or just being polite, if he was interested in her or he wasn't.

And she wondered if she was really interested in him, or if she was simply desperate for human contact, someone to touch and comfort and be afraid with, and she wondered if there was a difference and if it really mattered.

Burke made to stand. "Yeah, okay," he said, still not really looking at her. "I can sleep down there."

She shook her head. "What good is that going to do me, Burke?"

Now he had to look at her, and she held his gaze and studied his face, and she realized that she was nervous, too, that this brave and decent man who'd found his way into her life wasn't desperate for contact the way she was desperate, wasn't feeling that same intimacy she'd felt on the dock, wouldn't believe she was someone worth letting down his guard for.

And she was afraid, too, that if he *did* feel that intimacy, and if they gave in to it, Burke would wind up just like Afia and Ty. But she was more afraid of loneliness now, even though she knew it was the wiser course, and she looked at Burke and waited for him to say something and hoped he would let her into his bed.

"I don't want to be alone right now," she said. "I can't. So can you just lie back down with me and not make a big deal out of this?"

Burke blinked, like he knew that she knew it really was a big deal. "Sure," he said. "No problem. No big deal at all."

He lay back down on the little makeshift bed, edged over to the window, and lifted the thin blanket for Jess to join him. She lay down beside him, turned her back, and rested on her side, facing the stove and the sink, her knees hugged up close to her chest.

Lucy watched them both for a moment or two. Then she grumbled and circled a couple of times and collapsed into a pretzel on the carpeted floor.

Behind Jess, Burke lay still as plywood, and she could tell he was trying not to touch her, trying to give her space. Trying to be polite and decent and accommodating when that's not what she wanted at all.

"Will you hold me?" she asked without moving.

Burke hesitated again, but then he inched closer to her, slipped his arm under her pillow, and the other around her waist, and Jess snuggled back into him. She tried to think of the last time she'd done this, just been held by someone, and she knew it must have been Ty, but she couldn't remember. Ty hadn't been much for cuddling, not toward the end—or maybe that was her fault. After what she'd seen in the valley, after what she'd lost, Jess hadn't wanted to be close to anyone for a long while.

She suspected Burke hadn't been this close to a woman for a long, long time either, and she could tell how her proximity was having its effect. She pushed back against him, slipped her legs against his, and she could feel him getting hard against her, and she knew that she should leave now, go back into the fo'c'sle and pretend this had never happened, keep some distance between the two of them so nobody would get hurt. But she didn't.

She reached back and pulled him closer again, reached around with her arm and found him with her hand, and he groaned a little bit and took her hand, lifted it away. "You don't want to do that," he said.

She pressed her butt back against him. "Sure I do," she said, and she did, and she wanted it to be now, and she wanted it to be Burke.

"No, you don't," he said. "I don't want to take advantage. It wouldn't be right."

"Burke." She rolled over to face him, frustrated. "I'm a grown-ass woman. The last thing I need is some man telling me what I shouldn't want to do." She slid her hand down between them, found his cock. "Anyway, it seems like I'm the one taking advantage here. Though it doesn't exactly feel like you mind all that much."

Burke closed his eyes at her touch, and she could see that he did want this, as much as she did or maybe more.

But she needed to hear him say it.

She drew her hand back, waited until he'd opened his eyes. Until he'd reached for her, almost shyly, and she'd held his hand still.

"Are you okay with this?" she asked.

"It's been a long while," he told her. "Hell, I can't even remember the last time . . ."

He trailed off. She waited. His hand brushed her bare hip and she could see how his breathing quickened, and when he reached for her again, she let him pull her closer.

"I want this," he said, breathing rough. "I just don't want to disappoint you—"

She shut him up with her lips, pressed them hard to his. Slid her hand down beneath his shorts and took him in her hand fully and felt his body respond to her touch.

"Shut up," she said, and she kissed him again. "It's like riding a bicycle, Burke. Just relax."

It didn't last long.

Jess shucked her shirt and pulled Mason's over his shoulders, and then her mouth was on his again, and her tongue, and Mason closed his eyes and kissed her back, hungrily, felt her body move on top of his and his body respond, and Jess was right, mostly—he hadn't forgotten how, though it had been nearly half of his life since he'd done this.

He'd spent fifteen years waiting, and it was over too soon. Mason held out as long as he could, and then he couldn't anymore, and when it was over and she was climbing down from on top of him, he reached for her, not wanting to deny her the same as she'd given him, but she took his hands instead, stilled them, and nudged them gently away.

"I'm sorry," he said, and Jess groaned and rolled her eyes.

"Never apologize to a woman after sex," she told him. "Nobody wants to hear 'sorry' after they just hooked up."

"But you didn't—"

"I didn't want to, Burke," she said. "That's not what this is about."

She lay back beside him and stared up at the ceiling, and he edged over to make room and looked out at the lagoon and the island beyond.

"Why?" he asked after a while.

Jess let it sit there a moment. "Use it in a sentence?"

"Why us?" he asked. "Why right now?"

She rolled onto her side, propped herself up on her elbow, the blanket falling away from her body. "Are you complaining?"

"No," he said, still watching the water.

"But you still want to know why." She sighed and lay back again, studied the ceiling some more. "Okay, Burke, I'll tell you. But you might not like the answer."

He said, "I don't mind."

"I was lying down there in my bunk, thinking about a whole bunch of shit I didn't really want to think about," Jess said. "But this isn't the kind of shit I can just forget, either. Not any way that I know of, at least, and I'm about sick of trying."

"So this was a distraction."

She glanced over at him. "We're probably going to die, Burke," she said. "I don't know what you're thinking about this whole mess we're in, but to me, I can't see us walking away if those guys do too. This isn't the kind of disagreement that gets resolved peacefully."

He said nothing. He figured she was right, figured he'd known it for a while. He wasn't ready to give the game away to Kirby Harwood, though, not yet.

"I don't necessarily have a problem with dying," Jess continued, in a voice that could have convinced Mason she was telling him the truth. "But if it's going to happen, I'll be damned if I'm going to spend my last days on Earth reliving all the foul shit I've seen. There's better things I can do with my time, and as best I can tell, you shared my enthusiasm."

He nodded. "I wish I could have given you a better time of it, though."

"Hell," she said, "I haven't been this close to a man who knew more about me than my first name and adult beverage of choice since Ty washed up under that dock. If I'm dying tomorrow, at least I can say my last time was with somebody who actually gave a damn."

"Gave a damn," Mason said. "About what?"

"About *anything,* Burke," she said, exasperated. "About Lucy. About me. About doing the right thing. You might be dumber than a box of rocks for sticking around in this mess, but at least you're man enough to stand up for something. That matters a hell of a lot more than if you can give me a good ride for a couple, three minutes."

He laughed. "That might even be generous."

"Mason Burke." She rolled her eyes at him. "You've got to get over yourself, dude. Look around."

He did.

"We're on a deserted island. You want to make something up to me, you've got plenty of time."

She was still making like she was annoyed with him, but there was something playful in her eyes, and a warmth besides that Mason hadn't seen before. She tilted her head up toward him, and this time he knew that she wanted to be kissed. He kissed her, slow, rolled over and pulled her closer to him.

Beside the settee, Lucy grumbled, stood up, and retreated down into the fo'c'sle—but at that point neither Mason nor Jess had any inclination to care.

FORTY-SIX

Kirby Harwood stared at the helicopter and wondered yet again how he'd taken so many wrong turns in his life.

Okafor's man, Joy, had been waiting when Harwood and his men had finished filling out the paperwork for the Shelby Walker shooting. There was a shit ton of it too, took Harwood until dawn to get things squared away. And then Joy was waiting outside the detachment in that Suburban of his, spinning some yarn about Jess and her boyfriend had escaped on a boat.

There was no good way to spin what had happened last night. Harwood had sent a statement to Sheriff Kirk Wheeler in Neah Bay, and he knew there was a better-than-good chance that the state police would get involved, investigate the whole deal. Harwood had talked to the neighborhood, run through the official account—Shelby shooting first and all—and the neighborhood, by and large, had taken his word as gospel. Harwood had decent dirt on just about everyone on the block, and he knew for a fact there were a couple of households with outstanding warrants in Clallam County next door.

Nobody would cross the sheriff's chief deputy, not to stick up for some tramp and her invalid mom. But if they *did,* Harwood knew he was screwed. And just that thought alone was giving him a bad case of situational acid reflux.

And now the goddamn helicopter.

They were standing on an airfield near Port Angeles—Harwood, Joy, Cole Sweeney, and the pilot, a stocky man in a leather jacket and a big, bushy mustache who looked more like a cop than anything else. They'd left Dale behind in Deception Cove to keep order, though if a Whitmer boy ever kept order in his life, Kirby had yet to hear about it.

Mostly, Harwood figured it was because Joy had spattered Bryce Whitmer's brains all over the family kitchen. The shooter probably didn't trust Dale not to do something silly in the aftermath, and justifiably so. If Kirby knew his deputy, Dale would find a way to make things right—even if it fucked the whole lot of them with the Nigerians.

"They sailed west," Joy was saying. "I watched them go. You and your men were occupied, but no matter. We'll find them."

There was something absurd about using a helicopter to recover eight hundred grand's worth of product—though, granted, that was the wholesale price. But Harwood figured it wasn't about the product anymore; this was a grudge match for Joy and Okafor as much as it was for the Deception Cove deputies. It was just that Okafor had a bigger imagination.

"We'll have the helicopter for two hours," Joy continued. "The price will come out of your end, of course."

"Of course," Harwood agreed, though Joy didn't look like he was waiting for agreement.

"We'll find them. We will kill them. And we will recover the product." Joy looked at Harwood, looked at Sweeney. "Any questions?"

Neither Harwood nor Sweeney answered, but Sweeney sure looked like he was having second thoughts. Joy picked up on it. "Something you'd like to say, Deputy?"

Sweeney went red. Kicked at the tarmac and averted his gaze, like he, too, was wondering how he'd wound up in this spot.

"It's just one lousy shipment," he said finally. "You couldn't just, you know, write it off? Cost of doing business? You all look like you're gearing up for a *war* right now."

Joy studied the young deputy. Harwood waited, hardly daring to breathe, his right hand slipping down toward his holster just in case the drug man decided to get cute.

"One shipment, yes," Joy replied. "One stolen shipment, and on its face, only a minor inconvenience to an organization like ours, yes?"

"Well, yeah," Sweeney said.

"But an organization like this one has competitors, enemies," Joy continued. "Ambitious men who'd like nothing more than to seize Ateke Okafor's position at any sign of weakness. A stolen package, a missed delivery: these men wait to see how Okafor reacts. Is he a man who will tolerate incompetence? Is he a man who will brook *thievery* of any kind?"

Sweeney opened his mouth to reply. Joy waved him silent.

"This is more than one shipment, Deputy Sweeney," Joy told him. "To Ateke Okafor—and, if you're smart, to you and your colleagues as well." He straightened. "Are there any other concerns?"

There were no other concerns.

Joy produced his car keys and pressed a button on the fob. The Suburban chirped, and the back gate opened slowly. There were boxes inside, hard plastic cases. Joy crossed to the truck, reached in, and opened the first box, and Harwood saw a couple of rifles inside, packed in protective foam.

Joy studied them for a moment. Then he closed the box, latched it, lifted it out of the truck. "Bring the others," he told Harwood.

Harwood and Sweeney did as instructed. Each brought a box to the open sliding door of the helicopter, where Joy took them and placed them inside. The pilot was already aboard, the engine spooling up. Joy climbed into the chopper, gestured for the deputies to follow.

"Come," he said. "The clock is ticking."

Which clock he meant was unclear. But as the helicopter's engines roared to life, and the rotors began to spin, Harwood decided the shooter could have been counting down for the helicopter, for Jess Winslow and Mason Burke, or for Kirby Harwood and Cole Sweeney and Dale Whitmer themselves, and all would have been accurate.

The clock was ticking. Somehow, Harwood knew, this would all be over soon.

FORTY-SEVEN

Jess and Burke didn't sleep much, though they didn't try very hard, and it was early afternoon by the time they stepped back out on deck, the air cool and refreshing after the stuffy warmth of the wheelhouse. Lucy followed them out, nosed around the back hatch, steadfastly ignoring both Jess and Burke like she held a grudge over what she'd just been forced to witness.

Burke went up onto the roof of the wheelhouse and untied the three-person rigid inflatable skiff that Ty had kept stored by the dodger. He tied a rope to the bow and eased it over the starboard side of the wheelhouse, where Jess was waiting to help guide it down to the water. When the skiff was in the water, Burke handed down the rope, and Jess walked it toward the stern and tied it off, left the skiff to bob alongside the troller as she and Burke gathered supplies.

They didn't talk about what they'd done. But they didn't *not* talk about it, exactly; Jess could have predicted that Burke wasn't the type to pour out his heart to a girl after he'd slept with her, but she could sense his mood in how his fingers traced her skin and how he smiled, self-conscious, when his eyes lingered on hers a half second too long. She didn't regret what they'd done, and she could tell Burke didn't either, though in the back of her mind that fear still remained, that she'd just dragged him deeper into the hole that would bury him, that by giving in to her impulses, she'd ensured he would never escape.

She pushed the thought from her mind and tried to focus on what came next.

They filled the skiff with supplies: tools for digging, enough food from the galley's lockers to last a night onshore, warm clothes and blankets, matches for a fire. Jess had a good idea where Ty had hidden the package, but she decided it was better to plan ahead. They had a whole island to search, and the quicker they could cover ground, the better.

They brought the guns, too: Hank Moss's supply, Jess's shotgun, the pistol Burke had bought from Rengo in the woods.

"We'll stick you with the shotgun," Jess told Burke. "Easier to hit something at close quarters, and you look like you could handle the kick."

He nodded, stoic as ever. "You mind giving me some pointers with those pistols?"

She could have fallen in love right there. Not that she particularly cared about teaching him to shoot a gun, but because he had the balls to ask. She hadn't known many men who'd feel comfortable taking shooting lessons from a woman, and she'd known a hell of a lot of guys who couldn't shoot half as well as she could.

"Of course I don't mind," she told him, handing Moss's bag of guns down to him in the skiff. "We get to the island, I'll set you up with some targets. We'll make an Annie Oakley out of you yet."

Lucy wasn't sure about the rowboat, but they got her aboard. Jess hoisted her up to the gunwale, forklift style, and passed her off to Burke as she squirmed and snorted her complaints, Burke nearly swamping the boat, the whole process extremely undignified.

Jess laughed as Burke set Lucy down and the dog struggled to the bow of the boat, where she collapsed in a heap and stared back at them, traumatized. Burke steadied the boat, stood and held out his hand for her, and Jess rolled her eyes and passed down the oars, slipped into the boat while he was stowing them away.

"Don't go getting chivalrous," she told him, untying the line from the troller.

"No, ma'am," Burke said. "I wouldn't presume."

She couldn't tell if he was being serious or sarcastic. Figured that was going to be an ongoing problem.

She let Burke row anyway. Sat in the bow and comforted Lucy, the dog a lot less secure with this rowboat than she'd been on a vessel with a kitchen and bunks. She trembled the whole way to shore, cuddling up against Jess and licking at her face and staring out at the island in the distance like it was the very jaws of dog hell awaiting her there, instead of a nice patch of forest to sniff and a bunch of new places to pee.

But the dog's fear disappeared when they hit the beach, Jess jumping out into water to her calves, pulling the bow of the boat in to the narrow patch of shingle on the western side of the lagoon. Lucy leapt off as soon as the boat scraped the bottom, landed on the beach, and immediately set to exploring, dashing off between the trees and vanishing into the forest, her collar jingling with every step, the sound diminishing but never quite disappearing.

Burke and Jess unloaded their supplies from the skiff, brought them up to the tree line, and stashed them there. They dragged the skiff up to the high tide line on the beach, tied the rope off to a tree at the edge of the forest. Then they armed themselves—Burke the shotgun, Jess the rifle, a pistol for each, and ammunition for all—and then Burke looked at Jess and asked, "Where do we start?"

"Follow me," Jess told him. She shouldered her rifle and set off west through the forest, the narrowest part of the island, where the blue sky and open ocean were just visible through the trees, the surf plainly audible as it crashed on the black rocks. The island was maybe a hundred feet wide at this point, and there was a vague trail that bisected it, the product of locals like Jess and Ty escaping civilization for a deserted-island getaway.

Jess could remember following Ty through these trees, pushing the ferns aside and listening to the waves crash, the raven call, seeing Ty grinning back at her, and the sun hitting her face. It was a painful memory, but not as much anymore. Mason Burke was a better man than Ty Winslow; Jess knew it now for certain. If anything, she hated how young and naive she'd been to fall in love with Ty in the first place.

She pushed through the last of the trees, and then the forest was gone and she was staring out at the vast blue sky, ragged clouds racing overhead and sun rays shining down between them. The ocean spread out before her, darker blue than the sky and mottled with whitecaps, a bitter wind blowing in, the mainland extending out on her left like a finger of green, falling away at Cape Flattery. Here was the smell of tidal pools, salt water, and seaweed, the sound of the ocean overpowering now.

There was a beach here, a small one, sand ringed on either side by more black rock, sheltered farther out by half-submerged reefs. The waves crashed over them, sending white water exploding into the air with a sound like a mortar bomb. You could, conceivably, land a boat on this beach, though Ty said getting in through the maze of shoals was like suicide. You'd have to get lucky, or you could die pretty quick.

Burke stepped out of the forest behind her. He stood beside her and surveyed the vista, one hand shading his eyes, the other rubbing at the back of his neck.

"Jeez," he said. "I've never seen anything like it before."

"It's not so bad when it isn't raining," Jess said. "Just happens to rain about eight months of the year."

"Those other four months, though."

"Yeah, they're something," Jess agreed, and she meant it. She'd missed Deception Cove when she'd left it, every damn time. There'd been nothing to come back to but rain and rain forest and Ty's damn schemes, but she'd never been able to find anything she liked better. Even now the prospect of leaving to flee Kirby Harwood made her anxious.

"Come on," she said, starting up the beach. "I've got a hunch I know where Ty left that package."

They picked their way through the rough sand and over the rocks, dodging tide pools filled with urchins and tiny hermit crabs. Worked their way north around the end of the beach, a little rock outcrop and a couple of flat rocks like tables where Ty said you could suntan if the weather was good.

The going got tougher when you got past the table rocks, the forest encroaching almost to the water, the overgrowth dense and the land beneath unforgiving. Jess and Burke had to edge their way over the booming surf; she looked back and saw Lucy on the table rock, staring after them, her big brown eyes wide and concerned. For a moment Jess feared the dog would try to follow, but the dog wasn't that dumb; she circled a couple of times and lay down on the table rock, her head on her paws, watching Jess and Burke navigate the terrain and no doubt thinking how foolish they were.

There was another rocky point up here, as the land curved north toward the top of Dixie Island's C shape. The forest fell back a little, and there was a cradle of rock, and in the middle there was weedy dune grass studded with rocks and driftwood and dead trees. And there was something else, too, in the middle of that grass, something Ty had been eager to show her.

"Check it out," he'd said, helping her down from the rocks and into the grass, leading her across to where the trees blocked the sunlight. “Did you ever see anything like this before?”

For a moment she didn’t see anything, just grass and rock and the forest beyond. But she looked closer, went into the shade and let her eyes adjust, and she realized that what she’d thought were dead trees were actually something else.

Ribs, they looked like, a massive, mossy rib cage, and for a second she thought Ty had found a whale’s skeleton. But the ribs were wooden, and here and there she saw iron. This was man-made. Farther into the forest, more and more planks of wood curved up from the spine. This was a ship, or it had been. Now it was a wreck, and a big one.

Burke figured it out much faster than she had. “Must have been some ship,” he said. “How old, do you figure?”

Jess shrugged. “A hundred years, maybe more. Ty said this was a secret wreck and not many people knew about it. I figure if he hid the package anywhere, it’d be here.”

“Makes sense to me,” Burke replied, setting down the shotgun and walking to the closest rib. Jess watched him peer underneath, and she shivered a little bit. She wasn’t sure she wanted to be right, wasn’t sure she wanted to find this package after all. But she knew she couldn’t bail out, not now. There was no good path forward but the one they were walking.

She set down the rifle. Followed Burke to the wreck.

FORTY-EIGHT

Mason and Jess found the package easily. It didn't take more than four or five minutes.

The shipwreck was nothing but keel and sun-bleached wood at the beach end, but farther inland it grew more substantial, mossy and rotten, as the forest gradually reclaimed what had once been trees. Mason watched Jess push through the ferns and deadfall, lean into the loamy dark between the ribs and the trees surrounding. He waited, poking around in the tall grass on the other side of the wreck, and then Jess came back out into the sunlight and looked across at him and shrugged.

"Guess I was right," she said.

The package was stashed underneath what had once been the bow of the ship, wedged into place such that Jess had to crawl into the underbrush to retrieve it. She dragged it out, and Mason leaned down and helped her, and together they carried it out to the grass.

It was the size of a carry-on suitcase. Didn't weigh a great deal—twenty, twenty-five pounds—and it was wrapped in plastic so thick it was impossible to see what was inside. Mason figured you didn't need to be a genius to get that it was drugs, and a fair decent haul of them.

They set the package down on the rough shingle at the edge of the high tide line. Jess produced a knife and cut into the plastic wrapping, a long slice down the top of it, and then they peeled back the plastic like they were doing an autopsy, peered in and studied what they found.

Ten individual bricks, more plastic wrap, light tan substance underneath. From the color Mason surmised it was heroin, Southeast Asian or South American white, quality product compared with the Mexican black tar or brown powder. Ten bricks, each one probably a kilogram, each package stamped with a Playboy Bunny logo inside a black poppy. Nothing else.

Jess stared at the logos. "That son of a bitch," she said slowly. "That no-good, piece-of-shit son of a bitch."

Mason looked at her, waited until she met his eyes.

"This stuff is from Afghanistan," she explained. "Kandahar. I recognize the trademark from the briefings they gave us." She gave him a beat to figure it out. "This shit," she said, "is fucking propping up those same Taliban motherfuckers who're fucking killing us over there. And that piece of shit Harwood is helping them do it."

Her voice was low and even, her eyes dark. Mason had heard some scary things, seen scary people in the last fifteen years, but he reckoned he'd never seen anyone as dangerous as Jess looked and sounded right now.

"They grow this shit in the south," she told Mason. "They ship it through Pakistan, and they put it on boats, and they send it around the world and buy guns with the profits. RPGs. Body armor. Trucks. Everything they need to make my life miserable. And meanwhile, Kirby's at home with his monster truck and his big old boat, cashing in on this very same shit."

Mason didn't say anything. There wasn't much to say; he didn't like Harwood, but he knew Jess had to be feeling another level of hate. This made it personal, even beyond the death of her husband. From what she'd said about Ty, Mason figured Jess had lost people she cared a heck of a lot more about overseas.

He studied the package, and the smaller packs within. Tried to remember the jailhouse math. A brick of Southeast Asian white was worth about eighty dollars a gram, at least how he'd heard it. That clocked this package in at about eight hundred grand wholesale, far more on the street. But Kirby Harwood wasn't selling on the street, and neither was Ty Winslow. The whole rotten mess had been the death of three people and counting, all for less than a million bucks.

Jess was off in her world, staring out at the ocean, and Mason was going to try to do something, say something to comfort her. He didn't have the first idea how, but he was going to try something anyway. And then they'd pack up the heroin and bring it back around the shore and find Lucy, bundle everything back up into the skiff and head back to the *Better Days,* and maybe he'd find something to cook on the gas stove for dinner and they could decide what to do next.

He didn't get the chance to do any of that, though, because before he could speak a word to Jess, she stiffened and looked up. She looked back into the trees toward the lagoon and the anchorage, and after a second Mason heard it too.

The sound of an engine, a low, rumbling throb. At first Mason thought it was a boat, thought Harwood and his boys had somehow followed them up the pass. But it wasn't the lazy *chug-chug-chug* of a diesel or the lawn mower whine of an outboard motor. This was something else, something more advanced, something ominous and deadly.

This, Mason realized, was a helicopter coming near them, and he knew right away it was coming to the island. And at the same time, he knew those three bodies he'd been thinking about weren't the only folks who were going to have to die for this shipment of heroin.

The helicopter came in low over the water toward Dixie Island, and Kirby Harwood looked out through the front windows and shook his head.

"No way," he told Joy over the sound of the rotors. "There's no anchorage there but up inside the lagoon, and there aren't but three or four men in Deception Cove who could get a troller up there."

Joy met his stare with eyes as black as polished stones. "Was Ty Winslow one of those men?"

Harwood frowned. "Well, sure," he said. "But his wife isn't."

It was good enough for Joy. He tapped the pilot on the shoulder, gestured straight ahead. "We'll survey the island."

"You're wasting your time," Harwood said, but the conversation was over. He sat back and stared out the window toward the mainland, wishing he were anywhere but here.

They'd cruised up the coast from Deception Cove, taking it slow, checking every cove and inlet all the way to Neah Bay, searching for any sign of Ty Winslow's old boat. But it didn't make sense for Jess to keep the boat so close; the state highway to Neah Bay ran right alongside the beach. She'd have been better served driving if she were staying close to shore.

From Harwood's perspective, there were two places the widow could have run to. First was Canada, just across the strait, where on the southwestern coast of Vancouver Island there were no roads and practically no people. If Ty hadn't gone to Canada, Harwood expected he would have rounded Cape Flattery and gone down the west side of the peninsula, the open-ocean side, about thirty miles of wilderness and wildlife preserve, until you hit La Push and the Quillayute River. There were places to hide along that stretch of coast, Flattery Rocks and the islands around

Point of Arches, and if Ty Winslow had been smart, that's where he'd have gone.

But there was something lacking in both of those options. Ty Winslow had aimed for a fast turnaround, hold the package for ransom and get paid off quickly, and a run across the border or around the cape would have stood to lengthen the process considerably. He'd have made things a lot easier if he'd stashed the package on Dixie, but Jess Winslow couldn't think she could make it up that pass, could she?

Could she?

The helicopter flew closer, and Harwood saw the pass open up, a thin, jagged scar through the black rock and trees. The tide was going out now, rushing through that narrow opening and over semisubmerged rocks, and from the way it churned and roiled, Harwood decided only a maniac would attempt to head through.

He turned to Cole Sweeney. "When's high tide these days?"

Sweeney, an avid fisherman, looked up at the roof of the helicopter and thought for a second. "About oh eight hundred, eight thirty," he said. "Why, boss?"

Because the timing works out, Harwood thought, *if she was trying to make a move. But if she did, we'd see wreckage somewhere.*

But then the helicopter climbed a little bit to get over a rise in the terrain on Dixie Island below, and when it crested, Harwood saw the pilot point out through the forward window and descend again. He crowded beside Joy to look out where the man pointed, and there, smack-dab and sitting pretty in the middle of Dixie Lagoon, Ty Winslow's old troller sat bobbing at anchor, everything peaceful, like it wasn't no thing whatsoever to be in there at all.

"Well, I'll be damned," Harwood said, more to himself than to anyone else. "Jess Winslow, you're just a constant surprise, aren't you?"

FORTY-NINE

"Put us down," Joy instructed.

The pilot shook his head. "Where?" he said, gesturing outside the helicopter. "There's not a flat piece of ground on this whole goddamn island."

"On the boat, then."

"Can't do that, either," the pilot replied. "See that mast sticking up in the air, all those stay wires? We get too close to that crap, we're crashing. Unless you want to jump, you're not getting down there."

Joy wished he could strangle the pilot, but the man was right. The island, small though it was, was covered in trees, and what wasn't trees was steep, jagged rock. There was no place for a helicopter to land.

He studied the little fishing boat from the window. There was nothing moving aboard, no sign that the widow or her companion had noticed the helicopter. But they must have. The woman was a former marine. And she wasn't going to simply surrender just because her adversary was airborne.

Then the chief deputy, Harwood, touched his arm. Pointed out his own window at the western edge of the lagoon. *"Look."*

Joy looked. Saw what Harwood saw, an inflatable dinghy pulled up to the high tide line, half hidden against the shore.

"They're on the island somewhere," he told the pilot. "Let's have a look."

Lucy.

Jess's first thought was the dog, and she could tell by Burke's expression that he was thinking the same. Together they moved the package into the woods by the shipwreck and hurried back along the shore toward the table rocks, where they'd left Lucy.

Somewhere through the trees, the helicopter's engine roared like machine gun fire, and Jess knew it was Harwood, and she knew he'd seen the troller, and this was probably it. She clambered along the rocks after Burke, her rifle swinging against her back, her mind racing. The Taliban didn't use helicopters. She'd never had to deal with this kind of assault.

They rounded the shore to where the table rocks lay in the sun, and Lucy wasn't there, and Jess panicked.

"*Burke,*" she called out, and he looked back at her. "Where is she?"

Burke pointed ahead, stepped aside so she could see, and she looked down across the sweep of the little beach and saw Lucy running best she could on the rocky, uneven ground, her tail between her legs and her ears flattened back. Shit.

There was no sense in calling her. The chopper was too loud, and the dog wasn't going to listen in that state. Jess and Burke hurried after her, down across more jagged rocks to the beach, and across the shingle to the other side. Lucy was trotting in circles now, scared, unsure where to go, and through the trees the chopper's engine revved up, suddenly amplified.

They were coming.

Jess hauled ass to the dog, who cowered now against a rock face, all but given up. Jess reached her and pulled her away and into the forest just as the helicopter roared overhead, big and black and flying low, banking hard to trace the shoreline, the sliding side door open and faces peering out.

Jess held Lucy tight to her, the dog shaking hard, resting her chin on Jess's shoulder, the sheer weight of her blocky little head as surprising as usual. Jess held the dog close as the chopper disappeared down the shore. Knew it was a temporary reprieve at best.

Beside her, the ferns rustled, and Burke appeared, shotgun in hand. "I don't think they saw us," he said.

She replied, "Not yet."

"They're down there somewhere," Harwood told Joy after the helicopter had surveyed the perimeter of the island. "We know that for sure."

"Indeed." Joy's expression was grim. "And we can assume the package is there with them."

"Definitely. We just can't get down there."

Joy looked at him with those black eyes again, and Harwood looked away involuntarily. The sooner he didn't have to deal with the Nigerian, the happier he'd be. Hell, he'd be perfectly content never to do business with Okafor again. There had to be easier ways to make money.

"Call Mr. Whitmer," Joy instructed. "Tell him to meet us here with your boat. We'll attack from the sea, if we can't do it by air."

The pilot had overheard. "I don't have the fuel to hang around while your buddy sails his boat from Deception."

"He can drive to Neah Bay," Harwood said. "Launch there."

"Still going to be tight. You want to risk it, that's fine, but I reckon this helicopter's worth a hell of a lot more than whatever you're chasing down there."

Joy didn't react visibly, but Harwood could feel the man's anger burning. "Listen, they're trapped in that lagoon until high tide anyway," he told Joy, trying to diffuse the situation. "Means we have until dark at the very least to get our shit together, come back with a plan."

"They could paddle the dingy to the mainland," Joy said. "Or swim."

"Not with those currents. Those tide rips are wicked through the strait. They'd get swept out to sea or capsized, real easy, and Jess knows it. Swimming'd be even worse."

Joy thought about this. "Call Mr. Whitmer," he said. "Tell him to hurry."

"We're going to wait?"

"Not necessarily," Joy replied. "But there's no sense in dawdling, Deputy, is there?"

"So what are we going to do?"

"We're going to keep the widow and her friend where we can handle them," Joy replied. "If we can't get onto the island, we'll make sure they can't get off."

The helicopter had circled back to the lagoon, and Mason could see it through the trees as it dropped into a hover over Ty Winslow's boat. Together with Jess and Lucy, he inched his way through the forest, keeping as low as he could, until he'd nearly reached the waterline. He unslung the shotgun and kept it close at hand as he stared out through the trees at the helicopter.

The sliding side door was open. Mason watched the machine sidle down until it was directly alongside the little boat's stern, a hundred or so feet in the air.

"What are they planning?" he wondered aloud.

Jess said nothing, her expression grim, just gestured back to the helicopter. Mason turned and looked just in time to see Kirby Harwood poke his face out from the open door. Beside him, the man who'd come out of Shelby Walker's house was also visible. They both held long guns, aimed down at the troller.

As Mason and Jess watched, the men opened fire.

The guy had a grenade launcher mounted on the bottom of his M4. Harwood didn't want to know how or where Joy had obtained it, but shit, he sure did look comfortable with it.

They raked the hull of the troller with 5.56 NATO rounds, the sound of their rifles erupting over the noise of the helicopter, the shells pitting the white hull of the boat, painting a crazy pattern, but not, to Harwood's eyes, doing much damage.

But he guessed that was what the grenade launcher was for.

As Harwood turned his attention to the wheelhouse, shooting out every window in turn, Joy switched to the heavy artillery and dropped a grenade round plumb into the fish-killing cockpit at the stern. With a muffled thud and white water, the round blew a big hole out of the back of the boat, mostly below the waterline, and the painted BETTER DAYS, DECEPTION COVE, WA lettering was straight obliterated. With any luck, the explosion had destroyed the rudder and the propeller, too.

Joy reloaded. He nudged Harwood aside and aimed another round at the wheelhouse, missing the windows but making a big hole in the superstructure. He reloaded again, put a last round through that hole—wreaking some kind of special havoc inside—and then he stepped back from the open door and shouldered the rifle, apparently having decided the troller was pretty well taken care of. Harwood hoped he was right, because it was just about then that Jess Winslow must have gotten fed up. A muzzle flashed in the trees, and the helicopter rocked and jolted forward like a spooked horse. The pilot swore at the controls and veered skyward, nearly sending Harwood tumbling out the open door.

Then Joy was pushing past him, to the door again, with that M4 of his, and Harwood thought the Nigerian meant to engage the crazy bitch down there, maybe put a grenade in her lap. But Joy had switched back to bullets, and he sent a sharp, fast barrage down at the inflatable skiff where it lay at the tree line. Then he reached past Harwood and tapped the pilot on the shoulder, and the helicopter was suddenly gaining altitude very quickly, Jess Winslow's rifle sending parting shots skyward, none of them, to Harwood's knowledge, connecting with shit.

Joy slid the door closed. He sat back, laid his rifle across his lap, and looked across the helicopter at nothing.

"There," he said, and he wasn't smiling, but damned if he didn't look pleased with himself. "That should keep them contained until we're ready to deal with them."

Harwood looked out across the channel to the mainland, white-caps and swift current, knew there was no way Jess or her boyfriend could escape Dixie with their lives. Figured that meant she'd be right hopping mad when they came back in the Grady-White, hoped Joy was planning adequately for a pissed-off marine.

They would find out, Harwood knew. One way or the other.

FIFTY

Lucy was gone.

Mason pushed himself to his feet, brushed dirt and pine needles from his knees, his chest. He picked up the shotgun and looked around the forest, listening to the drone of the helicopter fade away into nothing.

Beside him, Jess stood as well. "Where's the dog?" she asked.

"Ran off." He gestured to his right, along the south side of the lagoon, where the terrain rose gradually toward the pass and the dogleg. "Soon as that asshole blew a hole in your boat."

"Ty's boat," Jess replied absently. "Not mine."

Mason rested the shotgun on his shoulder and started off toward the waterline, the landing where they'd tied the skiff. He imagined he knew what he would see when he got there, and sure enough, the skiff was destroyed, shot clean through with six or seven rounds, lying deflated and ragged there on the rocks.

Shit.

Jess was calling Lucy's name in the forest. Mason worked his way back to her, found her tracing the dog's path around the south side of the cove, her rifle slung across her back and both hands to her mouth as she hollered.

"Skiff's ruined," he told her. She didn't answer, just kept pushing her way through ferns and bog, climbing up the incline and calling for the dog.

"You hear me?" Mason asked her. "That skiff is destroyed. The troller's settling in the stern too, where the grenade hit, and the wheelhouse is matchsticks. I don't know that it's not going to sink."

Jess still didn't respond. Took hold of a root and swung herself up a four-foot patch of wet rock, looked around the top and kept going.

"You sure she went this way?" she asked over her shoulder. "That damn dog is such a baby sometimes."

He pulled himself up the rock after her. Muddied his pants, his hands. "Jess," he said. "Are you listening to me? We need to find another way off this island, before they come back."

She took another step. Then she turned around, slow. "There's no other way, Burke." There was something flat in her tone, in the way her eyes met his. "That's the point. We're stuck here until they come back to get us."

"Bullshit," he replied. "It's only a mile to the mainland. We salvage what we can, make some kind of raft."

"Current's too strong. Even in the skiff, we'd get swept out to sea." Jess turned around again. Pressed forward. *"Lucy!"*

"So, what?" Mason hurried to catch up to her. "You just want to sit here and wait?"

She didn't answer, kept moving. Kept calling for the damn dog. Mason put his hand on her shoulder, light, and she spun around fast and knocked that hand clear.

"Yeah, we're going to wait," she said. "They're going to regroup and come back in a boat, and they're going to try to kill us for that heroin, and I'm going to try to kill them all first. No civilians to get caught in the crossfire, no police to break it up. Just me against Harwood and his friends, and then that'll be the end of it."

He stared at her. "We could just leave the heroin out for them," he said. "Let them take the package and they'll leave us alone. Hell, Hank Moss knows we're out here. He'll—"

"We're not getting rescued," Jess said. "You need to understand that right now, Burke. We're not getting rescued, and we're not leaving them the package and hoping for a truce. That's not how this works."

She started through the forest again, hollering for the dog. Mason kept pace. "You want to think this thing over," he said. "That was a grenade launcher they just pulled out back there. These guys—"

"Aren't fucking marines," Jess said. "End of discussion."

She sped up a bit, called "Lucy" again. Came up around another rock face to where the forest cleared out, and the dogleg at the pass spread out beneath them. A ways down the rocks Mason could see the end of the pass, and the open ocean stretching back east toward Deception Cove. But Jess wasn't looking that far. At the edge of the rocks, hemmed in between the forest and the edge of the cliff, Lucy stood, cowering, tail between her legs, looking for all the world like she was just about convinced she'd be better off jumping.

"Lucy." Jess hurried over, wrapped her arms around the dog, who wagged her tail, once, and gave Jess's face a cursory sniff. "I'm sorry, girl. Those assholes are going to pay for it, I promise."

The dog looked about as unconvinced as Mason felt inside, and all the hugging in the world wasn't going to change that—for Lucy or for Mason.

But shit, neither one of them was about to tell Jess.

It was a bad situation, but it wasn't the worst.

If Jess knew Kirby Harwood like she thought she did, there wasn't a chance in hell he would try an assault on the island before high slack water. That meant he would come either tonight after dark or tomorrow morning. Jess expected Kirby wasn't fool enough to try to run the pass at night. His friend with the fancy toys was a wild card, but anything other than high slack in the daylight would probably mean disaster for the deputies, and Jess figured she was better off preparing to fend off an attack than expecting to watch Kirby drown in the channel.

She would sleep up here at the dogleg anyway, just in case Kirby tried to get cute. But a part of her was hoping he would have the good sense to wait until dawn.

There was no way onto the island except up the pass, even in Kirby's Grady-White. That would make defense easier when Kirby did come. She would camp up here with her rifle and pick them off as they motored up toward her, hopefully kill two or three before they knew what was happening.

One ex-marine with a good rifle and an elevated position against a handful of peckerheads in a confined shooting alley. If it played out like Jess hoped, it wouldn't even be a contest, the grenade launcher notwithstanding. Her biggest problem would be making sure Kirby's pretty little boat wasn't destroyed on the rocks.

But if they brought the helicopter, too? That would complicate things. That asshole with the M203 could camp out above her firing position, wait to see muzzle flashes, and then drop little bundles of death down from on high. If they brought the helicopter, Jess wasn't sure she'd be able to send up enough flak to keep the pilot on his toes while picking off the Tweedledickheads down the pass at the same time. She wouldn't be able to handle the situation alone.

If you don't win this fight, she thought, *Burke and Lucy die. And you probably can't win it without them.*

She met Burke's eyes across the small clearing. "I need you with me on this," she told him. "I need you to know that there's nothing in the world I want more than to get you and Lucy off of this island safe. And I need you to believe that I can get us out of here, but I need you to hear what I'm saying. There's no rescue, Burke. We need to make a stand."

Burke chewed his lip and studied the forest. He didn't say anything for a time, and then when he did, it sounded like something he'd memorized, something he was saying for himself, not for her.

"'Who rises up for me against the wicked?'" he said softly. "'Who stands up for me against evildoers?'"

She waited, and he met her eyes again. "You know I'll fight with you," he told her. "But I guess you'd better teach me how to shoot a little bit first."

FIFTY-ONE

Jess and Burke went back down to the shoreline where they'd stashed the duffel bag full of guns. Kicked at what remained of the skiff until they both agreed it was perforated beyond hope. Out in the cove, the *Better Days* lay half-sunk and listing, the whole stern underwater and half of the back deck, the wheelhouse collapsing in on itself. It might have been a sad sight to Jess, but it wasn't; Ty's boat had brought them this far, and she was maybe actually glad it wouldn't take them any farther.

There was no running now. Only fighting.

She laid out the guns for Burke and let him fire for a while, not long enough to use up too much ammunition, but enough that he'd stand a fighting chance in the woods against the likes of Dale Whitmer. He wasn't ever going to be Annie Oakley, but then, Jess didn't need a sharpshooter. What she needed was distraction.

"We'll put you at the entrance to the pass, north side, across the water from me," she told him after she'd laid out her plan. "You'll stay hidden until the boys are well into the pass and you hear me start firing. Your jobs are to harass that helicopter and to make sure those boys in the boat don't make it out of the kill zone and back into open water. I'll handle the rest."

Burke was breathing heavy from the shooting, not the exertion necessarily but the visceral thrill. She'd seen it before, knew the adrenaline was running, the heart pounding, the brain caught up in some lizard burst of pleasure, unable to really focus. You couldn't teach focus under pressure, not in a couple of hours, but Jess hoped to keep the plan simple and direct, give Burke something easy to take care of.

"Most important thing is you stay hidden until they're in the pass," she said. "If they see you too early, they'll realize what they're in for and bug out, and we'll lose them. And we really don't want that to happen. Understand?"

He nodded. "Understood."

"Second most important thing is you take care of that chopper. You don't have to shoot the thing down, but you do need to scare the pilot enough he stays out of grenade range. If not, we're both fucked."

Burke nodded again.

"Any questions?"

"No, ma'am." He looked at the pistol in his hand and rubbed his chin. "Heck, I'm sure glad you're here," he said finally. "I'd have been proper hooped if you'd asked me to ward off these assholes by myself."

"Yeah well," she said. "You wouldn't even know these assholes if it wasn't for me."

"Still," he said.

"I had a lot of practice."

"Yeah," he said. "I guess you did."

There was a pause, and Jess could sense by the way he was looking off across the water that he had something to say, and she waited a little bit, and then he said it.

"What exactly does the female engagement team do, anyway?" he asked. "I didn't think our military sent women into combat, but you sure seem to have a knack for it."

Well, there it was.

She kept her head down, fooling around in Hank's duffel bag, reloading spent clips from the boxes of spare ammunition he'd packed. Something to keep from meeting Burke's eyes, having this conversation.

"Just waiting for the right time, huh?" she said. "You figure we're alone on a deserted island, got a bit of downtime, probably going to die tomorrow, now's the time to tell you my war stories, what it was that got me fucked in the head?"

He didn't reply. She looked up at him, and he was studying her, his lips pressed tight together.

"You don't have to tell me anything," he said.

"They have this new thing called *Google,* Burke," she said. "*Wikipedia.* You get curious about something, you just type it into a computer and you'll get your answer."

He let out his breath. "Listen, I'm a dumb-ass."

"That's a fact," she said, and they didn't either of them say anything else for a while. Jess packed up the bag with the guns in it, and she headed back into the forest, and Burke fell in behind her. They crossed the isthmus to the west beach, where they found Lucy waiting, cowering and curled up behind a piece of driftwood log. Up above, the sky was beginning to cloud over, gray rolling in from beyond the cape, and the sun was going down somewhere beyond all that gray, the wind picking up and the rollers crashing against the shoals offshore with great white explosions of foam.

Jess went to comfort the dog, the poor thing shaking and shivering all over again, terrified from the shooting she and Burke had just done. Burke went to Lucy too, and they found themselves on either side of her, scratching behind her ears and stroking under her muzzle, speaking soft words of comfort to the dog and steadfastly avoiding each other.

It was awkward as hell, and Jess had had about enough of it. She wasn't going to spend her last night on Earth ignoring the only ally she had, no matter how dumb his ass was. She sighed.

"What it is, these places we're fighting, we need to gather intel from the locals, the villagers," she said, still scratching behind Lucy's right ear. The dog leaned into her knuckles, groaned a little bit, visibly relaxed. "But the way it works, the women in those villages won't talk to our men, it's a cultural taboo. But just because they won't talk doesn't mean they don't have good intel."

"So they send you to talk to them," Burke said.

"It was everything I wanted." Lucy was practically sitting in Jess's lap now, gazing up into her eyes with those big, gentle brown eyes of her own, sad and anxious and content at the same time, and the dog's warmth against her body was a comfort to Jess, too, and she guessed that was the point of a "companion animal," someone to calm her nerves down, keep her centered.

To Jess's chagrin, it was working.

"I grew up believing a soldier's role was combat," she said. "Even if I was a girl, I didn't want to get stuck behind the front line, some stupid support position. And my team, they embedded us with an infantry unit, rotated us to the front and sent us out on patrols like we were regular marines. It was action, and I liked the action, and I liked the job, too."

"Working with the local women."

She nodded. "They'd tell me stuff that no man would tell our men. They *knew* stuff their men didn't, stuff they would only tell another woman. And once I got them to trust me, I really felt like I was making a difference over there."

"Sounds like a good thing you had going on," Burke said.

"Who knows? In the broad scheme of things, it never amounted to much. Our guys made advances, took up forward positions; their guys would ambush and try to take it back. People died on both sides, and nothing ever seemed to change. As far as I can figure, they'll be fighting over that little nowhere valley long after we're all dead and gone."

Burke looked out over the water, seemed to be considering this. "They teach you Arabic?" he asked after a beat.

"Pashto," she said. Something stirred in her chest, something uneasy and miserable. "Pashto is the language."

"Do you speak it?"

"No." She could feel that something in her chest coming to life now, and she could feel her mind withdraw to compensate. "I had an interpreter."

"What, like a local woman? One of the villagers? How'd they sign her up?"

Afia.

If she went down this road, she'd be gone again. Checked out and flatlined while that evil still lodged in her chest tore her apart even more. She held Lucy close to her, and the dog squirmed a little bit. Jess didn't relent. She couldn't hear the surf anymore, couldn't feel the wind. Her eyes burned from hot sun and gritty road dust, and she could almost hear the soldiers at the gate calling out their warning to the woman on the road.

In a moment, Jess knew, she would hear the shot.

"Hey."

Burke reached out and touched her. Gentle but firm, he eased her arms loose from around Lucy's body, freeing the dog to twist around and lap at Jess's face with her big, sloppy pink tongue. Jess blinked. She could still feel it in her chest, but Burke's touch helped, and the dog, too.

"Fuck," she said.

The valley faded away, but it was still there in her mind. It wouldn't disappear completely. She knew it.

"Damn it, I'm sorry," Burke was saying. "This is nothing we need to be talking about right now."

His voice sounded like water, and she knew she wasn't entirely back. "It's okay."

"No, it isn't." He stood, held out his hand. "Come on. Let's go get that package before it gets too dark to find it. Then maybe we set up for the night. Wind's picking up."

"Storm's coming," she said. She took his hand, and he pulled her to her feet, and he held her there, tight and close, and she closed her eyes and held on until she could feel the salt spray again, hear the crash of the surf, and she knew the valley was gone again, if only temporarily.

FIFTY-TWO

Mason and Jess worked their way around the edge of the little bay and across the table rocks and the point, and then down to the grassy beach and the shipwreck. It didn't take long, but by the time they'd returned to the beach and found Lucy again, it was near dark and slate gray and the wind had kicked up something fierce. Sooner or later the rain was going to come back, Mason knew. He didn't look forward to the night ahead.

He was worried about Jess. She was still quiet as they led Lucy back across the isthmus to where the skiff lay shot up and ruined. She handed Mason the bag of guns, and they divvied up the food and clothes and other supplies they'd stashed, and Jess picked up what was left of the skiff and motioned back toward the forest, toward the cliff that overlooked the dogleg in the pass where Jess intended to set up with the rifle when the deputies came back.

There was a little cave there, on the far edge of the clearing, and they'd decided it would do to keep them dry when the storm started in earnest. At the very least, they could stick the guns under the shelter of the rock and keep them out of the rain. The wind would drown out the sound of any approaching boat until it was dead on top of them, but they would hear a helicopter from a distance. They had energy bars and plenty of water, warm clothes; they wouldn't need a fire.

They hiked up through the forest to the clearing in the last of the day's waning light, and by the time they'd made it to the cliff and the little cave, it was night and the pass wasn't visible, the forest just barely. Lucy stuck close to Jess as they navigated by flashlight, though whether it was fear that kept her close or some comforting instinct, Mason wasn't sure. The dog needed Jess as much as Jess needed the dog; that much was clear.

"Is this what you thought you'd be doing?" Jess asked, breaking a long silence as they knelt by the rocky outcrop and slid the guns into the dry. "All those years in your jail cell, did you figure you'd be hiding in the woods from a pack of dirty lawmen before you'd been a free man for even a couple of weeks?"

It was impossible to see her face, but there was humor in her tone, dark as the night outside.

"Truthfully, I didn't know what I was going to do," Mason replied, thankful for the conversation. "I guess I still don't." He gave it a beat. "I wasn't ever the kind to have a life plan, not before I went inside. I was mostly just running with Dev, trying to keep up."

"Yeah, and how'd that work out for you?"

He shrugged. The wind howled through the trees, and he laid out a mat of spare clothes on the dry rock beneath the overhang, and laughed as Lucy promptly curled up in the middle of it.

" 'Rescue the drowning and tie your shoestrings,' " he said.

She made a face. "What is this stuff, Burke, the Bible? You found God?"

"That one is Thoreau," he said. He shrugged, feeling sheepish. "I had a lot of time to read these last few years."

"Yeah? And what's it supposed to mean, 'rescue the drowning'?"

"I guess it means you're supposed to help anybody who really needs it, but otherwise mind your own business," he said. "At least, that's how I read it."

Jess didn't say anything, so after a beat he continued. "Like, I didn't come out this far because I wanted to meet a marine or see the ocean. I came because that dog needed help. I stayed because I could see that *you* needed help. But once all this is over, hell, I expect there's a good chance I'll spend the next forty years swamping toilets or maybe hammering nails, and that'll be fine. Better minding my business than causing more trouble."

Jess remained silent. She nudged Lucy deeper under the rock, stretched out on the clothes, and killed the light.

"All right, so that's what you believe is most likely to happen," she said once she was all comfortable. "But you mean to tell me there's nothing in the world you *want* to do with your life?"

Mason sat at the edge of the cave, resting his back against the wall and looking out into the bleak night. He hadn't spoken this much about anything to anyone, not in over fifteen years, and maybe not ever.

"I've thought about helping out," he said, every word feeling clumsy and heavy. "Guys like me, you know, how I was as a kid."

"What," Jess said, "like teenagers?"

"Sure, yeah, teenagers," he agreed. "Guys who got on the wrong path, maybe need someone to talk to. Someone to make sure they don't end up like I did."

Jess didn't say anything. Mason felt the moment stretch, wished he'd never said anything at all.

"That's what you should do," she said finally. "Forget swamping toilets, working construction. You can do better than that."

He laughed, derisive, looked across the cave toward her, though he couldn't see her at all. "You really believe that?"

"I believe you have something to say," she said, and he heard her clothes rustle and knew she'd sat up. He knew if he could see her, she'd be looking at him, her eyes earnest. "You did a bad thing,

Burke, but you've got forty, fifty years left to live to make up for it. You're not meant to waste them as a janitor."

He didn't know what to say. "Assuming we even get off this island," he said. "We could both die tomorrow and that would be it."

"You let me handle that," she replied. "You do what I tell you, and we'll get out just fine."

"Yeah," he said. "All right."

He believed her, about that part, anyway. Wasn't sure what to make of the rest of it, her faith in his broader purpose, but he figured that wasn't a question that would need answering for a good long time. In the meanwhile, they had more pressing concerns.

He set his head back and looked out at the night, and felt the first raindrops on his face, blown into the cave by the ever-building wind. The storm was coming; it was almost here. He wondered how they'd be able to sleep through it.

Jess's voice in the darkness: "Mason?"

He looked toward her. "Yeah?"

"Are you just going to sit there all night?"

He tried to find her in the dark, but he couldn't, and he couldn't see the forest outside the cave, either. The wind blew harder, and the rain came faster. His muscles ached from sitting like he was, and he realized suddenly he was tired, very tired.

No," he said, shifting his weight, crawling to where he'd last heard her voice. "No, I guess not."

He found the dry clothes and felt her warmth beside him, and he lay close to her and felt her move closer, heard the dog snoring somewhere deeper in the cave, and he closed his eyes and tried to forget the storm for a short while, tried to rest.

FIFTY-THREE

Later, after the rain had come on in earnest, blowing into the cave and through the shot-up, ruined skiff Mason and Jess had mounted at the entrance in a vain attempt to make a weather door, after Mason had lain awake, dog tired, on the rock beside Jess, the darkness the same whether his eyes were open or closed, his thoughts refusing to quit even though his body was about finished; later, after what might have been minutes, or it might have been hours, Jess rolled over onto her back beside him and spoke like she knew he was awake, like she couldn't sleep either.

"Her name was Afia," she said. He didn't say anything, and she continued. "My interpreter, in the valley. Afia; she was a young widow who'd learned English after her husband died. The marines hired her to work as an interpreter, and they placed her with me."

"Afia," Mason said, thinking it was a pretty name, knowing from the way Jess struggled to keep her voice matter-of-fact that Afia was at the heart of what it was Jess was wrestling with.

"She was pretty well my best friend over there," Jess continued. "We were about the same age, in an outpost full of men, so we had to stick together. She practiced her English reading old Archie comics; she told me I was Betty and she was Jughead."

"Jughead." Mason smiled. "The guy who ate all the hamburgers?"

"She liked food more than she liked falling in love, she said." He could tell Jess was smiling too. "But that didn't stop her from asking about me and Ty, or pointing out the hot guys at the outpost, to tease me. Me and Ty were already having trouble, and Afia didn't think so highly of him, based on the stories I told."

"Sounds like a good judge of character," Mason said.

"Yeah, well." Jess was quiet for a bit. "Anyway, we were friends, good friends, and we worked well together too. She was tough when she had to be; she could bully her way into a room full of women who didn't want to talk to an American, even a female, and by the time she was done yelling at them and giving them shit, they'd be offering me *piraki* and a place to spend the night. Plus all the intel they could muster."

"Perfect," Mason said.

Jess didn't say anything for a couple of beats, and when she did, the smile was gone from her voice.

"She was too good at her job," she said. "That's what it comes down to. She was too good, and we didn't protect her."

Mason let it sit.

"We went on a big winning streak," Jess said. "Thanks to Afia, we got advance word the Taliban was moving guys in for a raid on our forward outpost, nipped that in the bud. Then she got us word one of their big guys was passing through the valley on his way to Pakistan, and this guy was a *big* freaking get. We sent in a strike force and a couple of Apaches, took him out and three or four of his lieutenants. Really messed up their day."

"And the other side didn't like that."

Jess shifted beside him. "No," she said. "They didn't. They found out it was a woman who was screwing them up—and a Pashtun woman besides—and you can imagine how mad it made them."

"Sure," Mason said. He figured the kind of guys Jess was fighting weren't exactly on board with feminism.

Jess went quiet again. Rain lashed the ruined skiff and dripped into the cave. Lucy shifted position and stretched out and grumbled. And Mason could hear how Jess's breathing had changed, quickened pace a little bit, and he knew she was going away again.

"You don't have to," he said, finding her hand in the darkness and squeezing. "It's okay if you—"

"We were ambushed," she said, cutting him off. "We were ambushed, and they knew she'd be with us, knew I'd be there. Someone in the villages sold us out; we were supposed to check up on some intel about enemy movements. But hell, Burke, it was a setup from the start."

Mason said nothing, kept hold of her hand. And he squeezed again, and she squeezed back, weakly, but he could already tell she was slipping away.

And then she was back in the valley again. The air still and silent, the sun beating down. The village rose like a citadel in front of her, the village woman, Panra, waiting at the narrow stairs, gesturing forward to Jess, to Afia.

The rest of the patrol had spread out behind low walls for cover, only the barrels of their M4s and the tops of their helmets visible, the glint off of their sunglasses as they watched the women. Somewhere on the western wall of the valley, high above the patrol, Jess knew there were more eyes watching her, friendly eyes with .50-caliber machine guns and mortars. But she knew that if she followed Panra up those stairs, all the rifles and .50 cals and Apache helicopters in the world wouldn't do her much good, not if Haji was planning an ambush, not there.

Jess thought of the young child, Selab, at the village entrance, how he'd ducked away when she'd waved to him. She wondered why Panra couldn't bring the elders somewhere out in the open if they wanted to talk.

She wondered if she was climbing to her own death.

You're a marine, aren't you? Sack up.

Panra gestured again to the stairs, Come.

Get it done, Winslow.

Hoo-rah.

Afia went first, following Panra up the narrow stairway. Later Jess would wonder why she'd let her friend take the lead, why she hadn't cut in ahead with her rifle. But Afia always led; the locals responded better when they saw one of their own before the marine with the big gun. It worked just fine when the locals were inclined to be friendly. In this instance, though, it left Jess neutralized at the back of the line, that rifle of hers worth exactly shit.

Panra climbed. Afia climbed after her, and Jess after Afia. The sun bore down. Jess felt hot and dirty, her skin gritty. Her heart pounded. The stairs were steep and uneven, and she couldn't see much but the walls beside her, and Afia's backside. She couldn't see where they were going. Even turning around would have been precarious.

Panra said nothing as she climbed. Nor did Afia. Jess couldn't see where the stairs ended, couldn't see what waited for them. Couldn't see how much farther to the top.

They reached the end, maybe twenty feet from ground level, and the houses backed away into a small courtyard. Panra waited at the top for Afia and Jess to join her. She gestured across the courtyard to an open doorway. Said something to Afia and gestured again.

"She wants us to go in there," Afia said. "That's where the elders are, she says."

Jess looked at Afia, then back at the doorway. Nothing moved inside. "Why isn't she going first?" she asked. "Tell her lead the way, make the introductions."

Afia relayed this. Panra shook her head.

"She says there's no need. The elders are in there," Afia said.

The doorway was dark. Still nothing moving. Jess looked at Panra, who met her eyes and nodded quickly. Gestured again and spoke Pashto to Jess, rapid, urgent.

The woman was shaking, Jess realized. And that about sealed the deal. "Bullshit," she told Afia. "This is fucked up. We're leaving."

It was right about then that the shooting began.

"There was nowhere to go," Jess said as she lay in the dark, listening to the rain fall. "It was a targeted hit, and we were the targets. Panra, too, though she must have planned on getting out of there clean."

She wondered if Burke had fallen asleep on her, but then he squeezed her hand and she knew he was there.

"They were on top of the houses," she continued. "Maybe a dozen of them. They cut Panra down first, as she tried to run. Afia just bolted; I think she panicked. She ran to the first open door, but I think she got shot at least once. I heard her cry out."

"What about you?" Burke asked.

"I was shooting," Jess said. "I was trying to grab Afia, drag her back down the stairs, returning fire at the same time." She slowed again, remembering how it happened. "I caught a round in my chest, right square in my armor, and it knocked me over the edge of those steep stairs and out of the kill zone. I guess that armor saved my life, but I've never felt grateful."

Burke didn't say anything. She was grateful for that, anyway.

"Yeah, so, my guys were already halfway up the stairs when I came tumbling down. They got past me, and I heard them open fire, but there wasn't much they could do, not with Haji all lined up on those rooftops like that. Grieves gave the order to fall back, and the guys hustled me back downstairs, and they called in the Apaches."

"And Afia?"

Jess swallowed. "She survived. The insurgents cleared out real quick as soon as we dropped back. We tried to chase them up the mountainside, but it wasn't any use. They knew the terrain better, knew the shortcuts. And they took Afia with them."

She knew she could leave it at that and Burke wouldn't press her, knew he would get the point or as much as he needed. But she'd been over there too much in the last couple of days, and she needed Burke to know what she knew. She needed to believe he would understand.

So she told Burke how Grieves had been forced to call off the hunt, how she'd cussed him out and fought her guys all the way back to the OP. They'd left without Afia, left her to die, and though Jess could see Grieves was distraught about it, she knew he would never have abandoned any of his marines.

But Afia wasn't a marine. She wasn't even American. Her life simply wasn't worth sacrificing marines for. That's how the brass saw things, anyway.

Jess told Burke how she'd cried, lain in her bunk and tried not to look at Afia's stack of Archie comics, tried not to think too hard about going out beyond the wire herself, going AWOL, back into the village and beyond to try to find Afia and bring her back, whatever was left of her.

She'd been pretty close to doing it too, and then Afia had turned up again, tortured and brutalized, struggling to walk the last hundred yards to the wire.

She told Burke about the shot, and how Afia had died, and how her men had dragged her back to the wire and left Afia dead on the road, her blood in the dust. She told Burke how she hadn't cried after that, not once.

"It fucked me up," she said. "After that, I couldn't have cared less why we were put in that valley. My purpose was one thing: kill Haji. And that's what I fucking did, Burke."

He didn't say anything. He was still holding her hand.

"I finished my tour and I came home to Deception, and I realized pretty quick that I had no reason to be there. My marriage was going to shit, there weren't any jobs, and I wasn't done killing insurgents yet, not by a mile."

"So you went back."

"I reenlisted. I pushed hard to get back to the valley. I got lucky; they needed more women for the engagement teams, and I had experience. I had a rapport with the women in the villages."

She snorted.

"I didn't give a shit about engagement, not at that point. I said the right things to my COs, and I acted the part, but all I really cared about was getting those bastards back for what they did to Afia."

"And did you?"

"Not enough of them. And then Ty went and got himself killed, and they sent me back home, and somewhere along the way some doctor had a look at me and pronounced me fucked in the head. They gave me some meds and hooked me up with Lucy, and it was right about that time that Kirby and his homeboys started sniffing around after their lost package. And that about gets us to the part where you showed up."

Burke hesitated. "Do the meds help at all?"

"The meds make me even number than I am without. I don't like being numb, Burke. I stopped taking them."

"All right," he said.

She let out a long breath of air. "Honestly, I've spent a long time wondering why I didn't have the good sense to die over there with Afia. Everything that came after has been absolute shit."

He started to talk. She squeezed his hand to shut him up.

"But on the plus side," she said, "I sure learned how to kill people pretty good over there. And that's going to come in real handy tomorrow."

He tried speaking again, and she knew whatever he tried to say would be heartfelt and sweet and utterly useless. She leaned over and kissed him. "Don't try and fix me, Burke," she said. "Just try and get some sleep, if you can."

FIFTY-FOUR

Mason and Jess woke in the predawn, when the darkness outside began to fade, and the forest and rocks appeared as vague silhouettes beyond the cave entrance. The rain had stopped falling, but the wind was still blowing, and the ground was wet where they lay inside the cave. Lucy had weaseled her way between them, but she stirred when Mason did, grumbled and moved back toward the rear of the cave again.

Mason propped himself up, looked outside, watched the light grow, inexorable. He heard Jess rustling beside him, and then she sat up too and rested her head on his shoulder.

"Burke?" she said.

He glanced at her.

"I don't really want to die today," she said. "Not anymore."

Now he really looked at her, and she was watching him, and he leaned in and kissed her, took her in his arms and held on to her.

This time was different from the first times, on the troller. This was something more intimate still, like they both of them knew to hold on to this, savor it, before the violence to come.

They moved slowly, wanting it to last, drawing warmth from each other, and strength. The cave seemed to shrink around them, as if time had slowed or even stopped altogether—but of course it hadn't; the gray daylight seeping into their cave was proof, and soon enough the tides would turn and Kirby Harwood and the others would be here. And anyway, Lucy groaned from the back of the cave, like she couldn't believe they were going to make her endure this again, and that was enough to break the spell and send Jess into fits of laughter, and Mason had to laugh too, and when the laughter died away, Jess wrapped her arms around him and pulled him deeper into her, her hands on his back, urging him faster, and she laughed again as she came, and then he was coming too, driving down into her and seeing stars behind his closed eyes.

They lay there together for a few minutes, but not very long. It was shortly thereafter they heard the sound of the motor.

Kirby was early. The tide wouldn't turn for another half hour, but there he was; it had to be him, not too far away now, not if they could hear the motor with the wind blowing like it was.

Jess hurried to get dressed in the cramped space of the cave, Burke doing the same beside her. Every now and then he'd glance at her, she could feel it, or she would glance at him, but they didn't exchange words and barely even made eye contact. There was too much to do now, and they were running behind.

She finished dressing and crawled to the edge of the cave. Peered out and across the rock and cocked her head and listened to the motor. It was a boat, that was obvious, and she couldn't hear the helicopter. Maybe they were lucky, and Kirby had left the bird behind.

Burke poked his head out beside her. "Can't be in the pass yet," he said. "That engine would be louder."

"Not yet, but soon," she replied. "You have what you need?"

He reached back into the cave, came out with the shotgun and two of the pistols. "What about Lucy?"

"I'll tie her up somewhere the fighting won't reach her," Jess said. "She'll be okay. You just worry about doing your job."

He saluted, saying, "Yes, ma'am," and she had to smile.

"Go," she said. "And stay out of sight until you hear me start shooting."

He hoisted the shotgun. Leaned over and kissed her, hard, on the mouth, and then he was gone, skirting the rock face to the forest and disappearing within. He would circle around to the northeast end of the island, wait to trap Kirby and the boys in the pass. If all went to plan, Jess didn't think she would need him, but even if she did, the fight was going to end quick.

She called for Lucy. Heard the dog stretch, and the jingle of her collar as she made her way out of the cave.

"Good morning, girl," Jess told her. "Things are going to get weird for a little while here, but I don't want you to worry. Everything's going to be fine."

Lucy looked at her with worried eyes.

"I *promise,*" Jess said. "We'll take care of some business, and then we'll get on back to the mainland and I'll buy you a steak, okay?"

Lucy licked her face, and Jess figured that was as good an agreement as she was likely to get. She reached over to the ruined inflatable, untied the line from the bow, and tied it around Lucy's collar, and then, crouching low, she hurried the dog into the trees and circled up and around to the top of the rock wall, above the little cave. Found a nice little spot far away from where the shooting would happen, sheltered by rock and nestled in the ferns, and tied Lucy's line to a tree.

"You stay here," she told the dog. "I'll come back for you soon."

Lucy looked at her a beat, then took to surveying the area; she nosed up to a fern and took an exploratory bite. Jess watched the dog, suddenly reluctant to leave her. The damn mutt the cause of so much of this chaos—her very existence leading Burke here and thus leading them all to this island—and the dog was more concerned with eating her greens than with the reckoning that would come.

Shit.

She loved the dog, and she was glad Burke had come into her life to help get her back. She reached over and scratched Lucy's flank, once, and then she straightened and studied the dog, and hoped they would see each other again. She couldn't remember ever getting this hung up on a goodbye with a human being, but hell, who on earth needed proof that dogs were better than people?

"Bye, dog," Jess said. Lucy looked up, wagged her tail a couple of times. Went back to eating her fern, and Jess decided that was her cue. She turned and left the dog there, made her way back down toward the cliff overlooking the pass. The tide would be turning soon, and she needed to get into position.

Mason hurried through the dense forest, the shotgun in his hands and the pistols at his waist. He couldn't hear the boat, but he knew it was out there, and he could see that the water in Dixie Lagoon was lapping at the tree line. He knew the tide was going to have to turn soon.

He had no time to think, and no time to be worried about anything other than Kirby Harwood driving that little boat up the pass before he was ready. He made the isthmus and glanced west at the open water, big, rolling swells coming in, pounding the beach and the outlying rocks with surf. He pressed on.

There weren't any paths to the north side of the island, none that Mason could see, and the trees went right to the shoreline, so there wasn't any beach to follow either. He had to slog his way through the middle of the forest, tangled overgrowth and deadfall, the ground muddy and soft beneath his boots, the trees saturated with rainwater. He was soaked through his jacket before he'd made it ten yards.

It took him a full half hour to struggle his way around the top of the island to the point, the terrain rocky and uneven, rising and falling and rising again. He was winded by the time he was close, and he slowed down to catch his breath and so that Kirby and his boys wouldn't hear him crashing toward them, wouldn't see the trees move and know he was coming.

The island stretched north and east a little farther from the entrance to the pass, but Mason figured he might not ever set foot there. He was only interested in the pass and the boat waiting offshore, fifty yards from the rocks.

The Grady-White was almost as long as Ty Winslow's troller, but it was sleeker, whiter. It sat streamlined in the water with its twin engines burbling. Mason ducked away as soon as he saw it. He'd seen men aboard, dark jackets clustered by the console and standing guard at the stern, but he didn't dare stick around long enough to count them. It wouldn't matter how many Kirby had brought with him, so long as Jess could catch them with their pants down.

Mason backed away into the forest again. Retraced his steps along the north side of the pass until he found the outcrop he was looking for, a piece of rock he and Jess had spied from her cliff. From the outcrop Mason could see up the pass toward where Jess would be set up, but he'd be blocked from Harwood's sight by the forest behind him. It was a good spot, and it was where he would set up to ambush the deputy.

He looked west toward the face of the cliff, searched the top for any sign of Jess and her rifle. He wondered what she'd done with Lucy, whether she'd kept the dog close. He wondered what Harwood would do if he got hold of the dog again, and he wished he'd brought her to this side of the island instead.

It was too late now.

The noise of the boat's engines increased. Mason looked again for Jess on the cliff, but he couldn't see her, and he supposed that was a good thing. He ducked back into the forest and checked and rechecked his shotgun, listened to the boat approach, and waited for his time to act.

FIFTY-FIVE

Kirby Harwood squinted up the narrow stretch of water as he idled the boat closer. Searched the shore for any sign of Jess Winslow or Mason Burke. He hadn't seen them yet, but Harwood knew they had to be out there.

Dale Whitmer came up behind him. Stood beside Harwood at the console. "Tide's turning, Kirby," he said, his hand shading his eyes as he searched the pass. "We're losing our window."

On Harwood's other side, Joy shifted and fixed Harwood with those unsettling black eyes. "What are we waiting for, Deputy?"

Harwood didn't answer right away. They'd set out from Neah Bay at first light, made Dixie Island with plenty of time before slack. It was rough in the strait, a small-craft advisory, but the Grady-White could take it and there wasn't any other choice.

If any man in Deception Cove wanted to go ahead and kill someone or rob somebody's store, now was the day to do it. Harwood had brought his whole team. He'd armed Whitmer and Cole Sweeney with Remington model 700P rifles, deployed them to the stern of the boat, and told them to shoot anything that moved on the shore. Joy had brought the M4 with the grenade launcher, and Harwood had an M4 as well. In the little galley up by the bow, they'd stashed the rest of Joy's weapons—a couple of shotguns and some pistols—plenty of ammunition. By the numbers, the job sounded simple. Three cops and one scary Nigerian motherfucker with big guns and unlimited ammunition should have no trouble taking over the island. But by Harwood's way of thinking, the math just didn't add up.

Whitmer nudged him. "Kirby."

"I heard you, Dale," Harwood said.

"We don't move now, we don't move at all, boss. We need to get in there."

Harwood scratched the top of his head. "Get in *there,* you mean?" he said. "Up into that pass?"

He could feel Whitmer staring at him. "Where else?"

"Take a look up in there, Dale," Harwood said. "Tell me what you see."

Whitmer didn't answer right away. Then he spat. "I see the tide's turning, is what I see," he said. "Now listen, Kirby, if you're too chickenshit to—"

"To what?" Harwood looked at him, hard. "That's a US Marine waiting for us in there, Dale, and as best we can surmise, she's heavily armed. When we get up in that pass, there's no turning around, and if she's half as smart as we know she is, she's already figuring she can trap us in there, pick off each and every one of us from up on one of those ridges." He cocked his head. "Are you seeing that, Dale? Because that's the first thing I fucking see, and if I'm thinking about it, you can be damn sure the goddamn marine is thinking it too."

Whitmer went silent. He looked away, spat again. Joy picked up the thread. "You said that pass was the only way onto the island, Deputy."

"Maybe it is." Harwood searched the rocky walls of the pass one more time. Couldn't see movement, but he knew—just *knew*—Jess Winslow was out there, somewhere, waiting on them. "But we're not going in there."

Joy made to reply. Harwood shifted the engines into reverse, drowned him out with one thousand horsepower.

"I'll find another way," he hollered over the roar. "That bitch hasn't seen the last of us yet."

Mason heard the engines rev and realized quickly that something was wrong. He ducked off the outcrop and back into the forest, hurried up the pass to the entrance rocks, where the waves from Kirby Harwood's wash were just hitting the shore. The boat itself was just curling out of sight south, tracing the edge of the island on a plane, pounding into the swell. Within thirty seconds, it would be gone.

Mason counted the bodies aboard. Four of them. Too far away to figure out who, but by Mason's count, there were five working against them—six if you counted the helicopter pilot. That meant at least one man was missing, and the other four were deviating from Jess's expectations.

Mason didn't like it.

He worked his way back through the forest to the rocky outcrop where he'd planned to back Jess up with the shotgun. Stood tall and waved the shotgun over his head toward the cliff down the pass, hoping to get Jess's attention. But nothing moved on the top of the cliff. If Jess was up there, she wasn't letting him know it.

Damn it, Mason thought. *Just what are those boys up to now?*

Down the pass, Jess was thinking Kirby Harwood was either crazy or he was dumber than she'd thought.

She was gone from the top of the cliff before the sound of the engines had stopped reverberating against the rock walls around her. Someone aboard Kirby's pride and joy must have pointed out to him that idling up that long, narrow pass was probably going to end badly. And there was only one other place on the island even remotely worth trying to land.

Now he'd be headed for the little beach on the west side of the island. And judging from the noise of those engines as he'd taken off, he was aiming to get there fast.

Jess slung the carbine over her shoulder and hurried off the back end of the cliff and into the forest, beating her way down the rocky declination toward the isthmus, picking her path more confidently now, knowing the best route. She was thinking they might have to rename this island after her, or Lucy at least, assuming they made it out alive. There couldn't be too many people who'd spent this much time marooned on these rocks and lived to talk about it.

She peeled off toward the western shore before she'd fully reached the isthmus, found her way through the trees to where the forest gave up and the sheer rock took over. There wasn't much margin between flora and a twenty-foot drop into the roiling surf; she picked her way carefully along the edge, looking out at the big, rolling swell coming in, breaking over the offshore shoals. She kept looking for Kirby's boat and not seeing it.

Then she rounded a little point to a rocky peninsula just wide enough for her to stand and look north toward where the island curved inland toward the beach. And there, a hundred yards off that beach, the Grady-White idled, rolling in the trough of what must have been six-foot rollers, pitching from side to side as the men aboard studied the beach.

They hadn't seen her. And though they were a hundred yards out from where they were thinking of landing, they were only about fifty yards from where Jess was standing on the peninsula. She lifted the rifle to her shoulder, surveyed the boat through the scope. There were four men aboard, all of them holding on for dear life as the swell had its way with the Grady-White. Jess studied all of them in turn.

Kirby at the controls, gesturing inland. His nameless buddy with the helicopter and the grenade launcher riding shotgun, his expression eerily calm. Dale Whitmer, sullen as always, holding a long gun at the stern beside Cole Sweeney, who just looked seasick.

They all would have looked ridiculous if they hadn't been aiming to kill her. And Jess didn't know the man beside Kirby, but she knew enough to know she would have to respect him. If the boys made it onshore, he'd be the one to watch out for.

Well, she thought, *let's make sure that doesn't happen.*

She found the man in her sights again. Followed him as the boat rose and fell on another big wave. He was about Burke's age, she figured. Slim, with a scar across his cheek and black, lifeless eyes. He carried that M4 with the grenade launcher below, and as she watched, he was saying something to Kirby, and she could tell from the way Kirby reacted that even the deputy was afraid of him.

Let me do you a favor, Kirb.

Jess kept the rifle trained on the newcomer. Slipped off the safety switch. Waited as the Grady-White dropped down into a trough, followed it back up again. Let out her breath as the boat seemed to hang there, waiting on the next wave, as time seemed to slow.

Then she pulled the trigger and watched as the newcomer went down.

FIFTY-SIX

Joy was flat on the deck before Harwood's mind had even processed the shot. The Nigerian gripped his shoulder, writhing at Harwood's feet and cursing unintelligibly, and Harwood stood slack-jawed and stupid at the control panel, trying to piece it all together.

The next shot shattered the Grady-White's windshield, and Harwood didn't hear that one either—the crash of the surf sounding like artillery fire—but he knew Jess Winslow wasn't going to miss twice. He jammed the boat into gear and pushed the throttle full bore, knocking Sweeney and Whitmer on their asses at the stern, nearly sending Sweeney over the rail.

The boat roared and launched forward, Harwood ducking down low, trying to figure out where the widow was shooting from. He guessed to his right, on the rocks that curled out from the little bay, but he couldn't be sure, wasn't going to risk his life. He knew they had to move or she would pick them off one by one.

"Find her," he hollered back at Sweeney and Whitmer. "Get off your asses and take the bitch out."

The boys were still rolling around back there, fumbling for their rifles, and Joy had pulled himself up into a sitting position, keeping pressure on the big fucking hole in his shoulder, still saying something that Harwood couldn't decipher.

Harwood had bigger questions to answer anyway. Like how the hell he was going to get the boat through the shoals and to shore under heavy fire and on a huge, breaking swell. Even now, as the boat rocketed forward, Harwood could see white water in his path, washing over the jagged reefs that guarded the little bay, just waiting to tear the bottom out of his boat.

If they went in the water, they were dead, Harwood knew. The surf would smash them to bloody pieces on the rocks, and if they somehow survived the trip, Jess Winslow would be waiting to cut their balls off on the beach. He had to dodge the rocks somehow and get the boat to shore. And he was only going to get a single shot to try it.

Harwood pulled back on the throttle as much as he dared, felt the swell pick up the boat and carry it in toward the bay, the waiting rocks. He knew he couldn't slow down too much, not with the waves carrying them; he needed to keep the propellers churning water if he wanted to maintain any kind of control. But damn if those rocks weren't coming at him fast.

Harwood dodged a nasty patch of black rock, skirting to the right as another wave caught them and hurtled them forward, the wave exploding against the rocks and soaking Sweeney and Whitmer with salt spray. But the Grady-White was clear of that first shoal, and Harwood didn't look back. He kept the little boat moving, kept his eyes on the rocks, looking for a way through. The bay was a maze, choked with half-submerged hazards, but Harwood knew his boat, and he knew his own ability. He had ample faith in both.

So long as that bitch doesn't start shooting again, he thought, *we might just be all right.*

As soon as he had the thought, though, he heard another shot ring out from shore—and this one caught Whitmer in the chest. The deputy swore and toppled overboard, disappeared in the wash, and Harwood called his name and turned around to look for him. He didn't see Dale, but he damn sure saw the breaker.

It was a beast of a wave, and it was fixing to kill them. Harwood watched it rise, a thick black wall of water, saw the lip curling over high above the stern, and he knew they were finished just as soon as it came crashing down.

"Hold on," he told Sweeney and Joy in the split second before impact. "This here's going to suck."

She'd fucked up.

Jess watched the wave build behind Harwood's boat, and she swore to herself and wished she'd been smarter.

As soon as Kirby had decided to make a run for shore, she'd have been better off letting him through those rocks unmolested, she thought now. Let him have the little bay, the calmer water, and then open up on him and his boys, put them down without risking the boat.

She needed the boat to get Burke and Lucy off the island.

But she'd had a clear shot at Dale Whitmer, and she'd taken it and hadn't missed, popped him center mass and sent him into the drink. One down—two, if she was lucky, though she didn't think she'd hit Kirby's friend with enough to put him out of the fight permanently. Mind you, it would be a miracle if any of them survived what was about to happen, that monster wave breaking over the stern, picking up the Grady-White and surfing it out of control toward mountains of sharp rock. It would be a miracle if the boat survived too.

Jess watched from the southern edge of the bay as Kirby tried to outrun that wave, as he couldn't do it, as it spun the Grady-White sideways and nearly tipped it full over, hurtling it toward the reefs on the bay's opposite shore. The boat rode the wave up and onto the shoals, ten or fifteen feet across the rocks before the wave ran out of steam and the boat went aground.

She could hear the hull rip and tear from across the water, watched the little boat shudder violently as the wave's last momentum dragged it farther into the bay. The boat stayed upright anyway, and when the white water receded, the boat stayed where the wave had left it, marooned in two or three feet of turbulent water, the white hull scratched to shit, the twin engines still roaring.

There was no movement from within the boat, and for a brief moment Jess wondered if the wave hadn't killed them all. But then she saw Cole Sweeney poke his head up from the stern and look around, dazed. He seemed to say something toward the cockpit, so she figured Kirby and the other guy were still aboard too.

So be it, she thought, leveling her rifle again. *I was kind of looking forward to messing these guys up anyway.*

The bitch was shooting again.

Harwood stayed as low as possible in the cockpit of the Grady-White. The boat was aground; they'd survived the ride somehow, but he couldn't imagine how the hull would react if he tried to reverse back into open water.

Dale was gone too. He'd disappeared over the side and hadn't come up, and Harwood figured the odds were pretty good he'd drowned.

At this point he had bigger things to worry about. Like a pissed-off ex-marine putting 5.56 NATO rounds through the hull of his boat.

"Sweeney," he called back to the stern, where Cole was ducked low, his rifle lying forgotten on the other side of the deck. The deputy was spitting blood, but he looked okay otherwise. He locked eyes with Harwood, and his vision was clear, if a little bit terrified.

"Pick up that rifle and give me covering fire," Harwood told him. "We have to get off this boat."

They had to get their asses in gear, is what they had to do. Every second they stayed here was another yard Jess Winslow could close with that rifle of hers, and Harwood didn't want to be on the beach when she showed up at the tree line. They needed to get to the forest before she cut them off, then find somewhere to hide and regroup, take advantage of their numbers and mount a counterattack.

Mason Burke was out there somewhere too, Harwood knew. He didn't know what the ex-con was up to, but he had a hunch the guy would show up at the least opportune time.

Sweeney crawled across the deck and retrieved his rifle. Crawled back to the starboard side and hesitated there like a private too scared to climb out of his foxhole. Harwood gave him a look, nodded toward the forest, and Sweeney swallowed and looked pale and did as instructed, laid his rifle across the gunwale and began laying down fire.

Harwood was moving as soon as he heard the shots. Grabbed his M4 and some spare ammunition, and then he was crawling to the port side of the Grady-White, away from where Jess's shots were coming from. He muttered a quick prayer and climbed over the side, threw himself down to the water below, his rifle aloft to keep it out of the spray. He landed hard, wincing and swearing, the rock cutting through his clothes, the water soaking them, waves trying to drag him farther into the bay.

He circled around to the bow of the boat and aimed his own rifle toward Jess's patch of forest.

"Come on," he told Cole, who dropped back just as soon as he heard Harwood begin shooting. Pretty soon the deputy was crouched in the water beside Harwood, his hands bloody and clothes shredded from another hard landing.

Harwood locked eyes with Joy, who remained in the cockpit. The Nigerian had been shot, but he wasn't quitting the fight.

"Come on if you're coming," Harwood told him. "We gotta get off this beach."

He set up his rifle and fired again, and Cole did too, and as they fired and Joy made his move, Harwood searched the forest for any sign of the widow and her rifle, but he couldn't see anything. He hoped they'd hit her with a round or two, neutralized her, but he knew they wouldn't ever be that lucky. She was probably just taking cover.

No matter. Three rifles and only fifteen yards to the safety of the forest. Harwood motioned to Joy and Sweeney to make the run for it while he continued to rake the trees with rounds from his rifle. When the two men were safely off the beach, he ducked behind the bow of the boat and found Cole where he'd hidden in the forest, gestured to his deputy to start shooting.

Cole took a position and aimed across the bay, and when he pulled the trigger, Harwood stood and ran, stumbling on the wet rocks and nearly falling on his face into white water, expecting any minute to catch a round in his back. He covered the last three or four yards in the air, leapt into the forest and landed in a pile of deadfall, came up spitting moss and covered in mud, but hell, he was alive, and he'd made it off the beach.

"Let's find her," he told the others. "Put her down fast, and then we take care of Burke."

Joy nodded. Sweeney peered out at the beach, the wrecked Grady-White sitting battered in the swell. He nodded too.

The men stood in unison. Stayed as low as possible and crept into the woods, rifles at the ready, scanning the forest for any sign of Jess Winslow.

FIFTY-SEVEN

Jess had screwed up something bad now, letting Harwood and the others off of the boat and into the woods. She'd hoped the waves would take care of them, or that she could pin them down in the wreck and pick them off, one by one. But someone on the team had a decent sense for tactics and had pretty well kept her ducking while they worked off the boat and across the beachhead. And now they were in the woods, and they were going to spread out, and killing them all had just become a hell of a lot harder.

For the first time Jess wondered if she might lose this fight.

She chased the thought. Burke was out there too, somewhere, with a big freaking shotgun. If he could neutralize just one of the surviving attackers—preferably the scary guy—Jess was reasonably certain she could take care of the other two.

She dropped the empty magazine out of her rifle. Slammed another one in. Whatever happened, she would need to conserve ammunition. She slipped through the trees toward where Harwood and the others had landed, and hoped Burke was at least savvy enough to provide some kind of diversion.

Mason plowed his way through the forest, bullying through the overgrowth with the butt end of his shotgun. He'd heard the shooting, a staccato conversation, and he'd realized very quickly that things weren't going as planned.

Jess wasn't figuring on having any kind of back and forth, he knew. She'd hoped to deliver a sermon from on high, Old Testament style. But Harwood and his boys had clearly interrupted.

The woods were rough going. Branches tore at his clothes and clawed at his face, left him scraped and bloody, and the rocks ripped at his pants and into his knees as he climbed up and over yet another obstacle. He could hardly be sure he was moving in the right direction. He caught glimpses of the little lagoon and the wrecked troller through the dense brush now and then, but he was more following his ears toward the sound of the gunshots than he was navigating by sight.

The rifles kept popping off. Mason guessed Jess was the single shots, slow and methodical, and the jackhammer repetition belonged to the deputies. He hoped so, anyway; it meant Jess was still far enough away to be picking her shots.

Sooner or later the deputies would close in on Jess, though. So Mason kept plowing through the trees. Tried to keep his movements quiet, so the boys wouldn't hear him approach, but hell, they were shooting real loud and the surf was crashing anyway. With any luck, he'd be able to walk up behind them and near tap them on the shoulder before they knew he was there.

With better luck, they wouldn't know at all.

He kept moving, following the shots. Hoping Jess could fend the men off for as long as it took for him to swing in behind them.

Deliver me from my enemies, O my God; protect me from those who rise up against me.

Behind Jess, on the southern side of the island, Lucy could hear the shots too. They boomed through the forest around her, resonating through the tall trees and bouncing off the rock faces, filling her ears with apocalyptic noise.

She whined, paced, tail between her legs, wanting to escape but unsure in which direction, the sound ceaseless and deafening, her panic mounting. She fled to the end of her tether, cowered there, shaking, as the gunfire fell silent. The silence did nothing to calm her; the sound had come before, and it could come again.

Sure enough, within seconds, the forest exploded in sound again. It was enough to scare her into action. She pulled at her tether, wriggled her collar loose, squirmed her head through it, and pawed it clear with her foreleg. The collar dropped to the ground. She was free.

Lucy didn't waste time. She ran.

FIFTY-EIGHT

Dale Whitmer washed up, bleeding and spitting seawater, on the north side of the bay. Felt a monster breaker scrape him over a boulder like a bed of nails, then draw back, leaving him high and momentarily dry, confused and in pain and more than half drowned.

He lay there on the rocks, his clothes torn to shreds, his hands and face, too, and he wanted nothing more than to go back into the water and die peacefully. But it wouldn't be peaceful, he knew. The sea would batter him against the rocks until he broke, and it wouldn't be instantaneous, and it sure wouldn't be pretty. He had to move, quickly, before the next wave pulled him back.

Whitmer pushed himself up, the rock slicing open his palms where they weren't already cut. His rifle was gone; it would be useless by now anyway. Kirby's Grady-White lay aground in the surf a few yards away, beat to shit itself and probably a total loss.

The boat was upright, though, and Whitmer hoped that meant Joy's stash of guns in the little cabin was intact. Whatever happened next, he wanted to be armed.

Christ, but that Winslow bitch was a hell of a shot. Whitmer could feel the welt on his chest where she'd hit him, almost square in the sternum. If she'd aimed a little higher, he'd be dead right now, but that Joy fella had packed body armor for everyone, and Whitmer was glad for it.

There was no sign of Joy or anyone else, and Whitmer surmised that Harwood and Sweeney had made it into the bush. He'd heard gunfire from somewhere on the island as he lay bleeding, but as he made his way to the wrecked cruiser and climbed over the hull to the cockpit, the shooting stopped and the forest was silent.

Jess Winslow could still be out in those trees on the south side of the bay, scoping you with her rifle. Any moment she could realize her mistake and blow your head clean off.

But nobody fired on him, and Whitmer descended into the galley, the boat rocking as another wave hit. He found the plastic cases where Joy and Harwood had stashed them, found a whole squad's worth of .40-cal Smith & Wesson semiautomatic pistols staring him in the face when he opened the first box. He took two. Scrounged for ammunition, found a stack of spare magazines, and brought a few of those along too.

In a locker by the stairs he found one of Kirby's fishing jackets. Whitmer tore off what remained of the body armor and pulled the jacket on, stuffed the spare magazines in his pocket. Then he climbed out of the cabin and back up to the cockpit, and began to devise a strategy.

Whitmer wasn't sure he cared anymore whether Jess Winslow and the convict lived or died. He wasn't even sure he cared about the package Winslow's husband had stolen. He hadn't tagged along on this bullshit mission for the sake of a few hundred grand's worth of heroin.

Whitmer had other priorities now. And he wasn't going to leave this island until he'd accomplished what he'd come here to do.

He stashed the pistols in his waistband. Dropped over the side of the Grady-White and into knee-deep water, waded in toward the beach and the tree line beyond, stealthy as he could. Then he disappeared into the forest and began to stalk his prey.

FIFTY-NINE

Bad things were going to happen on this island.

Kirby Harwood gripped his rifle tighter and pushed through the low branches. Ten yards to his left, Cole Sweeney was fighting through trees of his own, matching Harwood's pace, step for step. Another ten yards or so away was Joy, and the men walked in unison, slowly and cautiously, circling around the edge of the bay to the south side of the island, where somewhere Jess waited.

Her rifle had gone silent, and that wasn't at all comforting. She wasn't dead; it wasn't going to be that easy. For all Harwood knew, she was watching them now through the scope of her rifle, waiting for the perfect kill shot.

Go ahead, he thought. *Shoot. Give away your position.*

He searched the forest ahead of him, ears pricked for any sound, eyes alert for any movement. Kept his finger on the trigger and swung the rifle around as he moved, knowing if he saw Jess, she'd probably see him, too, and then it'd be a race to who could shoot the other first.

Damn it, he hated the bitch.

He hated her for making him follow her to this island, for shooting at him and ruining his boat. He hated her because Bryce Whitmer was dead, and Dale probably too, and he and Cole were at the very least going to get fired over this shit, if they didn't wind up in jail.

He hated her for marrying Ty Winslow, whose stupidity was

matched only by his greed, and he hated her for going over to fight the towelheads and coming back so fucked in the brain that she needed a goddamn support dog who'd been trained by a fucking convicted killer.

He hated her for not rolling over like she was supposed to, for ruining his life and the only good thing he had going for it.

Fuck, he hated her bad, and he was going to make sure she paid for it, no matter what it cost him.

He *wanted* her to start shooting. He wanted to know where she was hiding. She was one woman, after all, and they were three men.

They would take her. They would take that rifle from her. And then they would make sure she hurt.

A noise behind Harwood scared him out of his thoughts. He spun, ready to open fire, wondering how Jess had outflanked them, but Jess wasn't there.

Nobody was there.

He realized the sound had come from deeper in the forest on the north side of the island, a branch falling over, a loud report like gunfire as a piece of wood must have cracked. Harwood met Sweeney's eyes, but Sweeney, as usual, was no help at all. The kid looked thirty seconds from pissing his pants, or not even.

"Burke," Harwood whispered. "Must be coming around behind us."

"Should we go back?" Sweeney replied.

"I'll do it." This was Joy. He'd closed the distance faster than Harwood had registered, and now he stood beside Sweeney, his busted shoulder packed tight with bandage and bloody fabric, a look of calm determination on his face. "You two find the widow. I will take care of her friend."

The look in the Nigerian's eyes was enough to keep Harwood from arguing, even as his mind hollered that the plan didn't make any sense. Joy was the most capable of the men; Mason Burke was a nobody. Surely, even Sweeney could handle the criminal, leaving Joy and Harwood to flush out Jess with their carbines.

But Joy was already gone, slipping back through the trees, and Harwood couldn't call out to him, for fear of alerting Jess, and so instead he locked eyes with Sweeney again and gestured him onward, toward the south side of the island.

Shit, he hated that woman.

Joy made his way north to where the island narrowed between the western bay and the little lagoon. He moved quickly and quietly through the forest, listening closely for any sound he might hear over the roar of the surf.

He wasn't listening for Mason Burke.

Joy wasn't concerned about the murderer. He hadn't seen any sign of him since he watched the troller leave the dock, back in the little shit town Kirby Harwood purported to rule. There had been only one person shooting at the helicopter; Kirby's boat the same story. For all Joy knew, Mason Burke had died on board the troller from one of Joy's grenades. Or maybe he was curled up in a ball somewhere, terrified.

Or maybe he was still out there, plotting his ambush. But he hadn't showed up yet, and Joy was still hunting Jess Winslow.

The marine was a sharpshooter. Joy was wearing the proof on his shoulder. *In* his shoulder, and out the other side. He knew he was lucky he'd lived, knew it was only the unpredictable roll of the ocean swell that had saved him from a kill shot to the head. Joy didn't want to give the widow another chance to kill him. He didn't relish the idea of advancing on her hiding hole, letting her see him approach.

But he didn't feel any allegiance toward Kirby Harwood or the other one, Sweeney. Those men were going to have to die anyway, no matter what happened next. Better they die doing something productive.

Harwood and Sweeney would seek out the widow Winslow. Probably she would kill at least one of them. But she would reveal her position when she did. And then Joy would take her, alive if possible, and she would take him to the stolen shipment.

Joy walked north until he'd nearly reached the trail that bisected the isthmus. He stopped and turned south again, searching through the forest he'd just walked for any sign of the deputies. He couldn't see them, and that was fine. He would hear them loud and clear when the shooting started.

He took a step in Harwood's direction, intending to retrace his path and stalk the deputies from behind. Before he could go any farther, though, he sensed something behind him, and he half turned, thinking maybe Mason Burke really *was* out there, plotting some big rescue.

"Stop right there."

It wasn't Mason Burke's voice. Joy stared as Dale Whitmer came out of the woods, his face scratched and bleeding, his clothing soaking wet and torn, his hand holding a Smith & Wesson semiautomatic aimed square at Joy's head.

"Deputy, you survived," Joy said. "That is excellent news. We're going to need you to help us flush out that widow."

Whitmer smirked back and the pistol didn't waver. "Don't either of us have to worry about Jess, not just yet," he said. "We've got unfinished business between us, and I'm about ready to put things right."

He motioned with the pistol. "Drop the gun, Mr. Joy, and let me tell you a few things about my brother."

SIXTY

Joy didn't drop the rifle. He stood still, eyeing the deputy over his busted shoulder, watching the man's gun, and trying to calculate his odds.

"You didn't think I was just going to let you walk away after what you did to Bryce, did you?" Whitmer was saying. "I mean, shit, you shot him in the head in his own goddamn kitchen, Joy. You didn't even give yourself a chance to get to know the poor miserable bastard."

Joy said nothing. He kept his grip on the rifle. He would have to duck and turn, fast, he decided. Throw himself to the ground and come up firing. He had reloaded with a fresh magazine when they came into the woods off of the boat; if he played this right, he could surprise Whitmer, take out his legs. The deputy had relaxed a little bit. He was already thinking he'd won.

Stupid.

"Got nothing to say for yourself, huh?" Whitmer continued. "I guess where you're from, that kind of behavior is normal. You all just kill a man, instead of talking things out."

"It worked," Joy replied. "You and your colleagues needed motivation. I provided it, and now we've nearly solved your problem."

"*My* problem." Whitmer spat. "Mr. Joy, I don't give two shits about that product you all are trying to move. You attacked my family, and if Okafor takes offense with how I choose to deal with that, he's welcome to come up to Makah County himself to square up with me like a man. But in the meantime, I'm fixing to solve *my* problem right now, with this gun in my hand."

Joy kept his voice calm. "If you lower that pistol now, Deputy, I'll forget this happened. We can continue to seek out the widow and her companion, and we can find your missing shipment. I won't bring this back to Mr. Okafor, and you and your friends can carry on with your lives. If not . . ."

He shrugged, and the pain in his shoulder was real, though he forced himself not to show it.

"If not, Deputy, then I'm afraid you won't like how this problem is solved."

Whitmer sneered. "You've got a real way with words, Mr. Joy," he said, advancing a step. "But I'm afraid you can't talk yourself out of this one."

Now was the time. Joy tightened his grip on his rifle, tensed his legs, and prepared to drop. Found a nice place to land, a clear patch of dirt. Whitmer was still speaking. Joy tuned him out.

Three.

Two.

BOOM.

A gunshot. Deafening. Joy ducked, instinctive, rolled away like he'd planned. Came up twisting around on his wounded shoulder, swearing from the pain, curling around with the rifle to find Whitmer and bury him. But Whitmer was gone.

Correction: Whitmer was already on the ground, howling and clutching at his midsection. He'd dropped the pistol, his hands bloody where he gripped at his stomach. He writhed on the ground, screaming. Another explosion, and a sapling near Joy's head disintegrated.

Whitmer hadn't fired, Joy realized. Those weren't pistol rounds. This was a shotgun.

The last thing Mason had expected to see when he reached the isthmus was two of Harwood's boys pointing guns at *each other,* but when he'd made his move on Dale Whitmer, he'd realized a little late that it wasn't Jess Winslow the deputy was trying to preach to. It was the new guy, the other guy, and Whitmer had him in a hell of a bind.

By that time it was too late to change strategy. Mason followed Whitmer's voice and figured he had to act fast, spotted a faded orange fishing slicker through the woods and knew it had to be his man. He came in hot, stopped as close as he dared, aimed the shotgun through the trees and prayed, and pulled the trigger.

Whitmer went down, dropped his pistol, and focused on trying to keep his guts in his stomach, but Mason figured out pretty quick he had other problems to deal with. He stepped out into the clearing toward Whitmer and caught movement to his left, turned with the shotgun just in time to see the new guy coming up from the ground with that M4 in his hands.

What the what?

Mason let off another blast from the shotgun, missed the new guy but sure taught that tree, and then the new guy was firing back, and Mason was ducking away and searching for cover.

Damn it, this idea had gone ugly, and it'd gotten there real fast.

Joy let off a burst and watched Mason Burke fall back. He stayed low, found cover behind a massive fallen spruce, breathed in the moss and the smell of gunpowder as he searched the forest through his scope for any sign of the murderer.

Dale Whitmer was still crying out like a gutshot man ought to. But if Mason Burke was hit, he wasn't making any noise about it. Joy scanned the forest, but the forest was thick. Burke had dropped away, out of sight, and he could be dead, or he could be playing possum.

One thing he wasn't doing was shooting. Joy thanked his stars the murderer wasn't much of a shot; at that range, with the shotgun, any half-competent gunman would have blown his head clean off. As it was, Joy imagined it was a small miracle the murderer had managed to hit Dale Whitmer. He'd at least solved that problem, anyway.

Now let me properly express my gratitude, Mr. Burke.

Burke wasn't coming. Joy realized he would have to hunt the murderer. He wished he had something for the pain in his shoulder; his left arm was going numb, but that fall to the ground had still hurt like fire.

Be a man.

Joy used the barrel of his rifle to lever himself into a crouch behind the fallen spruce. Slowly, stealthily, he eased his way around the far side to where Whitmer lay dying. He leaned down for the pistol, tucked it into his jacket. Stared down at Whitmer a beat and wanted to say something, but from the look in Whitmer's eyes, Joy could tell the deputy already knew.

Hate. Frustration. Anger. Fear. The deputy would die hurting, and he would die unhappy.

But he would die nonetheless.

"Goodbye, Deputy." Joy stepped across Whitmer's body toward where Mason Burke had disappeared. Somewhere out there the murderer waited, and Joy intended to find him.

Then Whitmer coughed behind him. Rasped something out that Joy didn't quite catch. Joy turned back.

"I beg your pardon, Deputy—"

BANG.

This time Whitmer didn't bother with soliloquies. He'd dug another pistol from somewhere Joy didn't know about, and with the last of his strength, he'd unloaded the weapon into Joy's midsection, sending Joy staggering back into the trees and down into the brush.

SIXTY-ONE

The men were killing one another, somewhere else on the island. Jess hunkered down and scanned the woods, and hoped Burke was all right.

She'd heard the boom of his shotgun, a couple of times, and then some rifle fire, and now small-arms stuff. No more shotgun, and that didn't bode well.

The fuckers were wearing body armor. Jess had figured this out when she watched Dale Whitmer emerge from the Grady-White in an orange rain slicker and hobble his way to the woods. She'd caught him square when she shot him, she knew it, and he should have died in the water, if not sooner.

But he was alive, and he'd rearmed himself. And she'd watched Joy fall back from where he was patrolling with Kirby and Cole, and now she knew Burke was probably fighting both of them. And if he hadn't learned to shoot since last afternoon, he was probably losing bad, or he was about to.

He's dying. Just like Afia.

Like Ty.

But Jess didn't have time to worry about Burke. She couldn't help him until she'd dealt with the problem at hand. And right now that problem was Kirby Harwood and Cole Sweeney, advancing up the incline toward her and hidden by a wall of trees.

If they were as smart as Dale, they'd be wearing body armor, she thought, watching as Sweeney swung out from a tall Douglas fir and dashed up to take cover behind another. And that complicated things just a tad.

But not much.

She waited, kept her breathing steady, her rifle trained on the Douglas fir that hid Sweeney. She could see where the barrel of his rifle stuck out, watched it move up and down as the young deputy caught his breath. She waited. She could fall him with a head shot as soon as he took a step, and that would be the end of Cole Sweeney.

Damn it, she knew Cole's mother. Jess gritted her teeth, tried to push that fact from her mind. The kid had known what he was getting into, coming here. He'd have no compunction with killing her.

Sweeney made his move. Jess tracked him with her rifle. She didn't pull the trigger.

The kid hadn't killed Burke when he'd had the chance.

Damn it.

Sweeney stuck his head out from behind another tree. Emboldened, he stepped out from around it, scanned the forest ahead of him with his own rifle. Jess swore softly and lowered her sight. Put a round through Sweeney's left knee and watched the kid fall.

You're getting too soft, marine, she thought. *Too damn soft.*

Then the forest blew up around her.

Jess was losing her touch.

Harwood had her pegged the second she blew out Sweeney's kneecap, watched the muzzle flash from sixty feet down the hill and opened fire accordingly, emptying his magazine into the trees where she'd fired from.

Sweeney was down, and from his screams, he was hurting, but Jess hadn't killed him. He was out of the battle, but that didn't matter. She'd lost some of her accuracy, apparently, and now he had her pinned down.

Harwood slammed a fresh magazine into his rifle. Advanced up the hill running, maintaining steady fire at Jess's hiding hole, fully aware that when he stopped to reload, she'd be up again and shooting back, and she still had the advantage.

He closed the distance, hurdling fallen logs and scrambling up wet rock, nearly falling backward but catching himself, squeezing off more rounds, keeping her pinned.

Damn it, but he could have used Joy right now.

He was coming around the side where Jess was dug in, her cover not so great on this side but perfect for Sweeney's position. Didn't matter now, except she wasn't quite set up to defend from this angle, and Harwood figured to overrun her. He was about out of breath when he reached the top of the rise, a couple of fallen logs making a nice little pillbox, and he was just about out of rounds, too. No time to stop now, though. Not with Jess on the ropes.

Harwood pulled out his pistol. Came in over the logs and kept firing, heard Jess open up from somewhere else, and ducked down until he heard her rifle click empty.

Harwood smiled. Gulped a breath. Stood up again and made for where she'd been firing from. He had the bitch dead to rights now.

Perfect time to run out of ammunition.

Jess had conserved her rounds after neutralizing Cole Sweeney. Knew she couldn't waste too many trying to tag Harwood through the trees. But Kirby was smart; he'd kept her pinned down, forced her to play defense. She'd guarded her last bullets until he reached the top of the rise, fired a couple of times and missed by quarter inches, and then she was out.

Jess dropped the rifle. Pulled a pistol from inside her jacket and let off a couple of shots to show Harwood she wasn't done yet. Nearly caught him too; she heard him curse, loud, as bark flew by his ear, and then he leaned out with his own pistol and squeezed off a couple of shots of his own.

She backed off, farther up the rise, farther into the island. Found cover and held it and waited for a shot as Kirby advanced, fired and stayed low as Kirby fired back.

He was better than she'd expected. He stayed low and out of sight, kept out of her crosshairs, edged around the side of her cover and nearly blew her head clean off. She fell back some more, scrambling up the slope on her backside, legs churning, aiming the gun down the rise and hoping Harwood didn't catch her first.

They traded shots again. Jess had the elevation, but Harwood had the advantage. He was gaining, close enough that Jess couldn't turn and run, for fear he'd put two in her ass. She clawed her way backward instead, sweeping the forest, feeling in her pocket for another magazine, knowing she'd be empty again soon.

So would Harwood.

Jess backed up, found rock. Wet rock, a wall of it, and she knew where she was, knew she was in trouble. There was no way to back up this wall. No way to get away now that she'd backed into it. She was going to have to climb for her life.

She emptied the last of her clip at where she'd last seen the deputy. Then she turned and scrambled up the rock, feet struggling for purchase, her knuckles scraped raw. The rock was wet and dangerous, but she'd done this before, she and Burke on their way to the cliff, and Jess knew the path. She made the top just as Harwood came out firing some more; she dashed into the clearing and heard Harwood click empty.

Now was her chance. Jess dropped out the spent magazine. Felt in her pocket for the spare, couldn't find it. *Fuck.* She looked around the clearing and saw it lying on pine needles where she'd mounted the wall. It must have dropped out when she ran.

She hurried back to the magazine. Could hear Harwood fighting the climb, slipping, swearing, getting closer regardless. She had only seconds. She picked up the magazine, jammed it into the pistol just as Harwood came over the top. She swung up and fired, caught him center mass—but of course the bastard was wearing armor.

Harwood didn't even blink, though Jess knew from experience it must have hurt like a motherfucker. There was something bad in his eyes, something mean and full of venom, something like she'd seen in the men who'd tried to kill her and stolen Afia in that little village in the valley.

This was personal for the deputy. This wasn't just about a million dollars anymore.

This was a fight to the death.

Harwood came at her. She fired again, at his head this time, but missed low and found armor again, and then the deputy was on top of her, knocking her back with a forearm like a grizzly bear, sending the pistol clattering across the clearing and flattening her to the ground.

Harwood kept coming. Went down with her, pinned her on her back. Rained punches at her head as she struggled to fight back, clawed at his eyes, his mouth, tried to block the blows.

He was too strong. She was strong for a woman, but he was strong, period, and he weighed double what she did. She couldn't move him from atop her chest, couldn't get the leverage to hit him back.

All she could do was lie there and try to grab at his arms, fight the best she could and try to stay conscious, hope somehow Burke found her before Harwood beat her skull in.

SIXTY-TWO

But Mason was in some trouble of his own.

He felt his chest burning as he backed off into the forest. When he looked down, he saw blood on his jacket, a hole in the material a couple of inches above the bottom of his rib cage. He hadn't felt it at first, with the adrenaline rushing. He'd taken a round from the other guy's rifle.

It hurt, and hurt bad, but there was no time to get upset over it. He was bound to hurt worse if the new guy caught up, and he retreated back into the trees, listening to the hellfire erupting on the other side of the island and hoping Jess was making out okay.

You've got to get over there.

The other guy wasn't even trying to keep quiet. Mason could hear him crashing through the trees as he came in on the chase. As far as he could tell, the guy wasn't shooting, though. He'd heard a couple more shots from back toward the isthmus, heard someone cry out and wondered if that was the end of Dale Whitmer. But it was about that time that Mason realized he'd been shot himself, and he decided to stop worrying about the corrupt sheriff's deputy and focus on saving his own ass.

Dang, but this sucked, and it wasn't just the pain. Mason could feel himself slowing, feel his body getting weaker, as he fought his way through the brush and over more deadfall. He'd been fighting his way through this forest all morning; even if the new guy hadn't shot him, he figured he'd have been about ready for a break. But now he felt *beat*. He felt slow, heavy. Clumsy. He climbed a fallen trunk and crashed down on the other side, nearly dropping the shotgun, couldn't muster the focus to stay upright, stay nimble.

He couldn't run forever. Hell, he wouldn't last another five minutes, not at this pace. He stopped. Leaned against a tall fir. Touched the gunshot wound at his side, cautiously, winced as his fingers came back bloody.

The gunfire had stopped on the other side of the island. Mason didn't know if that was a good thing or not. He couldn't just lie down and die, though, not until he knew that Jess and Lucy were safe. He had to get up and go find them.

Mason steadied himself. Wiped his bloody hand clean on his shirt and forced that hand to grip the shotgun. Then he started back toward Jess, straining to listen for any sound from Kirby's accomplice. He couldn't hear much but the wind in the trees and the waves breaking offshore. Even Jess's gun stayed silent.

He climbed over a fallen tree, slid down the other side. Tried not to cry out from how the movement burned at his rib cage. He was still bleeding, and the blood was coming out dark. He was exhausted, stumbling through the trees, propping himself up on whatever he could find. It was still a long way to where Jess was.

Then he heard something. A grunt, a man in similar distress. A patch of ferns shook fifteen feet away. A branch snapped. And then the other guy stepped out into the open.

The man looked plenty messed up himself. He'd been shot in the shoulder, that Mason already knew, but there were two or three fresh holes in the side of his jacket, and he was fighting to stand upright just as much as Mason was. The man's dark eyes were ashen; he breathed ragged through his mouth. But he still carried that M4, and he still scanned the trees like he was hunting to kill.

The men saw each other at about the same time. For a long moment neither did anything, and time seemed to slow to an endless, surreal pause.

Then the other man raised his rifle, and the world moved in fast-forward. Mason swung up with the shotgun and pulled on the trigger, and both guns let off simultaneously. The other man staggered backward. Mason slumped to the ground. The forest went quiet again.

SIXTY-THREE

He'd wanted to play football. He'd wanted to raise a family. He'd wanted to move out of Deception Cove with Terri-Lee and live the kind of life they were meant for, the all-state-quarterback and head-cheerleader life, the sweethearts-in-the-city life, a beautiful, successful life. He'd wanted to be envied by every sad, failed motherfucker who stayed stuck in Deception Cove, nothing to live for but reality TV.

He'd wanted Ateke Okafor to make him rich. He'd wanted Kirk Wheeler to retire and make him sheriff.

He'd wanted Ty Winslow to not fuck with his package. He'd wanted Jess Winslow to do the same.

He'd wanted Mason Burke to mind his own business and fuck back off to wherever he'd come from.

He wanted his package. He wanted Joy to go home. He didn't want Bryce Whitmer and Dale Whitmer and Cole Sweeney to be dead. He didn't want to leave this island in handcuffs.

Hell, Kirby Harwood just wanted to go home to Terri-Lee and forget this had ever happened. Sell the house for whatever they could get, the truck and what was left of the boat, too, resign his position and catch a bus somewhere else, forget about Deception Cove and every miserable person in it.

He wanted this to end. But it hadn't ended. And deep down Harwood knew it wasn't ever going to end, not the way he wanted.

Harwood didn't want to be here, but here he was, and he took out his anger and his frustration and, damn it, his *fear* on Jess Winslow beneath him, beating her blindly as she fought to get free, as she grabbed weakly for his hands and his throat.

She couldn't escape. She couldn't fight back. No matter what she did, Harwood knew he was going to kill her before he stood again.

Some marine you turned out to be, Jess.

He could feel her strength draining. Her body relaxed some, and her hand swiped at him, feeble. He swatted it away and stared down at her.

"You should never have tested me, Jess," he said, panting. "I told you I'd win."

She spat blood. "Fuck you."

"I'm going to kill you," he said. "I'm going to bash your head in right here, and then I'm going to find your boyfriend, and I'm going to drag him up here to see what he did. And then I'm going to kill him, and I'll find your dog, and I'll kill her, too. What do you think about that?"

Jess was gasping for breath too. Harwood could feel her chest rising beneath him. Her face was badly bruised, and she was scratched up and bleeding. She was beaten to shit, but apparently, she hadn't figured that out yet.

"You always did talk a lot, Kirby," she said. "But you're the same limp-dick nobody you always were. You're going to die on this island." She smiled at him, showed him bloody teeth. "What do you think about *that?*"

The woman had heart; that was never in doubt. But she was going to die anyway. Harwood felt around on the ground beside Jess. Found a rock big enough for what he planned next.

"Game over, Jess," he told her. He raised the rock high. Held it over her head so she could see it, and he mustered as much anger and hate and sense of cosmic unfairness as he could, and prepared to slam the rock down and end this whole fiasco.

And then something attacked him from behind.

Jess didn't believe she was seconds from dying. Even as she lay there, beat to shit and exhausted, staring up at Harwood and that big fucking rock, Jess couldn't believe it was ending this way. It just didn't feel right. It didn't feel final. She'd always figured she'd know when her last breath was imminent, and this, right here, this wasn't the time.

Turned out she was right.

Something knocked Harwood forward, and he yelled out in surprise, sprawled on top of her, and rolled back, swinging and kicking. Jess thought it was Burke at first, but then she heard the snarling and she knew Lucy had come.

The dog had her teeth gripping tight into Harwood's shoulder; she was growling in a way Jess had never heard before, her hackles raised and murder in her eyes. As Jess squirmed free from underneath Harwood, Lucy released the deputy's shoulder, and Harwood scrambled back, but the relief was just temporary. Lucy regrouped, and this time she came for his throat.

Jess rose to her knees, her head swimming, vision blurred. She watched Harwood swing his arm around, trying to fend Lucy off, but the dog simply bounced back and came at him again, forcing him backward and latching on to his arm, her teeth snapping, tearing flesh.

Harwood screamed and swore and kicked at Lucy. Lucy kept on him, backing him across the clearing toward the edge of the cliff, the elbow of the pass where Jess had hoped to stage her ambush. The dog's collar was gone; she must have wriggled out of it. Jess wondered how Lucy had known to come up here, how she'd known she was in trouble.

She's your dog, Jess. She damn well knows.

Harwood fell backward, Lucy on top of him. He kicked at her, and she bounced off and came at him again, and Harwood felt around, his hands reaching for a rock, for some kind of weapon.

Jess crawled across the clearing to where her pistol lay forgotten. She picked it up and looked across at where Lucy and Harwood still wrestled. The dog had him pinned, but Harwood's fingertips had just brushed another rock, and Jess knew the deputy would stave in her dog's head if he could just gain one more inch.

She raised the gun before he could get there. Aimed it over Harwood's head, over Lucy, and fired.

The shot did what she'd hoped it would: it terrified Lucy. The dog forgot about chewing on Harwood and bolted for the woods, leaving Harwood on the ground at the edge of the cliff. He was staring at Jess, trying to get his breath back, and she leveled the pistol at him from her knees.

"Get up."

Slowly, painfully, Harwood obeyed. He stood twenty feet away from her, hunched over, his clothes torn where Lucy had ripped through them, his face scratched and bloody. He was holding the rock he'd been trying to grab, though she couldn't tell if he was even aware.

Behind Harwood, the gray sky and the island and the pass, the wind overhead and the sound of the breakers far off. Jess stayed on her knees. She wasn't sure she could stand.

They looked at each other. The island was quiet, and Jess

wondered about Burke. Wondered about Dale Whitmer and the scary guy. Wondered if this was it.

Harwood was watching her, watching the gun. Like he was waiting for her to make up her mind.

"I got your package," she told him. She nodded across to the little cave where she'd spent the night with Burke. "It's in there."

Harwood followed her eyes. He said nothing.

"You know where it came from, that junk you were moving?" she asked. "You ever get the full history of that stuff?"

Harwood shrugged. "Asia, they said."

"Yeah, Asia," she replied. "Specifically, *my* part of Asia: Afghanistan. And you know what they do with the profits?"

He looked at her, blank eyes, hardly paying attention. Like he had no idea why she was giving this lecture.

"*Guns,* Kirby," Jess said. "Rocket-propelled grenades. Mortar bombs. IEDs. Any way they can think of to kill a US Marine, those opium-selling motherfuckers are buying it. And you and your homeboys are helping them do it."

Harwood kind of laughed. "We were just moving the stuff," he said. "We didn't hardly do anything."

Jess shook her head. "You ever see somebody with his legs blown off?" she asked. "Someone shot through the belly and trying to hold their guts in? You ever see a woman get beat up and raped and tortured, get sent back to you to die, just so you could watch?"

Harwood said nothing.

"All that stuff costs money," she said. "And you helped them get it. While I was over there fighting for this country, you were buying guns for the other guys. You ever stop to think about that, Deputy?"

"Jess," Harwood said. "Don't make this more complicated than it actually is, you hear me?"

"I guess that's a no." Jess steadied her aim, closed her bad eye, stilled her breathing. Focused on Harwood's chest as the deputy smirked a little.

"Aw, that's bullshit," he said. "You're not going to shoot an unarmed man, Jess. I know you."

She gestured to the rock in his hand. "That looks like a weapon to me."

Harwood went white. He let go of the rock. She'd put three in his chest before the rock hit the ground.

SIXTY-FOUR

The shots didn't kill Harwood. Didn't penetrate his body armor.

They weren't meant to.

Each round slammed the deputy like a freight train, staggered him, sent him reeling backward across the empty rock. By the third shot he was teetering on the cliff edge, struggling for balance and not finding it. He grabbed at air and it didn't save him; he opened his mouth to scream, and then he was gone.

Jess heard him fall, heard the grunt of expelled air as Harwood bounced off rock, heard a splash as he finally found water. She crawled to the edge of the cliff and looked over, saw him thirty feet down on her side of the pass, lying in the water with his ass to the sky.

He wasn't moving.

She watched him for a while. The tide caught hold of him a little, started tugging him out to sea. But Harwood didn't move, didn't look up and breathe, didn't paddle his arms and try to swim for shore. He just lay there, facedown, bobbing in the little waves, and Jess watched him and knew she should feel bad, but she didn't.

She didn't feel bad at all.

After a fair while, after Harwood's body had drifted down the pass a ways and nobody had come out into the clearing behind Jess to shoot her dead, Jess figured she ought to get up off her knees and go back into the woods and try to ascertain what had happened to Burke. She stood, though it hurt, and rested hunched over and blinking back tears, feeling every one of Harwood's sucker punches.

Every part of her ached. But the island was quiet, and that probably wasn't good. She stood straighter and wiped the blood from her face, started into the trees. Kept the pistol drawn and moved as cautiously as she could.

The forest was mainly silent, just the wind through the branches high above. Nothing moving at ground level, no sign of human life. The silence was eerie, and Jess didn't like it. She didn't like knowing that she might well be prey.

She happened upon Cole Sweeney first. The young deputy was lying where she'd shot him, leaned up against a tree with his head back and his eyes closed, and for a split second she thought he might be dead. But Cole heard her coming, and his eyes snapped open and he reached for the rifle beside him, but she was quicker with the pistol.

"Don't," she said, leveling the gun at his head. "Don't get stupid, now."

Sweeney glared at her. His leg was all bloody where she'd shot through his knee, and he winced every time he moved.

"You shot me," he said.

Jess scoffed. "In the leg, dumb-ass. I could have put one through your head if I wanted, you ever consider that?"

The young deputy did consider it. "Why didn't you?"

"I thought you might be worth saving," she said. "You could have killed Burke when you had the chance, and you didn't. I thought that maybe meant something."

Sweeney left the rifle where it lay. He rested his head back again and looked up at the treetops and let out a long sigh.

"I wish you had killed me," he said. "There's nothing waiting for me if I make it off this island anyway."

She shrugged. "You want, I can still shoot you," she said. "But I think you're giving up too easy. Burke served his hard time, and look at him now."

Sweeney opened his eyes, arched an eyebrow like he wasn't sure if she was joking or not. "The guy's a freaking murderer."

"Burke?" She shook her head. "He'd never even fired a gun before he came to this island. If he's killed anyone, it's since he ran into you."

Sweeney stared at her.

"The guy just loves his dog," she said. "He loves that damn dog enough to risk his life and his freedom over our stupid shit. You want a role model, Sweeney, you could do worse."

Sweeney let that sit for a beat. "So what are you suggesting I do?"

"I'm suggesting you stop trying to kill me," she said. "I'm going to take a look around and try to figure out what happened to Burke and your buddies, and if it all goes to plan, I'll make sure the Feds know you're not completely bad, if we ever get off of this island."

"What about Kirby? Dale?"

"Kirby's swimming home. And I don't know about Dale, but I'd assume the worst. I don't feel quite so charitable toward any Whitmers."

Sweeney stared up at the trees some more. Then he reached out with his arm and shoved the rifle away. "I'll probably bleed out before you get back anyway."

"You're not going to bleed out, you pansy," she scoffed. "I've seen guys walk miles on wounds worse than that one. You just stay comfortable, and I'll let you know when we're leaving."

"Shit," Sweeney said. "All right."

"All right." She picked up the rifle and slung it over her shoulder. Started off down the hill toward the isthmus. Then stopped. "Hey, where the hell's Bryce?"

Sweeney met her eyes, and his expression was flat. "Bryce is dead," he replied. "Joy blew his brains out."

"And who's Joy again?"

"Joy's the guy with the grenade launcher who fucked up your boat. He killed Bryce in his own goddamn kitchen about five minutes after he'd introduced himself to us. Said he'd help us get the package back, but one of us had to pay."

Jess thought about this. Wondered if maybe she was jumping the gun a little bit, expecting Burke to have handled Joy by himself. "Shit."

"Yeah, well," Sweeney said. "I never really did like Bryce anyway."

She left the deputy there and continued down through the forest, feeling every step and every time the rifle swung around and nudged her, wondered if she'd broken a rib or she was just getting soft. There was no sign of Burke or Dale Whitmer or Joy, and no sign of Lucy, either, and she sure as hell wasn't going to call out for any of them. She continued, her pistol ready, and tried to stay quiet as she descended through the trees.

She found Dale's body next. The deputy was lying just off the trail between Dixie Lagoon and the beach, still wearing that orange slicker he'd pulled from Kirby's boat, though Jess could see there were a fair sight more holes in it now than when he'd found it.

There was a pistol lying on the ground near Dale, and she kicked it away, but Dale had been shot more than a few times, and in bad places besides. He'd fired his last round.

She stood over him and looked down into his lifeless eyes and felt something come back to her, some kind of humanity she'd scared off when Kirby was kicking her ass. Dale, dead. Bryce, too. The Whitmers were mean as shit, but they were dumb; they hadn't come into this mess thinking it would end with the both of them shot. Hell, they'd probably bought every word of Kirby's big talk, believed they'd get rich, as they were supposed to, and nothing bad would ever happen.

And look at you now, she thought. *The end of the Whitmer lineage, shot all to shit in a dirty orange slicker.*

It was sad, and it was sad because she'd grown up with the Whitmers, and even if she hadn't much liked them, they'd always been a part of her town. She'd grown up with Kirby, too; hell, she'd almost been proud when she heard he'd made deputy, before all the shit with Ty had gone down. She'd been rooting for him to take over Kirk Wheeler's position as sheriff, just so she could say something actually good had come out of Deception Cove, just once.

But this was Deception Cove in a nutshell, right here. Big dreams dashed, and people dying young.

Something moved in the forest behind her, spooked her out of her reverie, and she spun with the pistol and curled her finger around the trigger and waited as the bushes rustled and a branch snapped, and then Lucy came out into the open.

"Lucy." Jess lowered the pistol, her heart pounding. "You nearly scared me to death, dog."

But it was Lucy who looked scared. She wagged her tail a couple of times, yawned nervously, looked into the woods and then back at Jess and yawned again and whined a little.

"What's up, girl?" Jess took a step toward Lucy, and the dog turned back the way she had come, started into the forest, and looked over her shoulder at Jess to make sure she was coming.

Jess got the point. She followed Lucy off the trail and down from the cliff, but closer to the lagoon side of the land this time.

Apparently, the dog had been over there, silent, as Jess had worked her way across to Dale Whitmer. Without her collar, Lucy didn't jingle when she walked, and the forest was thick enough that Jess could have walked right past her and not seen.

But she could see Lucy now, and she followed close, drawing her pistol and feeling her nerves start to wake up again. It had to be Burke, she knew, and the way Lucy was acting, it had to be bad.

She found the other guy, Joy, lying slumped over a rotten stump a stone's throw from the cove. He had his rifle slung around his chest, but he wasn't a threat anymore; half of his head was blown off, and he'd taken a few more rounds in places the body armor wasn't protecting.

Jess hoped he'd died slow, the son of a bitch.

Lucy skirted Joy's body quickly, her tail between her legs. She hopped up onto a fallen tree and looked back at Jess again, waited until she'd nearly caught up, and then jumped down again. Jess made the tree, and began to step over. Then she stopped.

On the other side was Mason Burke.

He'd been shot too, at least a couple of times. His jacket was bloody, at chest level and lower. He lay nearly flat on the forest floor, his head resting against the trunk of a tall pine, and he wasn't moving, and she thought as she looked at him that he was already dead.

Of course he's dead, stupid. That's how this ends.

But then Lucy went to him and licked at his face, whimpering, and Jess saw Burke smile weakly and open his eyes just a hair.

"Hey, girl," he said. Lucy wagged her tail fast and licked at his face some more. "Hey, girl, it's okay," Burke said. "It's gonna be okay."

Jess stepped over the tree and came down close to where

Burke lay, and he raised an arm weakly to fend Lucy off, looked up at her.

"Hey," he said.

She swallowed. "Hey yourself."

"Are we winning?"

"Yeah, Burke," she said. "We won."

He smiled a little bit wider. Leaned his head back. "Good," he said.

Then he closed his eyes, and Jess felt her heart break a little bit.

SIXTY-FIVE

Jess wasn't going to let Burke go that easy.

She left Lucy to keep an eye on him, figuring if the dog was nearby, he might think twice before deciding to die. She'd packed his wounds with dirt, wrapped them with strips she'd torn from her T-shirt, stabilized him as best she could. Burke needed more than battlefield dressings, though; he needed a hospital, no matter how many kisses Lucy gave him.

She wrapped her jacket around her and hurried back toward the isthmus and the western beach, where Kirby's Grady-White lay wrecked on the rocks, a few feet above the waterline now that the tide had fallen. She studied the hull as she approached, looking for any visible holes. She couldn't see any, but that didn't mean anything. She circled around the far side and climbed over the gunwale and into the cockpit, went down into the cabin to look for something she could use.

What she found was a half-empty first aid kit, a flare gun, and a shot-to-shit radio. And in one of the plastic cases with all the guns, $10,000 in cash. Whoopee.

The flare gun wouldn't do much with no one around to see it. The first aid kit was barely more than a handful of Band-Aids and some Polysporin. The radio wouldn't power up, and there wasn't any way Burke would live to spend that ten grand unless Jess could figure out a way to keep him alive.

Hell, Jess thought, *I'm just as well giving Burke a hit from that package Ty stole.*

She came back up into the cockpit and looked out over the ocean. The tide had turned again; it was coming in now, but it would take several hours to refloat the boat. For all she knew, Burke would be dead by then.

Jess pushed the thought from her mind. Focused on setting goals, things she could accomplish, things that probably wouldn't mean squat in the long run but that would keep her occupied in the meantime.

She took the first aid kit and a bottle of water and humped it back across to where Burke lay, not moving. He didn't stir as she approached, and she cursed herself, thinking once again he was dead.

But he was a strong piece of work, she had to admit. He opened his eyes a little bit and smiled up at her, and the dog looked at her and wagged her tail like she was hoping Jess had somehow brought the miracle cure.

Jess gave Burke water, and she treated his wounds as best she could from the first aid kid, though her T-shirt bandages were doing about as well as any Band-Aid. Burke drank the water and didn't complain as she checked up on him. When he'd drunk his fill and she was satisfied, she looked around and exhaled and pitched their only shot.

"We've got to get you back to that boat, Burke," she said. "It's going to hurt like a real bitch, but there's no other option."

He didn't answer right away. Finally he forced out a laugh. "You sure don't make it easy on a man."

"I can't see us getting off this island any other way," she said. "So you gather up your strength, and I'll be right back."

She took off into the forest again, climbing up the southern side of the island to where she'd left Cole Sweeney. He hadn't moved either, looked like he was sleeping. But he stirred when she approached, looked greedily at the water bottle she still carried. "You mind sharing that, Jess?"

She held it just out of his grasp. "I need you to do something for me first," she said. "I need you to get your ass up, and down this mountain to the beach and the boat. Can you do that?"

Cole looked at his ruined leg. "What, like this?"

She unslung the rifle from her shoulder. Emptied it, threw the shells into the woods. "There's your crutch," she said. "Only way off this island is using Kirby's boat, and the tide is coming in. You've got a few hours, but don't waste them."

Cole took the rifle. Looked at it, looked at her like she was crazy. Jess shrugged. "You'd rather wait here, be my guest," she said. "I'm just giving you options."

"Can I at least have some water?" Cole asked. "I'm dying here."

"You don't know what dying is," she said, but she handed him the water bottle and turned and went back down toward Burke, figuring you can lead a horse to water and all that. If Cole made the boat by the time she was ready, good for him. If not, she wasn't waiting around.

Burke was sitting a bit straighter when she found him again. Lucy looked concerned, but what else was new?

"I don't know why *you're* so worried, dog," Jess muttered, bending down in front of Burke. "Only thing hurt on you is your feelings."

She shooed Lucy away. Spoke to Burke. "I'm a little out of practice with this 'no man left behind' stuff," she said. "So bear with me."

She closed her eyes and got focused, sent her mind back to Parris Island, boot camp, a pissed-off drill instructor and a whole regiment of male recruits who didn't think girls like her belonged in the corps.

She sent her mind back to the defiance, the force of will, and the fear of failure that had pushed her to do the impossible over those thirteen weeks in South Carolina, and then she knelt down and hauled Burke over her shoulders, and forced herself to stand, the weight nearly breaking her, suffocating her, driving her back down into the dirt.

She leaned forward against Burke's pine, his body draped all over her, and she counted to three and focused her breathing, and pushed off and started through the forest to the beach.

It was slow, very slow, and it must have been torture for Burke. Jess had to stop every ten feet or so, adjust Burke's weight, find something to lean on. She wished she hadn't given Sweeney that water, wished Burke hadn't done all those push-ups. When the shit got *real* hard, she almost wished Burke were dead.

But that was a lie. She knew she'd rather be dead than live with Burke's absence, live with the knowledge that he'd died for her. She knew she'd see him with Afia every time she closed her eyes, more guilt and this time compounded by the fact that Burke was the most decent man she'd ever met in her life, and she couldn't even keep him alive long enough to tell him.

This kept her going. Kept her struggling, slow and steady, through the dense underbrush, Lucy beside her and ahead of her and constantly underfoot (the damn dog), the wind in the trees and the sun sinking low, already touching the horizon. And the tide crawling over the rocks, slow and inexorable, coming to lift Kirby's boat and take them away.

Cole Sweeney caught up with them on the beach, limping along on that rifle of his, wincing every step of the way. His eyes went wide when he saw Jess and Burke; he stopped and stared and coughed a little bit, self-conscious.

"I mean, you need a hand with him?" he asked.

She didn't look at him. "Can you stand up on that knee without toppling over?"

"No," he said. "But you—"

"You just worry about you, Cole," she said, gritting her teeth. "It'll take us a while, but we'll get there."

The tide continued to rise as they struggled across the beach. By the time they reached the rocks, seawater once again covered the shoal that had trapped Kirby's boat. Jess waded through, exhausted, more tired than she'd been since Afghanistan, her head swimming and her mind fighting to keep focused. She nearly dropped Burke, staggered under his weight, fifteen feet to go and it felt like infinity.

"Put me down," Burke told her. "I can walk from here."

She snorted. "Bullshit. You'll drown on these rocks."

Sweeney came alongside, then passed them, and she watched him hobble up to the side of the boat and throw his rifle over and hesitate and then pull himself up, heard him groan in pain as he rolled over the gunwale. All too late, she remembered there were guns on board, ammunition. If he wanted to, he could go down into the cabin and come back shooting, kill them all.

But Sweeney only propped himself up in the cockpit and leaned over the rail toward Jess and Burke, his arms outstretched.

"Bring him this way," he told her. "I'll pull him aboard."

She muscled Burke the last few feet, ducked low enough that Sweeney could wrap his arms around Burke's armpits, and then she lifted with her legs as Sweeney hauled. Together they muscled Burke into the boat. Sweeney lay him down at the stern, crawled down into the cabin and came back with a couple of pillows and blankets, then tended to Burke like they hadn't been trying to kill each other just hours before.

Men.

Jess picked up Lucy, who didn't like it one bit and complained more than Burke and Sweeney put together as Jess hefted her over the side and dropped her into the boat. The dog gave Jess an aggrieved look, then went back to the stern and curled up beside Burke. Jess lifted herself aboard with the last of her strength, sat splayed in the cockpit, and wondered if she would ever stand straight again.

There was nothing to do now but wait. The tide continued to flood, and Burke was still breathing, and all that remained was to hope the tide lifted the boat before Burke stopped breathing, and that the hull wasn't too damaged to get them to the mainland.

It was a ridiculous fantasy, but it was all Jess could cling to. She lay in the cockpit and listened to the water and waited as evening turned to night.

SIXTY-SIX

The rocks clawed at Harwood's boat, but the rising tide lifted her. The twin engines turned over. And in near pitch-black conditions, Jess somehow managed to navigate the Grady-White over the treacherous shoals that ringed the little bay and out into the open ocean. All that in itself was a miracle, Jess knew. But their luck began to run out again midway across the channel.

At least, she hoped they were midway. It was full dark by now; Dixie Island to the north was nothing but the sound of waves crashing in the blackness, and the mainland to the south was just more of the same. She'd been going easy on the throttle, sailing as fast as she dared but not so fast that Burke felt it every time they caught up with the swell. The engines weren't running smooth, either; she could hear something was wrong with the port-side propeller, and there was smoke coming out of the motor on starboard. But the boat was moving, and if Jess could keep it that way, she knew they'd make Neah Bay in an hour.

Then Sweeney ducked down into the cabin to look for fresh water, and when he came back, he was swearing, and he didn't look right.

"We're flooded," he told Jess. "There's about a foot and a half of water in the galley, and it's rising fast."

"Damn it." She poked her head down the stairs and saw he wasn't lying. If anything, it looked more like two feet of water down there. There was a breach in the hull somewhere, and from what Jess could tell, it was too late to do anything to fix it.

"Guess we're racing," she told Sweeney, and opened up the throttle. "Go back there and make sure Burke is comfortable."

The boat's engines roared, and not in a good way. The starboard motor sounded like death throes, and there was a rattle from the port side that didn't portend good things. But the propellers churned the water, and the boat rose on a plane, punching through the swell with a violence that sent Lucy scurrying forward from where Burke was lying, to the stairs into the cabin and the rising tide.

Jess could feel the boat wallow, how sluggish it seemed when she pulled on the wheel. She kept the wheel straight. She knew there were lights up ahead, somewhere, that would guide her into Neah Bay.

But the water kept rising, even as she raced the boat up the channel and the navigation light at Chibahdehl Rocks came into view, midway between Dixie Island and civilization. The boat's nose was planed so high she could hardly see the light, had to twist her head outside the cabin and peer forward to find it, choose her path. From the stern of the boat, Sweeney called up with a situation report.

"These engines are almost drowned," he told Jess. "We sink any farther, we're going to start taking water on over the sides."

She glanced back and saw what he meant. The pitch of the deck was thirty degrees now, with Burke in his bundles wedged tight against the stern wall and Sweeney holding on for dear life.

Jess eased back on the throttle, let the boat come down off its plane a little bit, redistribute the water in the hull farther forward. It was probably futile—the water was still flooding in and the boat was moving slower now—but she had to do something.

They motored on like that for another five or ten minutes, the light at Chibahdehl gradually getting closer. Then Jess heard a cough from the engines astern, and Sweeney swore, loud, as both engines cut out.

"They're done, Jess," the deputy called up, his voice fairly shaking. "Those engines are fried."

She forced confidence into her voice. "Guess we're paddling, Sweeney. Go on down below and find us some oars."

Sweeney looked at her like she was crazy, but he did as instructed, and Jess took advantage of the sudden quiet to go back astern and check how Burke was doing.

He still had a pulse, she discovered. He was tangled up in blankets and near soaked from salt spray, but he was alive, and he even opened his eyes a little bit, seemed to recognize her.

"You can go," he said weakly. "I'll be fine here."

She shook her head. "It's not you I'm worried about, Burke. You ever see that dog try to swim?"

"Not many pools where I came from," he said.

"Yeah, well, she hates it," Jess said. "She hates the water something fierce, especially if there's waves. The damn dog's a diva, and I really don't want to have to pitch her over the side."

He met her eyes. "You won't have much choice soon."

"You shut up," she said. "Me and Sweeney are going to row you two princesses to shore."

Up forward, Sweeney had come out of the cabin soaked to the waist, holding a pair of black plastic paddles that would have struggled to move Ty's skiff, much less a damn cabin cruiser. Jess sighed. "It's just going to take a while, Burke. Bear with us."

At this point there was no hope in making Neah Bay. Jess figured their best bet was to angle the boat toward the light at Chibahdehl, hope the waves brought them in through the rocks and landed them on the beach. She'd seen the rocks, though; they were as bad as Dixie's, and they'd claimed as many ships. It was suicide going near them without a chart, full stop, much less trying to navigate through without power.

But what hope did they have? Jess took one side of the boat, Sweeney the other. They set up at the stern as the cruiser settled in the water more or less uniform, the breach in the hull clearly somewhere amidships. Jess leaned down into the water and paddled, and the water was closer than she'd expected, and the paddle flexed and nearly snapped with her first stroke. She swore in her head and knew it was useless, knew they were all going to die in that water, cold and black and unforgiving, the way so many from Deception Cove had died.

I guess it's kind of fitting, she thought. *But I doubt many guys from Deception died quite like this.*

Lucy had curled up with Burke again. The dog was terrified, Jess could tell, and Burke was too weak to be of much comfort. She watched as Lucy got up and started to pace, her tail between her legs, her body hunched over and bent like a paper clip, and Jess's heart ached. It wasn't so much that she didn't want to die, it was that she didn't want the dog to die, not like this, that dumb diva dog who'd been kicked around by every manner of human scum on this earth, and who'd never wanted much more than a warm blanket to sleep on. The dog was going to drown, just like they all were, and the difference was that Lucy hadn't ever chosen to get involved in this mess.

I never deserved you, girl, Jess thought as she continued to try to paddle. *None of us did.*

Then the lights went out, a battery dying somewhere or a wire shorting, and the boat was plunged into darkness. There was only the intermittent red light on the rocks in the distance, and the noise of the ocean as it clawed at the cruiser.

They didn't say anything, any of them. Jess figured she might have done different if Sweeney weren't there; she might have bundled up with Burke and watched the floodwaters rise and kissed him one last time before she brought out her pistol and took the easy way out, Burke and Lucy first, and her last—but Sweeney was here, and the kid was still paddling hard. She could hear him breathing, hear how scared he was, and it didn't seem right to just give up with him there. The mood wasn't quite right for melodramatic goodbyes.

So they waited in silence, left to their own thoughts. Jess tried to make her peace and discovered she couldn't, not after everything she'd been through, everything she'd risked and lost, every battle she'd won.

Damn it, it made her angry, fighting so hard and it all being for nothing, finally opening herself up to someone and him dying too.

It pissed her right off, and she couldn't do anything with that anger but just keep paddling harder, even as she felt the first fingers of cold water wrap around her boots.

She paddled, sweating, breathing heavy, busting her ass and nearly busting that flimsy paddle—working so hard she nearly missed the sound of the engine in the distance, the lights on the horizon.

But Sweeney heard, Sweeney saw them. "There," he said, standing and nearly falling overboard. "There's someone out there."

They were north in the strait, about a mile away, headed west toward Dixie Island and the cape beyond. From the sound and the speed, Jess could tell it was another powerboat, some kind of cruiser, and she felt sudden relief as she watched it, imagined they were all as good as saved.

But the cruiser kept going, and she realized it couldn't see them, not with the lights out. It came abeam of the Grady-White and continued without slowing. *Just another colossal fuck-you,* she thought. *Kicking us when we're down.*

But then she remembered the flare gun.

"Come on back here," she said, scrambling up to the cabin, now two-thirds flooded, the water rising quickly. She muttered a quick prayer and dropped down into the cabin, which was choked with detritus, garbage and guidebooks and loose fishing gear, and she prayed the gun had somehow stayed dry.

It had.

She'd left it in a locker above the galley table, far removed from the rushing water, and she swam her way over, navigating by memory in the dark, and reached high and searched and nudged it with her fingertips, every second more distance between their boat and safety.

Finally she gripped the gun and swam it to the stairs, climbed up into six inches of water sloshing around in the cockpit. She hurried back to where Burke lay with Lucy, Burke's head above water but not for much longer, Sweeney still paddling like it would do any good, the lights of the cruiser receding now.

"If God owes you any favors, Burke, now's the time to call them in," she said, and she raised the flare gun and pointed it in the air above the lights in the distance, muttered a quick prayer of her own, and pulled the trigger.

The flare screamed skyward, the sudden light blinding, and she could see the fear on Sweeney's face, and the resignation on Burke's, see Lucy scrambling for somewhere dry, somewhere safe, and finding nothing.

Jess watched the flare, and she watched the lights in the distance keep moving, wondered if the people on board were even looking in her direction, if they'd even notice.

Come on, she thought. *We're over here. Come on back and get us, please.*

The lights kept moving westward. The flare burned overhead. Jess heard Sweeney sigh and reach back for his paddle, but Jess didn't move. She kept watching the lights, and she kept trying to pray. She kept watching, and praying, and the lights kept receding—and then, almost imperceptibly, the lights seemed to slow, and the pitch of the motor changed.

Yes, yes please, please, God, *send them our way.*

Gradually the lights came about. The engine in the distance revved higher. The flare burned high above, and Jess handed Sweeney a flashlight to wave over his head as they watched the boat turn and speed toward them. Then she sat down on the deck beside Burke and held on to his hand, and it might have been her prayers, or it might just have been sweet relief, but she knew all of a sudden, just *knew,* that this rescue here was the last one they'd need, the last miracle, that everything from here on out was going to be better.

SIXTY-SEVEN

Sometime later Mason Burke and Jess Winslow sat across from each other at a small table outside a small coffee shop in Neah Bay, sipping good coffee and nibbling on some kind of pastry and steadfastly avoiding eye contact with each other. The sun was shining for once, and the air was warm enough to make sitting outside almost pleasant, and Lucy lay curled up between their feet, her head on her paws, catching a sunny snooze.

Across the street, a Greyhound bus idled outside the Shell station, waiting on a departure time that was approaching too quickly. Mason and Jess sipped their coffees and didn't say much.

There wasn't much left to say, Mason figured. The story was over; the book was closed. He'd passed out about the time the rescue boat arrived, heard from Jess it was Hank Moss in his old Hubert Johnson thirty-two-footer, spotlight shining blindingly bright on the wrecked Grady-White, a rifle on his shoulder.

"Hands up," he'd called over the water. "Put them up, all of you, and no sudden moves."

It wasn't until he'd idled closer that Hank had figured it out, seen it was Jess and Burke and Lucy at the stern, and not just Cole Sweeney and the boys. He'd lashed his cruiser to the wreck and, with Jess's help, wrestled Burke across the rail and into his cabin, a settee and a blanket. He'd helped Lucy aboard too, and Jess, and then—grudgingly—Sweeney, and they'd untied Kirby Harwood's pride and joy and left it to drift or sink, and Hank had hauled ass for Neah Bay.

He'd told Jess he'd come to retrieve his guns, instead of reporting them stolen; he'd suspected Jess and Burke and Lucy might need a hand, given how every deputy in Deception Cove had vanished that morning. He'd set out from the harbor in the cruiser at dusk, made steady time, and was just about at Dixie Island when he happened to glance back and see the flare over the water.

"Luck," he'd told Mason later. "Just dumb luck, all it was. Another ten minutes and you all would have been swimming."

They'd woken up the nurse in Neah Bay, Sheriff Wheeler, too, and hauled Mason up to the Indian Health Center on the Makah reservation, beaten the door down and set about saving Mason's life.

According to Jess, it hadn't turned out to be much of a challenge, the bleeding all but stopped, and the rounds in his chest and stomach having missed anything *too* important. She was a marine, though, and her standards for "life-threatening" were apparently pretty high; he'd been out three or four days before he opened his eyes, and it was another three or four more before he was walking around.

Even now, sitting at this little table in a rare patch of sunlight, Mason could feel in his side where the first round had hit, shattering a couple of ribs and glancing off to parts unknown. He could feel in his stomach where the second round had passed, the entry wound like a bad itch when he shifted around, the exit wound dull and ever present.

Still, he was lucky to be alive, and that was more than could be said for Kirby Harwood, or the Whitmer boys, or the other guy, Joy. Or Shelby Walker and her mother, for that matter, or even Ty Winslow. All things considered, Mason figured he had no cause for complaint.

There was still the matter of the law, of course, and those bodies on Dixie Island and the million-dollar package hidden there too, and if Cole Sweeney hadn't survived, Mason knew, the federal agents who'd descended upon Makah County might have been somewhat less inclined to believe a story peddled by a convicted murderer and a war veteran with severe PTSD, especially when the opposition party was composed of lawmen. But Sweeney was alive, and he apparently held Jess in some kind of esteem for not blowing his head off, because he'd copped to the whole fiasco when the DEA got him in an interview room.

Sweeney would walk with a limp for the rest of his life, but he wouldn't do all of his walking in prison; the prevailing opinion in the coffee shops and watering holes in Makah County put the young deputy out of prison around the time he'd turn fifty. Which was bad, definitely, but it could have been worse, in just about every way.

Lucy shifted beneath the table, her collar jingling, and Mason bent down to rub her flank. The dog sighed and stretched out, content, her black fur warm in the sunshine.

"She's going to miss you, you know," Jess told Mason. "She'll think I scared you off, and she'll hate me for it."

Mason didn't look up. "Nah," he said. "She's your dog. She'll be happy enough when you get a new couch."

"That'll take a while. There aren't too many competent builders left in this county, and there damn sure aren't many good furniture stores."

She'd been staying at Hank Moss's hotel with the dog while she figured out what to do about more permanent accommodations, the house she'd shared with Ty being a total write-off.

"Plenty of builders back east," Mason said, and he still couldn't look at her. “You all could join the party and come home, meet my kin.”

Jess sighed a little bit, rueful. “I wish I could, even just for a visit,” she said. “But they want me in the office first thing Monday morning, see how the whole system works.”

He looked up. “Who, Hart?”

She nodded, and he saw she was nervous, but she was pleased, too. The events of the last month had inspired Sheriff Wheeler to finally pull the trigger on his retirement, it being strongly suggested by the county commissioners that a sheriff who couldn’t keep his deputies out of trouble might be better suited spending his time fishing instead. In Wheeler’s place, in the interim, came a man named Aaron Hart from nearby Clallam County. Hart would take over until the next election, still two years off, and his first order of business was filling the office in Deception Cove, replacing Kirby Harwood et al.

Hart had chosen Jess Winslow, with the county’s blessing. Who better than a war hero to whip a lawless town into shape? And Mason figured Jess was perfect for the job, even if it meant she had hard days ahead, cleaning up what remained of Harwood’s little empire. She wouldn’t be taking any vacations, not anytime soon.

Across the street, the Greyhound bus driver emerged from the gas station, zipping his pants and wiping his hands on them. Mason finished his coffee, checked his watch. “I guess it’s almost time,” he said.

She looked across at the bus and didn’t say anything. He watched her and felt rotten, and then she turned to him and took his hand across the table.

“I guess it’s better that you’re going,” she said. “Who knows what kind of mess we’d make if you stayed?”

He smiled sadly, knew she didn't mean it. "Not too many jobs out here for a guy like me anyway."

"Not cleaning houses, that's for sure."

"Not sure I'm qualified for much more," he replied. "Plus, I owe my sister and her husband a fair pile of cash; I've got to make right on my debts."

She reached below the table, into the bag at her feet. Came out with a sheaf of money and laid it on the table.

"Ten grand," she said. "I found it on Kirby's boat. I didn't think anyone would mind so much if we split it."

He stared at her. "I can't take that."

"You can damn well take half, Burke. You earned it."

He didn't say anything. It would have been easy. The cash was just lying there, $10,000 in hundreds, and half of it, by some logic, rightfully his. Enough to pay Glen and Maggie back, start a new life. Enough to stay here with Lucy and Jess for a while.

But he knew what Kirby Harwood had done to earn that money, and he knew he'd never feel right making a profit off of all that blood and misery.

He shook his head. "You keep that money," he said. "Rebuild your house with it, or heck, donate it to charity if you want to. But I can't take that money, Jess. It just wouldn't be right."

She held his gaze for a long beat, and then finally she blinked. Reached out for the money and took it back, shaking her head. "I guess you can suit yourself," she said.

"I'm sorry," he said, standing. "I have to do this part honest."

She watched him stand, squinting up at him a little bit, her mouth twitching like she wanted to say something but she couldn't decide what. Finally she let out a long breath. "I lied, Burke."

He looked at her and she was looking away now.

"I don't want you to go and I don't think it's better," she continued, quick, like she was rushing to get the words out before she thought better of them. "I know if past is any precedent, then I'll fuck this up, but God help me, I still want to try. And I know it's selfish of me, but I don't want you to leave yet, not until we know dead to rights that we can't make this work." She met his eyes. "You know?"

He came around the table. Took her hands, pulled her up into his arms. "You don't want this," he said. "Not with someone like me."

She slipped away. Slapped him, light, but hard enough to sting. "Don't you go telling me what I want and don't want again, Burke," she said. "I've said my piece now. If you're walking away, it's on you."

He made to reply, couldn't think of an answer. Then the bus driver honked his horn, and the moment was gone anyway, and he bent down and kissed her, and scratched behind Lucy's ears, and turned and walked across the street to where the bus waited.

He'd made it almost to the door when he heard Jess call his name, and he turned around and she was standing there, radiant in the sun, the dog beside her with ears perked and tail wagging, watching like she, too, was waiting on him to turn around and come on back.

"There's plenty of kids in this county need guidance," she said. "Probably just as many as Michigan. Not too many positive role models around here anymore."

He didn't say anything, and she shrugged. "You think on it," she said. "Think about that kid Rengo, alone in the woods. If there's anyone in this world who needs a kick in the ass . . ."

"I'll think on it," he said. He waved goodbye, and then he stepped onto the bus and handed over his ticket, walked up the aisle and found a place to sit down. Looked out the window to see Jess turning to leave, trying to pull the dog along behind her.

Lucy didn't want to go, though. She stayed staring at the bus no matter how Jess pulled at her, staring and wagging that tail, until the bus driver shifted into gear and pulled out of the lot, and even then that dog was still waiting.

SIXTY-EIGHT

It wasn't going to end like that. Of course it wasn't.

As soon as that bus started moving, Mason Burke realized he'd made about the dumbest mistake of his life, realized he'd gotten caught up in some bullshit self-pity, telling himself Jess was better off without him.

He was trying to escape Makah County because he was scared, like she'd said. Because he was worried he'd never be the man in real life that she'd seen on that island, the man who'd fought beside her when no one else would.

He was afraid that he wasn't much to be proud of when there wasn't a war to be fought, that when it came to normal life, buying groceries together, cooking dinner, going on dates, she'd see right away he was still something less than a man. She'd realize her mistake and curse her shit luck all over again.

He was afraid she would figure out he had nothing to offer, nothing except strength and a bullheaded stubbornness that worked fine in a street fight but meant nothing at all when it came to balancing a checkbook and remembering anniversaries.

He was afraid he would disappoint her, and he wasn't sure he could stand taking the risk.

Easier to escape. Get on a bus and ride two thousand miles and take a job cleaning houses, live in Maggie's basement. Pay Glen back his money and gradually build a life, maybe rent an apartment, buy a used truck. Work an honest day, and come home and eat dinner, watch a hockey game, drink a beer. Shovel snow in the winter, try to forget the rain.

Keep to himself, keep his eyes down. Avoid looking at people, avoid conversation. Stay out of trouble, and just try to survive.

He'd done it fifteen years. He could do it some more.

That was his thinking, and he played with those thoughts as the bus trundled east, ran his mind over them like how you run your tongue over a sore tooth, testing the pain, playing with it, trying how it feels.

Then the bus rounded a corner and drove past the old Whitmer compound, now put up for sale, and continued down the highway into Deception Cove proper. And Mason stared out the window and wondered how he was ever going to forget this place, and then the gas station went by, and Hank Moss's motel, and parked out front was the Chevy Blazer Jess had purchased from Hank's cousin. Somehow she'd beaten the bus here, though Mason couldn't see her anywhere.

Still, he knew she'd sped home on purpose, knew she'd parked in his line of sight just to tease him, give him one last painful thought to mull over in his mind. And then the motel was gone too, and the Blazer gone with it, and shortly after, the town faded into the forest and it was highway again, nothing but highway and the odd dirt road disappearing into the woods. Nothing but the apparitions of old houses, torn, ragged nets, someone's beached troller: the ghosts of Deception Cove come to watch him go.

Hold fast to love, Mason thought. *Hold fast. "Above all, love each other deeply, because love covers over a multitude of sins."*

And before he knew what he was doing, he was standing up, walking down the aisle of the empty bus to the front, where the driver sat listening to Springsteen, watching the two-lane macadam unfurl ahead.

He was the same driver who had taken Mason into Seattle the night Cole Sweeney ran him out of town. He recognized Mason in the rearview mirror, eyed him, suspicious, and Mason met his eyes, sheepish, and then he took the plunge.

"I'm real sorry," he told the driver. "But I need you to let me out here."

ACKNOWLEDGMENTS

First and foremost, thanks to RainCoast Dog Rescue Society for bringing the real Lucy into my life. Jesse Adams and Brielle Turpin found Lucy in a California kill shelter with only days left to live, and they scooped her up and brought her to Canada, and I'll always be grateful for it. RainCoast rescues and rehomes dogs from all over the world, and their work is in every sense a labor of love. Visit them at raincoastdogrescue.com to learn more (and donate!).

Thanks to my agent, Stacia Decker, who earned her commission on this book by including cute pictures of the real-life Lucy in her pitch letters to publishers, and who landed us a wonderful home at Mulholland Books.

Thanks to my editor, Emily Giglierano, for coaxing this book from its rough beginnings to the polished product you're holding in your hands, and for doing it with humor, irreverence, and an astute editorial eye. I look forward to plotting out many more Lucy, Jess, and Mason adventures together!

Thanks to Reagan Arthur, Josh Kendall, Betsy Uhrig, designer Marie Mundaca, and everyone at Mulholland and Little, Brown for welcoming me into the fold. It's a privilege to be part of your family!

Thanks also to copyeditor Erica Stahler for keeping me honest, and for saving my bacon more times than I'd care to admit.

Thanks to Chris and Katrina Holm; Josh Christie and Emily

Russo at Print: A Bookstore in Portland, Maine; Paul Swydan at the Silver Unicorn Bookstore in Acton, Massachusetts; Ed Aymar; Bill Bride; Erik Arneson; Lynn Pellerito Riehl and George Riehl; Robin and Jamie Agnew at the dearly departed Aunt Agatha's Mystery Bookstore in Ann Arbor, Michigan; Nick and Margret Petrie; Erica Ruth Neubauer; Jon and Ruth Jordan; Daniel Goldin at Boswell Books in Milwaukee, Wisconsin; Mara Panich-Crouch and Chris LaTray at Fact and Fiction Books in Missoula, Montana; Jim Thomsen; and Jane and Dave Danielson at Eagle Harbor Books on beautiful Bainbridge Island, Washington.

I'm also very grateful to McKenna Jordan, Sally Woods, and John McDougall at Murder by the Book in Houston; to Michelle Turlock Isler and her husband, Tommy Isler; to Barbara Peters, Patrick Millikin, Patrick King, and everyone at the Poisoned Pen in Scottsdale, Arizona; to Jim Thane and Steve Shadow; to Meg King-Abraham, Devin Abraham, and Dennis Abraham at Once Upon a Crime in Minneapolis; to Dan and Kate Malmon, Kristi Belcamino, Lynn Cronquist, Julie and Mike McKuras, and Alex Kent; to Anne Saller at Book Carnival in Orange, California; and to the rest of you lot: all of the readers, booksellers, and friends who've stuck with me on this ride.

Thanks especially to Alexis May Tanner, who has my back in matters big and small, and—more importantly—has Lucy's.

Thanks, as always, to my family—Ethan Laukkanen, Ruth Sellers, Andrew Laukkanen, Terrence Laukkanen, Laura Mustard, and Little E—for love and inspiration.

And thanks, of course, to Lucy. It was on walks together through the city that I rediscovered my love for writing, and so I owe this book to the hound, and so much more besides.

ABOUT THE AUTHOR

A former commercial fisherman and professional poker journalist, Owen Laukkanen is the author of six critically acclaimed Stevens and Windermere FBI thrillers, the nautical adventure *Gale Force,* and—as Owen Matthews—two highly inappropriate novels for young adults. A native of Vancouver, Canada, Laukkanen spends nearly every waking hour with his dog, Lucy, a six-year-old rescue pit bull whose hobbies include hiking, napping, and squirrels. Laukkanen and Lucy are currently at work on the second Jess Winslow–Mason Burke adventure.

MULHOLLAND BOOKS

You won't be able to put down these Mulholland books.

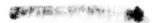